Carousel Court

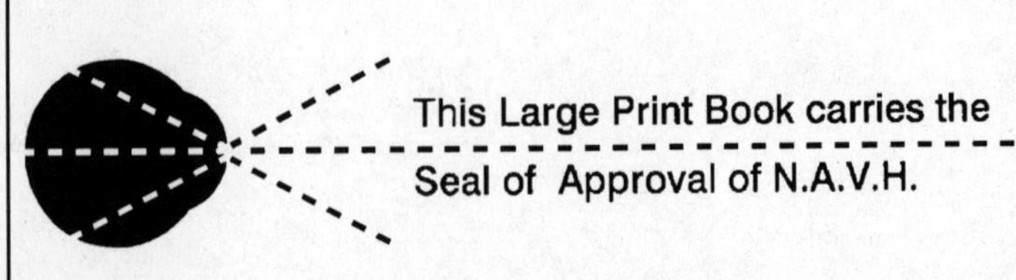
This Large Print Book carries the
Seal of Approval of N.A.V.H.

Carousel Court

Joe McGinniss Jr.

THORNDIKE PRESS
A part of Gale, Cengage Learning

GALE
CENGAGE Learning®

Farmington Hills, Mich • San Francisco • New York • Waterville, Maine
Meriden, Conn • Mason, Ohio • Chicago

Thorndike Press, a part of Gale, Cengage Learning.

This book is a work of fiction. Any references to historical events, real people, or real places are used fictitiously. Other names, characters, places, and events are products of the author's imagination, and any resemblance to actual events or locales or persons, living or dead, is entirely coincidental.

Thorndike Press® Large Print Reviewers' Choice.
The text of this Large Print edition is unabridged.
Other aspects of the book may vary from the original edition.
Set in 16 pt. Plantin.

LIBRARY OF CONGRESS CATALOGING-IN-PUBLICATION DATA

Names: McGinniss, Joe, 1970– author.
Title: Carousel court / by Joe McGinniss Jr.
Description: Large print edition. | Waterville, Maine : Thorndike Press, 2016. | Series: Thorndike Press large print reviewers' choice
Identifiers: LCCN 2016036133 | ISBN 9781410495150 (hardcover) | ISBN 1410495159 (hardcover)
Subjects: LCSH: Large type books.
Classification: LCC PS3613.C4832 C37 2016b | DDC 813/.6—dc23
LC record available at https://lccn.loc.gov/2016036133

Published in 2016 by arrangement with Simon & Schuster, Inc.

Printed in Mexico
1 2 3 4 5 6 7 20 19 18 17 16

FOR MY FATHER, WHO I MISS
AND JEANINE, JULIEN, AND V, ALWAYS.

I felt very still and very empty, the way the eye of a tornado must feel, moving dully along in the middle of the hullabaloo

— SYLVIA PLATH

Slither up just like a snake upon a spiral staircase

— KURT VILE

Dream Extreme. Those words welcomed them to Serenos months ago, in June, before the heat. It's August now and they don't see the white sign anymore, don't pay attention to it. If they did notice it as they race along the Corona Freeway heading home, what they'd see instead would be the red graffiti tags defacing it. Nick and Phoebe Maguire make a sharp turn and pull their dirty white Subaru Forester in to Carousel Court. Jackson sucks a blue pacifier. Nick pulls his Mets cap lower, shields his eyes from the wind. Everything is bathed in this orange hue, like a vintage photograph. Looking around: abandoned new construction homes, kids playing outside on a yellow lawn despite rumors of mountain lions and bobcats, pit vipers, and Latino gangs trolling for new turf. The flap of an orange tent pitched in front of a house flutters wildly in the relentless wind that roars down mountain passes and through the valley on a straight trajectory toward them. A bullet train. A single spark these days — the dry season — will burn the whole place to the ground. And there's the house. Bigger than it should be. It's not on fire, though Nick wishes briefly it were, because what it is, is worse. It's underwater, sinking fast, has the three of them by the ankles, and isn't letting go.

1

Phoebe opens her eyes before the alarm. She does this lately, since they arrived. On low-dosage days the ground beneath her hardens, common sounds are shrill: Jackson's cries more urgent, Nick's words more hollow. Above her, the blades of the ceiling fan rotate too fast, send chilled air across Jackson's exposed arms. He sleeps fitfully next to her and she pulls his small blanket over his shoulders. Last night he was inconsolable or she was. She could remove the pacifier from his mouth and wake him, but watches him instead. There are fourteen bones in the human skull; eight surround the brain. She brushes his forehead where the bruise yellowed then finally faded.

It's almost seven and Nick still isn't home. Knowing how exhausted he'll be, she scrambles eggs and slices ripe mango for him and leaves them on a plate in the microwave and sends him a text telling him they're there in case he feels like skipping the morning rush at Starbucks on the way home. When she leaves the house it's already hot and Phoebe holds Jackson to her chest with one arm while her free hand pulls the heavy red front door closed behind her as the ADT chimes. Her day will be spent driving. Always driving.

At day care, she kisses Jackson's warm forehead. She says "Duck, duck" and he says "Goose!" and laughs. She looks back once, as she does each time she leaves her son in this strip mall three miles from Carousel Court, and blows him kisses. She pushes against the glass door, out into the heat and glare of another day. She should be home with him. She hates herself.

Just after ten in the morning she's alone on a freeway that connects her to the other side of the city and all the ugly retail strips and offices, and despite the heat and harsh sunlight and the cool air-conditioned car and the helicopter buzzing overhead, this middle part of each morning is a gentle breeze: the zenith of Klonopin highway happens an hour after she swallows the last of four pills. She sends Nick a rambling message, coasts and descends into the valley, and laughs at the woman in the silver Jaguar leaning on her horn because Phoebe won't leave the left lane and let her pass. You need to be on this, Phoebe thinks, and continues in the left lane doing seventy and considering another caramel macchiato. With whipped cream this time.

Soon it's one and the sun is a beast and directly overhead and she needs to eat something but she's buzzed, shaky, from two caramel macchiatos and the anticipation of her afternoon appointment. Her ten milligrams of Klonopin from this morning have worn off completely. The Effexor is losing its effect as well. The tingling in her fingertips, which feel cold in the morning, is a sign. So is her appetite: She has none. She feels empty but the thought of food makes her queasy. The front seat is littered with parking receipts, MAC lip liners, her badge, a suitcase full of pharmaceutical samples and glossy brochures, her iPhone, and a stuffed Elmo doll. Normally on the floor of the passenger side would be the goodies. Mocha frappuccinos with whipped cream for the office staff, a dozen doughnuts from Krispy Kreme. Bribing the gatekeepers is the way the game is played, access to the doctors is everything, the only way to push product, improve her numbers. Show up, perform, and close.

Performing and closing: What happens in

the office stays in the office unless he wants to text about it later and send crude photos after midnight. That's where she's struggling. The energy is gone. The playfulness and flirtation are labored if not missing entirely. Except today. Today, she will meet a young physician with a new practice and she is energized, sharper than she can remember. She also has a new strategy.

Phoebe breezes into a crowded, cool office and feels the eyes of tired mothers and frail seniors and men moving over her strong, tanned calves and smooth thighs, the thin fabric of her form-fitting lavender skirt. This used to be the most entertaining part of her job. A physician back east once propositioned her in his office, offered to leave his wife and kids for her. Another put a thousand dollars in cash on his desk and asked for her panties. The female office manager of another practice accused her of stealing samples from their closet and had her banned. Phoebe knew the real reason: She was too distracting.

Today a plain-looking office manager working reception hands Phoebe a clipboard and asks her to fill out both sides of each form for new patients.

"I don't have a ton of time," she says and

waits for the doctor's eyes to drop to her legs. When they finally do, she scratches her knee, slowly uncrosses and recrosses her legs. "So," she says as she feels her skirt slide up — clumsily, though, too high — until the yellow lace edge of her panties is showing. She starts to adjust it, then stops. He stares. She's off her game; the mood isn't right, the room is too bright, her thoughts bounce from one unrelated topic to the next. Does she have anything left in her checking account? Did the lock click when she pressed the button on the handle? His eyes are too blue. She should stand, go check the door, but her skirt is still too high and he's still staring. Then she realizes she doesn't care what he sees or who walks in or what she does because all that matters right now is getting what she came for.

"I need you to write me a prescription." She interlaces her fingers on her lap. She's trying too hard to look calm.

"For what?"

"Klonopin. You know, Clonazepam." She closes her eyes. "The good stuff."

"Are you anxious?"

She laughs and wipes her nose for some reason. "It's the driving. It's bad out here. I'm not used to it."

The doctor is forty, his brown hair flecked

with gray, clean-shaven. His wedding band is silver and thick. He wears an expensive-looking pale blue button-down shirt and black slacks and shoes. He sucks on a mint. He takes no notes as he listens to her explain her medical history.

"I know I scheduled a physical but actually I just need the 'script."

"Where is it coming from?" he says, meaning her anxiety.

She sighs. "You know, the usual tribulations. Can you write me something?"

"What other medications are you taking?"

"Effexor."

On her way here, stuck in traffic, Phoebe had watched a skinny, wrinkled woman with bleached-blond hair in a floral bikini and Coke-bottle shades push a stroller with two big kids in it along the side of a six-lane thoroughfare. Those kids, she thought, had to be at least seven years old. The woman looked fifty. The exhaust and heat and sun beat down, and Phoebe had wondered how far she herself was from that, how much debt and desperation until she would be reduced to walking through the vapors.

"Where are you from?" the doctor asks.

"Boston. Delaware before that." She exhales and crosses her legs again, and the doctor's not looking. "We were moving to

New Orleans."

"And?"

"At one point. Now we're not."

"You don't sound too happy about that."

"We had other plans."

He stares at her with a sympathetic smile. "What brought you out here?"

The question makes her femur throb, and she feels a flash of pain from the fourth and fifth vertebrae to the top of her skull. "See this?" She pulls up her top, touches a long thin scar along the right side of her torso.

"Ouch."

"A UPS truck I didn't see."

"What does your husband do?"

A long pause. "A PR firm. He's a filmmaker," she says, referring to Nick's position that prompted the move here. "Produces films for corporate clients, mostly."

"Get undressed." He hands her a white paper gown and walks toward the door.

Phoebe watches him go, sees the exam table on the other side of the large office. Before she can say anything, the door closes and he's gone.

Hung on the wall: a framed spread from the *Los Angeles Magazine* Best Doctors issue. As she undresses, Phoebe studies the picture of the physician and his wife, casually seated together in an oversize white Adirondack chair. Wrapped around them are two beaming blond children, a pair of Chesapeake Bay retrievers at their feet. She loses herself in the lush green lawn and the sprawling estate. She's pretty sure they're not staring down a readjusting ARM. Their smiles are so easy and infectious that she feels the corners of her mouth begin to rise as the physician knocks on the door and pushes it open in one motion.

With Phoebe on her back, the physician slides the paper gown to her hips, leaving her upper body exposed. He presses his fingertips too firmly into her midsection, checking for organ swelling, unusual masses. "What is that?" he asks, breathes in through his nose. "Like cotton candy."

"Like a teenager?"

He laughs. "Is that the goal?"

"Some days."

"You have how many children?"

"A son. Two and a half."

His hands hover over her abdomen. She feels warm and sleepy. Her throat is dry.

"I can't stand in line at Whole Foods without getting dizzy and my heart racing," she says.

"Are you sleeping?"

"I keep dreaming about water. About my

son drowning. Is that normal?"

His finger traces a thin scar. "Cesarean?"

Phoebe nods. She shifts on the table.

He rests both hands on her forearm. "Recovered nicely. My wife struggled after."

"She looks well-rested. What does she do for a living?"

"Bikram yoga," he says flatly. "Spinning. Swimming."

"I hate her."

"She gets bored."

"With which part?"

"All of it."

"Let me guess: his-and-her vanities."

"Of course."

"Hot nanny."

"Check." He laughs.

"You're a cliché. Did she have work done, too?"

"Right here." His hands press softly against the area just below Phoebe's navel, where they stay. "Some excess here. Not on you, though."

She stares overhead, connecting the dots in a single ceiling panel. "I try."

He stands back, arms folded. "You know what I think?" he says.

Phoebe grips the edge of the exam table with both hands.

"I think you need to give yourself a break."

"Funny, I was just thinking I've been too easy on myself."

He turns away. Phoebe clears her throat. He pulls on a pair of white latex gloves and says, "Would you prefer that a nurse be present?"

Phoebe shakes her head.

"The anxiety," he says as he slides his fingers inside of her, "is something worth keeping an eye on."

Phoebe considers the physician and his firm fingertips. She could lie here for just a bit longer, his fingers inside her, gently being encouraged to give herself a break.

She flinches. Her eyes open. "What are your thoughts about Advair?" she asks.

His fingers slide out. He removes his gloves. "Do you have asthma?"

She sits up, light-headed, the paper gown still at her hips. "The black-box warning from the FDA: Has that impacted your thoughts about prescribing?" She pulls the gown up.

He's laughing. "This is a first," he says. "You're working me?"

"Because it's really just a product of the stricter FDA guidelines. There's no new science or interactions that you need to worry about."

He's shaking his head with a tight-lipped

smile, almost disbelieving, then suddenly with a stern expression, "You're clearly not playing for the set of steak knives. This is a Cadillac-worthy effort."

She dresses. He makes no effort to avert his gaze.

"Your practice is about to triple in size."

"It is?"

She nods.

"What if it is?"

"Any concerns or questions you have about Advair, I'm happy to discuss now or any time. Allergy season is around the corner, we have the number one med, it's in my portfolio, and" — she exhales — "have I not earned it?"

He laughs. "I do love you guys," he says. "But this — you've set a new standard."

She mentions the Dodgers and luxury boxes and dinner and other perks, anything he'd like, as she jots her cell on the back of her GSK Pharmaceuticals card.

He takes it and nods. Then he says, "Do you want a name, Phoebe?"

She tilts her head, plays dumb.

"To talk to. To help with these episodes, the anxiety."

She pauses. "I just need a refill," she says. "And one that won't force me to come back every other month for more."

"I can't just write you 'scripts without giving you someone's name."

"You can do whatever you want." She's pressing now.

He's standing with his arms crossed, leaning against his desk, not buying it.

"It doesn't stop," she says. "I go a little nuts. I put a thousand miles on the car in the past two weeks. And no, I don't sleep. The more tired I am, the more impossible it is to sleep." She's lying to him. She won't admit to the Klonopin blackouts, the inability to drag herself up the stairs, to lay her son down in his crib with a dry diaper and his pacifier and a night-light. She won't tell the physician that her son falls asleep instantly on the living room sectional, sitting up, then tipping over, falling to the plush carpeting, knocked out from his own marathon days. "It never, ever, ever stops." She exhales. "This was amusing, though. This was —" She almost says "nice."

"Get a nanny," he says, and hands Phoebe a single slip of white paper.

Their hug is tight.

"It's generous," he adds. "But you have to watch these. Driving as much as you do."

"Strong, too," she says, finally letting go of the physician. "Nice shoulders. Nice life."

"See you in three months," he says and

smiles. "Rest assured: You're a very healthy young woman."

She unmutes and checks her iPhone. There are texts and a missed call from Nick.

"Tell me again," she says.

"Tell you what?" the doctor asks.

"To give myself a break."

"Do you really need one?"

She laughs. "Someone's going to get hurt."

"Are you a danger to people? To yourself?"

"You sound like my husband."

"You're a stellar rep, Phoebe. Best I've seen today."

"We do it right at GSK." She winks at him.

"They give you those lines?" he asks, laughing.

"Drilled in. The Blue Army. We've always got your back."

As she passes through the doorway, for no reason that makes any sense to Phoebe, the doctor says in a clinical voice that is so unsettling to her that she freezes: "Be careful out there."

Phoebe keeps her back to him, slowly pulls the door closed behind her, walks to the elevator, and presses the button. Then presses it again.

She steps onto the elevator. The doors close. She presses a clean, raised circular steel button: double L. *Your Life Starts Now.* That's the headline of an osteoarthritis prescription-drug advertisement on the wall. A grinning silver-haired couple cut through a sun-drenched landscape on matching red bicycles. The elevator drops. *We won't grow old together.* She can't picture it. She can't see Nick losing his hair, gaining weight, swallowing more pills, medication she'll remind him to take, that he'll always ask her about: as though these past four miserable years spent peddling GSK pharmaceuticals make her an authority on his physiology. They already sleep in separate beds. Nick ends up on the red IKEA couch in Jackson's room. He says it's because of their different schedules; he doesn't want to disturb her sleep. They've stopped having sex. They avoid the topic altogether. She knows this about Nick: He carries the burden of this failure, this home that is crushing them, and will until he's stooped and broken.

The elevator shudders, picks up speed.

Phoebe considers another path. A way out of debt and away from Carousel Court and nights spent curled up sleepless next to Jackson's crib listening for shattering glass and footsteps, the next home invasion. Debt and routine and down and down. She sees white Adirondack chairs and chocolate purebred Labradors and a thick lush lawn adorned with children's toys, short drives to school and smiling teachers and Jackson's bright eyes and a little wave good-bye and the swell of emotion, and her eyes well up thinking about hot yoga and a call from Nick about a babysitter because they have dinner plans.

Your Life Starts Now. The silver-haired couple is rotting from the inside out: brittle bones and failing organs. If heart failure from too much of the pharmaceutical cocktail doesn't kill them, the corrosive regret and denial will.

It's all a fraud. She gets that. They bought the stock at just the wrong time, long after the private-equity investors pocketed their profits. That's why she sees their situation the way she does now. She's made her choice. Her insides free-fall. The rush of blood to her head as the swift movement of the elevator eases, gently delivers her to the lower lobby.

The doors open. She nearly grins at the inevitability: This was always going to be the resolution, if not the answer. She's not twenty-six this time. Unlike then, there is no emotion, no adolescent longing or lust for some other glossy life. Now she has Jackson, Nick, a need to be addressed directly and with conviction.

She shoulders open the tall glass door and leaves the cool, shimmering office building. Ripples of heat rise from the black asphalt. The parking lot is a field of smoldering briquettes and she's walking through it.

2

Phoebe's Explorer, her company car, won't start. She turns it over again and again and gets no response. Red lights flash. A crude clicking sound. This happened before. She left the iPod charging and drained the battery. It needs a jump. In the parking lot, she sits in the driver's seat, door open, hot.

She can call AAA or just ask someone for help. There's a frozen-yogurt place and a Panda Express in the strip mall across the street. She can wait there until help arrives. That's when she sees the young man with thick arms and a white T-shirt and jeans, a clear blue jug of water on his shoulder. He's sweating through his shirt and keeps his head up and a pleasant expression on his face, aviator glasses and tattoos wrapped around both arms.

• •

The second time Nick took her out, they were both twenty-four and living in separate parquet-floor efficiencies. He showed up at her building early and she was late. It was the hottest day of the year and he was talking to her short Thai neighbor, a mother of three who lived on the sixth floor. Nick held an enormous jug of water on his shoulder and some daisies in his other hand. The elevator in the building had been broken for a week and the Thai woman had two babies in a stroller. The water was hers, three more jugs on the sidewalk. He didn't notice Phoebe halfway down the block, watching. He was like Benicio in *Traffic,* she thought. Hot. Jeans and sweating through his pale blue button-down shirt. And the flowers. Come *on.* And maybe he knew, but none of it felt contrived with Nick. Four trips up and down the five flights of stairs. Neither could Nick mask his excitement when he discovered the oldest of the Thai kids was some kind of ice-hockey prodigy. He decided he'd document the kid's life and budding career like a Thai hockey version of *Hoop Dreams.* He wondered aloud to Phoebe if he should submit the finished project to festivals, maybe pitch it to PBS. She not only said he should, she would eventually make him a list of other potential outlets and producers with their contact information, as well as a list of five agencies she thought he should query.

When he got a call back from a producer at the Boston PBS affiliate about the forty-four-minute final product (which ended with the Thai kid getting kicked off the team for drug use, becoming a small-time dealer, then getting locked up for knocking out his pregnant girlfriend, the last scene with the mother visiting the incarcerated hockey prodigy in jail, introducing his infant son to him) Nick chalked it up to good fortune. "Their pain, my gain."

"You made this happen," she said. "You could have blown her off."

"Instead I just exploited the woman."

"It's called ambition."

"I was trying to impress you."

• •

Phoebe sends a text to Nick: *Need you*

The way she taps it out is casual, and she almost adds a smiling emoticon to soften it, because he'll read it differently. A command, demanding. Like calling up from the kitchen on a Saturday morning when he's still in bed, drained from work. She's agitated, Jackson's cranky, dishes are piled up like their debt, and someone has to take the car in, the rattling from underneath is getting louder and nothing is going as planned, and she'll call out his name and add "I need you."

That's how he'll read it.

When he shows up, he brings her iced coffee, which she doesn't need or want.

She thanks him, sips it, and puts it down. She's peeking in the rearview and side mirror, eyeing the office entrance, suddenly aware of their filthy Subaru that rattles, even when idling. "It's getting louder."

Nick is rubbing his eyes, not really listening.

"Should we stay with it?" He means the Explorer.

"Hell with it. Let's just go," she says.

"Can't jump it if we're not here."

"Let them figure out how to get me a car that works." She puts the keys under the floor mat, the doors unlocked. "We're not sitting in a parking lot waiting for a tow."

"You'll have to pick it up."

"And?"

"I'll have to drive you."

"That's a problem?"

"I don't know my schedule," Nick says. "Jackson has day care."

"It's Friday. We can pick up a rental on

Sunday if mine's not ready."

"We could do something," Nick says. "I'm beat, but we've got a couple hours."

The handsome physician appears and walks to a shiny black Lexus. Two empty parking spaces separate him from Nick and Phoebe in their rattling Subaru. He gestures to Phoebe, who raises a hand in recognition. There's no hiding: She's riding shotgun.

"Friend of yours?" Nick says.

"Not quite."

"Nice hair."

The physician disappears inside his black car with tinted windows, leaves them behind.

"Where to?" Nick asks.

The realization that they could and should want to get Jackson early, go somewhere as a family, hangs over them.

"It's three thirty."

"Nap time," Nick says.

The weekend lies ahead: no day care for Jackson, two days to fill, the heat insane, the pool dirty, and the beach miles and hours in the car, something she tries to avoid on weekends. And Nick will work both nights. He's always been good about taking Jackson for the first hour or more, letting Phoebe sleep, the only two days she can. He'll change and feed Jackson, and she'll hear her son giggling because of Nick, who will keep the TV off and play with him in the living room. They'll kick his Nerf soccer ball or throw sticky rubber bugs against the high ceiling, watch them dangle, peel off, then plummet to the floor, Jackson laughing, trying to catch them when they fall.

• •

They drove down to Delaware two months after they met. Phoebe's mother was visiting family there, had come up from Florida.

"Should have seen that FBI agent thing through. Should have followed through on that. Do some good in the world. Teaching. Weren't you going to teach? What happened to that?" There were deep creases in her mother's forehead, and she chain-smoked and stared out the living room window, overlooking a well-kept lawn and chain-link fence. The presence of a bird feeder surprised Nick. A squirrel hung from it, upside down, looting.

She cursed the animal and left the room. As she did she delivered one last stab, "Follow through on *something,* for Christ's sake."

She was unapologetic about the past: "You made it this far," she said to Phoebe. "So obviously, I did something right."

Phoebe refused to see her mother in Florida, where she lived surrounded by glossy tabloids and unfinished cigarettes. The house in Delaware was Phoebe's uncle's place, surrounded by bland white and yellow homes with dirty aluminum siding and cracked, weed-choked driveways. Phoebe's uncle was doing Thanksgiving. Nick insisted they go because Phoebe's mother had claimed she had terminal lung cancer and it might be her last Thanksgiving. It was Nick's first introduction to her family.

"She's lying. She needs money," Phoebe said.

"We go."

Nick bought two nice bottles of wine and a ham and two pumpkin pies.

"They don't drink wine."

"We do." He held the bottles up and smiled.

"You're pretty great about this," Phoebe said. "About everything."

He shrugged. "Family. You know. You do it."

"It never happened" was what he said to

her after the visit went south, predictably, when talk turned to Phoebe's father and all the ways he failed the family and why Phoebe wasn't sufficiently bitter. They left before dessert. Nick kind of ushered her out and pulled the door closed and turned onto the parkway that would take them home. He grabbed her thigh and laughed and said, "Buckle up," and she apologized and he said, "It never happened. And look, goodies." He placed a paper bag on her lap. In it was the unopened bottle of wine and a pumpkin pie.

• •

Now Nick and Phoebe and their dirty Forester idle in a sunbaked strip mall parking lot, contemplate their options for filling the couple of hours of free time they just found.

"Beach?" Nick says as he turns right into traffic, looking around for signs. "This goes west," he says.

"I'll feel guilty," Phoebe says, "going without him. He loves the beach. I love that he loves the beach." She trails off, closes her eyes against the late-day glare.

Just over a year ago, when Jackson managed his first faltering steps, it seemed that everyone had a house or was buying one. Deb and Marty, their neighbors from the seventh floor, bought one in Needham. Matthew and Caroline, on the ninth, bought one for themselves, another to restore and sell in Marblehead.

Young married professionals buying and selling houses for six-figure profits. So why not them? Of course them, finally them. For months they'd spent their weeknights staring at these shows, new ones every week, and Nick and Phoebe watched them all: *What You Get For the Money, Designed to Sell, What's My House Worth, Stagers, Flip This House, Flip That House.* It never rained on those shows. Nick commented on the production values, which tended to be high. He said he could do it cheaper, make it look just as good, if given the chance.

The animated tally-board at the end of one of their favorites on HGTV flashed money down, money spent, money made, along with the cash-register sound effect that had been echoing for weeks inside Nick's head.

After the accident, after Jackson's recovery and Phoebe's return to work, Nick knew it was time. Together they spent hours cycling through property listings online. They narrowed the scope of their search. They calculated the cost of mortgages, the expense of upgrades. In February, they quickly negotiated an interest-only, zero-down, 125 percent renovation mortgage on the house in Serenos. It was doable because of the twenty-two-thousand-dollar salary increase Nick negotiated with his new job, combined with the eleven thousand that remained in savings and Phoebe's inheritance from her aunt.

They chose the new construction with room to grow. Granite countertops, double-ascending stairways, and a double garage. More stainless steel. More square footage. More landscaping. And the pool: in-ground free-form hourglass with ice-blue Quartzon rendering, natural stone waterfall with solar heating. The cabana and wet bar. Nick and Phoebe spent as much as they could to drive up the value. Something else Nick insisted on: the rock-climbing wall. It was simple, clean, and something to make their place pop: One interior wall of the double-ascending stairway hid the bonded two-part application of granite-like panels. Phoebe admitted: It was cool. Studded with bright primary-colored modular rocks, it had six unique challenge courses to the top. They decided it would attract a more discerning buyer, would set their property apart from the rest of the houses on Carousel Court. It was virtual home-building, images on their laptop, point, click, purchase. Phoebe sat on the barstool in the kitchen and cycled through images and upgrade options. Nick stood behind her, close, and her optimism made him flush.

"We can do both colors downstairs," she said. "Banana crème and honeydew."

"We make it all back and then some," Nick promised effusively, and Phoebe agreed because the numbers made sense: low-interest loans and rising property values, but also because the scenario he presented was irresistible. They'd flip this house for a huge profit. They would have more income from Nick's new job, which would afford Phoebe three full months off in a furnished oceanfront rental in Los Angeles. This, the gift from Nick to her for the rough stretch she'd endured, the exhaustion. A summer to herself, walking distance to Hermosa or Manhattan Beach, to breathe new air, to fill mornings and days with Jackson. With more excitement in his voice than seemed rational, Nick drew Phoebe's attention to a landscaping company's website, the emerald rolls of TifGreen Certified Bermuda. Her laughter was the reaction Nick wanted. And it was genuine, the last time since Jackson that they were in sync.

He's working hard, Phoebe tells herself as Nick drives. His sunburned visage softens in the afternoon shadows as the freeway snakes through and around steep hillsides in the direction of home. Maybe, she thinks, it can still work. "Hey," she says. She extends a closed fist. He bumps it.

3

The orange glow from across the street is a lit cigarette. Nick and Phoebe's neighbor Metzger smokes in front of his tent. He's in uniform, same outfit every day: khaki shorts, clean white New Balance sneakers, white socks pulled up over thick calves, and despite the heat, a white oxford, sleeves rolled up, left over from his days working at the bank.

"Fucking Kostya," he calls out, meets Nick on his side of the black, windswept street. Whatever he carries by his side is dark, a crowbar or baseball bat maybe. Nick doesn't want to know.

Kostya didn't fasten the lid on his recycling can and the wind knocked it over, spilled plastic two-liter bottles of Mountain Dew and Sunny D and beer bottles all over the street.

"And his park job." The truck is half backed out onto the street. "Is it that hard to pull your fifty-thousand-dollar Tundra up the driveway? Fucking Armenians."

Nick laughs. "Ukraine. I think."

Metzger's pissed off about a lot of things: the pain in his partially torn Achilles that will require surgery he can't afford. The weight he can't shed. Gas prices. The deserted house next to his. The insane neighbor next to Nick and Phoebe. Kostya's dirty, skinny kids. One night Metzger's thick green lawn was empty; the next morning the orange tent appeared. His is a military-style double-wall combat tent with a vestibule providing twenty square feet of storage space. The atomic orange structure rests a few feet from the curb, putting the neighborhood on notice: Things have changed and aren't changing back anytime soon.

"Close your eyes," Metzger says.

The gun Metzger puts in Nick's hands is a Mossberg 500 twelve-gauge pump-action shotgun. It's black and cool to the touch, and Nick likes the feel of the matte finish, of the butt and pump, though he's never fired a gun, so he says very little about it.

"Nice," Nick manages. It's heavier than he would have expected.

A lone, illegible graffiti tag recently appeared on the wall of the drained pool in the house next to Metzger's: a five-bedroom, three-bath new construction left behind a month ago. It was the first house to drop on their cul-de-sac. Cars, three or four young men deep, recently started appearing, crawling along Carousel Court on weekend nights. Nick gets the sense, and confirmed with Kostya and Metzger, that they're surveying the terrain, zeroing in on the next target. Metzger in his tent with his new Mossberg is the first and maybe only line of defense so far. For that much, Nick is grateful. Metzger worked at Bank of the West until last month. Nick doesn't know what he did there.

"Keep an eye out tonight?" Nick asks. This is the favor he needs.

Instead of responding, Metzger says, "Look at that mess," and trains the beam of light from his police-style flashlight on another spilled recycling container. The mess is in front of the house belonging to the Vietnamese family. The mother is a former teacher and apparently now a very good nanny, someone Nick and Phoebe have been saving money for, wanting Jackson somewhere other than Bouncin' Babies. The Vietnamese family's recycling is all one-gallon plastic water bottles and newspapers, no soda, no beer.

"Kostya's mangy dogs." Metzger spits.

"Or kids."

"Same difference," Metzger says, and laughs. "Russian mutts." Both men instinctively direct their attention to Kostya's house, the biggest on the block.

A string of white lights dangles from a tall palm at the edge of Kostya and Marina's property. Of all the generically grand properties erected in the last five years, theirs is the grandest. All of the houses went up cheap and quick, but theirs sits slightly above the rest, on a modest incline with a winding stone walkway and a wide sloped asphalt driveway big enough for his Tundra and her Suburban. The lights that mark the top end of the cul-de-sac are the first thing you see when you turn on to the street at night. Kostya, obsessed with the palm trees, saw a Corona commercial that came on around Christmas — that's where he got the idea for the lights. But they were such a pain in the ass to string up that once he'd done it, he decided to leave them, lighting only one tree. So they have a lone skinny palm at 45900 Carousel Court towering over all the other houses on the street. The white lights flicker when the sun goes down. Yes, Phoebe finally agreed when Nick pressed, it's a nice effect.

Nick hears music, too loud, coming from the house next door.

"Believe this shit?" Metzger glares at the new construction identical to Nick's. "What goddamn time is it?" He shines the flashlight on the house.

"Late," Nick says. "Good song, though."

Metzger reports that the neighbor has been in and out of his garage for the last hour, carrying boxes from his truck. This seems to agitate Metzger, for some reason. "And now this shit," he says.

"Connie Stevens?" Nick says quizzically.

"You think this is funny?" Metzger turns away from Nick and says under his breath, "Just watch."

The man living next to Nick and Phoebe looks about thirty. He has close-cropped blond hair, always wears a hoodie and shorts no matter how hot it gets, lives alone, and talks to no one. In the three months since Nick and Phoebe moved in, they've had one exchange: The man was ripping tiles from his roof and tossing them onto their driveway, where they shattered. Phoebe asked him to stop; he ignored her. His patchy yellow lawn has a couple of wilting date palms and a eucalyptus tree. Red spray paint recently appeared on the front door, a signal from the lender to interested parties:

This house is dead and ours. The man added to it — a fuck-you to the bank — a red X on the wall next to the door, a white O and another red X, and a blue tic-tac-toe board separating the letters. His black pickup truck has huge wheels and looks new but, unlike Kostya's, is filthy.

Metzger tosses his cigarette toward the street, orange ash on black asphalt, squashes it. "Vietnamese are rotten," he says, pointing at a house by the entrance to the cul-de-sac. "Mexicalis are rotten," he adds, pointing out another house. He lights a new cigarette. His cadence is caffeinated, jittery. "Mormons are rotten to the core. That's three houses right there about to get tapped." He draws three fingers slowly across his thick neck, indicating a throat slitting. The cigarette dangles from his dry lips as he speaks. He's flicking invisible ticks from his thumb at each of the nine homes in their cul-de-sac, referring to their neighbors who are still, after three months in Serenos, California, forty miles east of Los Angeles, mostly strangers to Nick and Phoebe.

"Sucked dry," Nick says.

Metzger shines the light on Kostya and Marina's house. Aside from Metzger, and waving and smiling at the Vietnamese couple in passing, Kostya and Marina are Nick and Phoebe's only friends.

"They're fine," Metzger says, "for now." He shines his light on Nick's house, the thick green grass. "Lawn looks good."

Nick nods.

"But these idiots," Metzger says, gesturing around the street. "If they can just talk to someone at the bank!" He laughs. "Guess what? I *was* the bank. You owe what you owe." He's following Nick to his car, and Nick isn't sure why. He walks with a limp. He wipes perspiration from his forehead with his thick hand. Nick has his keys out and the driver's-side door open.

"Keep an eye out?" Nick says. He grabs Metzger's thick shoulder and motions to his own home. "Tonight. While I'm gone."

"Find any bodies yet?" Metzger says, and laughs.

Nick starts the Subaru. He plugs in his iPod, cycles through tracks until he finds the song he wants.

"Bring me something. A flat-screen. Some golf clubs."

Nick laughs.

Metzger is unmoved by the heavy bass from T.I. spitting lyrics to "Ready for Whatever."

"Knives. Good knives. I need some steak knives."

He's standing over Nick with a thick arm draped on the roof of the car. Heat radiates from his heavy face, a rash on his left cheek. His hair is thinning and slicked back with sweat. The first time they met, Metzger felt compelled to inform Nick that he's lived in his three-bedroom house for twelve years, longer than anyone on the block. Before the street was even paved, before the nine identical strips of asphalt and houses were thrown up, before everyone came scrambling in like the little ticks they are to suck the soil dry. There's not enough water, he said, and his yellowing middle-aged eyes were glazed over. Welcome to the neighborhood. Nick promised they weren't staying.

"Wanna bet?" He laughed and left.

Metzger's dog and his wife both died in that house. Metzger had the dog stuffed, and it stands at the foot of the stairs by the front door. He also kept his wife's body in their bed for four days before calling anyone. And that's when Nick sees it: Whatever crawls along his shoulder is thick. Metzger brushes at it without looking, and Nick nods absently, waiting. Metzger finally sees it, pinches it, and holds it up in the light from his flashlight. It's a cicada and it's buzzing, trying to free itself. Metzger balls it up in his fist, turns, and hurls it into the blackness. He finds a brown shell on the lawn. "They're everywhere. Look through it." He holds it up and Nick sees the vertebrae, the eye sockets. "That split on the back, see it, that sliver, that's where the little shits slither out." He laughs and crushes the shell in his palm, dusts himself off. "Going to Kostya's thing?"

"Wouldn't miss it."

Metzger's shaking his head. "Neighborhood barbecue with this bunch. Now, that's some shit I want to see."

Nick grins, close to pulling away.

"I'm an OG!" Metzger yells, laughing, inexplicably using black Southern California slang.

Nick laughs out loud, pulls away, and then says to himself, "And I'm the new breed."

He rolls past the dark and deserted house next door to Metzger's: The family of four who inhabited it disappeared in the night four weeks ago, leaving behind most of their possessions. They were the first family to drop on Carousel Court. They slipped away before they were locked out or chased out. There would be more. Nick hopes one will be the man next door, suspects it might be the Mormons. He knows Phoebe wanted it to be their own house, to come home one night from ten hours in the car to find a U-Haul backed into the driveway, Nick and Kostya filling it. It wouldn't matter where they were going, just that they were leaving. Nick knows it's just as likely that Phoebe will come home to find the locks changed, a conspicuous Day-Glo orange notice on the door from the county sheriff's department to match the young neighbor's. It's a matter of time, months or weeks, he doesn't know. It requires only one or two late payments these days. It isn't whether or not it will happen but what he can do that no one else has already thought of or tried, some way to bow out gracefully, his marriage and balls intact.

Traffic is light on the wide streets leading out of Serenos. At a red light, Nick removes a worn black-leather pouch from the glove compartment, drops into it his multi-tool with the three-inch blade and a pair of heavy-duty pliers, and removes the pepper spray and a box cutter. He spent an hour last night on the back patio by the pool sipping Heinekens, a white towel at his feet, his tools aligned just so. With one of Jackson's old cloth wipes and a small tin of Red Devil oil, he cleaned each of them. He heard nothing when he cleaned his tools: not the young neighbor playing his music too loud; not the plaintive wails of dogs (or were they coyotes?) from the barren hillsides; not the dry brush in the wind. A crowbar, bolt cutters, a multi-tool, and a short blade. He was some kind of benevolent failure. Or madman. He was a thirty-two-year-old college-educated father drowning his family in debt but energized by a simple prospect: proving to Phoebe that he alone, not a New York banker or some handsome young physician, was the winning play still.

4

Phoebe can barely hear the music coming from next door over the incessant chorus of cicadas as she walks around the house with Jackson held to her chest, turning on all the lights. Nick left for work an hour ago, his third night this week. The last two words from him as she closed and locked the door behind him and set the ADT were "Lights on."

She carries Jackson and his clean laundry upstairs to his room. A CD of international children's songs plays from his Bose box. Jackson fills a Tonka truck with Matchbox cars while Phoebe hums along to his songs. She folds his size-2T shirts and shorts and places them neatly in his blue three-drawer dresser. The blinds are closed and the ceiling fan turns slowly as she arranges his books neatly on the shelf. She straightens a framed illustration from *Where the Wild Things Are* that hangs over his crib. She turns on the light and dims it. The room is bathed in orange light and peaceful as she sits on the plush beige carpeting with Jackson. Downstairs, the refrigerator hums, churns: a fresh batch of ice cubes. The LG stainless steel behemoth is restocked with organic raspberries, blueberries, kiwi, mangoes, and strawberries. Thick slices of bruschetta brushed with olive oil. She'll eat both, one side rubbed with a cut garlic clove while it's still hot, the way JW showed her once when he took her to a long lunch three months after she was hired at twenty-four, a perk and a leg up that she surely hadn't earned yet.

All good? comes the text from Nick.

Fine

Is he sleeping?

Just now

You should see this place — insane

She doesn't respond. She has nothing to say about whatever he encounters on the other side of the door, all these rotting five-bedroom corpses and their Bermuda grass, yellow from neglect.

Before Nick left the house, he had her by the jaw. Something he's done since their first weeks together, when he held it in bed, perched over her. "There's something about you," he'd say. It had a calming effect on her until recently, because now they're thirty-two with a son and debt and tumbling down the face of something they never anticipated and the gesture sends all the wrong signals, draws attention to his limitations. Like a grandfather doing the same lame magic trick for the grandchild, who is a teenager now and bored, because that's all he's got. Tonight, when Nick was lacing up his boots, giving her instructions, she knew he was feeling guilty about leaving them alone again.

"Kostya and Marina are home." The neighbors, who might be considered friends, were also in their early thirties, with two sons and a daughter, all somehow named after pickup trucks, Titan, Tundra, and she always forgot the third. "Call them, obviously . . ." Nick trailed off. "If anything happens." His back to her, he sat on the stairs in the clean marble foyer. His voice echoed when he called out: "It's Loma Linda. Maybe an hour from here."

But Phoebe didn't hear Nick because Jackson was awake again and wailing. He hadn't slept through the night all summer, since they arrived in June. He knew something Nick and Phoebe only suspected. His fitfulness was an alarm they'd heed if they could. Phoebe was at the top of the double-ascending Couture by Sutton buttercream-carpeted spiral staircase. She was headed to their son's powder-blue bedroom with its crown molding and accents of textured glow-in-the-dark galaxies of stars and moons. She turned and studied Nick, who had climbed back up the stairs, looking shorter than his six-foot frame when set against the sixteen-foot ceilings.

"You feel good," he said as he gently massaged one of her breasts even though she held their son between them. "Really fucking good."

She closed her eyes and rested her chin on his shoulder and exhaled. "Tired," she said.

"When do you leave in the morning?"

"Early," she said. "Maybe seven."

"We'll miss each other."

"Again," she said.

Dirty dishes top off the kitchen sink, wet laundry clings to the inside walls of the washer, musty from neglect, forgotten last night or the night before. The landline never rings. They turned it off because all the calls are from lenders or collections and there's no point in answering. The days are tough and grinding, long needles scraping bone.

It's just past one A.M. In the upstairs bathroom, Phoebe swallows her last five milligrams of Klonopin because even curled up next to Jackson's crib under her old comforter with his night-lights and hushed breathing, she couldn't sleep. The pillbox she keeps in the Explorer (they drove to North Hollywood to pick it up the day before, a new battery installed) is empty. So, too, is the bottle in the bathroom vanity.

Did you take my klonopin? That's the text she sends Nick.

There's no immediate response.

She studies herself in their sweeping vintage Astoria pivot mirror, finds a single long silver hair, and pulls it from her scalp. Nick's right: She's too thin. And the thinner she gets, the older she looks. She runs her fingers lightly along her collarbone, then smiles weakly at herself, full dry lips and almond-shaped eyes and eyebrows that Nick traces with his thumb when they're getting along.

The vibration is her iPhone.

No. You finished them. You just lost track. You're not paying attention.

While she tries to think of a response, he writes:

Again, Phoebe.

She possesses an ability now, since the

move, if not months before, to tune him out. Nick playing the role of concerned, engaged husband, her partner, looking out for her well-being: Watch yourself, careful, keep an eye on this because these are serious drugs. Want another reason why? Run your finger along the raised pink scar on Jackson's scalp.

What Nick doesn't know, what he can't possibly grasp, is the interaction with the second glass of wine or the Maker's Mark she sneaks in the afternoons when she finds herself home, skipping appointments while he works, wandering their bloated new-construction house, considering picking up Jackson's toys, then deciding that their presence, scattered across the plush carpet and glass coffee table, gives the place warmth. She lazily undresses, runs a bath, places the bottle of Maker's Mark on the cool tile floor.

And tonight, even with the low dosage, she has enough in her system to effectively complement the Maker's Mark. She wipes condensation from the face of her iPhone, taps out another message to Nick after sliding into hot water.

Do you know how comfortable I am right now, Nick? This very instant?

Klonopin cocktails don't go well with warm late-night baths.

I'm not trying to hide it.

As evidenced by the empty little MM bottles in the recycling bin.

Eco-friendly ;)

Careful Phoebe

Afraid I'll go under?

Afraid you'll want to.

Nick is also right when he prods her about work. She *is* slipping. The allergy and anxiety products she's been selling for GSK are the same she sold for four years back east. Now she follows the GPS directions to medical office campuses and hospitals from Santa Ana to North Hollywood. She's been back at it since they arrived, makes only some of her appointments, rarely tends to her cold-call list, occasionally dropping in to the doctor's offices with her sample case and sales pitch, flat and without conviction. She makes the appearance, reads the script she's memorized, leaves the office before the physician's second glance at her legs. She's doing enough to stay employed, barely, the handsome young physician she courted recently a unique exception.

What she also does is linger in the produce section at Whole Foods, watching brown men in black aprons thoughtfully arrange and tend to red, gold, and deep-green vegetables. Whole Foods trips trigger a uniquely intoxicating blend of adrenaline rush and sedation. Or maybe it's the Klonopin. Or both. Since the move here, she's learned that the fine mist showering the mustard greens, arugula, and summer squash is on a forty-second cycle — ten seconds on, thirty seconds off. Lentils, red beans, omega-3–enriched milk, brown rice, and kale: It is all there, aisles of superfoods, a road map to cultivate the healthiest child on the planet. Jackson deserves nothing less. On that much, she and Nick agree.

She'll come home with too many organic red bell peppers, asparagus shoots. They can't afford the food, don't even always cook it. She'll throw out the same bunches of kale and broccoli, never getting around to steaming them. Her attempt last Sunday at fennel with leeks, roasted red peppers, marinated feta, and Greek olives was a disaster, stuffed down the garbage disposal before Nick got home.

The down comforter is from the master bedroom, the same comforter they've had since they moved in together eight years ago. The faded stains are spilled wine and soy sauce. She clings to it like a child. She curls up with an oversize blue pillow next to Jackson's crib and stares at her iPhone, listening to her son's fitful breathing. She sends a message to Marina, apologizing for blowing off shopping the other day, and asks if she's going to the playground this weekend and if they're still on for *Desperate Housewives* Sunday night. The response is immediate.

Hell Yes, girlfriend! Juicy Couture. U like?

The image is of Marina: pouty, too tan, bleached blond, with her wide forehead and bright red lipstick and pale blue eyes. She wears a too-low-cut camisole, her swollen breasts spilling out.

Hot, Phoebe lies.

ciao, skinny thing

Nick's right about her losing weight. But Nick's wrong, too. She does not obsess about what didn't happen. Of course, she considers where they were supposed to be instead of Carousel Court. After Jackson's asleep and Nick is working or knocked out upstairs or on the patio throwing rocks at shadows on the dry hillside behind the house or walking the block playing vigilante, she spends idle hours Googling Redondo and Hermosa Beach and child-friendly restaurants and playgrounds within walking distance of where they'd planned to live.

It wasn't a breakdown, but it was close. Her exhaustion sent her into the back of the idling UPS truck, then spinning helplessly into oncoming cross-traffic, and on that January night thirty minutes south of Medford, Massachusetts, she nearly killed Jackson. But it wasn't the pastel pink, blue, and yellow pills, it was fatigue. That much she knew. And fucking Nick. It was all on her, Phoebe felt, to run this thing. To keep them going. If they were going to ascend, plateau at a level she could live with, it was all on her. Phoebe knew and resented it. Nick's grand solution: Move them to a beachfront rental on the West Coast, secure an investment property to upgrade, flip for enough profit to secure their future. All the while giving Phoebe what she desperately needed, if not deserved: a summer off to spend with her son. An undisturbed period of rest and regeneration. Time and space to figure out what she wanted next for herself. Nick, though, can't deliver on his promise once again. His overreach astounds her. The realization that he's simply not up to this is too much to contemplate alone on a windy night.

5

Bank-sanctioned home invasions. When Nick and his crew of six from Everything-MustGo! arrive at a location, it's never a surprise, but it's always unwelcome. Men hauling and tossing leather sectionals and flat-screens from a home into Dumpsters or the back of a pickup truck makes neighbors uneasy, even suspicious. Nick keeps work stories to himself because there is nothing about his vocation that Phoebe wants to hear.

On a hot Wednesday morning last week on a cul-de-sac in Chino, a gold minivan slowed to a crawl while the men worked. The driver stopped, got out, and without saying a word, started whipping cans of tuna fish and then a full bottle of marinara sauce at Nick's crew. She missed everyone. As she threw, Nick noticed her diamond engagement ring and wedding band. One of the tuna cans went through the living room window. Out of breath, unsure of her next move, she yelled, "*Fuck* B of A!," and the crew laughed, relieved, having learned to expect worse.

The next day, a hot morning, the crew was rushing through a trash-out on Del Torino in Lake Elsinore. On the front lawn of every house on their side of the street was a freshly planted *Bank-Owned* sign. The car that crept to the house where they worked, turned slowly into the driveway, was a red Dodge Challenger. It idled for too long; the driver leaned sideways into the passenger's seat. From the airless, empty living room, Nick watched as the crew stood in the shade from a thicket of wilting palms, drinking Red Bull. They all studied the car. A man got out; forty, maybe younger. He was shirtless and walked casually through the open front door of the house. Around his head, like a turban, he'd wrapped a blue towel with white stripes. Nick realized when he saw it that it was from the set of towels that he and Phoebe had at home, purchased when they first arrived, along with emerald-green tumblers and a wicker patio set from Crate & Barrel that they couldn't afford. It had something to do with the heat, Nick thought. Maybe the towel was soaked in cold water. The man fumbled with his keys, pointed them in the direction of the car, set the alarm, dropped them on the marble foyer floor. He was barefoot, unshaven, and he carried something sharp in his left hand. In the other, a silver revolver. Before the ambulance and police arrived, it was Sean who found the keys to the car, opened the driver's-side door, pocketed something he pulled from the center console. Loose change? A cell phone? Nick didn't bother asking.

Nick can't understand why he froze in the narrow hallway between the kitchen and the man. He should have run. Turned a corner, found the back door, barreled through it, and run. But he did nothing. He watched as the man, who acknowledged none of them, took the sharp object — a small blade — and sliced his pale, hairy chest from the left shoulder to his abdomen. He winced, and the blood distracted Nick until he realized that the man was swallowing the barrel of the gun, and Nick's hands rushed involuntarily to cover his ears and head and all he heard was the explosion. There was no mess. The towel trapped the skull and bits of brain. Nick gave a statement to the police. Trying to push the image away, the man's bloodshot eyes, the echo from the single shot, the dull thud of the body collapsing on the dirty marble floor.

All Phoebe wants to hear from Nick these days, all she can handle, is news of a job prospect comparable to the one they came out here for: his production manager position with the boutique Encino firm. The career he trained for. But no one is hiring, he reminds her. His voice will rise when he's defending himself: "There is no position to *pursue*!" And when they exhaust the subject yet again, Phoebe moves seamlessly to the next item on her list: reassurance that their own investment experiment on Carousel Court is appreciating well beyond the eighty-seven thousand dollars in upgrades. Because if it's not, or won't be soon, what are they doing? The answer is clear: It isn't and won't be anytime soon.

Tonight's work goes quickly. The house in Agoura Hills lies on a deserted street of matching middle-class houses. It's late and dark, the electricity still flows, and all the lights are turned on inside.

Nick's not in charge this time, just helping out. This is not his regular crew. He's never met these guys. None of the four men except Nick speaks English, and even though the men don't speak, there's a sense among them that they dodged a bullet tonight. If the house were somewhere else, somewhere harder-hit, with no power, the mood would be tense.

A neighbor in a bathrobe appears with two Weimaraners. The dogs sense something, seem agitated, growling, pulling on their leashes.

"What the hell?" the neighbor says, eyeing the green Dumpster, the furniture, and the rolled-up carpets being carried out of the house. He's cursing his dogs before Nick can answer. They're ignoring him. The dogs don't want Nick but whatever is around the right side of the house, which is all blackness.

"Just tidying up," Nick tells him.

"They've been gone a week," the neighbor says.

"Two, actually," Nick corrects him.

The man surveys the items, a stained red leather recliner, a walnut entertainment console, a Dyson vacuum cleaner. "Help yourself," Nick calls out over the insane barking of the dogs. The man shakes his head, yanks the leashes hard, disappears down the orange-lit street.

The sound coming from behind the house: voices, urgent. Nick finds the other three members of the crew, one directing the beam of a flashlight into the dry brush at the edge of the property. Another man hurls a rock in the same direction. Whatever set the neighbors' dogs off is back there and has everyone on edge. The third member of the crew, young and skinny, produces a black pistol, points it at the brush. The oldest of the three slaps him.

"Pendejo!"

The gun disappears. A bottle is thrown, shatters against a rock. There's no sound. The oldest, the crew leader, instructs the others to go inside, finish the job.

When they're gone and Nick is alone in the backyard, he turns on his own flashlight, approaches the dry brush. Chained to a headstone-sized boulder is a terrified, emaciated black dog. The animal makes itself as small as it can, low to the ground, squirms toward Nick, cowering. Three dirty Tupperware dishes and a porcelain bowl with a trace of brown water surround the animal. Nick cleans caked yellow crust from its eyes. The animal wags its brittle tail, ears tucked back. Pink and festering red skin where the collar was pulled too tight around the neck. Nick loosens the choke chain.

He takes a picture of the neglected thing and sends it to Phoebe with a message:

Owners left it behind.

The image: a sickly dog that is all matted

fur and bones with white flecks around his chin and muzzle and his pleading brown eyes.

Nick calls Phoebe. "What do you think?" he asks.

"About what?" she responds.

"He's sweet. Well-trained."

She sighs.

"We have plenty of room. Jackson would love it," he says.

"Where does it come from?" she asks.

"What?"

"A dog, Nick?"

Silence. He lowers his voice. "There are so many of these houses, Phoebe. Deserted."

"So what?"

"People are scared," he says. "They're desperate and have nowhere to go. You know what they need?"

The dog drinks from the hose Nick has turned on.

"A place to collect their thoughts, make a plan," he continues. Nick directs the hose on the back of the dog, fresh cool water cascading over the infected skin and matted fur.

All someone would have to figure out was the logistics: how to get the houses ready, how to get people in, how to collect and move on. All the homes are new construction. All he has to do is slap on fresh coats of paint, clean the carpets, drain and refill the pools. Where would an anxious family rather plot its next moves: some Motel 6, a friend's basement, or a three-bedroom house with a pool and Nick as their landlord?

"Houses," he says to Phoebe. "I know where they are. They're all sitting empty and clean, and there are too many for the banks to track."

"I don't know what you mean, Nick."

"It's a disaster out here. No one's in charge. I can put people in these houses, and we can get something going."

"Renting vacant houses? Just so we're clear. That's your idea?"

"How badly do you want to get off of Carousel Court?"

• •

Nick had called the number from the orange flier the same day he tore it from the wall. EverythingMustGo! was the name of the company, but the voice that picked up just said, "Yeah." When Nick said why he was calling, the voice started firing questions: Was he in shape? Yes. Did he have his own transportation? Yes. From? Boston. Did he know the area? Not yet. Education level? College graduate. That slowed things down, the answer unexpected, and the rest of the responses led to a half-hour meeting at a diner in Chino Hills, where the questions continued.

"Why do you need this job?" the boss asked him.

Then: "When you stumble on a corpse in some bedroom, will you pull the diamond ring from the finger?"

Nick stared at him. There was nothing to say.

"Messing with you." The man laughed. "What did you do in Boston?"

"Film production."

"You can't find that out here?"

"Had an offer that fell through. And now no one's hiring."

"That's for sure."

"But you are," Nick said.

"I am."

The man, for some reason, studied Nick's résumé, seemed genuinely interested in if not impressed by Nick's background, and peppered him with more questions, none of which had anything to do with the job. Nick told the man about his trip to New Orleans after Katrina, when he'd driven down to document the aftermath, pitch to cable networks, piece together a documentary short. As he showed the man his driver's license and a pay stub from his last job, Nick studied the thin gold chain and shaved fat head of the man his employees called "Boss" and wondered what other angles the man was playing and how soon Nick could find his own. The world around them was sliding into the sea, furnished houses left behind in the dark of night. Everything was folding in on itself, yet Boss wore a soft pink polo shirt with his collar up and Ray-Bans and a fresh cigar he lit only when he started the ignition of his white convertible Lexus and said, "Welcome aboard. Have a hunch you'll do well here." It took under three months for Nick to earn the promotion to crew chief.

"You married?" Boss had asked him that warm spring morning in Chino Hills.

"Six years," Nick said without hesitation. He sipped his coffee, which was cold. The man stabbed a greasy sausage link with a fork and, without looking up, said: "She scared yet?" The question caught Nick off guard. Its precision cut like the sharp edge of the dry palm fronds that scraped Jackson's bedroom windows at night.

• •

Nick races by a refinery he can't see, breathes in the warm, oily air that whips through the Subaru. He smells his fingers. It's not the refinery, it's him — the Red Devil he used to clean his tools, a task of questionable utility aside from its meditative qualities. It helped him slip into character, readying himself for whatever awaited them inside the dead house in the darkness. Nick keeps the windows down so he can hear whether or not the rattle is getting louder.

Before he left their house on Carousel Court for the overnight job, he shot a look through the foyer window: the orange military-style tent on Metzger's lawn; the lighting he helped Kostya install along the front of his house; and the feeling that no amount of security devices could undo what was done, or worse, prevent what was to come. Jackson squirmed and giggled between him and Phoebe; a game, Mommy and Daddy closing in around him before Daddy headed out for the night. That was when Nick brushed Phoebe's strong jaw. He could have squeezed it until it cracked, but what good would that do? He'd rather hold it, marvel at its bold lines and angles, the faded little scar on her chin, the perfect symmetry of her face. Hers is a face people steal when they create fake online profiles. They actually found her face on three social media accounts. (She deactivated, then reactivated, then deactivated her own account when they arrived in Serenos.) Hers is a face that sells Advair to physicians who don't need it. A face that deserves granite countertops and recessed lighting and the excess of rooms that require designers to come up with new names like "double-bonus room." Boss likes him. Nick thinks he'll have this gig as long as he wants. What he can't wrap his mind around, what he dreads: facing her in the quietest hours of the night when he's the reason she can't sleep.

6

Phoebe stands on the hot pavement, drinking a cold Fiji water. The sun is a blistering yolk. Phoebe will be in the San Fernando Valley all day. She looks up when a helicopter roars overhead, too low, giving chase. She finds the sun, which momentarily blinds her. Her eyes adjust as an impossibly thin blond woman in tennis whites and sunglasses pushes two bleached-blond Ethiopian kids effortlessly across the black asphalt in a Bugaboo Cameleon double stroller, two thousand minimum, Phoebe thinks.

Nick bought them a Bugaboo last year, spending money they didn't have and wouldn't earn anytime soon, and she was fourteen pounds overweight and spent every weekend in her purple sweatshirt, and the living room was a disaster and this thousand-dollar stroller they didn't need and couldn't afford sat there like part of some kind of disdainful Puzzle Time quiz on Nick Jr.: Which of the objects in this room is laughably out of place?

The small Korean woman massaging Phoebe's feet in warm water is completely silent. The nail salon is nearly empty. Phoebe turns off her iPhone, closes her eyes, and tries to sleep behind her sunglasses.

Back in the car, the air-conditioning dries her French manicure. She's spent five hundred hours in the company Explorer. The mileage reads 10,303. It read 789 the day in June when Nick drove her to North Hollywood in the dirty Subaru to pick it up. They spoke six words to each other that morning:

"You missed the exit," she said.

"Fuck me."

It's the middle of August now. She inherited all of her clients from a rep whose job she got when the other woman quit to spend more time with her three-year-old daughter. The colleague reminded Phoebe that with so many hours in the car, she should have a second agenda, some other project to fill the hours. In the Notes app on her iPhone, stuck in traffic, the woman wrote a children's book about a boy who ate his blanket and it turned into a cape, as well as a treatment and three episodes of a TV series about a young professional mother whose daughter was dropped on her head as a newborn and now speaks only Japanese, despite being raised by white people and having a Salvadoran nanny. It's a comedy, she explained. Phoebe insisted she had enough to keep her busy, but the woman pressed the point: Be damn sure, because five years can slip through your fingers.

More Starbucks and Krispy Kremes for the office staff. Phoebe can do more of what she did back east. More explicit pics for the docs sent from the Bebe dressing room. But she can't bring herself to drive two more hours to a few more offices to fill bins in sample closets and make nice with moody office managers to get a few minutes in the office of a new doc who simply doesn't need what she's selling. A year ago she was Diamond Status: ten-thousand-dollar bonus (over three months' rent) and a four-day cruise to the Bahamas that she gave to her mother who never did use it. Now she's slipping. She's unranked. Her bonus this year if nothing changes: a navy GSK fleece pullover, bathrobe, and slippers.

The email that arrives on Phoebe's iPhone is from Citibank. A check has cleared. The email is for Serenos Montessori. The amount is a hundred dollars.

She forwards the email to Nick along with: *???*

Her cell rings.

"A deposit," Nick says.

"For what?"

"It's small and affordable. Ten-minute drive."

"From where?"

"It's an option."

"Not for us. Not here," she says.

"Come January?"

"We won't be here, Nick."

She ends the call.

The tank is nearly empty, but Phoebe doesn't like to refill it until the end of the day, so it will be as full as possible in the morning. She can get through an entire day on a full tank, not have to refill once, if she stops at the 76 station near the house. To get through one day without having to stop for gas is a challenge she sets for herself every week. But there's no way to wait that long today, so she pulls in to a Chevron station. The gas card her job gives her still isn't working.

She sends two texts to her district manager:

Card's not working again. How many times? Still haven't been reimbursed for last two tanks. This makes three

He doesn't respond.

She uses her own credit card, has no idea how close to the limit they are. It works and the tank is full. She checks the pressure on all four tires. Two need air, and she pulls the Explorer over to the air pump but doesn't have quarters, so she leaves, will do it later.

She counts the six lanes of traffic. She has no more appointments, is dizzy from withdrawal and counting the white lines on the gray freeway. Her head is light from not eating. She's on the 101, passes signs for San Bernadino and Santa Ana. The 405 is what she needs, but she's not paying attention and is pushed into the right lane. She has to get left, and there's a green light, but it's a flashing X, which makes no sense, telling her to go but it's wrong, there's clearly no room at all for her. As tractor-trailers and Harleys roar past her in the far right lane, there's simply no opening. Phoebe's gripping the wheel tightly when she guns it. A black Dodge Charger is feet from her rear bumper. There's nowhere to go. She speeds up. The Dodge swerves, passes, cuts her off. Her throat is tight. She can't swallow. The traffic won't slow. She accelerates. Texts pour in and she can't resist the urge to look down and click the icon, then looks up, hugging the concrete divider, pulls the wheel to the right, charred remains of a crash lie in a heap on the shoulder. The text is from a doctor with *a raging hard-on until I had to shoot all over my wife while picturing you.*

Another from Nick that says *Nice list* in response to a Post-it with tasks for the rest of his Friday and the weekend.

You do realize I worked overnight last night and am just getting home. Will be sure to squeeze this shit in before the four jobs I have this weekend.

The sunlight around a sharp bend momentarily blinds her. Without seeing, she swerves, switches lanes. Two more lanes and she's over, brakes hard, and is off the freeway. The engine idles, the company car in park on the shoulder as traffic flows past, indifferent. She exhales and starts tapping the steering wheel that she still grips with her thumbs until she's pounding it. Her extreme dream.

• •

At yet another post-college party off of Boylston Street, Nick complained to an Emerson friend about getting stuck with a water bill because a running toilet went unaddressed by the landlord (along with two faulty outlets, a leak in the ceiling, and mold). The bill was a week's salary for Nick, whose days were spent in a windowless basement office managing the schedules of unpaid interns and cataloging the PR firm's client reels.

The words that introduced Phoebe into his life he said more to himself and were less about the apartment or job than his life: "I might just burn it down and start over."

"Sounds like a plan."

He took her in: athletic with thin shoulders, green eyes, and a jaw he wished he had. Her lips were full, her cheekbones sculpted, and her eyebrows thin and arched; there was a sharpness to her.

"Two words: tenant's rights," she said. She instructed Nick to stop paying rent and file a claim with the help of the public advocate's office.

"There's such a thing?"

"I have a friend."

"And if I'm evicted?"

"Won't happen. Landlords feed off tenants' fear. Especially kids. Smack him upside the head and watch what happens."

The landlord caved, paid the bill, and

replaced the toilet.

They quickly fell into an easy rhythm of weekend mornings with bagels and coffee while Nick read the *Globe* and Phoebe went online or scheduled her week and paid bills and returned calls to friends. They went to the farmers' market and movies at the Outer Circle or the Uptown. Nothing they did together ever felt like work. They'd stand in line outside Pasta Mia on thirty-degree nights, sniffling, holding each other, her cinnamon breath visible. Invitations always poured in for Phoebe. Yet there was no party or event Phoebe declined that made her feel like she was missing something. Instead of taking the party cruise down the Charles, they welcomed the new millennium on the roof of her building in a sleeping bag with a bottle of wine. She wondered what Nick would look like with his head shaved, so he let her do it. He liked that she always seemed to smell as though she'd just stepped out of the shower.

"You have really long fingers," he told her one morning in bed, not long after she shaved his head. "You should let your nails grow."

She stared at him and said, "You look better with hair."

She was self-conscious about her overbite

and the slight gap between her front teeth. Nick loved it. What he was less fond of but also appreciated was her forthrightness: Phoebe's tendency to goad Nick, accuse him of settling too easily, accepting average outcomes for himself. When he didn't follow up on a production assistant gig for MSNBC in New York, she was livid and wondered aloud if his lack of killer instinct might be their undoing. She had rough edges. She had ambition and volatility that aroused Nick. She knew people: bouncers, managers, bartenders. She seemed to know everyone. They once brought home a friend of hers with the intention of having a three-way, but the girl got sick before anything happened and spent the night on the bathroom floor. Phoebe twisted his balls once during rough sex, and he spent an hour nude, in the fetal position, battered by tsunamis of pain. She grabbed a blue gel ice pack from the freezer and tickled his back with her fingernails.

She could pull off any look: Nick's Mets cap and V-neck T-shirt and jeans or strappy little black dress from Bebe. She was the most gorgeous woman Nick had ever dated. She was tall and angular. On their couch (she moved in after five months), she ate ice cream from the container with an appletini, her phone constantly buzzing, someone always asking a favor: Could she cover a shift, pick a person up from Logan, let her crash on the floor for a night after a fight with the boyfriend? She always said yes. Favor asked, favor granted. Up and out the door. She knew Nick felt slightly intimidated, and she liked that, reveled in it.

Her father, the merchant marine, volunteer firefighter, and finally, driver for UPS, who left the family when Phoebe was twelve and had been in touch only three or four times, called her on September 12, 2001. It was the first time they'd spoken in six years, and the call lasted twenty minutes and ended with Phoebe in tears, her father still talking, cursing the women in his life, who were all leeches and takers. Within a week she'd applied for a job as an FBI agent. She trained relentlessly: On days when she bartended the lunch-to-close shift at the boutique hotel in the city she woke up at six thirty to get to the indoor pool to swim, lift weights, run a few miles. Nick called her "Special Agent" and bought her a fake badge. They drove to a shooting range and blasted holes through Osama bin Laden. She ate a Paleo diet: leafy greens, nuts, and fish. She cut her hair shorter than Nick liked, but he was so turned on by the whole mission that it didn't matter. Nick would come on her as she clenched, and he'd watch it slide down the smooth surface of her taut stomach. But Phoebe's pursuit of a career in law enforcement sputtered. Dark winter mornings made getting out from under the covers with Nick more difficult. More shifts were available at the bar, and they needed the money, so she took them. Worked later, slept more. Her hair grew back. She craved Pasta Mia and Belgian waffles for Sunday brunch at the diner. Nick didn't mind. There was no shortage of adventure, she said. They'd find another mission.

"This is going to be fun," Nick said when he asked her. They were twenty-six. It was the weekend after Labor Day. They'd driven to the Cape. He had an artsy handcrafted silver ring with an emerald-green stone that cost ninety dollars. They'd each gotten a week off from their jobs: By then Nick was at a small PR firm with mostly commercial clients, and Phoebe had just completed orientation for new hires at an investment firm downtown. She was meeting partners, she told Nick. The first week. She was having lunch the next week with a senior manager. She was making an impression. She worked insane hours. She was up at five thirty, at the office by seven. She had a new mission.

Their after-tax income was stable. They had Saturday-morning co-ed soccer and Sunday Pats games with a keg and wings and mutual friends. There was an easy rhythm to their life together that allowed Nick to overlook the lull Phoebe hit when the FBI thing came to an end. There was a month, maybe two, during which she withdrew, sleeping too much, watching daytime TV, letting calls go to voice mail until the box was full and you couldn't leave a message. She gave no more rides to friends. She and Nick fucked, but it felt strange; she was indifferent, never saying no but never seeming to enjoy it. Once or twice he stopped and told her he wouldn't finish until she did. "Then don't finish." And it was winter and she hated winter and Nick wanted to think that was it but he knew better.

What he'd learned from spending those years together and what gave him some peace of mind about the lull was this: She would find something else and the fire would return and calls would be answered, rides given, television turned off, fucking until they both finished, like it mattered to her. What he didn't concern himself with then and what would surely become relevant to him in ways he couldn't begin to anticipate was this: Where would she channel her manic energy if she didn't find another mission? When it was time for Phoebe to cycle up again, all of that drive would have to go somewhere. And Nick couldn't see or refused to recognize an unavoidable outcome: She would eventually turn it on him, and he better be ready.

• •

It's almost four. She's in Hermosa Beach because she had one more appointment today, but it was in Tustin, and when she saw how far that was on the GPS, she canceled it. Seagulls cry out overhead, steady themselves in the wind while the surf rushes over Phoebe's bare legs, her shoes dangling in her right hand, iPhone in the other. The sun has burned through the marine layer and the sky is bright blue. She doesn't want to leave the beach, refuses to return to the car, head east, two hours with traffic. Picking up Jackson is her only motivation. When they found the house on Carousel Court, went all in and bought it, Nick promised: "And we'll have a summer rental on the beach." But they aren't on the beach. They're nowhere near it. She resolves to bring Jackson back here this weekend whether Nick's working or not.

There's a small team of people shooting footage of a surfer. When they were first living together, Nick was showing her all this footage from documentaries and newsreels he most admired, from far-off places ravaged by war or natural disaster. "On the ground," he would say. "In the middle of it," he'd add. "Someone has to be there, go there, put the pieces together, and bring it to life. That's all I want to do. Be in the middle of it." It could be a tsunami or some civil war or famine or disease-ravaged place; he ticked off a list of topics for pitches he'd already written and sent off to production companies in Boston, New York, and Los Angeles. The quiet certainty in his tone convinced Phoebe that it was realistic: He would be going overseas to make documentary films, and she would go, too, and their reality, their life together, would revolve around immunizations and efficient packing, checklists and emergency procedures, local militias and rogue fighters, moments of sheer terror — lawless states ravaged by civil unrest, the stench of human remains — all so Nick could capture it, bring the tragedy home, raw and unfiltered. And Nick and Phoebe would live to tell about it. She'd go with him. When she got pregnant, Phoebe simply added a nanny to the fantasy. They'd skip the dangerous trips but tag along for the others. When Nick traveled alone, Phoebe would immerse Jackson in French classes. She'd find them a cabin in Maine or the Shenandoahs where they could spend Christmas, chopping wood for the stove. But after Jackson was born, even a move to New Orleans or long weekends in the mountains felt beyond their reach. Worse, Nick seemed okay with that.

And Nick killed it, slowly, with purpose, Monday through Friday, eight thirty to six, week after week. He was in Hartford instead of Havana, calling her to say the commuter flight was canceled and he was renting a car and driving home to Boston and could she record the Celtics game and reminding her that tomorrow was recycling day and to bring the cans down to the basement of the building.

He snapped at her once in Boston, before their new plan took shape. The ones who made a career of it, all those documentary filmmakers, were trust-fund kids, he hissed, staked by their parents. He was convinced, and Phoebe didn't argue, that the young filmmakers could afford to travel the world and shoot footage of disasters or soccer teams because, unlike Nick and Phoebe, they didn't have to earn money for a living. Options are limited, he said, when you have to work for a living.

Her iPhone vibrates. She reads the text:

You didn't leave a message.

It's JW.

She doesn't respond. She called an hour ago, hung up after one ring.

She's at her car, brushing sand from the bottoms of her feet. Two surfers pass by with longboards, oblivious to her. A man with a boxer on a leash ignores her, studies his handheld. She's anonymous here.

I'm flattered that I'm still in your contacts, she writes.

Top of the list and it's alphabetical

How's that?

AwesomePhoebe What about Amanda?

Who?

Ana? April? Araceli??

Funny

Let me guess: Martha's Vineyard. Maine. Lisbon?

My ex's basement apartment. I have nowhere else to stay.

There's nowhere you can't afford to stay

It's a divorce thing. Complicated

Don't you have layoffs to recommend?

Some lives to wreck?

;)

How were the Galapagos?

You still read my emails. Thought you tuned me out.

White noise.

The yoga instructor: breathtaking. Older woman, too. Like fifties and just stunning. And her grad school daughter . . . and two other women. Have you been to Sardinia?

She doesn't respond.

You sent me that SOS in June. And two months later I respond, you're thinking, Typical, right?

And another: *Are you ok? Do you still need me? You had me worried when you wrote that.*

And another: *And yet . . . do you realize how hard it gets me to think about you needing me?*

And one more: *Totally inappropriate but honest, right? Can never be too honest.*

And a last message from him in the string: *Of course I don't expect a response. I never do. Your self-restraint is commendable. Can I take some credit?*

Will try you again when I'm out there, which will be soon.

Days, not weeks.

She taps out a response: *Nearly three*

months, not two. And you're not hiding out in a basement apartment. Who are you really with?

But she doesn't send it. Instead, she deletes it. She's sure he's somewhere else, with someone else, and not his wife or one of his ex-wives. She doesn't care who he's with. It doesn't matter. That's what she tells herself as she turns off her iPhone. Her neck is stiff. She rubs it until the skin burns.

7

The semiautomatic pistol Nick found in the uncovered toilet tank of a house they trashed out in Loma Linda had no rounds in it. He'll never load it, but he's glad he's got it. Despite the gun and Metzger and the floodlights and ADT, Nick and Phoebe stay awake late, leave most of the lights on inside until morning. It has nothing to do with the strange noises they hear, something metallic, scraping, from somewhere inside the house, as if it's alive, or the relentless moaning winds and anguished cries coming from the bone-dry hills that surround and seem to close in on them. He lies awake because he knows the fracture never healed between them. It's a matter of time before the nerve is struck.

He hung wind chimes their first week here, took them down because they kept clanging and getting tangled in the wind. Even with the heat and lack of rain, Nick takes pride in keeping the lawn thick and green. He applies all sorts of synthetics to beef up the turf, keep it lush. The three white chaises by the pool are arranged just so. He swims laps daily. He brings Jackson in with him. When he does, Phoebe warns him to please avoid the deep end. Rings from Phoebe's tumblers of her special-recipe mojitos dot the glass table. Jackson's toys gather neatly around his playhouse, which is finally free from wasps after Nick sprayed it and hosed it down, yet again. Nick habitually circles the perimeter of the house with a flashlight and the unloaded pistol. The water in the pool glows; sharp ends of palm fronds scrape the windows. The dead ones are easily torn loose by the wind, end up floating on the clear water until Nick fishes them out. Cicadas clutch the screens on all the windows, land on the chaises, pelt the living room and kitchen windows. When Jackson was floating on his back in the pool yesterday, a cicada landed on his face. Before his son could react, Nick carefully plucked it from his forehead and crushed it on the poolside concrete.

He checks entry points and blind spots. He finds a living room window unlocked and secures it; one of the ten motion-sensor bulbs is out, so he climbs a ladder two stories and changes it. He scales the fence separating their property from the young neighbor, whose backyard smolders from a recent fire he set: computer monitors, athletic equipment, garbage, end tables. All the lights are on and music plays from inside the house. It will be like this well into the night, and Metzger will call the police, but they won't come or will arrive hours too late. Metzger cursed them out once: "This isn't goddamn Compton! Taxpayers live here." Nick has an eye on the neighbor and Metzger, too, like everything else. He misses nothing.

8

"Did you feed him?" Nick asks Phoebe. There's no response. "Did he eat?" She's facedown on the sectional, passed out again. The house is quiet and cool. She's bathed in seven-thirty twilight that floods the living room on a hot Thursday in August. Nothing's changed since June: a ten-hour day for Phoebe spent in the car means a Klonopin blackout at night.

Summer is almost over, but it's now clear the heat is here to stay. It's the seventh consecutive day over ninety-five degrees. The forecasts warn of no break from the dry, hot pattern. Wildfire and high-wind warnings every day. Nick's been working since nine this morning on a house in North Hollywood after two consecutive night shifts. She can't hear him, and he knows it but asks again: "Did he eat?" *He* being Jackson, who is slouched against Phoebe's ass, his pacifier dangling from dry lips, his diaper bulging, heavy with urine. "Did he eat?"

The television is on, the sound muted. The loop of On Demand coming attractions is the sign that they were watching Jackson's shows. Nick could figure out whether or not his son had dinner with a simple check of the kitchen sink for the plastic cow dishes, empty jars of little meats, pasta twists. But that's not the point. Nick shouldn't have to play detective. He drops to his knees, inches from her face. "Did he eat?"

Nothing. Maybe she's trying to sleep through it all — the night, the summer, this season of their lives together. It's no accident that she's up before the sun, gone before Nick is home or awake, and more often than not, passed out before sundown.

He could scoop her up, carry her to the Subaru, strap her in the passenger seat, and drive her up the coast to Monterey Bay. A bed-and-breakfast. He'd check her in. She'd wake up and ask first about Jackson — where is he, is he okay? — and Nick would tell her he's fine, he's with the Vietnamese supernanny, eating sticky rice and broccoli. Then she'd look around and see the huge trees and gray skies and swatches of blue where they were thinning and ask where they were.

But Phoebe is not Nick's immediate concern. She's passed out, high on Klonopin and Effexor, Ativan and whatever else. She should be someone's priority, just not Nick's, not now. Jackson is the one who needs to be put to bed the same way, at the same time, every night.

"It's not even eight," Nick is saying to himself. "This is why he's always tired. His whole rhythm's messed up." He picks up his soggy son, turns off the television. "Routine. Every night. It's not fair to him, Phoebe." These conversations are so much easier when she's passed out. He actually prefers talking to her when she's blacked out. He can tell the truth. Nick wonders what isn't easier when she's passed out. It's a win-win. Except for Jackson. When he's changed, cleaned up, a fresh dry diaper and pacifier dipped in apple juice slipped in and the night-light and Mozart turned on softly, Nick returns to Phoebe's side and asks again, "Did he eat?" until she jolts awake, confused, sitting up in the dark, Nick still asking the question not for the answer but to make the point, quietly, in the darkness: She is failing her son.

9

Drop-off takes longer than it should. Jackson is a mess. As usual, he is the first child here, along with one employee, a heavy hippie chick from Altadena who wears thick red glasses and a scoop-neck T-shirt that is too small. Jackson is bawling, red-faced. The girl sits down, tries to soothe him, rocks him, sings into his ear a song Phoebe doesn't know. But he wriggles free and falls to the carpeted floor, runs to the door, and slaps it over and over, his silent screaming the last image Phoebe has as she leaves the building.

She fires off a text to Nick:

Yes the nanny would be nice, right? You'd think by this point, right? I know, right, I'm sounding like a raving bitch.

His reply is instantaneous and catches her off guard, though it shouldn't.

Brilliant Phoebe. Spot-on framing of the situation. OUR situation.

Whatever

Remember, babe: every page of the mortgage has TWO signatures on it. But facts and shared responsibility aside: just what IN THE FUCK do you think I'm doing?

• •

Nick was impressed that Phoebe had achieved a starting salary twice her age at twenty-four with full benefits straight out of BU. She assisted a humorless woman with short blond hair and halitosis, but that wasn't the point. The associate analyst position she secured with a leading financial services firm would look solid when she applied to business school, especially if she'd found a mentor. When she started at the firm, she was no different from the other new hires without MBAs: always borrowed, assigned short- and long-term projects, pulled off, put back on, a pawn in a larger chess match between managers, directors, and partners. There were unspoken endurance contests among the new hires: who arrived first, who left last, who came in on the weekend, who spent the most time with the senior analysts, whose phone vibrated the most, who was never found at a desk after being pulled into a meeting, who made any impression at all on a partner. And the crown jewel of achievement: who got a turn with the lead partner, JW.

Laughter was rare in the firm, was rare for JW. But Phoebe made him laugh. When he wasn't on calls or in meetings, he was walking around his cool, bright office with his shoes off. Somehow Phoebe found herself on his soft leather couch, taking notes on her laptop, next to a pair of blades, gloves, two white helmets, pads, and three hockey sticks. He had games on Thursday nights.

"You look better with makeup," she said. He'd been on CNBC that week and she'd watched. He'd invited her to come. She'd laughed and lied and told him she had Bruins tickets.

He asked her how she slipped through the cracks and ended up down in the pits with Jane. He said he was going to look into doing something about that. Maybe he'd bring her on staff, his staff, make her an analyst. "Instead of floating around unclaimed," he said.

"So do it," Phoebe shot back, which made him smile.

"Come watch me play."

"No."

The next week, Thursday, before his hockey

game, he summoned her to his office. It was the third consecutive afternoon he'd called her in. She brought her laptop, was taking a seat on the couch, when he motioned her over to him in the center of the room.

She held the open laptop awkwardly between them. She could smell his aftershave: lighter, almost floral.

"Want to come watch tonight?"

She cleared her throat. "Why do you want me to watch you?"

"Only if you want to. Do you want to?"

Nick is home, she thought. He's home by now and on the couch watching *SportsCenter,* eating leftover Thai or the rest of his burrito from lunch.

"Watch you play hockey with your friends?"

She studied the flecks of white and reddish-brown stubble on his chin. Through the sweeping window behind him, the electric-blue bridge against the night sky.

"This is weird," she said.

He took the laptop from her, placed it on his desk, and returned to her. "What is?"

"I don't even know what this is," she said.

He took her hands. She considered what she'd say to Nick, how she'd rationalize the decision: Do you realize what someone like that can do for someone like me?

So you're some kind of whore? he'd say.

This is our life, Nick. I've made my choice, and I chose you. And it wasn't a mistake. This thing with JW was a calculated risk, and I took it. And the last part would be less than truthful. There was very little calculation involved. Only the adrenaline rush when the door closed behind her and they were alone.

"Close your eyes," he said. "Open your hand."

She followed his directions.

He placed an object in her right hand. "Open your eyes." It was her smartphone. She'd left it in his office. "If you *ever* leave this anywhere other than this office or your home, you will lose your job."

She said nothing.

"You realize the sensitivity of the information on there."

"The password —"

"Forget the password. Anyone can bypass that."

She apologized and started to leave.

"Phoebe," he said. "You have to earn trust."

The following night, after he returned her smartphone to her, Phoebe was again in JW's corner office. It was after eight. The floor was nearly deserted, hushed. Only the cleaning staff made any noise. His shoes were off. He wore a blue oxford, untucked, no tie. He tapped out a text message on his personal phone.

He brought a hand to her face, her jaw.

"The door," she said.

"What about it?"

She moved past him to the window. There were so many boats in the harbor. All the red and white lights drifting across the black water. "So do something." The voice that came from her was steady. Without hesitation and before she could manage to turn around, she felt all the weight of him lean against her, pressing them both against the glass, and she wondered how much force it could withstand.

After, he talked about his family. He smiled when he showed her pictures of his son building sandcastles on a beach, wearing a life vest in a boat on some lake. He seemed to listen when he asked about her relationship with Nick and how they met in college and their apartment and the stupid details of life with no real money as newlyweds and nonstop sex and no sense of where the hell life was taking them. God, he missed those days.

"And these?" she asked. "Will you miss

these days when they're gone?"

"I'll miss this."

"What is *this*?" she asked him.

He laughed. "Hell if I know."

A routine developed between them at work. She'd be at her desk, having called Nick to tell him she was going to yoga or drinks with friends, and she'd have spent twenty minutes in the ladies' room applying MAC eyeliner and Sephora powder that she'd picked up at lunch because it was Thursday and that worked best for JW. His office was always dark except for his desk lamp, and he'd be on his cell and in the middle of things and it was after seven, almost eight, and she'd lock the door behind her and stand at the sweeping glass window and stare out at the new bridge, glowing blue and stuffed with red taillights and white headlights and the cold black water she couldn't see flowing beneath it, and she'd feel her heart race when his call ended and keep her back to him and close her eyes the moment his hands moved up and under her skirt until she was guiding his fingertips gently, easily, inside of her. The thought occurred to her, irrational as it was: This is rubbing off on me. This life and world, the small details of JW, his measured but intense breathing through his nose, the ease with which he maneuvered them across the room, the crispness of his shirt, the warmth of his neck and the faint lines around his eyes and the flecks of gray in his sideburns. She was satiating an appetite she didn't know she had, an appetite that seemed to border on compulsion.

It was bullshit, she thought. She told him this, laughing, one night in his office. "This is ridiculous," she said. Her warm forehead pressed against cold glass.

"What is?"

"This view." She held her hands wide, palms spread, pressing hard against the window as she found his eyes in its reflection.

"Tell me to stop," he said, and slid his hand around her tight waist and pressed himself against her. "Tell me I don't deserve you."

How could Phoebe know what this man deserved? She knew enough not to answer.

"You have everything in front of you," he said. "To be twenty-six again. Jesus."

"Come inside me."

The decadence with JW was somehow irresistible. It felt mature and otherworldly. Town cars dropped them off and picked them up. He chopped spruce trees for the woodstove in his family's cabin. He took Phoebe there on a Saturday morning (when work had kept Nick stuck in Hartford for the weekend) and drove her back to the city the next morning. He spoon-fed her frozen cherimoya that seemed to melt on her tongue in his dimly lit office. He made no apologies or excuses for himself and never once told her he loved her or said a disparaging word about his wife except that she tried too hard sometimes to keep everything in order.

"You," he said a year or so after their first time together in his office, "need a mentor."

"Are you volunteering?"

"Produce," he said. "That's what you tell yourself. Produce. If you do, you'll be fine. If you don't, you won't last."

"Is that a yes?"

"Of course."

"Make me a senior analyst," she said.

"With no MBA."

"But with you as a mentor."

"You're on track," he said.

"For what?"

"There's a path. Don't overthink it. Follow it and you'll have everything you want."

"That's a cop-out."

"You remind me of —"

"Don't say your daughter."

"Me."

She wondered briefly if there was something special about her, some intangible quality that cut through — her aggressiveness, the innate ability she'd always seemed to possess to use her looks, her sexuality, in any situation, with just enough subtlety not to offend or embarrass herself. So many others underplayed or overplayed their hand. She never did. She managed it every time, and this time, when it mattered most, she was nailing it.

"Can we make a deal?"

"Name it."

"Something significant. When I've got my MBA. Help me land somewhere."

"If you earn your MBA, I'm all yours," he said.

"I'm not walking away from this without something real. Understand that."

• •

Idling in the Explorer, air-conditioning blasting, before pulling out of the Bouncin' Babies lot, she taps out a text message:

Well it's late summer so . . . you're in Maine at the lake house with the wide dock and blue sailboats. You're in khaki shorts, gray T, and leather sandals, and your Tag Heuer is wrapped around your thick tan wrist as you sip your second mint julep, and you haven't decided yet: lobster or crab or maybe a Chilean sea bass, and there's nowhere on the planet you'd rather be . . . with maybe one exception.

There's no response.

10

All the night jobs are scheduled late, in the quietest hours, for a reason: High-risk properties require an element of surprise, and the less attention they call to themselves, the easier the work. There's been talk at EverythingMustGo! of moving all the work to overnight hours, but there are too many houses now, springing up like weeds, too much money to be made not to work day *and* night.

Tonight feels different. It's Rialto, not as nice as Agoura Hills. And tonight, when he left the house with his clean tools, he and Phoebe weren't speaking since he can't take Jackson to the pediatrician tomorrow because he's working all night and she can't because she has appointments all day and he called bullshit and told her to skip Equinox for once and she asked for the last five film production positions he applied for.

The Hondurans can't keep the dog they

found, and he says he'll take it even though Phoebe called him a bitch from the top of the stairs as he left the house, so he left the front door wide open and Metzger was standing outside of his tent and Kostya was walking his German shepherds off-leash past the house and Phoebe stood in the doorway and didn't care who was around: "I'm tired, too, Nick!" she screamed, slammed the door.

Outside. Nick sends the text to Arik at a little after nine. The street is wide and dimly lit, cluttered with Hondas and pickup trucks, shadowy apartments and condo complexes, Sunset Ridge and Savoy West. Arik is twenty-two and a fifth-year senior at UC Riverside. The long yellow fingernails distract from his tattoos around three fingers where rings would be and the others up and down the backs of his arms and the back of his neck. He's jittery like a junkie, though as far as Nick knows, Arik drops E, smokes weed, maybe some 'shrooms, but that's it. He says he can get twelve dollars a pill and give Nick half up front in cash if he'll fork over some of Phoebe's samples. Nick may have been tempted if things were getting worse or if he didn't have the new, potentially lucrative idea. A plan he'll keep to himself.

The text back from Arik: *Shit. Dude. Come in.*

Arik shares his apartment with Mallory, and Mallory looks barely twenty and is gorgeous, and Nick knows this about Mallory: She'll walk barefoot through a Starbucks, and the barista and the men on their laptops and even the young mothers with their City Minis and chai teas will watch her breeze through. She's tall and sleepy-looking, lets him in. Calls out to Arik after saying hey to Nick. Arik's apartment is filled mostly with possessions he took from abandoned houses: IKEA furniture, a guitar on the hardwood floor, a foosball table, an Xbox, two wall-mounted plasmas, a python in a red-lit terrarium. Everything's up on Craigslist and eBay. But it's the foosball table and the sleepy, pretty housemate that trigger a sudden wistfulness in Nick: What he'd give to be twenty-one again. He flops down on the chair, picks up the guitar, watches Mallory texting and smoking and fixing her hair in the kitchen. He could sit here all night. He could blend in so easily, he thinks. Days of vague promise and nights that start no earlier than eleven, never amounting to anything. Mallory is making plans for her night that starts at midnight.

"Have you ever heard of Deep?" she asks.

She's not wearing a bra.

Nick shakes his head. He could watch her thumb the white handheld until he comes.

Arik bursts from a room. "You *must* stop playing that track!" He's laughing, pulling a T-shirt over his head, boots on, untied. Two insane Chihuahuas charge Nick, and Mallory puts her cigarette down, walks over, and, apologizing, bends over to pick up the yapping dogs while Nick lazily stares down her scoop-neck T-shirt. She seems to hold the pose for a beat too long. Nick asks if she's ever heard of Charles Manson. She stands up with a quizzical look on her face.

"You look like a Manson girl," he says.

"I don't know what that is." She's shushing her Chihuahuas.

"The hair. Your whole look. It's working."

Mallory just stares at him. She's simultaneously pale and glowing.

"Promise me," Arik whines. "Let me download you some new shit."

"I like her voice," Mallory says, and kisses the head of one of her dogs. "I'll turn it down."

"Google it," Nick says. "Manson girls."

"I'll do that."

Arik's close-cropped blond hair almost makes him look like a skinhead, though he wears a black Bloc Party T-shirt and long green board shorts and leather bracelets and necklaces.

"God, I'm old," Nick says.

According to Arik, they all have to move out, and Mallory wants a place with two of her girlfriends. Nick knows this: An unfurnished four-bedroom lies vacant half a mile from campus, a mile from where they are now. It was abandoned weeks ago and, according to Boss, belongs to Bank of America and is a low-priority property. They trashed it out last week. It could sit idle for months. Mallory could be in there as soon as Nick changes the locks. Glancing at her flawless skin and the navel ring, he thinks he wouldn't mind helping her out.

Arik follows Nick outside and into hot, gusting winds. A woman shrieks. A man chases his trucker cap across the parking lot. Arik curses. Nick looks back and shields his eyes as he tries for one last glimpse of Mallory, but she's gone. Arik is texting someone as he gets in the car and says, "Take the 10," even though Nick knows this; he put the address in Google Maps before he left the house.

Arik laughs at something he's reading, sends another text. " 'Shrooms from Eureka. Down with that?" he asks.

Nick waves him off, distracted by the prospect of houses, renters, changing locks, painting and cleaning, listing. And collecting: deposits, first/last, monthly or bimonthly rent. Keys and addresses. And a time line: How long has a house been empty, and how long will it stay that way? How much risk is there, and is it worth it?

"Check it." Arik is shoving his handheld in Nick's face: a predictable image of Mallory making out with their other roommate, another long-haired girl, both in body paint. "Mardi Gras, dude."

Inhaling the scent of Arik's body spray and the winds rocking the car and the Chromatics track drifting from the speakers, Nick sees Mallory again, in his mind, bending over. Nick is seeing the girl's pale breasts and wondering what she smells like in the morning under the sheets.

"Tomorrow's Tarzana, right? Or Friday?" Arik looks up from his iPhone.

"Friday."

"Nice properties in Tarzana. Unlike tonight. Rialto's so ghetto."

But the houses aren't a concern to Nick. He accelerates, changes lanes. Images of Mallory flash across his mind. The surge of adrenaline he feels is from details that converge: three or four vacant houses, collecting first and last from renters, expanding from there. Arik is turning up "Miss Murder" by AFI and Nick returns to Mallory: Maybe he'll put her in that house.

The thriving business of trashing out foreclosed homes sends Nick and the crew through dry canyons and out along barren freeways past endless brown walls and wilted palms and bright yellow Union Pacific cars and weed-choked rail yards until they're in the middle of another neighborhood. AFI is pounding and the windows are down and he changes lanes without signaling and tall shadowy palms bend. The hillside recedes into the blackness of another night, and in his mind an overhead camera tracks them, zooms out, and it's just this dirty white Subaru moving no faster than the rest of the traffic. But he knows better.

Arik mentions yet again an idea he and Sean, an older member of the EMGo! crew, have been discussing for weeks. Arik wants Nick because they need a third and the deal is lucrative enough to split three ways. But Sean is a madman, forty and brooding with five kids, restraining orders still active.

"Sean wants to move on it next week," Arik says.

Nick laughs. "Good luck with that."

"I'm not going without you."

"You're better off."

"This house is loaded."

"I'm being recruited to stage a home invasion by a twenty-two-year-old I didn't know a month ago. And Phoebe worries about my trajectory," Nick says, addressing no one.

Arik looks at him blankly for a beat, continues tapping out a message on his handheld. "Have you been to Desert Blaze?"

Nick shakes his head.

"Like Coachella but hotter. Want to go? Mallory's asking."

Nick's counting houses and doing sloppy math. Shadowy palms and softly glowing hillsides loom over them.

"And it's not a home invasion, dude," Arik says. "More like a collection."

"Tell Mallory to text me," Nick says.

"Next right," Arik says.

Nick knows where to go. And he knows Boss respects and trusts him. He knows that's a way forward for now.

"You're out of uniform, soldier," Nick says to Greg, and leans over the driver's-side door of the black Maxima.

"Boo!" Arik slams the hood of the car.

Greg is from Baldwin Hills, grew up in Long Beach. He doesn't scare easily. In the glow from his iPhone, Greg's white tank top shows off his brown skin and tats and the Kappa Alpha Psi fraternity brand on his right shoulder.

"Give me a brand, bro," Arik calls out, pounds his chest. "We should all go in on it. EMGo! across the chest."

"You first, *bro.*" Greg glares at Arik, who grins.

"Fire it up, bitch."

Greg's the only one here not wearing his EMGo! long-sleeve T-shirt or polo. He's smoking a cigarette and texting his wife. He and Nick exchange a fist bump. Nick hands him a Red Bull. They're the same age. Greg works at Enterprise, played some football in college. His wife's a model, bartender, and caterer and wants to do interior design or fashion, but that's not working out, so now she wants to move back to Chicago to be closer to family, and Greg's running out of reasons for saying no. This job, he says, is not helping his case.

"How big?" Nick looks at the house.

"At least forty," Greg answers.

"So all night, then," Nick says mostly to himself. Any house with a volume of abandoned items that's more than thirty cubic yards takes at least five or six hours with a crew of four. They'll have five tonight but more volume, so this won't be quick.

Greg has his engine running and headlights on. "Lights just went out," he says. "Whole street's out."

"Good times."

It was Nick who jumped in the pool last month, freed Greg's foot from the drain when everyone else just kind of stood there, dumbstruck. The water was neck-high, green and thick, and maybe that was what kept the others from helping. Either way, now Nick's got this reputation among the crew and the Boss as someone to be counted on, someone who mans up. So now he manages three crews. He likes the way it feels and tries to focus on that image of himself and not the one in which he's a married father standing on some strip of asphalt in Rialto waiting to haul trash left behind by strangers out of a house they couldn't afford.

A huge gust sends a garbage can lid sliding across the asphalt, sets off a car alarm, and agitates dogs. A loud cracking sound makes them all flinch.

"Good Lord," Greg says. "They do not pay us enough." But he's laughing and shaking his head and sipping his Red Bull, still texting. Orange sparks crackle in the distance. A transformer.

"Fires," Nick says, a half-thought about

wildfires and this wind.

"Should burn this place down," Greg says. "Whole block."

"Don't stop there," Arik says, looking up from his iPhone.

Nick approaches the house. A police helicopter thunders past, too low. The wind gusts. Why is the garage door open? He looks back at Greg. "Did you open that?" Greg shakes his head, his cell at his ear, watching. Nick takes a few cautious steps. That's when it hits him: the stench from inside.

Most jobs they move right in. Boss will be there with the keys, get them inside, set the Dumpster in the middle of the driveway. Music will be on in the house. Someone always brings music. Lately it's been Jay Z, White Stripes, the Offspring. Anything loud, fast, hard. Boss doesn't care. Whatever moves the houses. Boss stumbled into it when a friend needed his help in a pinch. He got his contracting crew together, hauled out everything in under three hours. Now he's got major clients: Banks need their houses back from those who came up short. Clean 'em and green 'em, Boss says. Boss recently bought a new boat so he and his wife can take their kids fishing up at Lake Arrowhead. He drives a new Lexus and a fully restored metallic-blue Firebird convertible. He's got laminated maps, red and green circles marking new targets. He's on to something. He's just getting started. That much, he and Nick have in common.

Boss needs and trusts Nick because, unlike the Hondurans, he's college-educated and can speak fluent English, and unlike Arik and Sean, he's mature. Greg has Boss's trust, but Greg is leaving because Greg has somewhere to go. That's why Nick has the keys to the Rialto house tonight. EverythingMustGo! needed more sane white guys, Boss said. Nick didn't ask for clarification. There was an advantage to play, so he played it. Trashing out foreclosed houses gets him twenty-two dollars an hour plus anything of value they claim.

Nick and Arik set up the generator in the garage for the spotlights that will be trained on the exterior of the house. The more light, the less likely it is that anyone will bother to call the police, which slows them down. They set up two spotlights inside the house as well, making the house glow. A green Honda slows to a stop with the windows down. Jorge and Jaime are brothers from Honduras, work jobs like this, landscaping, painting, mostly in silence. They speak to each other in Spanish or respond to Boss when he addresses them in his broken Spanish. The brothers stay in their Honda, like they always do until Boss shows up or comes out of the house.

A red Kawasaki Ninja explodes onto the hushed street. It's Sean. He rides without a helmet, stops abruptly next to the Hondurans. Sean's always late because he says he's "putting some fear into my boy." (His fifteen-year-old son beat an Iranian kid unconscious at school and now has court dates and legal fees.) Aside from the trash-outs, Sean sells and rents Jet Skis at a surf shop in Huntington Beach, but with his son's issues and the attorney's fees and business down, he made a call and joined their crew. He has narrow bloodshot eyes and long brown hair; he squints and likes to deliver quick, hard jabs to Arik's chest or shoulders when they're on the job. He punches Arik as though they're brothers or cousins, but Arik isn't in on the joke, is not all that comfortable with the punches. Yet Arik tolerates it because, he tells Nick, the guy's a lunatic.

Everyone except the Hondurans is passing around the joint Arik rolled. They're all gathered around Nick's Subaru. The only time Sean isn't punching or manhandling Arik is when he's sharing his weed. There's an expression on Sean's face that registers with Nick. After Nick takes a hit from the joint, he sends a text to Arik: *I think he likes you ;)*

"Walk up the driveway and breathe in," Nick tells the group, exhaling.

Sean goes first.

Arik's response to Nick's message is immediate: *No shit. He keeps asking me to go camping.*

Nick doesn't respond.

Arik tries again: *So are you in? It's a sweet gig. I need you on this bro!*

I'm sure

Some dude owes Boss. So we're going to go pick it up.

Good luck with that.

All you do is drive and help us over the wall.

Have fun camping ;) Keep your tent zipped.

Nick sends a message to Phoebe:

I'm being recruited.

For what?

A job.

And? Tell me.

Couple guys need me to help collect some debt. Good times.

There's a long pause. Phoebe finally responds: *When is the last time you even*

bothered to check Monster.com?
Sweet dreams

Boss approaches, his pink polo shirt pulled up over his nose. He's heavy, sunburned, and bald. Now he looks pale, hacks up something, and spits. No one asks. They just wait. He wipes his mouth with the back of his hand. He's wiping spit from his nose and chin. "Something's dead in there," he says. "Find it." Another helicopter passes, and the eucalyptus and wilting palms are shaking from the wind drowning out the steady hum from the generator. In the darkness, no one moves. Sean eyes Nick and then Arik and then Nick again.

"Fifty to whoever finds it. *Cincuenta dólares.*"

Inside, Nick kicks a couple of dead rats, avoids what seems to be human feces in the same room, with white walls covered in graffiti tags. He could direct guys like Boss does, dividing up the labor, sending pairs of men to certain parts of the house. But they don't need to be told. So Nick just starts working. He drags three mattresses to the driveway, scoops up children's underwear and stuffed animals and mayonnaise jars and vacuum cleaners, two hard drives and three cardboard boxes filled with old cell phones. In a bedroom he finds soccer and T-ball trophies. A child's journal filled with stick-figure drawings and shaky writing lies on the floor. Inside an open closet, wrapped in a soiled sheet, Nick finds the source of the stench. Holding his breath, he picks it up, unravels it, and what tumbles out lands hard on the floor. It's a dog. The carcass has no eyes and very little fur, and the bones are visible or push through the skin. No collar or tags. Nick's face crumples from the stench. He texts Arik, eyes watery, squinting: *Guess I get the 50*

The men, filthy and sweating, gather in the bedroom around the dog. Sean pokes at it with the end of a pool cue. Some little girl's pet. The same little girl whose *Dora the Explorer* diary Nick found in the lavender bedroom with lavender curtains. No one moves. Arik stuffs money in Nick's back pocket. Sean sees this and punches Arik in the ass and calls him a twink. There's some laughter and the room clears. It's Nick and the rotting dog. He's talking to himself. "How many Emerson College media production majors does it take to remove a rotting dog from a bedroom closet?" He squats and reaches for a corner of the stained sheet and drapes it across the carcass. He does this with each corner until he's got the animal completely wrapped. When he drives his hands under the body, he does so with too much force, wanting to get it over with, and his fingers slip through a seam or tear in the fabric and the matted fur gives way, probably because the maggots and blow flies have worked through the flesh, and Nick recoils and wipes his hands spastically along the hard carpet.

The animal's front leg has slipped loose. And Nick is holding it.

Another transformer pops. Orange sparks shower the street. The wind carries a hint of smoke. Nick leans against his Forester, queasy. The Dumpster is half-full; the dog's remains lie wrapped in the sheet next to it. Another police helicopter passes overhead, another spotlight, another criminal on the run. It's the end of the world. But Nick stares at the uninspiring ranch house they just gutted. In a week or less, the house will shine; the bank will hire contractors (work Boss is bidding for), drain the West Nile water from the pool, paint the lawn green, hang new light fixtures, fill the holes kicked through in the bedroom and living room walls, two coats of white matte semigloss on the crown molding. Nick opens a new memo, calls it Rentals:

1. Initial assessment, get info on property
2. Monitor until they're renovated (Boss can do it??)
3. Week or 10 days, change locks, post on CL, put up signs with disposable cell #

Nick as landlord. He hasn't slept, and the headache he thought would fade with caffeine hasn't, and is, if anything, worse. Through the haze in his mind, a notion burns through: Maybe there is something approaching salvation to be found in all these dead houses.

11

The hose outside still works and Nick rinses himself off in the front yard. They all take turns. It's almost six. They've been here for eight hours. A silver lowrider filled with young men approaches, slows as it passes the house. Arik and Nick are shirtless, dripping, staring it down. Sean walks into the street like he's ready to start something. The car keeps moving. Nick feels a surge of adrenaline. The car is gone. Sean returns to the group, and whatever danger they may have been in seems to have passed, and despite Sean taking a piss on the lawn Nick realizes that he loves these guys, wants to hang out. He'll get Greg's cell. They can go out, watch the Pacquiao fight. Arik can bring Mallory and some of her friends.

Everyone wants to get home. Boss has cold Coronas for them. The stench from inside is stuck to the lining of Nick's nostrils, reaching down the back of his throat.

It's six A.M. and the men are drinking beer on an ugly street in Rialto.

The Hondurans make off with a leaf blower and an armful of clothes. Boss is standing in the middle of the lawn, making notes on his handheld. He's got a couple of properties farther inland for Nick to assess. Boss needs a minute of his time.

"I need you on Angel Duty." He keeps making notes on his handheld and, without looking up, continues, "Have a couple of nights coming up. I'll shoot you the addresses, get you the keys."

What this means is Nick will spend a night or two alone in a refurbished house to discourage anyone from trying to break in. The Guardian Angel keeps the lights on and the house secure so the bank can hand it off to the new owner without squatters pissing on freshly painted walls or cooking meth in the kitchen. Nick will do it because the pay is double. Though Angel Duty means he'll spend the night alone in an empty property, there's not much Nick will say no to these days.

Arik's watching Nick and Boss and inching closer. Sean sits on the porch, wearing a floppy safari hat he found inside and finishing his beer; he chucks the bottle toward the Dumpster and it shatters and Nick turns to him and he's leering at Nick. Arik moves closer to Nick and Boss, stands inches behind them. Sean walks past and says something to Arik that Nick can't make out, then mounts his motorcycle and revs the engine. They all watch as Sean glances over his shoulder, spits, then peels out, pulling the front wheel up off the street as he goes.

Boss gets in his white Lexus and leans out the window, hands an envelope to Nick, and tells him, "Thursday. Get me word that night. We're scheduled for Saturday morning."

Inside the envelope: two sets of numbered house keys, the address of each house on a corresponding index card. Also in the envelope: two tickets to Thursday night's Angels game.

Arik grabs the envelope then removes his iPhone and enters the addresses to the houses. Nick looks at the cards.

Arik laughs. "I got this house, dude."

"I don't think so."

"Have you been to Tarzana? You don't want this one. There won't be anything in there anyway."

Nick's search engine is slow, but he enters "Tarzana" on his handheld and waits.

"Meet me there."

"Pick me up," Arik says.

Nick reads about Tarzana: It's in the San Fernando Valley and, according to Wikipedia, is a wealthy community with average home values assessed at nine hundred thousand dollars. Nick realizes this property is a gift from Boss, a home stocked with goodies.

"Don't go there first," Nick warns him. The house is a four-bedroom with a three-car garage.

"You have the keys to the castle," Arik says, and shrugs.

Nick stares at his green eyes and wide forehead and bleached-blond crew cut and acne: He's a kid. He's alien to Nick. He's the offspring of some adults who found themselves in a soulless tract of ranch houses forty miles from Los Angeles. He may as well be an Eskimo. Somehow they speak the same language. Nick wonders: Was he this adrift when he was Arik's age? Nick produced a radio show at Emerson College when he was nineteen, carried a full course load, and a work-study job at the dining hall on the weekends. Nick was considering NPR, online journalism, something edgier. Phoebe at nineteen was enlisting the help of third-year Harvard law students to file suit against her mother's former employer for gender discrimination when DuPont fired her for insubordination. (Some workers were inadvertently exposed to hazardous materials in her plant, and she wouldn't let it go.)

Nick and Phoebe at nineteen weren't setting the world on fire, but, unlike Arik, something burned inside them. Arik's got this grin on his face that fades into a faraway gaze. Something occurs to him and his focus returns. "Will you give me the tickets, at least?" Arik says. "You're not going to use them."

Nick hands him the Angels tickets.

After dropping Arik off, Nick makes two calls. The first is to Jaime, one of the Honduran brothers, who gives Nick the number of the guy who took the black dog from the house the other night. When he calls the number, he gets voice mail, leaves a message, then sends a text explaining that he's willing to pay for the dog and to please give a call back.

The windows are down and warm air rushes through the car as Nick plugs in and cues the Black Keys on his iPod and "My Mind Is Ramblin' " comes from the speakers. Nick is turning over numbers in his mind.

In a Starbucks not far from Serenos, he

sips a double espresso, makes notes on his iPhone. Six houses. That's what he decides. He'll rent six houses to six families. He'll collect the first month's rent from each family and a deposit of one month's rent. He'll rent each house month-to-month for a minimum of a thousand each. He'll earn twelve thousand from six houses in addition to the monthly rent for as long as each occupant stays. Some will leave without warning, so whatever he collects in rent is a bonus. Six houses will be twelve thousand dollars. Double that and he'll have twenty-four. Can he handle twelve houses? If he can push it to twelve houses, for three months each, he'll be bringing in close to fifty thousand dollars in cash.

He scans the contacts in his iPhone, finds the name he needs. "Yes. Mai? Hi. This is Nick Maguire. Nick and Phoebe and Jackson from down the street on Carousel Court. Yes. Thank you."

He's up and sticking a finger in his ear and pushing the warm glass door open and stepping outside into the wind and heat. Nick saw Mai pushing an orange double stroller onto Carousel Court yesterday afternoon, one of the seats empty, and stopped the car and introduced himself. They'd always said hello in passing and waved, and she'd smiled at Jackson. He asked her now about rates and availability, whether the empty seat in the Graco is available. He's pacing the wide concrete walkway, smiling and nodding as he speaks, as though Mai is there in front of him. And he's grinning because the call goes well and she's available. She can start immediately.

He's still smiling when he's back inside the Starbucks, because with this move they can finally stop waking Jackson up in the dark and carrying him half-asleep to the car, dropping him off alone at Bouncin' Babies. Phoebe can sleep an extra hour in the morning. Neither of them will have to rush to day care to pick him up. And Phoebe can talk to someone about her meds, because Nick can't be the only one telling her she's playing with fire.

A moment later, a call comes that Nick was hoping for. The man who took the abandoned dog home the other night is returning Nick's call, responding to the message. Nick offers him fifty dollars for it. The man says seventy-five. Nick will call or text to arrange a pickup in the next week or so. It's falling into place, Nick thinks.

Twelve houses. Spread out across Los Angeles, San Bernardino, maybe the Valley, wherever Boss has properties lined up. Unlike the cicada shells littering the dry grass, the houses have just enough meat on the bone to attract the scavengers and jackals and birds of prey. He exhales. He surveys the Starbucks. Sunlight floods the place. A Latino kid in a Celtics jersey holds the door for a young mother pushing a yellow Bugaboo double stroller. The babies wear blue sandals and red sunglasses. Everything pops: the colors, the people, the thick warm aroma of coffee, the bright sunlight, the steady wind, and the trees shaking, bending in it.

12

The sticker on the back of the white Cutlass Ciera reads: *Ask Me About My AK-47.* Phoebe is stuck in stop-and-start traffic, midmorning on the 110. They have $2,998 in savings. There will be no Serenos Montessori for Jackson. There will be no nanny. No help at all, is all Phoebe can think. The Discover is their only working credit card. She's swallowing her second dose of Klonopin with Propranolol and Effexor kickers. Listening to her favorite Blondfire track as the first warm wave washes over her from the inside out, she is making a mental list for Whole Foods: sun-dried tomatoes, butternut squash, and the cherimoya she slices in half, freezes, then feeds like sorbet to Jackson. A series of texts flood her iPhone, breaks the spell. But not one is from JW. They're all from her regional GSK manager, because her quarterly sales numbers are in.

Got your first #s: not encouraging

Why aren't they ordering from you? Thought you were the star back east, Phoebe?

Ask yourself: what am I not doing out here that I could be doing?

Bottom third in volume this quarter

From diamond status to bottom third not good.

News flash: simply showing up for appt's isn't enough, Phoebe. Do what you know how to do and get them back up ;) SHOW THEM how badly you need them

When her handheld finally stops vibrating, she responds: *@ gym firming up ass.*

I know you're up to this.

You remind me of my last DM back east

How's that?

Better left unsaid

Is yours a job you can afford to lose?

Phoebe stands at the reception desk in a cold, shimmering medical office that's all glass and polished chrome edges, the samples in a small black case she pulls behind her. The girl behind the counter is taking calls and wearing too much foundation. It's caked on, concealing a breakout on her cheekbones. She's likely a temp, Phoebe thinks. Just starting out. Her fingernails are manicured and her handheld is open to a social networking app she keeps checking even though the calls are pouring in. She's not long for this job. And yet Phoebe can't shake the urge to trade places with her: to be twenty-six, untethered, apparently unconcerned about stability, marital, financial, or emotional. Phoebe grabs a lollipop from a crystal dish and pops it in her mouth and recalls exactly where she was when she was twenty-six.

Her iPhone vibrates.

• •

When she was twenty-six, Phoebe was stabbing an olive in an untouched dirty martini with a silver pick in a warmly lit restaurant across the table from the managing partner of the firm she was leaving. JW was ordering another and trying to convince her to stay, while Nick was at home with his blown-out knee, keeping it elevated, waiting for Phoebe to get home and the Percocet to kick in.

"This is a career-track position you're walking away from."

"Not without an MBA."

"I don't want you to leave."

"I can't handle it."

There was no nobility in ending an affair. It was simply stanching the bleeding. She'd sat in her cubicle untwisting paper clips at the end of too many workdays, waiting for JW to summon her to his office. She'd walked to the gym after and showered there, then sat on the T, always in the rear by the window, the rocking of the streetcar somehow soothing. She'd stared at the television screen next to Nick, who'd be asleep on the couch, their bodies idling in the flickering glow of their darkened apartment. There was no recovering from this. She was doing permanent damage. Sound sleep came only after Nick's surgery, when she found his Percocet.

Meanwhile, in the hushed corner of a dimly lit restaurant, JW was telling her there was something special inside her. He said it was something he needed to be around.

"We all have someone like that at work," he said. She was that person for him. He offered to increase her salary. He told her she could have an office of her own. He promised he wouldn't call her cell or text or expect anything.

She didn't care if any of it was true. She couldn't start a life with Nick like this.

JW made her a proposition. One without expectations or obligations. It was something he was returning to, a question she'd posed when she first started that he wanted to answer.

"I'm paraphrasing, but something along the lines of 'How do these assholes do it?' Right? You asked me about your colleagues, the twenty-five-year-old white boys who were all your age but somehow selling off condos, financing their first million-dollar homes. What *was* their fucking secret?" He held up four fingers, kept the middle one down. He said his father had lost a finger. He said his father also had a mouth full of cancer from chewing tobacco for the three decades he'd spent on his knees splicing copper wires and refilling Freon tanks.

JW described a quiet, hardworking, big-hearted father who would have made his sons whole when he died, left them equity. And before that, had he had the means, he would have paid JW's first mortgage so that when he sold, he could have used the cash to buy the million-dollar house. JW said his own father would have leveraged his relationships to get his sons started. That was how it worked. Not complicated, he said. "Now I have it and I'm using it. Like he would have. And like I will for my own family." He removed a checkbook and wrote something, tore it free, and placed it within arm's reach on the white tablecloth. "Your leg up." He leaned back in his chair, finished off his drink.

She stared at the black ink on the face of the pale green check. Phoebe knew JW relished the fact that he could write her a check for a hundred thousand dollars without hesitation.

"I'm supposed to refuse this. That's the right thing to do."

"Don't overthink it."

"What am I supposed to say?"

"Take a trip. Sardinia, maybe?"

"This is" — she held out the check — "inappropriate."

The 675-square-foot one-bedroom apartment with the pale blue carpet and cracked storm windows was the reason she considered it. Nick's desire to launch a film career of his own was the reason. Did she deceive Nick, betray his trust? Of course. Was she new to all of this and overwhelmed and young, entitled to a lapse in judgment without having to sacrifice her marriage?

"Don't tell me I earned it."

"I'll write you recommendations. I'll make the necessary calls for any business school you want." He finished his drink. He looked around the restaurant. He sighed, satisfied with himself. "This should change your life, Phoebe. If you're as smart as I think you are."

The olive in her glass was a shredded,

pulpy mess. She could feel the bits as she swallowed.

"And I'm sorry."

She waited.

"For pushing you to stay. You're doing the right thing."

"Am I?"

"You'll be fine. I'll find you something. But you're right. This thing between us —" He looked away. "It's no way to start a life with someone."

In the cab on the way home, she removed a small pill case and swallowed a Percocet. She removed the check and stared at the unusually large pale green rectangle before her, his signature illegible. She noticed the memo: *Because we don't all start from zero.*

• •

The message for Phoebe is from JW.

Just harvested my basil and pesto

He's resuming a conversation that he initiated with her years ago, when she was a twenty-four-year-old new hire. A decadent dialogue she thought she'd ended but willingly resumed. In his world, chocolate Labradors walk off-leash on residential streets. Town cars, not cabs. Warm almonds in the dish and two Range Rovers and the restored Alfa Romeo he's quietly proud of.

He details his casually elegant summer life in Maine. He's gardening. Harvesting bell peppers, basil, and tomatoes. They're hiking tomorrow, sailing if the weather holds. Phoebe doesn't ask who he means when he says "we," assumes he means his current wife and maybe a kid or two.

So the wife's in wine country. Why not hop on a plane?

Why don't you? You were coming, remember? In days not weeks. I'm here.

Where?

In the city. Come say hi.

In the elevator of the medical office, she turns off her iPhone, something she used to do before she ended things with JW. She did it not because she didn't want JW's messages or calls pouring in while she was sharing the couch with Nick, but because the suspense was a rush: powering it on, watching the screen, waiting for the vibration, the chime; an adolescent game with new technology. She'd outgrown it, she thought.

Later that night, after washing and folding all of Jackson's clothes and pouring out milk from a gallon jug a day before the expiration date and printing out a list of positions from Monster.com that Nick can apply for, she lies restless next to Jackson's crib and turns her iPhone back on.

No messages.

It occurs to her, watching the spinning, shadowy blades of the ceiling fan, that she could use a hundred-thousand-dollar check now more than ever.

She taps out a text to JW: *How long are you here?*

He doesn't respond.

The text that arrives nearly an hour later is just a link to a website for a place called Hotel Bamboo. Phoebe opens it. She scrolls through images of spare, clean suites accented with lush gardens and koi ponds, sunken bathtubs and open-air fire pits, set deep in the canyons of Los Angeles.

Then a message from him: *Zen Suite*

She doesn't respond.

Come say hello. I leave Sunday.

JW is here and wants to see her, but on his terms. That's something Phoebe can't do. Not this time. She doesn't respond to his last few messages. She finds Hotel Bamboo on Google Maps. She opens another page she bookmarked on her iPhone. The link she sends to JW is for a financial analyst position in management with D&C in Laguna Beach.

They used to be a client of ours, right? Can you make this happen?

There's no response. She knows all too well that it could be an hour or a week before JW replies, if he replies at all. He could joke with her or take her seriously. He could toy, tease, and treat her like he used to: some young tough-acting thing who reminded him of his youth. Or he could take her at face value: a professional seeking advancement, playing angles, capitalizing on connections. How he sees her no longer matters, if it ever did. All that matters now is that he not take a month to respond.

13

It's morning. Nick is driving through predawn darkness. He's sore and he stinks even after rinsing off. The stench of garbage lines his dry nostrils. He has two initial assessments scheduled in Chino Hills and Tarzana next week.

Last night he drove a gloved fist through a plate-glass window. He took a sledgehammer to armoires and overpriced bed frames that couldn't fit in the Dumpsters in one piece — furniture people could use. He plugged in the yellow Dyson vacuum cleaner. It still worked. He carried it past the Dumpster, dropped it in the backseat of his Forester. The grandfather clock. No one wanted it. "Don't you people have grandmothers who would kill for something this ugly?" Nick called out, and when the members of the crew who could hear him all yelled, "Crush it!," he swung the sledgehammer with such force that the clock exploded on contact, all splintered wood and glass. It used to be that some of the crew kept whatever was left behind, or sold it on Craigslist, but now there's no time. Too many houses to trash out, too many unwanted belongings. Their livelihood depends on working fast, doing away with the leftovers. Who has time to coordinate with Salvation Army to haul this shit away? The men work for profit, not charity, so Dumpsters and landfills are the only solution. Nick destroyed everything he could and felt satisfaction in the moment. The best he could hope for last night, what he kept in mind as he worked — that jaw of hers and crushing things.

14

She picked Jackson up early today. She had no appointments after twelve and got home at one and spent an hour online instead of napping or doing laundry, still overly caffeinated and anxious from driving. She decided, instead of being alone, she'd walk three houses down and take Jackson from Mai for the rest of the day. Whole Foods had everything she needed. Now she's in the kitchen, marinating three lamb chops in a blue ceramic bowl. Nick will be home by seven. They'll have dinner as a family, she told him on the phone. "You're cooking dinner?" he said skeptically. "Are you planning to poison me?" She slices a lemon in half. She chops garlic cloves with a long knife and adds fresh rosemary. Over the Harry Connick Jr. on the Bose box, she narrates for Jackson while she works, sprinkles Cheerios on his tray. The tablespoon of butter and canola oil sizzle on high heat, splatter, so she lowers the setting and the next song comes on and Jackson cries out and Phoebe drops a few more Cheerios on his tray and through the kitchen window glimpses the orange light off the surface of the pool.

The bubbles of blood splatter and signal the inch-thick fillets are ready to flip.

Nick messages that he'll be home early. She texts back that it's good timing because dinner is ready.

She mixes the Whole Foods–prepared asparagus salad and heats garlic mashed potatoes. She places two bottles of wine, white and red, on the dining room table. He's home.

Nick eats slowly, picks at the meal. He eats around the chop. After finishing his potatoes, he's unsure what to eat next.

"What is it?" she asks.

The music still plays. He says that it's a nice touch, they should do it more, play music during their time at home together.

"You don't like the lamb?"

"It's fine."

"Then why aren't you eating it?"

He hesitates, studies her plate. "Red meat makes me sick," he says finally.

"Since when?"

"I don't know. Recently."

"All red meat?"
"Can't eat it."
"At all?"
"At all."
"It was this or lobster ravioli. I wish you'd told me."
"You could have asked."
"Well, this is a huge fucking waste then," she snaps.

15

The calls start the morning after he posts the signs. The houses Nick selected are from Boss's list of bank-owned properties that have been trashed out and sitting vacant the longest. The voices from the calls that pour in all have the same inflection: hushed, urgent, joyless. Nick adopts the same tone of voice as the physician who explained to Phoebe and Nick what would happen, what to expect, when Phoebe had an abortion just after college. Neither Nick nor the people calling want to be on the phone any longer than they have to be. So they cover the essentials: times and locations for meeting, first at the house, then, if they want it, a Starbucks or Panera for the contracts and cashier's checks and keys.

Nick figured out the logistics days ago. The signs needed to pop, the lettering clean and bold, the message simple. He chose burnt yellow with black letters and candy-apple red with white lettering. The two versions he came up with:

NEED HELP? NEED A HOME?
LOW RENT, NO QUESTIONS ASKED

And the other:

There IS a Way OUT
RENT: Month-to-Month
NO Questions Asked

The signs were laminated plastic and started at thirty dollars apiece but lasted for six months to a year, he was told by the middle-aged black man behind the counter at Kinko's. Nick said thick paper, something durable, maybe laminated, asked about prices for twelve-by-eighteen and decided on a hundred, then changed his mind, ordered two hundred laminated plastic burnt yellow and red signs. Each sign had a phone number in stark black lettering with a 909 area code underneath the words. The numbers were different from each other and didn't belong to Nick, were disposable phones that he'd use to get started. With the stack in the passenger seat and a staple gun and clear packing tape, Nick spent two hours posting fifty of the signs on telephone poles and traffic lights at intersections. He circled a block, stopped at a red light, snapped a few pictures with his iPhone, decided the phone number was in fact large enough and the sign did pop, the white against red.

This morning he sits alone in a booth at a diner off the Foothill Freeway, staring out at traffic, waiting on new tenants — a young lesbian couple — for a house in Pomona. He's nervous. He orders only decaf and swallows one of Phoebe's Klonopins. He considers leaving. He can't rent a house he doesn't own. What is he even thinking? But when they appear, the couple looks as tired as the waitress refilling his coffee. And there's no turning back. He feels something bordering on sympathy for this couple: They wear their fear on their faces. He's putting them in a safer place, however temporary. He'll treat them well, offer help, be responsive to their needs. There's about a ten-second silence filled with the sounds of some familiar pop song playing on a jukebox in another booth and Spanish coming from behind the counter as tables are bused and orders are called back to the kitchen.

The women perk up. They're thorough, ask so many questions:

Why a cashier's check?

Why couldn't you meet at the house again?

Why no pet deposit?

For the first time he fears getting caught. They're on to him.

"Do you guys want the house or not?" Nick says. "It's not complicated. If you have reservations, forget it. No hard feelings." He removes a twenty-dollar bill from his wallet and places it on the table. "That should cover your tea."

They stop him, ask him to wait for a moment. They glance at each other. The heavier of the two sighs audibly. They look exhausted. They sign and date the one-page rental agreement that covers the first six months and which neither party has any intention of following. Nick keeps both copies and they don't even notice. They hand Nick a cashier's check for twenty-four hundred dollars, which covers first and last (he waived the deposit). He slides the check back to them. "After you get your keys."

16

All the neighbors wear brave faces. No panic in their eyes. No tight grins or faraway looks or awkward gaps in conversation. The mood is pleasant, if not festive. Marina's daiquiris help. The only flaws in Kostya's backyard design: mismatched western red cedar planks haphazardly nailed to the pressure-treated pine fence that surrounds his backyard, giving it a cheap two-tone look, and the single string of white lights hung from the branches of a dried-up eucalyptus tree nearest the pool. "Fly Me to the Moon" drifts from speakers Phoebe can't see. JW used to play the Harry Connick Jr. version in his Boston office.

It's the first week of September. Back here, behind the biggest, nicest house on Carousel Court, the neighbors are celebrating the end of summer, though they all know the heat won't end anytime soon. And an orange tent on a front lawn with a loaded pump-action Mossberg within thirty-five feet of the children is less of a concern than it should be.

Phoebe closes her eyes against the sun. Propranolol kick-starts the Klonopin. She's noticed the difference lately, how quickly things slow down for her. Phoebe sips her daiquiri from a blue plastic cup, and when her eyes adjust to the light, she is further reassured by the sight of Mai holding Jackson, sitting next to her husband. Nick sips his beer from a blue plastic cup next to Phoebe on a chaise longue, shirtless and tan, more muscular than he's ever been. And it's all from the job and climbing the living room wall, because he never did get a gym membership out here, too expensive.

"She was a teacher in Vietnam," Marina is telling Phoebe, just out of earshot from Mai. Marina is smoking a long, thin cigarette. "She was best nanny for us. Clean. Good core." Marina taps her breastbone. "She work weekend, too, for you?"

"Monday through Friday."

"She cook, too," Marina adds. "Better than me."

"She steams broccoli and this Vietnamese soup and sticky rice."

"It's called *pfo.*"

Nick says, "I see her jogging down the

street, pushing that monster stroller and singing."

"And the notes," Phoebe says. "I love the notes." The daily handwritten reports of their activities by the hour. "A godsend," she adds, her eyelids heavy.

Phoebe watches Mai apply sunscreen to Jackson's shirtless little body. Mai and her husband are in their fifties and say very little, but she smiles a lot and wears white sneakers and khakis. Phoebe closes her eyes; Nick is talking, but she's not listening. She wonders how much better off she'd be if Mai had been around when she was nine and thirteen and seventeen. How many rough edges smoothed over with that kind of nurturing. Jackson deserves that much. She wants to bring Mai home with her tonight and keep her there and make everything better.

She finishes her drink. Nick is smiling stupidly at her or the kids launching themselves into the pool, and now he has Jackson, is stroking his head, and says something about next weekend and a trip to the beach and Phoebe closes her eyes again and everything around her spins so violently that she's forced to open them and when she does Nick and Jackson are gone.

■ ■ ■ ■

Kostya hoists his son over his head and roars. The child screams with laughter. Kostya throws him into the pool. The child comes up laughing. Kostya grabs his other son, tosses him in, then his daughter, leaps in after them.

"They're zoo people," Marina says. "Belong in zoos to hump in public." She lies back and takes a drag off her cigarette. She's complaining about the men at the car wash, who are always staring at her tits.

"At least there's something worth looking at," Phoebe says, and her eyes close as she massages her temples.

"You too skinny, bitch. Still have your boobs."

Phoebe is lounging next to Marina by the pool, still saying yes every time she's offered another daiquiri. Phoebe reaches for Marina's cigarette, takes a drag, and surveys the property. The blue wooden playhouse with white shutters; the thick oleander bushes that obscure the eight-foot pine fencing surrounding the entire perimeter. A rectangular sandbox, a bar with stools, tiki torches, and a cabana, and still a generous amount of open space, a thick green lawn for the kids and dogs to roll around on.

"I like your house," Phoebe says flatly.

"I like your ass." Marina reaches over and smacks Phoebe's rear end, her short shorts showing off tan, toned thighs. "Fuck you, girl. No cellulites. You got work?"

"We'll have people over," Phoebe says, and sighs.

"What *we,* white woman?" Nick snaps.

"We'll host next time," Phoebe says without conviction. Jackson now sits on a blue towel spread out between Nick's and Phoebe's chairs.

"Would you like anything, Marina?" Nick stands over the women, stares at Marina's breasts spilling out of her white bikini top as he finishes off a beer, his third.

"No, darling." She lights another cigarette. "But if you see my husband, tell him he need to light torches."

"Gorgeous? Another daiquiri?"

Phoebe doesn't answer. Marina punches her shoulder.

Nick grins. "She's cranky. Needs a nap."

Phoebe's not smiling, though.

"I blame your daiquiris." Nick leans in close to Phoebe, his warm breath in her ear. He says nothing. He runs his free hand along the back of her head, then grabs it. His words slow and thick, he says, "It's all my fault. And it always will be." He looks down at their son, rubs his head, and walks away.

"Finally, we agree on something," she calls out.

"Father of the year!" he yells, not looking back.

The only other source of calm here tonight, aside from Mai, the daiquiris, and the benzos, is Kostya, with his thick frame, long black hair, and reassuring voice. Phoebe watches him hoist a keg over his head while explaining to his daughter how to set the DVR to record some movie she doesn't want to miss and reminding Metzger, who is working both grills, to flip the steaks.

"I wanted smaller," Kostya says to Phoebe. "Less house. All this is work and more work, more worry." He hands her a Corona and she sits up, finishes off the last of her daiquiri, then takes a sip from the cold bottle, and Marina laughs. Phoebe makes a sound of approval.

"Strong, no?" Marina asks.

Phoebe smiles. Nick sits down next to her with Jackson. He leans in, his dry lips at her warm ear. "What if we both self-medicate? How would that work?" He's clenching his jaw.

"Nope," she says, and resolves to switch back to daiquiris.

"More house, more can go wrong. But she want space and biggest house on block. What have you," Kostya shrugs and runs a hand through his hair.

"What*ever,*" Marina corrects Kostya. "Not *what have you.*"

"She and kids are home all day, so okay, we get bigger space."

One of their kids sneaks up, squeezes between Kostya and Marina, and says something softly, shy but urgent. Kostya continues with Nick and Phoebe. "You have fires still next door?"

Nick nods.

"We talk to him." Kostya nods; his unshaven face is red and acne-scarred. A faded bluish-green tattoo on his neck, unidentifiable characters. "He running scared. Like Metzger in his tent." He waves and grins at Metzger, who is staring at them from across the yard. "Like this one." He pinches Marina's soft, pale waist. She slaps his hand. Their skinny son is speaking fast Russian. Marina brushes him off. Kostya wheels, leans in to his son, stabs the boy's bare tan chest with a thick finger, says something. The child sulks, doesn't move.

"This one gets nervous." Kostya is now

affectionately rubbing his son's head while motioning toward his wife. "She hears things in the night. Sirens and noises from other houses, sounds she doesn't know what it is."

"I don't like the vibrations," Marina explains.

"Vibes," Kostya says, eager to correct her for once.

"Last week when all the lights go off," she continues.

Kostya interrupts, gestures at the sky as he speaks. "All streetlights go off, and ours in the house were flicking on, off, on, off. She bring the kids into bed, all three, and kicks me out and tell me, 'Go keep watch.' "

"As you should," she says, then, conspiratorially, "because tent man and his guns."

"You have a gun."

"I don't sleep on the yard."

"You make me sleep on yard." Kostya laughs.

"So how dangerous is he?" Nick asks, nodding in Metzger's direction. There's a pause. Marina looks at her husband, who shakes his head.

"What?" Phoebe asks. Nick looks at Kostya.

"Well," Marina urges her husband. "They should know."

"That is not the type of man to go quiet," Kostya says, rubbing the right side of his face. He meets Nick's eyes and nods. "He will come to you soon for money. He ask us twice already."

Nick says nothing.

"He say it's his duty to defend his home," Kostya adds.

"How much did he ask for?" Phoebe asks.

Kostya and Marina exchange a quick look as she responds, "Too much."

"But fate is fate," Kostya says. "So now this one say it is my job to protect her, us, the house. And it is the primary objective. As I say. Get through this time. This is home. But she has the gun!" He laughs too loudly and everyone else kind of smiles, unsure. "So there I am in living room, holding her pink pistol, watching for zombies. Watching the watchman."

Nick takes Phoebe's hand, which surprises her. She checks, but he's not looking at her. His skin feels callused, and he has a piece of moleskin wrapped around the meaty part below the pinkie where he cut himself at work. She likes it when he takes her hand at unexpected times. She usually feels tension release. Not tonight, though. Not lately. She has rings on three fingers today and he's playing with them. He thumbs the sterling silver engagement and wedding bands, the small stone he admitted to spending eight hundred dollars on in a dimly lit shop in New Orleans on their first trip down there. He leans over and says something about wanting to take her home right now, lay her back on the buttercream stairs. "Let's go." But she doesn't budge.

Kostya continues. "So who ends up sitting by window all night?" He slaps his chest. "Because now I freak out." He shoots a look at Marina, who just shrugs. "You lie," she says. He laughs.

"Home," Nick whispers.

"And the dogs, they can't sleep, so they are pacing round and round because," Kostya says, "there is so much goddamn *tenseness* in *this* house." He grabs Marina by the waist with both hands and bites her long neck. "I eat her up." She can't suppress her laughter. "She taste like oyster."

"Phoebe keeps a knife under her side of the mattress," Nick says loudly. "How scared should I be?" He's turning on her.

She stands as though leaving.

"It's a long one, too," Nick says. "Huge blade."

"You gave it to me!" Phoebe pantomimes a gun with her fingers and fires a round at Nick.

"Found it in a foreclosed Spanish revival in Yorba Linda . . ." Nick trails off.

Before she slips inside the house through the sliding patio door, Phoebe waits until Nick's eyes find her, and when they do, she stares, her sunglasses still on, and he blows her a kiss and she stands perfectly still and if he were within earshot she'd tell him what she thinks of him, the first thing that comes to mind as she looks at him sitting on the low chair in the shadows with their son. She'd tell him explicitly, so there was no confusion: He's failing.

17

She wakes up on the floor in her son's bedroom under a white down comforter. Nick keeps the house cold. "I just don't want to go," Phoebe says to him when he picks up. It's seven fifteen. Next to her, unaware that she's there, Jackson is talking to himself in his crib. Phoebe doesn't know where Nick is and doesn't ask.

"So don't. Go to the beach. Dig for shells," Nick says. "He loves watching the surfers." She can hear the lift in his voice that happens when he talks about things that make Jackson happy. "Get breakfast and just take the day," he adds.

"It's Tuesday."

"Wednesday," he corrects her. "It's a Mai day."

"Every day is a Mai day," she says, and sighs, content.

A measure of relief: no more Bouncin' Babies, waking Jackson from sleep, the anxiety around getting there in time at the end of the day, through traffic. Mai is coming. Mai walks three houses up Carousel Court and rings the bell. Phoebe lets her in, and after good mornings, Phoebe smiles and watches her ascend the stairs to Jackson's bedroom, where she coos and laughs and sings and changes and dresses him, carries him down to the kitchen and feeds him breakfast then straps him into his stroller and says good-bye and jogs away, guiding the stroller along the smooth asphalt, singing as she moves.

Nick messages to say he won't be home before Jackson leaves because he has a rush job, a small condo in Whittier.

Do you work this weekend? she texts back.

Of course.

He messages back: She should sleep in the bed. At night. She should set a routine. She should change out of her work clothes at night.

Sleeping on the couch in your skirt and blouse. Not a healthy pattern.

She doesn't message back. She will. She has already resolved to make those improvements, adjustments that will steady her. She will sleep in a bed. She will remove her clothes first. She will consume half to a whole milligram less of Klonopin daily and continue weaning herself off of it until her use is situational, not habitual.

It's just after eight P.M. Phoebe scrambled eggs for Jackson's dinner. They watched *Thomas & Friends.* She gave him a bubble bath. Nick isn't home. Jackson's room is cool and dark and smells floral, like his after-bath lotion. A soft green night-light glows in the far corner. His little body is facedown, arms and legs spread out wide, reaching, scaling rock-climbing walls in his dreams. She falls asleep with her hand wrapped loosely around the leg of his crib.

In the morning, the only message on her iPhone is from a client. Nothing from JW.

The client is an older primary-care physician she met Monday in El Segundo because he's new to the GSK roster and brought with him seventy-seven patients from his other practice, and Phoebe needs him to prescribe the Advair and Levitra to as many of them as he can. She gave him her cell number the first time they met, written in red ink on the back of her business card. The text message, in which he asks to see her panties, on or off, preferably on, reads like a seventh-grader wrote it. Most of them do. And all of them send her immediately, ruthlessly, back to Boston, the blur of days and highways and cold drizzle and the red glare of taillights before the accident, when she nearly killed their son.

Driven into her and every other new hire during a two-week orientation for sales reps six years ago, using mojito-fueled raucous late-night role-playing sessions at the Hyatt Regency in Boston, was a very simple and absolutely nonnegotiable edict: A HAPPY doctor with a LARGE practice will prescribe YOUR products to his patients and that's YOUR job. A happy doc is a happy rep. Make them happy. How goddamn hard is that?

Again she checks the display: still nothing from JW.

• •

He liked to call her late. Three years ago he called after midnight. He was traveling and had been drinking. He said it lightly: "You realize how many people I could call when I'm feeling like this? And I'm calling you, Phoebe Vero Maguire." After a while he said, "Get dressed. Get in the car and drive."

He was drunk.

She dropped the call. He texted: *You owe*

me that much. I miss us. Don't you miss us?

Not really

You've got such balls. Why I love love love you.

I'm somehow different from all the rest?

You were the first person I called tonight

He's sleeping next to me. The bed is warm. Life is good. I have no desire to be anywhere else.

Have you started trying?

I'm seven weeks.

Well well. Congrats.

Thank you.

That donation should come in handy

You should sleep it off, JWonderful.

He must feel the weight of the world on him.

He doesn't know.

She immediately regretted the disclosure.

It's the Regency Hotel on Park. No expectations. I'll check out, give you the suite if you want. I just want to see your face. He won't even know. Only we'll know.

She had no response. She wanted him to stop, get tired, bored, fall asleep, go another year or so without contact.

There's room in your life.

There's not.

Make some.

The bathroom door didn't close completely and she couldn't turn the light on without the fan coming on too and it was broken and made this horrible grinding sound that would wake Nick so she sat on the small step stool in the cold dark bathroom for nearly an hour, trying to find an answer: What was wrong with her that she was even considering this? She was numb and then tingling. Adrenaline coursed through her until she was convinced the sound of her own breathing would wake Nick. She found herself standing, opening the vanity, filling her purse with essentials for a weekend away. It was insane. She was insane. She glimpsed her shadowy visage in the angled mirror from the vanity she didn't fully close. The reality: She was doing it. Packing and leaving for two days in New York. Even now. After everything. There was no logic to it. She wasn't just crossing some line. She had located the fault line in their foundation and was about to obliterate it.

She was tiptoeing around the cold, creaky bedroom of the seventh-floor apartment they'd shared for five years. In the dark, she tried not to wake Nick. She moved with precision, slid a few things into her shoulder bag. She was a very responsible lunatic.

She found herself on a train, chewing spearmint Life Savers and sending text messages to Nick and lying, for the second time in their relationship, about JW. She mentioned her mother, said she was melting down again and was in the hospital and there was a six A.M. flight to Orlando and she'd call when she landed. She was twenty-eight years old, hadn't seen JW in two years, since the hundred-thousand-dollar check cleared. The hotel valet took her keys, the hum of Manhattan looming all around her; she moved with a surge of self-confidence through the golden lobby of the Regency Hotel on Park Avenue, the center of the world. Only when she arrived at the bank of elevators did she feel flushed, her fingertips damp, an impression left on the cool gold surface as she pressed the up button.

In the reflection of the elevator doors, she saw a girl immediately familiar and entirely unrecognizable, split down the middle. A young woman carried by the currents, not powerless to swim against them but giving herself over to them because of the tightness of her throat, the rush of it all. The gold doors opened. She should stop, let the doors close before she set foot inside. Simply turn around. She should get a cab back to Penn Station, get the next train back to Boston. Nick would never know. This never happened.

Phoebe stepped inside. This wasn't an

elevator that stalled, that skipped floors, or required constant maintenance like the one she and Nick took multiple times a day at home. This was an elevator for men with a second wife and a daughter and a son and everything to lose who wanted to spend some time with Phoebe. She was doing something right, it occurred to her, the moment the elevator launched her skyward. The only reason she was there, stepping onto that elevator, she told herself, was because her certainty about Nick and the life they were building allowed it.

It was only later, when it made less sense, when there was no rational explanation or justification, in the quiet of the steam-filled marble bathroom, that the cold rush of truth hit her like a wave crashing: Her entire life with Nick was bookended with JW. From the start of the relationship to this point, expecting their first child together, as she stood nude with the bathroom door open on the thirty-third floor of the Regency in Manhattan, the taste of him lining her gums like battery acid.

Phoebe knew Nick would come after her. He'd figure out where she was and come find her. She knew Nick wouldn't wait for a train, would drive instead. She could see him behind the wheel, staying left the whole way, flashing the high beams until the lane cleared and he saw Manhattan looming in the distance.

He called and told her where he was. She begged him to stop, to turn around, to go home. JW was gone. He told her she could stay another night, two, as long as she wanted. If it were up to him, he said, he'd keep her there indefinitely.

"You want me to go home? Whose home? Our home?" Nick said he knew she was in New York. He'd checked her search history and found the website for the hotel. "Looks expensive," he said. "Can I crash there, too? I promise not to get in the way."

"Come get me," she said, and she was dizzy. She leaned all of her weight against the window.

"You're not serious. You're not well."

She tapped her forehead against the cool glass. Harder and harder. "Please. Just come get me." She was a mess and she knew he was broken.

"We've never spent a year together, nine months, six, a week, without this —" He stopped. "You left your emails to him open for me to read. Why would you do that? Why am I bothering with you? How fucked is this?"

He told her that he'd stopped driving,

pulled off 95. She pictured him standing next to his car and screaming into his cell amid the polluted marshes and refineries around him. "You're killing me," he screamed into the phone over and over. "You're killing me." If she were on a bridge, she'd have jumped. She could have walked the stairwell up to the roof, seventy-seven floors. She pleaded with him. She didn't know what she was doing. She was powerless. She'd walk into traffic.

"There's no answer," he said.

"There is," she insisted.

"We have to end this . . . whatever this is."

"I can't."

"You're there. Why are you *there*?"

She said nothing. She paced. She chewed her lower lip, stopped, fingered the sharp edge of the soft leather-bound room service menu.

She met him downstairs, outside. He'd refused to set foot in the hotel. The wide concrete and din of the city threatened to drown them both out.

"I'm not doing this," he said. "Not doing this. Not —"

She tried lamely to take his hand, and he spat on the sidewalk. It was bitterly cold and he was out there on Park Avenue with an unzipped hoodie, no hat, black jeans, raw and red-faced.

He walked away. Then jogged. Never once did he look back to see if she was following.

Together back in Boston, in stride somehow, they idled in the car. Nick turned off the ignition. Sat behind the cracked windshield they couldn't afford to replace. Phoebe told Nick she was pregnant, then posed an impossible question. "Tell me what to do."

"About what?" Nick asked, exasperated.

"Him."

Nick punched the steering wheel with a closed fist, over and over, the horn blaring each time. Phoebe grabbed his shoulder, his forearm, tried to make him stop. "Tell me," she said.

"You can't seriously be asking me this! Tell *you* what to *do*?"

"Please."

"There's *nothing* to *do*! What is there to do? Do nothing!" He slammed his head against the window. He was the madman.

"Stop," she said. "Don't."

He would shatter the glass. The windows fogged over. He stopped. "I need to run screaming from you," he said, stared off into traffic.

Out her window, three bald blue men stared from a poster on the back of a bus.

Mind Blast was written under three sets of eyes that looked shocked open.

"I just don't get the appeal," Nick said. He hadn't heard her. "They're fucking blue. And?" He kicked open the door. Phoebe tried to grab him. He kept going.

The next few days Phoebe brought flowers home, replaced them when they wilted. The apartment was always fragrant. She knew little touches sent a clear signal to Nick: She had made her decision. She made coffee before he woke up even though she drank tea, filled the gas tank in his car, went down on him.

Nick passed her in the living room, stopped, exhaled, and fell back against the wall, slid to the floor. He held his head in his hands as if someone had kicked him.

Phoebe recounted the events for herself: She went to New York, spent the night in a Park Avenue hotel suite with JW, informed Nick that she was pregnant. And the night before, she left the email for Nick to find, the message to JW before seeing him, proclaiming her love for Nick, as complicated and dysfunctional as it seemed. And she was back in Boston now, asking Nick what to do.

They sat on the floor across the room

from each other. It was late, after midnight. They were sober and tired and hadn't eaten in hours. What did she know about him? His tired, bloodshot eyes, the drawn face, pale and unshaven, the same blue and white rugby shirt he'd worn for two days. She was terrified that he could never fully satisfy her. And knew he would never leave her.

She gave him all the power. Or pretended to. And she knew he hated her for it. He'd driven to Manhattan to bring her home. She'd read online that pregnancy triggered severe hormonal imbalances. Brain chemistry was affected. Balance needed to be restored. Yet consumption of SSRIs or benzos impaired the developing brain of the fetus. Madness, temporary or not, must be tolerated. She emailed the article to Nick. He wrote back: *Why didn't you cc JW?*

But something lay ahead, looming around a blind curve in the road they were careening down. And this kind of shit had to be reconciled before they hit it.

"Are you this weak?"

"No."

"Now, Phoebe? Have the decency to fuck us up when we're not about to have a child. What do you expect me to do now?"

"Tell me what to do. Tell me to leave. Tell me to tell him to never contact me again."

"I can't."

"Tell me," she said.

"I did. I made decisions. I've been decisive. Every time."

"Then do it again."

"I did," he said.

"For me."

"How in the hell can I decide this for you? What is there to even decide?"

"I need to hear it. I need to know."

"How does this make sense to you? I'll never understand it."

She was still. There were no tears. No pleading. Just stillness.

Nick turned to her. "I'm not leaving a child of ours. If you want to make that decision when the time comes, then *you* fucking leave." He stopped. "No." He stood up and walked from the main room of the apartment, across the creaky hardwood floor. "No, no, no, no," he said, and quietly closed the bedroom door behind him.

• •

Jackson is covered in white suds, the bathtub filled with toys, a giant rubber shark lurking near the surface. Phoebe sits on a step stool, legs crossed, taps out an email to JW:

If not D&C then something like it. Something

at that level. Help offset all the hell I'll catch when Nick learns how it happened. Has to be LA (or Maui). Consulting to financial services firms because I want to travel (international would be awesome) and not junior or associate but manager. Salary around 100k + bonus. I'm being direct because isn't that what you drilled into me for three years? Produce, produce, produce. Results matter. Nothing else. Exceed expectations. Is the offer you're making me, JW, of the quality that exceeds my expectations? If not, I can't justify it. There are other factors, obviously, that could complicate things. You asked me if this was a path I'm prepared to take. I've asked and answered the question, applied to this: not another gift from you, but THE gift. And all its associated potential complications and drama. But it's workable. Everything is. And I'm running out of options, patience, time, energy. This house is killing us, ok, too much??? So I can and will manage this if the price is right. Period. So I guess it's your turn to produce.

In bed, a remix of Moby's "Sweet Apocalypse" drifts from her headphones as she taps out one more message, this one for Nick:

I think somebody's dead and floating in the pool.

Nick responds: *??*

Sorry. Autocorrect. Something's dead.
Saw that. Will fish it out when I get home.

18

In the dream she drives with the windows down, Jackson strapped into his car seat and sucking his pacifier. Blistering sunlight and clutches of date palms and looming green signs until they reach the Salton Sea, and she's wearing her yellow sundress with a small tear on the hem and aviator glasses and JW's watch dangles around her thin wrist, Jackson in her arms, his floppy fishing hat pulled low over his soft forehead. He's slathered in sunscreen. He keeps slipping from her arms. But he's warm and happy with just his mother and sunlight. Jackson gets hotter and hotter until he's raving, inconsolable, and the small tear in her yellow dress is crimson now and growing. She's trying to nurse her son, blood from the dress smeared across his face, and he's sucking and pulling and insane with frustration when she produces nothing.

A woman from a magazine profile that

Phoebe read in a physician's office the other day appears in the dream, snatches Jackson from her arms. She is fierce-looking, short blond hair, piercing blue eyes, and high cheekbones. She wears a black suit and a thin pearl necklace. The woman from the story was the CFO of a Fortune 500 company and articulated her philosophy for success: Don't dwell on failure or shortcomings. It's a waste of time. Be tenacious in the pursuit of goals. Ruthlessness is not a vice. Phoebe watches the woman rip her blouse open and press Jackson's face to her chest.

The dreams have been more intense since she started substituting Seroquel samples for her Klonopin and wine.

The response from JW came overnight. Nick is next to her in the bed. It's seven A.M. Her eyes are dry. He sent a succession of text messages:

Want anything from Bangkok?

Btw . . . got your email.

LA, consulting . . . agree that's more your speed, a few people/places come to mind . . . salary bump . . . all good . . . let's make it happen.

She messages back, but six hours have passed since his last communication.

That's not going to work. I need concrete

info. If not D&C, what specifically do you have in mind? Deloitte and Booz have offices here.

The immediate response from JW surprises her:

Then get your ass over here like you mean it

Where?

My suite.

Nick shifts in bed; Jackson is calling out from his room. The day begins.

It's different now.

She has shortcomings and a list of failures too long to contemplate. JW chief among them. She feels herself sinking under the weight of them, so she chooses ruthlessness instead.

Is it though?

Quite

19

Nick stands alone in the backyard, staring at the surface of the pool. Despite the chlorine and the hint of smoke from next door (the neighbor set fire to his couch last night), Nick can smell the animal. It floats in the middle of the pool, pink and gray and wet black fur. Something devoured it. Nick figures it managed to escape but, disoriented, stumbled into the water. They have to keep the cover on the pool. Phoebe never remembers, and since his overnights began, he's also forgetting. He'll build a fence around it before Jackson falls in. There's so much they should do, so much they were going to do.

Nick extends the skimmer net, drags the animal across the water to the far end, lifts the waterlogged thing from the pool. What the hell should I do with it? he thinks, then walks around to the front of the house, crosses the street to the abandoned house next to Metzger's. From the side of the drained backyard pool behind the empty house, he dumps it.

The images Mallory sends are impressive: black and white, suggestive without being explicit. She wants Nick's opinion. Do any of them make him pause, linger a little bit? They all do, but he hesitates before responding, studies them a bit longer. He's sprawled out on a chaise behind the house, sipping Phoebe's Maker's Mark from a cracked tumbler. Mallory wants to model. She also loves to train. CrossFit is her thing, she says. She wants to compete. There's an Ironman in Oahu in March. Nick is stuck on one image: the girl lying nude facedown on a mattress, a sheet draped over her ass, hair pulled back to reveal the tattooed lyrics from a Pink Floyd song on the back of her neck. But the more Mallory says she wants to do with her life, the harder it is for Nick not to think of Phoebe and how she used to be when he fell in love with her.

Nick sends the question: *Are we still going running?*

Of course! Sooo . . . which one??

Nick has already downloaded the images of Mallory onto his iPhone, selects the one of the girl nude under the sheet and sends it back to her.

Really?

What are you doing now?

Lying in bed.

Did you run today?

Twelve miles. Sore

The sensation of someone behind him, peering over his shoulder, is overwhelming. Nick turns, finds no one, the sliding glass door still closed, dim recessed light in the kitchen. His iPhone vibrates.

Another JPEG: Mallory's hand in her panties.

Are you alone?

Yes.

Arik?

Who knows?

Nick is buzzed, tired.

I'm making so much $$$, he types.

Show me

My house is HUGE.

Is it?

Can't wait to put you in one

Come for me

Phoebe doesn't know he's home from work. She's passed out on the couch. It's midnight. He stood over Jackson's crib when he got home. The boy sleeps soundly, breathes clearly, allergies in check. Nick could drive forty minutes to Mallory's apartment and follow her to the bedroom, watch her crawl across the mattress until she's lying facedown, white tank pulled up over her breasts to the back of her neck.

You're making this too easy

U want to work for it??

We don't sleep in the same bed. I know she wants it that way. I can't solve it.

So have something easy.

We barely see each other. We fight all the time.

You think too much.

She'd be happier if I were dead.

Take this ;)

The image that arrives is Mallory, back arched, offering her ass. He masturbates on the patio. He stares at the black sky, and the words from one more series of text messages from Mallory ring in his thoughts: *It's fire season,* she wrote, *you can't see the moon. I'm sooo high. The lights are flickering in my room.*

And then: *When the fire comes they should let it go, burn it all down and start again.*

Silhouettes of dry palms sway in the wind. The cicadas are deafening. He's almost there when an image flashes across his mind: Phoebe leaning over JW's desk, looking back over her shoulder at Nick sitting on the leather couch in the man's office while JW pounds her from behind. It burns when he comes.

20

Why does she drive? Phoebe's trying to relax, but her breathing is short in the dry heat and she's overtired, her foot twitching, still pumping the brakes, and Marina is asking her lazily from the shade of an umbrella why she drives. She drives because that's her job. She drives because she's got no option; in debt with this economy, she's not in a position to gamble, to take it lightly, to play the games she played back east, push back against rude managers, skip appointments. They can't afford for Phoebe to do any of that out here. So she drives. And drives for Jackson is the easy answer, the most instinctive, the only one that makes sense.

Kostya wades in the shallow end of the pool, dunking and holding his son's head under, staring at the women, at Phoebe. She doesn't stare back.

Marina's sucking on a frozen banana.

"You must feel crazy." She dips the banana in her daiquiri, licks a trickle from her wrist. It's not that Marina doesn't understand. She knows what Phoebe does for a living. She knows the answer to her own question. Phoebe hears it differently. She sees the blood-orange sky and watches Kostya pretend to drown his son and the steady hum of cicadas and the burning wind on her face, and when she turns to Marina, the shadows have shifted and the woman is less a commiserating friend than some spectral presence posing unanswerable questions.

Why does she drive? What possesses Phoebe to think this time will be different than the last, when she rammed the company car into the back of the idling UPS truck, high on Klonopin, Jackson's spine twisted, nearly snapped, his soft forehead striking the back of the passenger seat like a ripe peach thrown against a wall?

The scream is the boy freeing himself from his father, coming up for air in the pool. The game is over. The boy is scared and crying. Marina calls out in Russian, chastens Kostya.

Phoebe's simple answer to the question: She drives for Jackson. If she tells herself this, that she spends the time on the road doing her job, earning what she does, for her son and his relative safety with Mai, then she stays between the two white lines in her mind, the serpentine but narrow path she follows until she sleeps (then the lines don't exist and there are no roads at all, just Jackson climbing their living room wall, stuck at the top, in tears, losing his grip, landing hard). When she loses focus, strays from her narrow lane, she drives for visits to an unnaturally dark, hushed office so that a sixty-one-year-old family physician can hug her and not let go and she can feel his erection through his cheap slacks against her abdomen as he presses his thin lips and unshaven face against her ear and his warm breath is stale, and the picture of his tired-looking wife on his desk as he hesitates before asking if Phoebe will watch him masturbate.

She drives because she's trapped, because she knew better but didn't find her voice when Nick dangled it in front of her: a summer off with her son by the beach. She drives with some hope that the hours spent alone will be enough time to piece together a solution, the sinkhole threatening to swallow them whole.

"It works," Phoebe finally says. That's the answer she offers Marina, who probably doesn't hear because, like Kostya and their son, she looks skyward at yet another police or fire helicopter passing low overhead.

Marina throws the last chunk of banana at her husband, who floats facedown on the water, looks dead. “For now,” Marina says as Phoebe watches the sky.

21

Phoebe waits next to Pink Taco on a busy street in West Hollywood. The late-afternoon sun feels warm on her neck. She left her car with the valet at the hotel across the street, per JW's instructions. He sent a series of texts overnight. Also for JW, she wears the fringed linen-blend skirt from Mint Collection on Melrose that he linked to in a text he sent last week. It's short and teasing, and her hair is pulled up in a ponytail the way he likes it. He has a couple of hours before he leaves for Thailand.

Nick left Jackson with her this morning, left the house without speaking. She called Mai. She messaged Nick: *She's bringing him home @ 4. I won't be back.*

The words *LIVE RADIANTLY* are stamped on a billboard below a woman who looks anything but radiant: The black-and-white image is faded. Someone has outlined her face with yellow paint and cut out her eyes, two black spheres that look nowhere, see nothing.

Phoebe turns away from the image and chews a fresh piece of spearmint gum. She'll get her car and drive home. Or to the beach. She'll get Jackson and take him to watch the seagulls. She's shaking when she hears a voice cry out. It's so filled with rage and desperation that she's sure someone must be dying. A madwoman in all black with white hair and bright red lipstick is accosting pedestrians. Her blotchy face is bloated and she's barefoot. Phoebe edges close to the curb, looks down at her iPhone screen, hoping to avoid the woman. Cross the street, she thinks to herself. But her feet won't move. The light turns, traffic slows, and the afternoon shadows shift. The intersection where she stands and its sweeping murals advertising flavored vodka and women's clothing and looming hotels and hills and the madwoman whose voice falls silent and the black eyes on the billboard telling her how to live all trigger a wave of panic in Phoebe. She swallowed ten milligrams of Klonopin before she left the house. Now she sticks her hand in her bag, finds a Seroquel.

The wind is the madwoman breathing, poised to sink her teeth into Phoebe's neck.

A flesh-eating zombie went on a rampage recently in Echo Park. It was on the news. They said he was high on PCP. He ate the faces of three homeless men before police shot him dead.

Her phone vibrates. It's JW: *Turn around*

She does. A black BMW idles on the corner; the passenger door opens.

Get in.

Phoebe notices that she casts no shadow in the refracted sunlight. A stillness settles over everything: the cars that idle at the red light; the eucalyptus and tall palms, motionless.

She can't do this. Not now, not again. She knows one thing if nothing else: She's incapable of managing another turn with JW.

The light turns and a bus roars past and breaks the spell. The madwoman is gone. On the white screen of her handheld, small letters tell her what to do.

Get In.

Live Radiantly.

The open car door is a mouth ready to swallow her whole.

22

Phoebe drives home past wilting palms behind walls that line the cracked freeways and choked traffic and the translucent brown air and hears the low-flying helicopters and Harleys and breathes the exhaust on Sepulveda and Moorpark and at every backed-up intersection in Pomona. Her veins are wide and loose from the Seroquel and Klonopin. She can feel the blood flow. Tension melts away. She reads the message from Nick about not paying attention. She refills the tank using her Discover card because there's no money on the company gas card. She sees the two boxers in the backseat of the black Land Rover in the full-service lane and doesn't quietly resent the young Asian mother but instead asks if the dogs are from a breeder. "They're great with kids," Phoebe says, and the woman nods and seems uneasy, and Phoebe notices the two girls in the backseat with the dogs and considers asking the woman about pediatricians, but the woman is on the phone now, windows up. Though it's impractical and unaffordable, Phoebe recalls the image of the dog Nick sent from the house, the animal left behind.

She taps out a message to JW: *Maybe the Polo Lounge for drinks when you return??*

No immediate reply.

You understand I'm conflicted. I wouldn't have been standing there waiting for you if I wasn't. I just couldn't get in the car. Do this again. Maybe if someone had pushed me. If you'd grabbed me and pulled me in. I don't know. It can't be like it was.

His response: *So then why that skirt?*

She ignores JW's question. She sends a series of messages to Nick instead:

OK. Let's try it. I want the dog.

Was there a collar on it? Can we find out the name?

You're right Jackson will love it. Can you still get it?

There's no response. She sends another message:

It would be good to do for Jackson. And for us.

Nick finally responds: *It's been nearly a month, Phoebe.*

Try?

Too late.
Why?
He's gone.

23

Nick doesn't know why he lied to Phoebe about the dog. He paid for the dog. They're getting the dog. He reaches for his coffee and apologizes to the couple across from him in the booth. She's a nurse. He's a teacher. They look tired, like new parents, minus the joy. Their kids are six and nine. Their house is a four-bedroom foreclosure in Corona.

"We're getting a dog," Nick says. "I think. Do you have pets? I'm fine with pets. It's not a problem."

They shake their heads.

"California's fucked. Teachers are fucked. We're fucked." The man looks out the window as he speaks. "Nurses at teaching hospitals are fucked. No money. State's defaulting. Everyone's fucked." He turns to Nick. "Except you, apparently. How are you not fucked?"

Nick presents them with his authentic-looking three-page rental agreement.

The wife places her hand over the husband's. "But we can pay the rent," she says. "We have income. We're just fucked in every way imaginable. This is month-to-month, right?"

"Right."

They'll likely be in the place for a month, maybe two, before they figure out whatever's next, some better place to land.

"We'll do a fresh coat of paint inside," Nick says. Panera is packed and quiet. Too many middle-aged men and women staring at laptop screens, looking for jobs.

The husband thumbs through messages on his iPhone. "Hang on," he says. He jots some numbers on a napkin, slides it in front of his wife, who glances down at it, gives a nod.

"We'll do something about the pool, too, the pump —"

"We don't give a shit about the pool," the man snaps.

"Okay. No pool. I'll take a hundred off the monthly."

"Fine," the man says.

"Okay," the woman says.

The man enters a number, holds the phone to his ear. He follows some prompts, enters more numbers, ends the call. He signs the rental agreement — as binding as the napkin he's writing on, Nick thinks.

The woman signs next.

Nick wants to get this over with, get their check, get home. But he needs to see it through. "Initial and date, here and here."

"So how'd you get so lucky?" the woman asks Nick.

"With what?"

"Everyone's pretty much screwed out here," the man says. "Except you?"

Nick is pleased with himself. He plays the part to perfection. "I'm not making shit," he says. "Whatever I collect goes straight to the bank that owns me."

The $2,998 Nick and Phoebe had in savings is now $21,400 and about to jump another thousand when the cashier's check the couple slides across the table clears.

24

The vibration on Nick's handheld is Arik. Nick is home alone with Jackson, who fell asleep on his chest ten minutes ago. Phoebe is out, still working, or not.

Guess who's lying like a half-dressed skank next to me on the floor drinking a kale smoothie?

Nick doesn't respond.

The next message is a JPEG: Mallory lying facedown on the plush cream carpet, sipping a Jamba Juice, wearing black-lace boy-shorts and nothing else. She has rings on her toes and an iPad open to TMZ.com in front of her.

Arik messages again: *Got something juicy.*

Go

Favor for boss. Don't ask him about it. He can't know we're doing it. He wants possible deniability.

Plausible?

??

What do you need me for?

You gotta drive us. And help. Boss wants YOU.

You said he asked Greg and the Hondurans

That was bs. Just come. Mallory and her girls want to chill after.

Nick carries Jackson upstairs and lowers him into the crib, but the boy grips the back of his neck and won't let go. Nick keeps him in his arm and walks to the window. Outside he sees Metzger smoking a cigarette, shirtless, pointing his shotgun at the sky.

So you down or what?

I don't think so.

EZ cash/merch.

No.

We need three, dude. This ain't no trash-out ☠

Then what?

Collection. Renter owes boss a shitload of money.

Call Sean.

We're not allowed to do this without you.

Nick inhales the clean baby scent of his son. He kisses his warm forehead twice as he lowers him into the crib, this time without waking him.

25

They've been driving for over an hour. Nick is sipping a can of warm Red Bull that Arik handed him when he got in, and a Dirty Beaches track drifts from the speakers. Arik approves by nodding. After calling Mai, despite the late hour and last-minute request, and asking if she'd stay with Jackson until Phoebe or he returned, Nick relented and said yes, he would join them tonight. The call to Mai was also after he'd spent hours online researching the quality of local pre-K and elementary schools and read nothing that gave him confidence they could do for Jackson what he and Phoebe both insisted they wanted for him.

Nick had to drive out toward Redlands to get Arik and then turn around and head down to Riverside to pick up Sean. He was rushed all night, and arrived late after he fell behind on laundry and cleaning the pool, walking Carousel Court with Kostya to check on the empty house next to Metzger's. (Marina was sure she saw three men in a white pickup truck idling in front of it, leering at her as she jogged past. Nick did find a few cigarette butts at the end of the driveway.)

The house Sean and Arik need to hit tonight is in North Hollywood: Toluca Woods. It'll be the three of them and a supposedly empty twenty-eight-hundred-square-foot five-bedroom gated villa that was rented to a man in his late twenties who left the house behind and owes thousands to the owner of the property, a wealthy colleague of Boss. The men — Nick, Sean, and Arik — are the muscle. They'll divide the cash or possessions among themselves, change the locks on the doors so the owner can rent it out again.

The property belongs to a casino owner in Rancho Mirage, the title holder of a handful of homes used for favors, bribes, for people who couldn't go through conventional channels to get a place to live legitimately. They all paid in cash. They were all men, here illegally or in hiding, who would fail background checks because of crimes committed or IRS issues. The upside for the owner was the huge cash payments up front; the downside was the inability to enforce agreements. Nick and the casino owner have that in common, if nothing else.

It's just after midnight. The moon looks swollen. Like it's going to burst. Arik rolls a joint and lights it.

"What if it blew up? The moon? Tsunamis, right? I mean, the tides. Wouldn't the oceans just roll over us? Waterworld."

Nick is driving tonight because he didn't share the address with Arik or Sean and asked Boss not to, either, even if they bothered to ask, because they would have gone to the house first and gutted it or, if the man were still there somehow, collected if they could, and Nick would have lost his cut. Because in the end, Boss doesn't care how the possessions are divided up, as long as the favor gets done. There will always be another job, another payout, according to Boss. And he's right. This thing is just getting started.

Arik gives up the front seat to Sean. "You're late," Sean says to Nick when he gets in. He smells like weed. All the lights are on in his ranch-style house. He's been here for a month: since his wife left. He's here for the schools, he says, and laughs because his only son, sixteen, is gone for good, went with his mother. Sean needs a lot of money and soon. So tonight Sean is missing his son's concert (he's in a band with some friends called Prisoner, and they're playing a warehouse show). He sends messages to his son's mother, who is uploading the concert on YouTube. "Bitch won't text me back."

It's almost one by the time they take the Universal City exit and Nick says, "Find Cahuenga, Cahuenga."

"There it is," Arik says from the backseat, window down, leaning out, the warm night air washing over him.

Nick says, "Ledge, Ledge, Ledge."

"There," Arik says.

"Take a left," Sean says. "When we cross Camarillo we're there. It's on the left."

"You know this how?" Nick asks.

"I do my homework," Sean says. "Toluca Woods. Keep going. About a mile."

The ranch-style houses on Ledge Avenue are similar to Sean's, only much nicer, with manicured lawns and white picket fences, oleander and silk floss and short palms. They're set close together, giving the street a neighborhood feel; Nick imagines streets blocked off for Fourth of July barbecues and Halloween parties or some kid's fourth birthday party.

Sean hits Nick's arm. "Stop here."

■ ■ ■ ■

The house is three stories and set farther back from the street than the rest, behind a ten-foot cast-iron gate.

Nick called the Hondurans, but they refused to help. Only for Boss, they said. They do work for his properties, not "the collections," too *peligroso.*

If they're able to collect the money owed from the tenant, he's told by Sean and Arik, they'll clear nine thousand. The three of them will split three thousand and whatever they can carry out of the house in one trip.

"How likely is that?" Nick asks.

"It's not," Sean said. "These assholes are never home."

Nick sighs audibly. "This isn't your first . . . job?"

Sean ignores him. "It's a wild card. You can say no. Drop us and wait."

"If they're home?"

"They've got security and won't let you get close enough to piss on the place. In that case, you just walk away."

"And if there's no one there?" Nick asks.

"Do us a favor: Stay in the car."

Ledge Avenue narrows where the house lies. The winds have slowed. The air is eerily still and so dry it seems to crackle. The bright moon seems larger than ever, closer somehow. Arik is staring up at it like a child. Nick breathes in the scent of smoke. Not a controlled burn, he thinks. Something started carelessly, like most of the wildfires, or with intent, and soon helicopters and sirens will fill the purple night sky. Stone walls and the black iron gate surround the property. Poised atop each of the two columns on either side of the gates: a pair of matching wild-eyed gargoyle statues.

"The only house for ten blocks that's gated," Arik says. "That's not a small gate, either."

Nick and Sean ignore him.

"We're going to get shot," Nick says.

"Then stay in the fucking car!" Sean roars.

Sean spits fierce instructions, warnings, into Arik's ear as they stand next to the car. Nick can hear Arik saying, "I know, I know," and he sounds like a boy, "I will." Sean runs his fingers through his long hair three times, walks around to Nick's side, the open window, inches from Nick's face, the liquor on his warm breath, skin pocked with acne scars and reddish-gray stubble, eyes glassy, as if they've been dipped in something yellow, translucent. "You're not calling the shots on this one, chief. Your nuts come off if you screw around."

Nick and Sean pull themselves up so they can see over the wall as Arik sits on the hood of the car. The floodlights are turned off; the lawn is green; the sprinklers are on, watering the patchy green turf; the driveway is empty.

"The bank could be turning the water on," Nick says. "Keeping the place ready to show."

"No signs posted," Sean answers.

"Place looks lived in."

They drop from the wall.

Nick checks the address again: 11290 Ledge. He calls Boss and gets voice mail. He leaves a message, then follows up with a text: *Sprinklers ON. Sure about this address??*

Sean wears a grim expression, takes a drag of a cigarette. He motions for Arik, and from the deep side pockets of his black cargo pants: three white latex masks. Sean and Arik slowly slip theirs on. The effect is terrifying. The eyes are black plastic circles, the heads misshapen and white, like executioners from a fever-induced nightmare that Nick used to suffer as a child. This feels completely out of control.

"Thanks for the ride." Sean's voice is

muffled and tinny through the mask. He asks Arik if he's ready.

"I'm not wearing that," Nick says.

"They will piss their pants," Arik says, too eager.

"Let's keep talking," Sean steps to Nick. "Until someone comes along walking their goldendoodle."

Arik leans against the car, rhythmically tapping the passenger-side window with his thumb, a thick silver ring making a clicking sound against the glass. Nick leans over to get Arik's attention, tells him to move when Sean motions for Arik to stop tapping the glass. A masked face presses against the smudged window and a hollow-sounding voice commands: "Now!" Nick grabs the white mask from Arik.

They're at the back door. Nick refuses to wear the mask. "These masks will get us shot," he says to Sean, whose grunt indicates a deeper, more fundamental issue with Nick. When they peer inside, they see the house is completely dark except for glowing red and green lights from various clocks and electronic devices and alarms. Someone's obviously living here.

Sean and Arik speak in muffled tones through their masks.

Nick says, “We don’t even know if this is right.”

They stare at Nick for a beat, clearly surprised that he’s wearing the mask.

“You don’t get it,” Sean says. “This is the house.”

“What if it’s not?”

“This is the house we’re doing.”

“And if it’s the wrong house?”

“No such thing.”

Sean wedges the end of a crowbar through the door and frame, pops it open. Nick pulls the mask over his head, adjusts it so the slits align with his eyes. He understands something the moment the glass door cracks open and he glimpses his reflection in the glare from moonlight, the stark white latex mask and blackness from the neck down: He’s not here at all.

Sean moves across the room to a small panel of lights on the wall and pushes some buttons, deactivates the alarm. It’s cold inside. The air-conditioning is on and Nick can’t hear well with the mask on, a steady hum in his ear. Sean and Arik move quickly. They pick up various pieces of electronic equipment: laptops, a juicer, two flat-screen televisions, a painting they struggle to remove from the wall, what looks like some kind of award, a Grammy or an Emmy. Nick doesn't know where Sean got the duffel bag, but he's filling it with cutlery and shoes and Nick finds a barstool and sits down because he's queasy, as Sean and Arik disappear upstairs and Nick stares at the flashing green light on the wall panel, watches it turn solid red.

He walks around in the dark, looking for a bathroom. A door he pulls open leads down a flight of carpeted stairs. The room he finds himself in is huge and dimly lit with orange recessed lighting. It's a game room. Pool table, air hockey, two pinball machines. There's a cotton candy machine in the far corner and vintage air travel posters in large black frames on the walls. Nick picks up the cue ball, slides it in the deep pocket of his cargo pants, finds a bathroom.

Nick hears loud voices coming from upstairs.

There's someone here. Men are yelling over each other. No one sees Nick, who stands in the stairwell doorway that leads to the great room. Sean and Arik still wear their masks, stand over a thin man, maybe thirty, in his boxer briefs, facedown on the leather sectional. His hands are bound with electrical tape. Arik stands back, waiting for instructions from Sean. In their white masks, they intimidate. Tonight is some kind of game for them. Maybe Sean will cash in, extort the man. It's clumsy and crude, seems haphazard. When Sean kicks the man twice, hard, and he falls to the floor, retching, it confirms something for Nick: The man may or may not be guilty of something, may deserve what he's getting, but they've crossed a line that he can't and won't. Nick grabs Arik by the upper arm. "I'm gone." A pause. "Are you coming?"

Arik is watching Sean press his knee against the neck of the man on the floor.

"Go then," Arik says.

"I'm your ride."

"We're taking the Land Rover."

"What Land Rover?"

"His." He motions to the man whose neck Sean is now straddling. Sean is bellowing, "Don't pick your nose. It's not polite to pick your nose and eat it!" He's sticking the man's finger up his own nose and forcing it in his mouth.

"No worries," Arik says, laughing along with Sean. "We're supposed to take the dude's Land Rover."

Nick tosses his mask on the passenger seat of his car, keeps the windows down, the air cooling his sweaty head and neck as he drives. He inhales deeply through cleared sinuses the faint smell of Arik's marijuana and something vaguely floral. He sends a message to Mallory. *Will have keys for your friends tomorrow. Let's get them in the house. Call me.*

He removes the cue ball from the deep front pocket of his jeans, white like the moon, and squeezes it. A text message from Mallory reads: *Awesome!! When are we going running?? Or whatever ;)* The approach to the freeway is deserted. Nick merges easily with the traffic. He grabs the latex mask off the passenger seat and slowly pulls it over his head until it's fully on again. The left lane of the freeway opens up. All blackness and bright white strips of light and wind. Nick feels a rush of adrenaline, the left lane somehow his alone. He guns it.

26

The elderly black couple from Torrance sits on a plastic-covered couch in a plastic-covered living room in a too-warm house on a deserted strip of asphalt in a place called Lakewood. The man, mocha-colored and bald, wears an ironed blue oxford, khakis, and clean white sneakers, and hands Nick cash: all twenties, fresh from the ATM. Nick tries very hard not to picture the couple standing at the bank machine, the husband pressing smudged steel digits with an arthritic index finger.

Nick met them last week. The man told him what they went through, about the Bank of the West representative who convinced them they should borrow against the house because real estate was safe: Values always rise. Nick wondered if it was Metzger who told them this. Nick offered to move their belongings to the new house, the rental he found for them from Boss's list in Lakewood, the neatly manicured lawn on the well-lighted street. Nick paid three of the Hondurans a hundred dollars each to help with the move.

"All that bank bullshit," the man says. He sits back in his plastic recliner, clears his throat. "All their tricks and products." He grabs a glossy blue folder and hands it to Nick. Inside are glossy photographs of housing developments in Nevada. "Lake Mead," the man says. "Swore to us it was going to explode. She warned me, of course." He motions to his wife, who is standing now. They were pressured into borrowing two hundred thousand against the new-construction mortgage they secured with an interest-only adjustable rate.

"Not one year in the past sixty-two that housing prices didn't appreciate," the man says to Nick, his eyes yellow and tired. "Four percent at worst. Then eleven, twelve. You're a fool not to cash in on that."

The wife carries a cardboard box of bathroom items past them, up the stained carpeted stairs. It's the two men now.

"They were so slick," the man says. "Too slick. I laughed at those assholes when they said, 'Everyone wins, Alfred.' " The man inhales sharply through his nose. "They use your name. Keep calling you by your first name to make you feel like you're in it together."

"I hear you, Alfred," Nick says.

Alfred shakes his head.

Nick counts out half the money that the man gave him: five hundred dollars. He places it on the glass coffee table. "This month is half price."

The man stares at Nick.

"Painters are coming by next week to finish up. Call if you need anything."

27

"Do you trust me?" Nick asks Phoebe.

"Of course not."

Nick stands over her, facedown on the unmade bed, and contemplates the arch in her back. A line of little knobs pushes through her tan skin from her neck to the small of her back. He's muscular now, stronger than he's ever been. T-shirts stretch across his chest and at the shoulders where they were once loose. Phoebe is withering away.

Nick rests his hand on her spine and presses down and, as he does, wonders how much more pressure it would take for him to snap it.

"Tell me again why we can't burn it down?" she says.

"Fraud. Prison. Might kill some people."

"Who would know?"

He kisses her lower back, moves up her spine. "Burn it down then," he says.

"I might," she says.

"Wake me before you do?" He slides his leg over her, pulls her underwear down. She doesn't react.

"Maybe."

He kisses the knobs of her spine, which feel sharper than they should.

"You should call them," she says.

"Who should I call?" he asks.

"Your employers. The reason we're out here," she says. He stops kissing her, continues, then stops again. She doesn't seem to notice or care. "The people who are responsible for these golden days." She exhales and lifts herself onto her elbows, staring at the pillow, stretching her face with the heels of her hands. "It's been three months."

"What's your point?"

"Would it hurt to call them?"

"There's no job. There wasn't a job. There isn't and there won't be."

"They gave you options."

"We couldn't afford those options." The PR firm offered Nick half pay for full-time hours.

"It's better than what you're doing."

"There's no position. Let it go." Nick is lying down now, legs extended, adjusting himself. He's sore and stiff. The buzz is long gone.

"Fuck it. I'll call." She rolls over, nimble, catlike.

"Please do." He offers her his phone. She considers it. "Exactly."

She snatches it.

There's a pause. Everything is hushed except the bathroom faucet, which one of them failed to turn off completely. They stare at each other.

"You never wanted it. And I know why. You were terrified of the expectations. They chose to bring you out here, and you were going to have to perform. I mean produce. Justify their investment in you. And that scared you. They're not idiots, Nick. They could smell your fear."

She finds the number in his contacts and holds up the phone so he can see it. "Ringing," she says.

"It's Sunday night. No one's there."

"Hello? Hi. Who's this?"

Phoebe stares at Nick, sticks a finger in her ear. "Hi. Yes. Sorry to bother you on Sunday. Phoebe Maguire. I am, thank you." Nick reaches for his phone. Phoebe slaps his hand away. "So, yes, my husband. Nick Maguire, yes, from Boston. Yes, he is. Thank you for saying so."

Nick grabs her arm and squeezes. She slaps him across the face. Her fingernails scratch his cheek. He lets go.

"He is. It is discouraging, but he's no less committed. I've never seen him quite this focused on making something happen, which is in part why I'm calling."

Nick grabs her again and pulls too hard. She falls forward and drops the phone. Nick reaches for it. Phoebe kicks him in the abdomen, hard, grabs the phone. "Apologies," she says, laughing. "My son. He's almost three. Quite the handful."

She kicks Nick again, twice, this time connects with his thigh and then his chest, rushes into the Labrazel Italian marble en suite bathroom with the cast-iron claw-foot antique tub, slams and locks the door.

"It's that kind of night," she says.

There's a long pause.

"Yes, extremely unorthodox, agreed."

Another pause.

"You gave him an offer. We moved our lives here for that offer. You offered terms that he agreed to in good faith and moved his family, my job, our son, across the country because you, Mr. Mason, asked him to. And now *you* are working on Sunday night and *he* is not."

Nick has his ear pressed to the door, hears it all.

"He's not. He is. He'd kill me. That's not

the point. Right now. Okay, then, tomorrow."

Nick is knocking on the door, lightly but persistently rapping his knuckles in a steady rhythm. "Not amusing!"

Her conversation continues. "Why not? No. Wrong." Then a pause. Then her voice rises: "Fuck that."

His knuckles are now fists, and he's pounding the door. "Enough!"

"A little. Okay, a lot. Vodka cranberries. Three. And two mimosas this morning." She laughs. "I know. Yes. Pharma sales. Oh, fuck you. Thank you. Do the same. Sleep well, too, asshole."

Nick is kicking the door.

"You'll break it, jackass," she calls out.

"Open it."

"No."

He's rubbing his dry eyes with his knuckles, drags his hands across his forehead.

"Can I have my phone?"

"Who is *Mallory*?"

"Now, please."

"She's hot. Young, though. Is she even eighteen?"

He gives up. He finds dental floss on the dresser, begins to floss.

"Have you been with anyone since we've been married? Tell the truth. I don't mind. I just want to know. Have you been with Mallory?"

The floss is stuck between two molars, both filled with silver. Nick is pulling it down, clumsily. He's all sunburned exhaustion and rage. "No," he says finally.

"I don't care. I like that name: Mallory."

"Come out if you want to talk." The tips of his index fingers are purple from wrapping the floss too tightly. "Come out and fuck me," he says. "Like you fucked him." He tugs at the stuck floss and it slips, not up but down, slices his gums. In an instant he's at the bathroom door, which he kicks. "Did you call them, Phoebe? Did you seriously?"

"They're pricks."

Nick rubs his hands back and forth over his scalp, hard and fast.

"Someone needed to man up." The door swings open. She stands before him in the doorway with a sympathetic expression. "Baby," she says, "you're the worst drinker." She brushes past him.

"You're unbelievable."

"Unpredictable? Yes. Unproductive? No. Unworthy. Unfulfilled?" She stops. She's not looking at Nick, who stands over his sink, checking his gums, which are bleeding. "Underwhelmed?" she says, and turns off the bedroom light. "Always. Which may have something to do with why I don't want to feel you pressing up against me."

He sees his cell on the vanity. He checks the call history and sees the number from the Encino firm and the call length: four minutes, twenty-two seconds. He considers her spine. Again. He's standing in the doorway.

Phoebe stares at him. "Don't move," she says. "You actually look tough like that."

"You're insane."

"I like that look for you. Like our first date when you were showing off, carrying those huge jugs of water for my neighbor. It worked. Very hot."

"You need help."

"Come lie with me."

"If I do, we aren't stopping."

"Come."

He sits next to her on the bed, stares at the wall. She takes his hand, pulls him until he's on top of her. She guides him inside of her.

"Apologize to me," he says.

She's silent. Her eyes are closed. He's still talking, but she's somewhere else. Then she snaps out of it and says, "We were supposed to be at Marina and Kostya's tonight."

He stops. "Apologize for what you did."

"But they barbecue every weekend," she says in a decent Russian accent. "Come inside me."

"Apologize."

"We'll see them Saturday. And we'll bring something."

"Now."

"This *is* my apology." She pulls him until he falls on top of her, and as she digs her fingernails into him, rips his skin, he feels it, the pointed, fragile thing, the spine that holds Phoebe together. He could snap it in two. And inside of her, he's realizing that may be one of the few things he could do that she'd respect.

28

She's on her way down to Newport, then Laguna Beach, and JW is sending text messages. She just finished ninety minutes at Equinox, mostly the StairMaster, then some core work. She feels strong, focused. She's looking for a house to rent, maybe a Craftsman, walking distance from the beach. A rental she and Nick can afford when she starts her new job, the one JW is delivering.

Polo Lounge is a bit passé.

No job news. It's brutal out there. Things aren't picking up like I thought. Could be a while.

She responds: *MOTU JW can't move mountains? What's next with me and D&C?*

She steers with her knees while she pulls her hair into a ponytail. She swallows and her throat is tight. This morning she upped her Klonopin. She was plateauing; all the signs were there: grinding her teeth at night; pitched forward in the Explorer as she drove, the hot tension between her shoulder blades, the gauze lifted from the brown sound-barrier walls and wilted palms that line the gray cracked freeways.

Today she was steady. Until now. JW cuts through the warm psychotropic fog, ruthlessly, right now.

His response: *Soon maybe.*

Rules don't apply to u. Your words. Don't start now with bullshit about what u can't do.

Easy babe. Wheels are in motion. Come see me.

Then when do I hear something?

Can we at least Skype? If you can't get away?

When can you tell me something real?

Very soon. Can you get away?

Maybe

When?

Soon

It's almost four. Phoebe pushes a full cart of groceries through a Bristol Farms she spotted on her way home.

Texts pour in from JW.

It's Saturday night. No Skype: get away. Come for drinks and sushi?

Monday, she responds.

When Monday?

It's not Saturday. Today is Monday. Labor Day.

I don't care if it's Sunday morning. I want your middle-class ass over here NOW!

She calls him. He doesn't answer. He sends a series of messages:

If my extended weekend comes and goes without a Phoebe sighting I'll just have to come back. Again and again.

There's a knock at the door: is it you??

Damn it, girl. I've decided: I need you NOW

Zen Suite. Hotel Bamboo. As late as you like

Want to go to Japan? My attorney just called and I'm free! One ex-wife down, one to go. No payments, no damages no debts. I.D.L.E.

She messages back: *???*

I. Don't. Lose. Ever.

She calls again. He answers.

"IDLE? Kind of childish. And don't make me the bitch who keeps asking."

"So don't be that bitch."

"Yes or no?"

"Do I ever lose? Is that your question? I think you know the answer, babe."

"Does that extend to me?"

"I. D. L. E."

"I'm not you. Same rules don't apply."

She drops the call.

He messages her instead of calling: *Answer one question for me. Can we without a condom this time?*

29

The barbecue is winding down. Outside at dusk, another hot Saturday in September, the two couples, Kostya and Marina, Phoebe and Nick, lie on chaises by the pool. They've been out here for hours. Kostya produces a joint, offers to share. Nick reaches for it and takes a long drag.

Kostya drops a cicada on Marina's head and she doesn't notice. Phoebe starts to warn her, but Nick grabs her arm. The cicada is grotesque, with bulging red eyes and orange wings. It crawls from Marina's hair to her neck, and she casually brushes at it, then realizes that it's something larger than a mosquito or a fly, and in one motion she pinches it, wraps her hand around it, pauses to take a drag from the joint Phoebe passed to her, then drops and crushes the thing with her bare heel.

"You're my hero," Phoebe says to her.

The charcoal briquettes are dimming.

Nick walks over and scoops up Jackson, holds the boy in his arms on a chaise longue while Phoebe helps Marina collect the red plastic cups and paper plates and empty beer bottles. Nick finishes off the rest of Phoebe's warm daiquiri. He closes his eyes. Jackson is calm, resting on his chest. He could lie like this forever. He feels the presence of someone standing over him but doesn't open his eyes, doesn't want to break from this. When he finally opens his eyes, he sees the wide silhouette, the ember of a lit cigarette.

"Jesus, Metzger," Nick says softly, not wanting to disturb Jackson. "What are you doing here?"

"He's out there," Metzger says.

"Does Kostya know you're here?"

"Fuck Kostya. He's all talk."

"I don't know what you mean." Nick lowers his voice.

"Forget it. So he's burning shit again."

"Who is?"

"Your neighbor," says Metzger, his voice rising. "He's loading up the truck."

Nick makes a shushing noise and says, "Do you mind?"

Metzger stares at Jackson for an unusually long time.

"Good night," Nick says.

Without taking his eyes from Jackson, Metzger says, "He's burning more of his shit."

"That's great, Metzger."

"We just sit back and watch until what? He burns the whole place down?" Metzger looks at Nick with disappointment on his face. "Well, I called it in."

"Fantastic," Nick says, reflexively wrapping both his arms around Jackson's warm body.

"They don't mess around during fire season. They'll be here." Metzger drops his cigarette on the concrete, steps on it, then struggles to keep his balance as he tries to light another. Nick is waiting for the request for money. He turns toward the sliding glass door that opens into Kostya and Marina's kitchen and breakfast nook. He wants to go inside, but not until Metzger leaves. He starts to say something about heading home when Metzger spits on the patio, then turns to Nick before he leaves and says, "Going to Buffalo to bury my father. The Mossberg's yours." Nick eyes him carefully and can't decide if Metzger is sentinel or symptom or both.

Inside Kostya and Marina's cool kitchen everyone is smashed. The kids are watching some Pixar thing in the living room that's clearly too sophisticated for Jackson, but the animation has him mesmerized. Marina and Phoebe lean against the emerald-green granite kitchen island. Nick sits opposite them, squeezing the last drops of juice from a wedge of lime into something Kostya mixed. Nick wonders how close he and Phoebe are to asking about summer camps and local schools. A couple of breaks, a few thousand dollars? What would it take to make this more than a wrong turn? To make it their home?

Kostya grabs his wife's breasts and she shrieks and slaps him and he growls and they're both laughing and he says, "Healthy woman here," and she punches his ass with a closed fist twice, hard, as he leaves the room to take a piss.

Nick tries to remember when he and Phoebe last felt so carefree, satisfied with the moment, their home life, their place in the world, their outlook. A few thoughts flash across his mind, teasing stretches of time around their wedding, their honeymoon in the French Quarter, and the plans each dreamed up in their king hotel suite after breakfast in bed seven years ago. A trip they took to Rehoboth back east when

Phoebe was pregnant, walking barefoot along the cool, wet sand, the lights of small boats glistening on the horizon as they narrowed down their list of names: Jasper, Jonathan, Rex, Sebastien, and Jackson. Two nights they spent on Nob Hill in San Francisco for a documentary film festival.

"We're not exactly where we planned to be," Nick says to Marina, responding to a question no one asked.

"Yet," Phoebe adds.

Kostya returns, drying his hands on his shirt.

"We're closer, though," Nick says.

"Closer to what?" Phoebe asks.

"I'm thinking about New Orleans again."

"You are?" Phoebe snaps, stands up, walks to the kitchen counter, and pours another drink. "That's news to me," she says, and laughs out loud.

Marina smiles. Kostya turns to Nick, then back to Phoebe.

"I told you this the other night," Nick says.

"Was I in the room when you said it?" She's baiting him.

"You were passed out on the sectional."

"Continue, Nickels," she says, her new nickname for him. "The next phase of our grand plan."

The expression on her face, with her

ponytail, reminds Nick of the Phoebe he wants to fuck. For some reason, right now, in their neighbors' kitchen with his wife emasculating him, he wants to fuck her.

"There's something about it down there," Nick says. Phoebe returns to her stool, carries it over to Nick's side of the island, sets it too close to him. With the kitchen island obscuring their lower bodies, Nick takes her hand and places it over his crotch and holds it there. "Right after Katrina, being down there," Nick continues, and Marina and Kostya actually seem to pay attention to his story about the footage he was putting together and the Discovery Channel and the bloated bodies he found in the flooded shotgun house and the dogs left behind, moving in packs, cannibalizing each other. Phoebe's hand, surprisingly, remains on his crotch.

Kostya laughs. "Sound like Ukraine."

"Why do you feel this compulsion to bullshit everyone?" Phoebe pulls her hand from him. She turns to Nick, inches from his face. "Your hair is thinning," she says, reaches for his head.

Nick slaps her hand away.

The room is hushed.

Addressing Kostya and Marina, Phoebe continues as if nothing happened. "We're not going to New Orleans. We're not going anywhere."

"We honeymooned down there," Nick says. "And housing is dirt-cheap."

"We have a house," Phoebe says. "Remember? The rock-climbing wall, the hourglass-shaped pool with quartz rendering? The Italian marble bathroom?"

"Well, I don't care where we go," Kostya says, and slaps Nick's back. "Camping, the beach, New Orleans, Vegas, we are going somewhere. All of us go together. Take week or two somewhere new and sexy."

"Anything to avoid his *zalupa* father," Marina says.

"Did he call?" Kostya asks, walking across the kitchen to help his wife put away dishes.

"He says he can have bonus room," she says.

The rumor around Carousel Court or, more accurately, coming from Metzger, is that Kostya and Marina paid cash for their house. Another rumor: They owned stores in Chicago that sold Russian groceries and liquor that did quite well. The rumor that Kostya was involved in loansharking is bullshit, Nick says, part of Metzger's conspiratorial fantasies. The truth is, unlike most on the block or the city of Serenos or the counties of San Bernardino, Riverside, and L.A., Kostya and Marina appear unmovable.

Kostya is shaking his head, his bloodshot eyes without focus. "I'll buy him his very own house before we move him here."

"Buy his dad a house, Nick," Phoebe says, voice rising. "But wait, can your garbageman job cover that?"

Nick grins and his lips are tight and instead of slapping the smug expression off Phoebe's face he says, "Eat something."

Kostya's laughter is uneasy. He interrupts, invites Nick to come with him.

Nick follows Kostya upstairs, down the long wide carpeted hallway to the master bedroom. Kostya keeps running his hands over his hair, mumbling something to himself. When he raises his voice, he says, "See this."

Opposite the unmade king-size bed is a walk-in closet. Hundreds of pairs of shoes are piled floor to ceiling.

"She is eBay shoe queen," Kostya says, and moves past the shoes to a framed black-and-white photograph of a soldier. Nick studies the face, young and dirty, a cigarette hanging from cracked lips. It looks cold in the picture, dark, lifeless. But the soldier's eyes are bright and there is the hint of a smile on his prematurely aging face. "Vladimir Savchenko, my father, in Dubai."

Nick doesn't get it. This is not Dubai, he thinks, studies the bare trees, the snow-covered landscape. When he looks up, Kostya has a black safe door pulled open. He removes something heavy wrapped in a white cloth. He hands it to Nick, who opens the cloth to reveal a gold slab. Imprinted on the face: a winged beast clutching a triangle flag, a swastika in the center of it. Nick stares at his brilliantly distorted reflection in the gold bar. He doesn't know what to do or say. He sees in the shadowy mouth of the vault three stacks of identical slabs. Kostya's blood-soaked safety net. He grabs it, clutches it with thick fingers and stubs, and stands too close to Nick. It's rigged. The game is corrupted. It's madness in the tight small space of haunted vaults and walk-in closets. It's very late. It's time to go home.

30

Nick takes his time walking home under a brilliant moon. The coyotes aren't so much howling as they are laughing. The orange tent lies dark, and the canvas door ripples in the wind that feels hot and almost, somehow, electric. Serenos is folding in on itself, eating its own. Nick shivers and he's hoarse and clears his throat as he studies his glowing phone and taps out a message to Mallory — *helter skelter* — that is ignored.

When he walks inside, Phoebe is on the sectional, bare feet propped on the glass coffee table, thumbing through images of Jackson on her iPhone. "Love this one," she says absently, doesn't show Nick.

"Did he go right down?" Nick says, chugging a glass of ice water. One childhood memory of his father before he died: watching him stand in the dark kitchen before going to bed, drunk again, guzzling large glasses of water.

"You don't have him?" she says, looking up. "You left him?"

"What the fuck, Phoebe?"

"You walked out of the house without —" She stops, screams: "Fucking incompetent idiot!"

"I'll get him," Nick says coolly as he sends a text to Kostya, who responds immediately. "He's sleeping," Nick says, holds up a picture Kostya sent of Jackson asleep under a white sheet on the sectional.

"I'll get him," Phoebe says.

"I got it." Nick raises his glass.

"Now, please."

"Roger that!" He salutes with a middle finger.

"I can't stomach you —"

"Slut," he snaps.

"— when you drink."

Silence. Nick starts to apologize, but Phoebe cuts him off.

"By the way, we're getting the dog," Nick says.

"Poor dog."

"I'll take care of it. You just do what you do. In fact, stay the fuck away from it."

There is silence. Nick doesn't care about the dog right now. Or even getting Jackson. Both can wait. He eyes her phone. "Show me your phone," he says.

"Go."

"Your texts from today, tonight. When you disappeared for half an hour and said you were in the bathroom."

"Since when do you *ask* to check my phone?" She sighs. "It's late. Go get our son, Nick."

"I can leave," he says. "I have cash."

She thumbs through more pictures of Jackson. "Are you getting him or am I?" she says.

He ignores her. "You know where I most want to go? It's weird, because I never thought much about it. Too crowded and rainy. Maybe it's all this fucking heat, but whatever it is, I've got this desire, this yearning, to go to Japan." He's shaking his head, his eyes avoiding Phoebe as he talks. "Yeah. Japan. Tokyo. From there, who knows? But start in Tokyo. A few days, a nice hotel suite, high-rise with views of the city. What do you think? Would you want to go?"

She says nothing, starts to leave.

"That's right, go get the son you forgot. Maybe you *should* go to Japan," he says.

Phoebe is now in the street. Nick is two strides behind her. She stops, wheels around, says, "Go home."

"You wanted me to read that. Like you

wanted me to read your email to him five goddamn years ago when you told him you loved him." Nick laughs maniacally, too loud. Nearby, Metzger sits on a low lawn chair smoking a cigarette, his orange tent glowing from the lantern inside. Nick doesn't care. He's a few feet from his wife under a full, heavy moon. A murderer's moon, he thinks. He can't manage a deep breath in the thick warm air. "I can't believe you even have him in your contacts. That's relatively new. I remember when you got that thing. Right before we left Boston. We were at the UPS Store, and then we went to Dunkin' Donuts and the Apple Store and you bought it on the spot. And I paid for it! What I did *not* pay for is you to stick that motherfucker in your contacts."

He rushes to her side and grabs her arm. She rips it free.

"Japan. Wow. You don't play around." He spits the words. She's got her head up, exaggerating good posture, that jaw jutting forward. "Are you crying? Oh, Jesus, Phoebe. Come on! You're fucking crying? You're going to Japan with your man and you're crying."

She stands in the middle of the street. The black asphalt is warm under Nick's sneakers, and that's when he notices: She's barefoot. She's wiping snot and tears from her face. She's breathing too hard, exhaling too much, hyperventilating. She stumbles to the side, away from Nick, rights herself. "Japan," Nick says, and turns away, heads home through a stiff hot wind, calls out to no one in particular, "And away we go again!"

• •

It was January, before the notion of the California move existed. Phoebe woke up before the alarm on a bitterly cold Boston morning. The bedroom windowpane was cracked from relentless arctic air. She had twelve appointments scheduled. The same bitter cold seeped through the vents of their Jetta, the heating system they couldn't afford to replace. She should have come clean about the hundred thousand, said that it was from JW and not some dead relative, but she didn't and never would.

By the end of the short gray winter day, all twelve appointments kept, the text from her manager asked her to drive to Medford to visit one more physician. In his fifties, large new practice, an easy target.

It was too late, though. She'd picked up Jackson.

Have son/reschedule

Medford — take u 20min

An hour at least to get there w/traffic. Then?? Have son. Can't.

100+ scripts hotness. Go get ' em.

Have SON!

Figure it out, Phoebe.

Will schedule a dinner/drinks w/him next week

Sending someone else. They get commission and points.

Whatever

You're trending down.

give me 30min

Good girl. Next time don't me make push. Just do the job.

"Quick stop for Mommy. You're going to be my helper, okay?" She reached back and squeezed Jackson's leg. She found her iPod and adapter, slid it in. She found "Zombie" by the Cranberries, a song she played on a loop in high school. Phoebe reached up and back and flicked on the overhead backseat light and dropped a Richard Scarry book onto Jackson's lap and surveyed the traffic. It was so dark. All she could see was the blur of red and orange lights of traffic and the rear of the car in front of her and the glare of oncoming headlights and those in her rearview.

She got a text message from JW.

He was in Maui. He wrote *Mahalo* and attached a JPEG not of the black sand beaches nor a sunset but of her from a couple of years earlier, wearing her dark-framed glasses, his unbuttoned oxford shirt, and nothing else, sipping room service coffee and staring at a laptop screen.

Have you seen this woman?

She deleted it. Turned off her phone, tried not to think about two years ago. She changed lanes without signaling, accelerated.

"Fuck it." She whipped her head around to meet her son's wide brown eyes: "Want to go to a restaurant with Mommy?" She switched the music back to the World Playground CD for her son, but the volume spiked. Jackson flinched. Phoebe clicked it off, changed lanes because the white box truck in front of them had its hazards on. She reached back for Jackson's leg again, some delayed impulse to comfort him after he'd flinched. She swerved back into the right lane. "Let's get dinner together, just the two of us." She wrapped her hand around Jackson's soft, cool calf.

She missed something, a signal or a flashing red light or a turn. She didn't know because the car seemed to float, almost fly, shot from a cannon, bursts of bright light and grotesque sounds: torn metal, exploding glass, shrill hissing and wailing. Gagging on thick, salty bloodied mucous and more lights, orange, blue, red, and white flashing. Urgent voices and bitter wind, and in her mind Phoebe sat on a white porch swing, holding Jackson on her lap. Someone was promising her something if she'd only stop screaming. Someone was losing patience with her. She needed to stop kicking. "Where is he?" is all she kept screaming. The last thing she heard before the black: a helicopter, landing.

Jackson slept on his back. They positioned pillows in a way that would keep him from being able to flip over. Not because the doctors advised this but because the blue contusion on Jackson's forehead over his right eye was the size of a golf ball and had a slit in it that was wide and deep. It glistened with a swatch of Dermabond that made it look like some kind of grotesque special effect. Nick burst into tears when he first saw it. They'd succeeded in the two years and two months since their son's birth in never once dropping him, never once allowing him to fall from the sofa or their bed. Now his head looked like it might burst.

They were convinced he'd lose something vital: sight, cognitive abilities, language. They spent a night in the ICU for observation. He was wired up. Beeping and flashing like some sort of fleshy plastic explosive. Nick wanted him to sleep through it all. But Nick was also terrified every time his son's eyes closed: They'd never open. Stay awake. Rest. Look at me. Sleep. He sang to him and blew gently on his face when his eyes grew heavy. X-rays and a CT scan were negative. He didn't vomit. They ruled out a severe concussion. It was mild at worst. He'd be fine.

But they were wrong, had to be. The doctors were overworked and just wanted the hospital bed for the next patient. Nick and Phoebe were convinced they'd missed something. At home, despite the pain and swelling from her own injuries, she fed Jackson every meal slowly, carefully. She limited him to soft foods, though it wasn't necessary. Mashed bananas, yogurt, warm apple-cinnamon oatmeal. He was fragile and vulnerable. She inspected his bowel movements for blood. Phoebe sat alone in the glow of her laptop as Jackson slept, Googling the worst.

So Nick and Phoebe stayed awake, watching their sliced and swollen son, restless, waking up, crying out, producing odd high-pitched whines they'd never heard him make in his two years of life, which terrified them. The same fears gripped them both.

"Call the doctor."

"Take him to the emergency room."

"No, he's not fine."

"You're holding him too tight."

"How *much* did you give him? It's clearly not enough."

"He's not breathing right. Listen to him. Feel his chest? It's not right!"

"You have no idea what to do, do you?"

And the truth she couldn't find words for lay on the bottom of her black leather Coach bag beneath the compacts and work ID and Altoid tins and validated parking tickets and loose change and gummy bears: the brown plastic prescription bottles, mostly empty, the reason her son may die.

• •

Phoebe messages Marina that she's at the front door. She rings the bell. The oldest is at the door but not opening it. Phoebe tells him who it is and that she's here for Jackson. The porch light is too bright, buzzing. Phoebe looks over her shoulder toward the empty street, the flaps of Metzger's tent zipped closed. A pale light glows inside it.

"My parents say there's a crazy lady running around stealing babies and I'm not supposed to open the door."

"I was just here, Titan! I live three doors down. Jackson's mom." Something pops. Phoebe flinches. "Can you get your parents?"

"Dad's not here. Mom's giving my sister a bath."

"I just texted her. Tell her it's me." Phoebe sends Marina another message. The door unlocks, the alarm beeps twice as the door swings open.

"He's watching *SpongeBob,*" the kid says, and disappears.

The living room is dark and it takes a moment for Phoebe's eyes to adjust. The huge room has high ceilings and an enormous L-shaped leather sectional that takes up most of the space. A fireplace with a fake fire and a sweeping wall-mounted flat-screen television provide the only light. Sitting alone in the middle of the sectional, the images from the television flickering on him like some kind of strobe light, Jackson appears hypnotized, sucks his pacifier.

"Jacks?" she calls out as she moves toward him. He looks so small and lonely in this giant room, his little head and body on the oversize piece of furniture, like some kind of massive sea creature about to swallow him. Phoebe says her son's name again. He doesn't hear her. He doesn't seem to sense that she's there; even when she sits down next to him, he doesn't turn his head. He won't look away from the images flashing in high definition. She looks up at the screen: It's not SpongeBob. Two bloody men fight in a cage, pummel each other. How long has he been alone in here, staring at this? She grabs him and tries to stand but loses her balance and they fall back onto the couch together. She might vomit. She swallows hard.

"Honey, honey," she says into his ear as she stands. "Let's go home." His body gives out. He's instantly asleep, head heavy against her chest.

She sends Marina another text: *I have Jackson.*

She leaves the house. Before she pulls the front door closed, she feels it being pushed hard against her, forcing her out, probably Titan, and the dead bolt clicks and then another lock and the chirp of the alarm being set and the string of white lights in the tall skinny palm is coming undone, dangling, whipping in the wind like the skinny bright tail of a dark beast she can't see. But it's okay, she tells herself, squeezing her son to her chest, walking fast along the deserted asphalt street.

The only sound is her bare feet slapping the warm pavement. And Jackson's breathing, made raspy from the dry hot air.

The shadows in the orange-lit street like misshapen dogs are three coyotes, and they freeze, not scared, more poised. A fourth appears and their yellow eyes glow like embers. Phoebe stops. The animals are blocking her path to the house. If she turns and goes back to Kostya and Marina's, she's sure they'll chase her. If there weren't four of them, she would have thought they were Kostya's pair of German shepherds. God, she wishes they were Kostya's dogs. The largest animal turns away from Phoebe first, disinterested, but the other three keep their eyes trained on her. They take a few cautious steps toward her. The click of their claws against the asphalt is the only sound. They don't want her, though.

She hears it: a low moan. They're growling, hungry. They want Jackson. She's placed her son only feet from the animals. She deserves what comes. Her legs are weak. The animals are so close she can smell them — pungent, like something decomposed. A hush. One of the animals, the smallest, looks like a pup. It has large triangle ears that are too big for its little head. The pup eyes Jackson, tilts its head ever so slightly, seems to sense a kindred spirit.

The shots explode and the echo reverberates around the cul-de-sac, ricocheting off the terra-cotta walls of the houses. Jackson is stunned, silenced by shock. The wailing is the animal sprawled out along the street in pieces. The shots are from the orange tent, Metzger. He killed one, for sure. Another tries to limp away. Another shot rings out, sending the wounded animal into the side of a recycling bin, knocking it over. Right, right, Phoebe is thinking. She makes herself small, clutching Jackson, whose screaming is pained, too tight. Right, right. Okay, okay, she keeps thinking. Inside, sweetie. Let's go inside. Everything's all right. Doors are opening, figures cautiously emerging from the few well-lit houses that remain on Carousel Court. Kostya and Marina. Mai and her husband. Phoebe watches their front door, now jogging toward it, sure it will swing open and Nick will appear, shirtless and ready.

31

In the bright sunlight, Phoebe stares at blotches of faded blood on the asphalt from the coyotes Metzger shot last night. The text that arrives is from Marina: *He toss them in his backyard empty pool. Skin them. Eat them??*

Phoebe responds: *I was holding Jackson when he fired the gun.*

Sorry honey I'd have done same thing.

In our direction?

They're savages. Lucky he sit out there and watch for all of us.

Nick hasn't said anything to Phoebe this morning. All he said last night was: "Why didn't you run?" But he wasn't standing at the door, poised to save them. He was half dressed, texting some girl from their bed.

Now he stands outside, shirtless, cleaning the pool. He has to work this morning.

"He's a professional contact," Phoebe says from the shade of the patio as Nick pulls the tarp tightly over the pool. "He is nothing more. It is not here we go again."

Nick kneels over the far end of the pool. Then he stands, walks around the pool once, pulling on each of the tarp's straps to ensure its stability. He stops a foot from her. Says nothing.

"Let's not get into some long-drawn-out —"

He presses two fingers over her mouth, but too hard. She recoils, slaps his hand away. He laughs.

"Fuck you," she says.

Protruding from the waistband of his shorts is the butt of a semi-automatic pistol. He could hold it up to his head or hers, even unloaded, scare her straight. She knows she looks like shit: limp hair, bloodshot eyes, and so thin.

"There's something out there." He waves his pistol at the distant hillside. "I can hear it at night. Kostya, too. He thinks it's a mountain lion. I think he's right. Go look. I dare you." He walks inside the house, slides the door closed behind him.

32

If the open front door of the Pomona house weren't white, the streaks of blood on it wouldn't look as stark as they do. Nick rented the three-bedroom new-construction house to a Lithuanian family last week. The call came in on one of Nick's burners, from the renter who had paid him three thousand so far for three months.

Now the man is bleeding and pale. A man and woman stand over him on the yellow lawn. The man standing up clutches something dark. The garage door is open. A pickup truck is idling with the driver's-side door open. The object is a long blade that he is wiping clean against his jeans. The woman is fat and sweaty and holds an aluminum baseball bat in front of her, shaking it, repeating some phrase in Russian.

Nick could carry the unloaded pistol as he approaches but decides against it. They're all agitated and sweating. The man on the ground is cursing back at the couple, clutching the bloody gash on his forearm.

The woman yells at Nick in Russian.

The bleeding man falls back, closes his eyes, exhausted.

The other man says something to the woman. She takes a wild swing at the man on the ground and connects, hard, with his chest. He cries out, balls up.

Nick grabs the bat, struggles with the woman, and the man with the blade waves the knife at Nick, spitting and cursing. Nick backs away without the bat, holds his hands up.

From his car, Nick calls Kostya, who doesn't pick up. He tries his landline. A child answers. Tundra, the oldest, Nick thinks. His parents aren't home.

"Tell me what they're saying," Nick instructs. He holds his cell in the direction of the cursing woman and man with the blade. He's a few arm's lengths from Nick but close enough for the kid to translate. It's made clear to Nick: They want their house back.

Nick is ready to hang up. He knows what this is: The owners who left have come back, not quite ready to give up or with no place else to go. Either way, they want the people who Nick put in their house to leave.

"They called police. The police are coming." It's the kid. He's still translating for Nick.

Nick turns to the wild Russian couple, holds up his hands. "We're sorry. We're sorry." Nick is tapping his chest. "My mistake. Not his. My fault."

The man and woman don't move. Nick hears sirens. He drops his iPhone on the turf and, bending over for it, keeps his eyes locked on the couple.

Nick decides the renter will be fine. Police are on the way. He considers what they have: the burner number, which is untraceable to him; his first name, "Paul"; no address; no copies of the rental agreement. He doesn't need this house. Nick has cleared, after trash-out and painting and lock-changing expenses, fifty-two thousand for all of his houses. He walks to his car, gets in, starts the ignition, and leaves.

The message that appears on his iPhone, the screen smeared with the blood of his former tenant, is from Mallory: *Want to get high?*

Nick is on a freeway heading east to a drive-in theater he passed on the way here.

Is Arik there? he writes.

I'm not home

Where? Are you alone?

It makes a difference?

Of course

Then yes. I'm alone. On the beach.

And you want me to come get high with you?

That is my desire, yes.

Can I bring my wife?

Don't fuck with me, mister.

I have blood on my iPhone. I may have witnessed a murder that I caused.

Sounds exciting. Come.

I'm not sure I can handle getting high right now. Want to see a movie?

I just want to put my head on your lap.

7:30 Mission Tiki in Montclair.

Yummy.

33

The houses surrounding the playground, a mile from Carousel Court, are all the same, exact replicas of Nick and Phoebe's: Spanish-style new construction. On one of the many bank-owned signs someone tied a bouquet of white helium balloons with bleeding yellow heads and Xs for eyes. No one is playing in the yards. No fathers doing yard work or carrying groceries in from the minivan. No landscapers. It's a hot Sunday morning and the cicadas are screaming.

Jackson cries out from the backseat, "Playground!" over and over. It's too hot to be outside. But he starts to whimper, tears streaming down his cheeks, when Phoebe passes it. He wails. She's gripping the wheel and shushing him and saying it's too hot to be outside.

"Fine," she says, taking him out of his car seat. "You'll see." She'll stay at the playground for fifteen minutes until he can't stand it anymore. It's not just the heat. Phoebe hates this place as much as Nick does, but it's the only one near them.

The equipment is all bright primary colors and the slides are wide and slick and the ground is blue rubber and the white wooden fencing that surrounds the perimeter was probably nice once but now is faded and splintered and an entire stretch is missing. No one bothered to plant any trees. The only shelter from the sun is a metal overhang behind two metal benches that sit side by side. A few women sit while the children burn. Unlike the playground with the pond and mallards and tall oaks and birches and blue herons along the Riverway, where she took Jackson nearly every day last summer, there is no water here, no trails or trees. The only birds she's seen are black, grotesque, drifting overhead, circling. She's not convinced one of them won't swoop down, sink its claws into Jackson's back, disappear with him.

Most of the women on the hot metal benches speak Russian and Spanish. Phoebe knows a couple of them by sight but not by name. Marina knows all of the Russian women, who sit in a bunch and smoke and sip sugary drinks and feed their skinny kids chewy Kopobka candy. Phoebe always ends up going home with a handful stuffed in her purse. There may have been Goldfish here once, but not anymore. Marina's not here today and Phoebe's relieved. She won't have to stay, and can carry Jackson away screaming, and who cares?

The boys here today are much older than Jackson and play on a random patch of asphalt that looks like a half-finished basketball court. Someone amassed a huge pile of cicada shells on the edge. Two older boys in white T-shirts and baggy jeans are trying to set fire to it. They flick a lighter over and over. Curse each other. Phoebe shields her eyes, watches one of the two boys remove something from his pocket; the other ignites it, and they lay the flame on the pile of shells and watch them burn.

Other boys form a mosh pit and take turns sending each other through. It's a game: The others prevent escape by any means. It's up to the boy getting pummeled to break through. If he falls, he's out. Jackson thinks it's funny.

The skinny monsters flail and shove so hard that Phoebe looks at Jackson, because if she watches the boys much longer, she'll start to see the barren landscape fold in on itself, this patch of earth swallowing her and

Jackson whole along with the rest of the debris. Massive electrical towers loom over everything from brown hills that separate them from the next ripple of homes. Phoebe rubs her temples. The headaches are from tension and the foolish decision (made Friday night when Nick found her passed out behind the wheel in the Explorer, engine idling, in front of the young neighbor's house on Carousel Court) to radically wean herself off the benzos, cutting the dosage to nearly nothing just to prove she could. Or maybe it's the electromagnetic waves from the towers generating the tingling down her spine, through her arms to her fingertips, until she's shaking out her hands like some kind of madwoman. She could be walking down Sunset punching the exhaust-filled air or pushing a stroller through the vapors or letting a physician finger her until she cries. What's the difference? She wants JW to bail her out again. It's not about her. It's another woman entirely, doing her bidding. She'll make them the young, beautiful family they should have been.

She sends Nick a text: *Not sure when we'll be home.*

She may go to the beach and spend the day. She may check them in for the night at the Beach House Inn or the cheaper one farther up the Strand. They'll have their own little adventure. Pretend they live there. They'll look for neighborhoods and houses they can rent near the beach, near Laguna, where she'll soon work if she handles this the way she should.

Another message to Nick: *Could be tomorrow. Don't know.*

There's no reply.

With the entrance of a chubby Thai kid into the melee, Phoebe hears the sound of slapping skin and rising voices from the skinny monsters. The shoving becomes punching.

A thin boy with shaved red hair lands a closed fist to the temple of the Thai kid, sending him into the asphalt. One of the Russian mothers yells something from the bench but remains seated. The Thai kid doesn't seem to have a mother here, rubs his head, slumped on the asphalt. Phoebe is ready to leave. The kid tries to stand, but another kid kicks him and the boys laugh as he falls again. Phoebe takes a step toward the boys but stops. "Enough!" she calls out instead.

A Russian mother snaps her fingers. Another stands. When the kid rises again, two boys shove him hard and he falls. They won't let him up. That's the game.

One of the boys stumbles backward into Phoebe, knocking her into Jackson, who falls from the slide onto the hard rubber surface below. The Russian boy who fell into her is laughing and within arm's reach, so she swings her elbow, hard, crushing the bridge of his nose, spinning the boy face-first into the ground.

Jackson is on his back, stunned. His mouth opens and stays that way. He either can't breathe or is crying so hard that no sound comes out. A dark pink swatch forms instantly on the left side of his face, where he hit the blue rubber surface. Phoebe clutches his little shoulders and shakes him lightly, trying to induce breathing, a sound.

Finally, it comes. A deep, piercing cry.

The Russian boy lies motionless on the ground.

No one else seems to have seen what she did. She leaves the playground.

The side of Jackson's face is red and he sucks cold apple juice from his sippy cup. His tears have dried and he seems fine, kicks his feet with excitement when Phoebe mentions the beach.

At the first red light, the AC on high, perspiration cooling on her neck and chest, a pulse of exhilaration courses through her as she taps out a text: *I just left the playground*

How was it?

The immediate response surprises her.

I knocked a Russian kid unconscious

Clarify

A wild kid too old for the playground hurt Jackson.

So he had it coming

He never saw it coming.

They never do. Did you truly knock a kid unconscious?

Phoebe sees the sign for Beach Cities, changes lanes without signaling, leaves one freeway for another.

When do I get an answer?

What's so special about Laguna and California? I'll be honest, that office isn't where the real action is.

Don't start being a bitch now, JWonderful. You gave me your word.

I've given you a whole lot more than that.

And without a definitive answer, or specifics about the date and time for the interview with D&C in Laguna Beach that JW promised, Phoebe is no longer interested in spending a night on the beach with Jackson. She no longer wants to explore neighborhoods, check out rental properties. Instead she drives another mile or so along this gray freeway, exits, and continues along surface streets in what she thinks is El Segundo until she sees it: the forest-green marquee and all-caps white lettering. The parking lot is packed. She doesn't care that she'll have to carry Jackson across the hot asphalt, through the vapors, to Whole Foods. She starts making the list in her head: South African wine, a bottle of El Perro Verde red, cherimoya. She'll linger in the wide, bountiful aisles, the cool air, the welcoming faces, and mist will cleanse fresh-cut kale, and time itself will stop.

34

It's a hot Wednesday night in September. Phoebe watches footage leading all the local newscasts of wildfires in Topanga Canyon and Riverside. She looks for Serenos on the mostly red "Fire Zone" animation on-screen. They're not in it yet. The story that follows the wildfires is about them: the countless families stranded in the Inland Empire. Reporters fan out across greater Los Angeles and walk nearly deserted streets dotted with abandoned new-construction homes.

Nick is climbing the wall. Jackson is laughing through his pacifier. The dog that Nick finally picked up, which they haven't named, barks wildly at him on the wall. The barking only makes Jackson laugh harder, and his laughter is infectious, so Phoebe's smiling, too.

"I can't laugh and climb. I'll fall."

"Don't fall, Daddy!" the little voice calls out.

"Yeah, don't fall, Nickels."

Phoebe's staring at his calves: They're muscular, tan, and hairless. She's sipping her wine and rubbing Jackson's head and realizing that she envies her husband's calves. "You do have nice legs."

"You know what's funny?" Nick looks down at her, sweat dripping from his nose. "How little respect you have for me."

"Could you still work with a broken leg? Probably not, right?"

"Do you appreciate anything?" He laughs. "Is there anything that satisfies you?"

"Jackson," she says. "And sleeping in. But really just Jackson."

He manages to ascend a bit higher.

"Is there something else? Was that a trick question?" she asks.

"This *is* the first home you've ever owned. Our first home. That means nothing?"

"Not really."

"Whether or not you want to acknowledge it. It matters."

Fall and get it over with, she thinks. Crack a femur, a trip to the ER, titanium screws and a cast and crutches. She'll take care of them, all of it, again. She eyes the hard rubber rocks, the yellow, red, blue, and green to the top, the summit he's never reached.

"Don't go too high," she says, and finishes her wine. "Stay right there in the middle. It's what you're used to."

He's nearly to the ceiling. He slips. Catches himself.

She spoons her cold cherimoya, sucks on the frozen ball of cotton candy–flavored fruit. A few weeks at home would force him to reengage the professional world, follow up with some of the production companies he reached out to before. Maybe some Emerson alumni searches in L.A., some networking. Get online. Get on track.

"Fall, Daddy, fall!" Jackson calls out. Soon both he and Phoebe are laughing and chanting. She finishes her fruit and picks up her son and walks upstairs and runs the bath, chanting in a hushed tone, "Fall, Daddy, fall, Daddy, fall, Daddy."

35

The messages from JW come at midnight. It's been three days. He sends three texts:

Lawrence De Bent

D&C

The one you talk to.

She's sitting upright in the middle of the king-size bed. Nick sleeps downstairs. She responds: *And?*

He has your CV.

And?

He's in Brussels

And?

Shall I spoon-feed it to you?

Like frozen cherimoya

I wish

And?

Set something up with his office.

And?

And I'll see you next time.

Sorry we missed each other. But thank you. How are YOU?

You don't want to know.

I do. Tell me one thing.

My son just got the boot from Dartmouth for cheating. My second wife is suing me for IIED. Don't know what that is? I didn't either. Am told by attorney it stands for intentional infliction of emotional distress. Are you serious? IIED?!

That was more than one.

Savor your days with a toddler. It only gets worse.

Will I get this? D&C in Laguna Beach.

Do you deserve it?

What happens when we see each other?

I already set you up. Not necessary, right? You got what you wanted.

Having nothing to do with that.

What then?

Oh lord, who even knows. I keep dreaming about your Boston office and the cold window against my face. What does that tell you?

I don't know.

Do you want me to spoon-feed it to you?

It's morning and the tank is full and she's on the freeway heading west with no major delays and the flow of traffic is like a flash flood. Her levels of Klonopin, Effexor, and Lexapro are all optimal and the surface streets get her to Wilshire and to the corridor in what feels like record time. She has eighteen new songs downloaded on her iPod and they're on shuffle and each sounds better than the one before it and after two effortless stops inside Wilshire Memorial, her next appointment cancels, so she's got time to kill.

She messages him: *Come see my working-class ass before it's firmly planted in the upper-middle class.*

The Coffee Bean is full, but everyone seems young and healthy and in a good mood, and she's wondering where the hell all these people live. It can't be Serenos. There are four men who all seem to look the same despite different color hair and varying heights and builds, and she can't pinpoint it, but whatever it is must be an illusion: They can't be as beautiful, tan, and pulled together as they appear. She's at the glass door, and the aviator glasses and short skirt and tight blouse and black strappy Jimmy Choos from her Boston days give her the confidence to smile at the one in the group who gets the door for her, and his teeth are bright white and she laughs and asks him, "What the hell?"

He looks puzzled.

"Your teeth," she says.

He's stopped in his tracks, still holding the door. He smells like a six-foot mimosa.

"They're insane," she adds.

"Thanks."

The business card he slips her reads *Interscope* and as she leaves the group of men, she feels their eyes on her, a familiar sensation, and decides then, on a wide, crowded sidewalk, gleaming towers and tall palms and fountains and buses and yellow sports cars and silver Maseratis racing on a nameless street, to text JW even though he didn't respond to the previous two. She Googles Lawrence De Bent. She Googles West Side Rentals and goes to their website and checks listings for rentals in Manhattan, Hermosa, and Laguna Beach. She rereads the last message from JW, the one he sent ten minutes ago. She lightly thumbs the screen. She knows how it was and this isn't that.

Remember I told you I felt like a teenager in the basement of my ex?? Well I didn't finish.

So finish, she writes back.

Wanna fuck you like you're a teenager.

36

It's the first week of October. It's the hottest week since they arrived in June. The heat is unrelenting. For some reason, Kostya and Marina have Halloween decorations on their front lawn already: a family of zombies that appears frighteningly real at night. Nick and Phoebe are exhausted. It's midnight and they've each been up since six. Nick had a nosebleed an hour ago from the dry hot air. Phoebe is premenstrual and cramping. Nick keeps the bedroom door open, as much to listen for strange noises as to keep from suffocating.

"Spell it out, Phoebe. What do we have left?"

That's easy, she thinks. She adjusts the volume on the baby monitor she keeps bedside. What is left is Jackson. What's left with JW? An answer, yes or no: Will he produce for her? His third wife, Japanese, lonely, must spend as much time as Phoebe would wondering who he's texting or calling or Skyping, who's taking the gold elevator up to his hotel suite or boarding a flight with tickets he paid for to meet him in Maui or San Francisco. Between the lines of her text messages with JW is a stark reality. She needs him more than ever. What's left? Closing the sale with JW. What's confusing her is the rush of adrenaline that comes with each text he sends, the resulting agitation and inability to sleep without copious amounts of pink and yellow benzodiazepines.

"I'll answer my own question," Nick says as he leaves the room. "Nothing is left. And there's nothing inside of you. It took me ten years to see through you because I'm an idiot."

Phoebe closes her eyes. She remains upright on the bed, legs crossed. She's nodding. She's waiting him out. She bites her upper lip. Another moment or two and the right words will ignite her. They don't come, though. Nick leaves the room, closes the door quietly behind him.

37

The rumors are all true, it turns out. Stories about a home invasion two blocks over by men with shaved heads from Tustin, tying up the Hamid family in the bonus room and stripping the house of everything — electronics, their two cars, all the granite and stainless steel appliances. They took the wife to the nearest ATM and made her withdraw the maximum. Brought her back to the house, lit it on fire, and left.

Saturday morning, in the predawn darkness, Nick watched from their bedroom window as a black Nissan Maxima with tinted windows and Nevada plates crept along Carousel Court, stopping at the edge of the young neighbor's yard. The car idled for twenty minutes before Nick walked outside, stood barefoot and shirtless in their driveway, a sweaty callused hand clutching a tire iron. He leaned back against Phoebe's Explorer and lit a cigarette, stared at

Metzger's tent, hoping he was inside it, awake, ready. The car turned around, left.

On Monday, the lead story on KCAL was about a home invasion/double murder ten miles from Serenos in La Habra. The image on the screen that made Nick get up off the sectional and leave the house without explanation to walk next door to the young neighbor's house: a black Nissan Maxima with tinted windows, Nevada plates. Next door, the house was dark inside. There was no car in the driveway. Nick pounded on the front door. Nothing. He walked around the side of the house and found the empty pool filled with charred remains: furniture, papers, books, dishware, clothes. A body could be buried in there and no one would ever know.

Nick is alone in the cool kitchen. It's four A.M. The house hums, electrical currents, the wind pressing against window frames, the central air flowing, keeping up with the demand for lower and lower temperatures. Nick sits on a leather barstool at the granite island, concentrates on the rhythm of his heart. Sticky beat, the physician called it when Nick went to the ER after working thirty-two hours straight last week, when he couldn't drive home, choking on his own breath, throat tightening. The Asian woman told him, "Sticky beat," and added, "You're young. Relax. Enjoy your life." The irregular heartbeat was simply stress, lack of sleep, nothing to worry about. Nick is bringing a third bottle of Dos Equis to his lips when his iPhone vibrates on the granite island. The message is from a number he doesn't recognize, a 919 area code: *scurrd yet?*

38

Phoebe's alone in the house. Blackjack sleeps at the foot of Jackson's crib. The man who found him called him Blackjack because he was lucky to be alive. So they stick with that.

She finishes a bottle of Beringer white zinfandel that Nick brought home, she thinks, as some kind of fuck-you. "We can't afford what you drink," he said when she placed two bottles in their cart the last time they shopped together.

She opens another bottle. Nick is working tonight, then who knows? She wonders if he's met someone else, that girl Mallory. Or maybe someone from the office he should be working in. Maybe they met when he came out for interviews and stayed in touch. Maybe he's been fucking her since they arrived. Maybe she's the reason he's insisting they stay out here. Maybe Phoebe's the victim in all of this. Maybe Phoebe should finally give herself a break. She is, after all, doing something about it.

• •

Nine months ago, it was Phoebe's thirty-second birthday. They were drinking alone. Jackson went down easily, early. A bottle of Stags' Leap with a pink bow on it was next to Nick's laptop on the glass coffee table between them.

She sat on the couch, Nick on the floor. She was still in her work clothes, Nick in torn black jeans and a gray Emerson T-shirt. The one-bedroom was quiet, drafty, and clean. The two coats of banana crème were still drying, the air thick with the scent of fresh paint. She asked why, and he said, "Happy birthday." Then he added, "Because it needed it."

Sheets were balled up in a corner of the main room, brushes, pans, and rollers. "You did it?" Phoebe said, and laughed.

"Of course not."

Nick waited until that day, her thirty-second birthday, to lay it out.

"Why now?"

"It was overdue."

She scanned the apartment. "Looks good."

It was Wednesday. Nick's new production-manager position with the Encino firm was confirmed the previous Friday. He'd kept it to himself. He could start as soon as they got out there. He asked for four weeks. He would have asked for longer because he knew this about the offer and the firm and the work, the expectations, uprooting his fragile family, the night sweats that left him drenched, shivering, thirsty, sitting up alone on the living room sofa, drenched underwear and a blanket over his shoulders, the gray light of dawn and the cold realization: He did not want it. Any of it. The job and the associated pressure to justify their faith in him. This was all for her. He was fine exactly where he was. Phoebe was the one who'd gone off the rails. Phoebe needed help. And if she'd taken fewer coping pills and slept a little more, she'd have seen the idling UPS truck in the right lane at dusk.

So Nick opened his laptop, double-clicked the link to a website, turned the screen to Phoebe.

Phoebe studied it. "What am I looking at?"

"We're Nobody Productions. That's their website."

"Great name. So what?"

"They do commercials, some short films."

She was nodding. "They're in Boston?"

"Nope."

Nick opened his Yahoo! account, double-clicked the email from We're Nobody Productions in Encino, California, one of three production companies offering him a position out of the forty-two he'd inquired with. He'd flown out there once, lied to Phoebe, said it was for his job recruiting a client. The interview had gone well enough, apparently.

She read the offer letter, the terms, which were generous. She reread it. She stared at Nick. Her lower lip did that thing it did when she was happy, disappeared inside her mouth.

Double-clicking websites and watching Phoebe absorb the news and seeing her expression soften, the distance in her eyes, made Nick forget for a moment how little he cared about this job, taking on new responsibilities, proving himself all over again, not to himself or some new firm but to his wife. For that, he resented her. But not now. She was tall and beautiful, with that jaw and that hair, and the confidence she moved with seemed like a test to Nick: See if you can keep up with me, keep me engaged, amused, in love, and this can work. He realized that as much as he wanted to win her respect, he loathed the part of her that expected him to try again and again. But not in that moment, that Wednesday night of her thirtieth birthday. The next phase of their life together unfolded in front of her on a laptop screen. It overwhelmed her and it was because of him.

Nick was buzzed from the validation that came from the L.A. firm's offer. It didn't matter that the production company was obscure, only four years old, and that he didn't want the position.

"We'll need a place to crash," Nick said, feeling playful, reacting to Phoebe's reaction, "and they're all, 'Start whenever' and saying they can help find us a place. And I'm all, 'I got it.' So there's this." He clicked a link to a real-estate website, turned the screen back to Phoebe. The image was of a pale blue bungalow squeezed in on a narrow concrete strip. The slide show cycled through various images of the property: the master with the hardwood floor, the child's bedroom with the ceiling fan, the living room, the kitchen with the small island, all-new appliances, granite countertops, the rooftop deck with the partial ocean view.

"Furnished. Three months. Near the beach. Collect our thoughts."

"Nick."

"The offer is generous enough. We can

swing it. They'd have me start this summer. The rental is in Hermosa Beach. And we have it. It's done. The money is better than what I make now, so I can cover the rent. Enough with our savings to switch things up. There's a lot more we can do. And I kind of think now is the time to do it. I kind of think when you pushed me out the door when I didn't want to go down there after Katrina, it was a bit of a wake-up call. And now I'm awake. And you're killing yourself out there, and it's just . . . time."

They could have left the next day. They could have packed their clothes and Jackson and just driven west. Or the following week or that weekend.

"Let's go sooner. Let's go now," Phoebe said. "Why wait?"

Nick laughed.

"You shouldn't wait. Just get started."

"We have time."

There was a sudden pause. It was tense and familiar. Nick took her hands. "It's your birthday, baby." It was Nick slowing things down, it was Phoebe pushing.

"Jesus, Nick."

They needed some time, though, to do it right, to maximize the payoff. They needed enough time to find and upgrade and flip the right property, then go all in and, when the time was right, cash out.

"Damn straight," she said. She had both hands on his face and just held it there.

The buzz didn't wear off. They lay awake in bed that night.

"I don't need it, Nick."

"We do," he said.

"I don't need two months off."

"Three."

"We can't afford it. And the house flip. It doesn't add up."

"Since when does that stop anyone? It can and will," he said.

"You think there's something wrong with me."

"Phoebe, you're tired."

"I can't do this. Spend a summer sitting —"

"A few months with your son. Some time to yourselves. Apartment hunting."

"You're not making that much more."

"It works. And with what we should clear from selling the house."

"Okay."

"We'll get a nanny, too. We can swing a couple days a week. You can hang out on the beach. Explore."

"You're treating this like it's a breakdown. I'm not sick."

"Time and rest. Jesus, you nearly died."

"That was months ago. I'm fine."

"And you've been working since. And it's crushing you. Enough."

She sighed. She still swallowed Advil by the handful, she still got migraines. She had three titanium pins in her left ankle that still had to be removed.

"Get excited."

"I am. I will."

"The summer is yours."

"I can do my job anywhere, too. I can talk to people, and it's no different out there. I can plug in and go."

"Not this summer. You're on vacation. Just hang out and be a mom." Nick sighed. And that was it. He delivered the words with genuine confidence in his voice. He felt a sense of calm he'd felt only once as an adult: in the delivery room with Phoebe, holding her hand, at her ear. Just like then, it felt as though everything had been thought of, nothing left to chance, and it was for her and them and he could read her, knew that when the faint lines on her forehead vanished and her shoulders dropped, the tension released, she'd never felt safer.

She seemed to process all of it, or she tried: three months in a furnished rental on the beach to spend with her son, teaching him to swim, shopping, apartment searching, weekend trips up and down the coast.

"We need another car."

"We'll get one."

"It's expensive. Insurance and registration."

"We'll get a hybrid. Save on gas."

"Three months?"

"Three months."

She exhaled. "I don't know —"

"I know," he said.

"So tell me again," she said as she slid her leg over him and sat up, straddled him.

"We do it. We go."

"Your stuff, Nick. It's so good. You deserve this."

"Don't."

"It is. Why do you think they hired you? This is your time."

"I love us. Like this. I love us," he said.

It had been a long time. He tried to remember the last time they were this optimistic about anything other than Jackson, and he couldn't. Nick had watched her Klonopin disappear and reappear and disappear again. He read the texts she didn't bother to delete from the physician clients who wanted her to get them off in exchange for more 'scripts. He found the JPEGs she sent: Phoebe in the dressing room at Bebe or Nordstrom, snapping images of herself, an arm across her bare breasts, topless with only her hair covering her, yellow lace boy shorts and French-manicured fingernails slipping under the waistband. Each image a piece of her sold off.

"Best case?" she said now.

Nick flipped her over and she let out a burst of laughter and he came on her stomach and chest and she cursed and laughed some more as he collapsed next to her.

"Best case is we make a killing," he said, and he was out of breath and she was laughing quietly and said, "California and you all over my chest. Best birthday ever."

It took Phoebe two hours online to learn what the comps sold for on Carousel Court, the other new-construction homes with similar square footage and pools but without the degree of upgrades they had in mind. What Nick couldn't know is that she would finance the move, the house, the expenditure on upgrades, ensure profitability, and invest in them with JW's money.

39

The early-morning mist is warm and thick and Phoebe is shrouded in it. She stands in the driveway reading a message from JW: *You last night: incredible. Almost like the real thing. Could taste you.*

And then: *Tell me this: did he get you the personal massager or did you pick it out yourself? Can I get you one?*

Then: *As I said, was only in town for a night but next time in person. Not that Skyping isn't amazing. Am checking out. Want the room?*

Yes.

According to the Explorer, it's 103 degrees, and Phoebe believes it. The sand burned her feet, and the moment she and Jackson crossed the Strand and left the crashing surf and breeze, the temperature spiked. She's an hour from Serenos, longer if the traffic doesn't clear, after a day spent at the beach, her second trip with Jackson in two weeks.

Nick is working. Nick is ignoring her invitations. It's five and Jackson is hungry and tired, played through his nap. She carried him into the waves. They watched the swimmers and surfers and lifeguards training, diving into the surf. They built a sandcastle and Jackson laughed when the waves washed it away. He was breathing the cool ocean air, the spray in his face. She could feel his mood lift with every wave that crashed. He chased the seagulls. She snapped pictures on her iPhone. She rinsed the sand from his little legs and feet under the shower as they left.

She won't be home until dark. She hates getting home after dark. Her iPhone vibrates, a message from Marina: *Desp Housewives 9 pm, bobcat*

Phoebe is now filling friendly 'scripts for Marina, who doesn't believe in doctors but needs something, anything, because she can't slow her brain down, she says. They have a loose Sunday routine — watch their show, smoke a joint, and soak in the outdoor spa — and Phoebe is surprised that it's something she actually looks forward to.

Stuck on some blocked freeway baking in heat.

Kostya 2. Had boyz at batting cagez now getting dinner somewhere so am here alone with princess. Come over!

Trying.

Car sitting outside the empty house. Just sitting there.

Are you trying to scare me??

Any crazy bitch comes near the house then it's over for her

The next message from Marina arrives two full minutes later and is a JPEG file. The image is the rear end of a black Nissan Maxima with Nevada plates, taillights glowing.

Leave it alone. Tent Man's there. Or just call the police.

Marina doesn't respond but sends another JPEG.

See that? That's my pink .38 pointed at these golovorez

Go inside. Lock the doors. Call 911 and I'll see you at 9 ;) And don't shoot anyone.

Going outside tell them bitches where to go ;)

Can't cope with two shootings on the block in a month.

She's home. Two helicopters pass low overhead. Jackson is asleep. Carousel Court is deserted. It's just after nine. Blue garbage bins are tipped over from the wind or Kostya's dogs or the coyotes, trash strewn across the asphalt. The orange tent ripples and sags. Two of Kostya's children run from a neighbor's backyard, shrieks of laughter, until they disappear around the other side of the house. And it's the slate-gray sky and the silhouettes of swaying palms and the loose string of white lights and the collapsing tent that make it plausible that the running, screaming children weren't playing.

But there is no sign of the black Maxima from Marina's pictures. Marina's not aiming her pink semiautomatic pistol at strangers from a bedroom window. The neighbor is, however, setting more of his possessions on fire. Phoebe smells the smoke from his backyard as she carries Jackson inside the house and upstairs, where she changes his diaper, kisses his forehead, and lays him down in the crib. Nick already refilled and turned on the frog-shaped humidifier and three night-lights. Jackson makes a tiny sound and rolls to his side under his pale yellow blanket. She draws the blinds and leaves his door open. Nick is sleeping in the master bedroom, facedown, jeans and no shirt, boots unlaced but still on.

She shakes him once. He makes a noise, but his eyes stay closed.

"I'm leaving. Nick, can you hear me? I'm going." He makes another sound. "Listen for Jackson." She places the baby monitor next to his face, turns up the volume.

She leaves the room. From the kitchen she takes a bottle of Fiji water and an apple. In her white Coach bag: her wallet, a Massachusetts driver's license, her GSK photo ID, four bottles of pills, and a new purple hairbrush.

She sets the ADT and locks the front door. She enters the address in her GPS and turns right as she leaves Carousel Court, turns onto the wider street, passes the banks and nail salons, T-Mobile and Jamba Juice, and the crisscrossed palms in front of In-N-Out Burger. The looming sign is like giant blue LEGOs: the Shoppes at Serenos, Forever 21, PacSun, and P. F. Chang's. She pulls in, parks. She wants stretch pants and a top or two, a short dress. All the stores are dark. It's ten o'clock on Sunday night. Everything is closed. She's tired and sunburned. She'll shop tomorrow. She'll go to Melrose Avenue and Mint Collection and that other little shop on the corner. She'll play juvenile games. She'll take pictures of herself and show him what he's missing. She'll treat him like the perverted client that he is: a mark. He may deserve more in exchange for what he gave her, but it's the fact that all that's required to course-correct her life, maybe salvage her marriage, is superficial titillation for him after all this time, and that enrages her.

She's driving, following green signs that lead west. She accelerates at the yellow light, pulls the wheel to the right onto the San Bernardino, and is alert with the windows down and her long dark hair tangled, shot through the currents of traffic like a hollow-point bullet.

40

The silence of the dark room only exacerbates the ringing in her ears. Sunlight seeps through the edges of floor-to-ceiling windows opposite the king-size platform bed. This morning the split in her skull is the hangover from too much wine and Klonopin. She checks the time on her iPhone. It's 1:13 P.M. She tries to lift her head but can't hold it up for more than a moment, drops it back to the mattress, out of breath. She closes her eyes to recall last night: She followed a narrow, ascending road after an hour on the freeway; at the ivy-covered gate she pressed the silver button on the call box and watched it slide open; the tan skin of the slight blond man who greeted her seemed to glow; his nonchalance when she said no, she had no luggage, and then he showed her to her bungalow; the glistening hillside lights; the messages from Nick asking where she was.

What did she say to Nick? There was a call. They spoke and she recalls her tone (harsh and dismissive) but not the words. She drank wine and ate JW's leftover bruschetta and swallowed three Klonopin because she had to sleep or she would die.

Now she sits on the edge of the low firm bed, and her throat burns when she swallows. All the contents of her Coach bag are spilled across the bed and floor, as though someone shook it out, searching for something. She has no recollection of doing it. The walls are purple. She slides the door open and steps out into the bright yellow sunlight of a hot afternoon. The wind moving through the canyon smells of smoke. The cicadas crying out. Even here, she thinks.

The messages from Nick are from last night and this morning and five minutes ago:

You coming home?

Where ARE you?

??? I have to WORK, Phoebe.

Are you passed out somewhere? You realize how dangerously high your threshold is now for that shit? You will sleep and never wake. Lame. Totally, completely pathetic way to go out. But what do you care? You won't be around to hear it.

Slip away, Phoebe. Slip away. What an example for your child.

She responds:

Take him to Mai's. He can spend the night. Or Kostya's.

You're still with us?

Phoebe lies back on the bed, holds the iPhone over her, taps out a response:

Sorry.

Not cool. Totally uncool.

Her phone rings. It's Nick. "Just say it. Say it. Tell me."

"There's nothing to say. I can't explain anything away. It's just not what you think."

"I'm not sure you should come home. I'm not sure it's safe."

"What is that supposed to mean?"

"Just being responsible. Being realistic."

There's a long pause. She's fingering the lip of a wineglass, nearly empty. Outside, tucked in the shade from a eucalyptus, she notices the koi pond.

"I'm not sure someone won't get hurt," he adds, his voice distant.

"You and me both."

"Keep thinking it's some twisted dream."

"It's not."

"Like he's bending you over a hotel balcony."

"Nick."

He clicks off.

Instead of leaving, Phoebe does the math: Jackson's fine until six, which is pickup time from Mai's house. It's two. The water is ready. She fills the sunken tub with lavender bath salts and slides in, closes her eyes, and slips underwater.

41

The message is from JW: *So tell me? Was I right?*

Phoebe responds: *I feel badass in here. You were right. To die for ;)*

She stands on the veranda, squints in the dry wind. It's almost four. She sips cool white tea. Her mind is finally still. She feels the organic jojoba, sunflower, and apricot kernel oil lotion seep into her skin. Her sinuses are clear. She considers calling for the Pilates instructor, who, according to the brushed nickel–covered hotel guest-services guide will conduct a seventy-minute session in the suite, but it will likely take at least an hour to get back, to pick up Jackson. It's time for her to go home.

Pick a handful of weekends or weeknights and it'll be there for you.

The two-foot cast-iron statue rests on the granite coffee table and depicts a man balancing acrobatically on one hand atop a smooth white stone. She rereads the message twice, slower the second time. What is he telling her? She runs her fingers along the iron statue. It's cold and smooth. She wants it. She considers taking it with her. It won't fit in her Coach bag. She'll get it next time.

No obligations.

Not sure

Minimal expectations ;)

Liar

Maybe I'll visit. Make sure they're taking care of you.

What else do I have to do?

Stay badass when I'm there

It's five o'clock. Shadows stretch across the hillside. She's wearing her white sunglasses, charcoal yoga pants, and peach top from yesterday.

Another text arrives: *Who's at the door?*

She doesn't respond. She's late. It'll take hours now, rush hour, to get home. Stress she doesn't need.

Is it the Pilates instructor? The concierge? Your husband?

The knocking is rhythmic and playful.

She knows before she opens the door.

He looks younger than before and thinner. Clearly, JW is avoiding any of the emotional distress he's accused of inflicting. His eyebrows are dark and his pressed blue-pinstriped Versace shirt is untucked. He's tan and smells like the beach, brown Ray-Bans perched on his head. She wonders if he just got a facial. She wants to push past him because she's late, her husband is working, her son is waiting miles and hours from here. But what is she going back to? Nothing is different, just slightly worse than the day before. Nick and his sweaty cash.

She wants it to be yesterday. JW does this to her. Every time. And it's not that he's unapologetic or unaware, and he doesn't press or make her feel bad when she doesn't or can't drop everything at a moment's notice. He is nothing if not understanding. The truth she avoids: She can never say no to him and make it stick. It might be considered a character flaw, a fault line at her very core, she thinks. A connection burned through or never made somewhere in her makeup, no clarity about what matters, what must come first: her family.

But what about her? She existed before Jackson, before Nick, and exists now, the slightest gap between her front teeth, the same chestnut hair. When her mother nearly died from what should have been a lethal cocktail of martinis and Xanax, went into respiratory failure, and was hospitalized for three weeks, Phoebe went to Florida to help salvage her mother's last good years. You can't live someone else's life for them, Nick told her when Phoebe was determined to stay down there until her mother was fixed. She's making her own choices.

Phoebe heard it as concession, typical Nick. You're not a fighter, are you? she accused. Your acceptance of failure is not much of a lesson for your child.

And you don't know when to quit. That could be a fatal flaw.

JW slides his sunglasses into his shirt pocket, casually surveys the suite, looks for something, maybe confirmation that she's alone, that Nick didn't come along for the ride.

"This is fantastic. It's really special," she says.

He crosses the room, pulls back a sheer curtain, then the sliding glass door, stares out at the dry canyon, dark from the afternoon shadows. "Isn't it," he says, his back still to her.

"Quite the gesture, really," she says. "A nice break." She smiles.

He turns to her. "Was he here?"

"Who?"

"Your husband."

"Do you care?"

"Makes no difference to me," he says, and wraps his soft hands around her forearms. "You're stick-thin."

She lets out a sigh. "I don't want to leave." She shakes her head as if trying to clear her mind. Her arms are free of his grip, which was loose. "I don't even know what time it is. It's Monday, right?"

"Tell me."

"What?"

"Why don't you just tell me once and for all to fuck off?" he says.

"I should be asking you that."

"So we deserve each other." He laughs.

He's closer to her than he should be. His warmth fills their space. She breathes him in, the familiar citrus that lingers on her clothes, remembers how she'd hold them to her face as she stuffed them in the washing machine when she was twenty-six, while Nick slept.

She's cycling through messages from Nick (*call . . . this is inexcusable . . . who the hell do you think you are?*) on her iPhone, not meeting JW's eyes.

"Why don't I feel guilty?" she asks, tosses her phone to the bed. "Something is really wrong with me, right?"

"Fundamentally."

She punches him hard with a closed fist on the side of his head. He staggers back and curses. She stares at him, poised to do it again, exhilarated.

He's still laughing, rubbing his head, when she swings, this time missing because he's ready and agile enough at forty-nine, so she scratches his neck with her other hand, slicing the soft skin. He grabs both of her wrists. He's strong, too, and she recalls the last time they were together, he was in the midst of a popular workout regimen that involved flipping over giant tires and dragging sandbags across dirty gym floors.

"Easy. Easy," he says.

She drops her head. Everything spins. She closes her eyes, which only makes it worse. It's the same as the dizzy spells that send her into strip-mall parking lots to climb into the backseat of the Explorer with the engine on and air-conditioning blasting as she pages maniacally through images on her iPhone of the last three years of her life: Nick clutching a wooden spoon loaded with Nutella, poised to spread it over her swollen belly; Jackson plugged full of all sorts of wires and cords, clutching Nick's index finger in NICU; the nurses and Phoebe and Jackson in his little knit hat; Jackson floating on a blue blanket surrounded by primary-colored plastic fish; Nick and Phoebe at the Boston premiere of some movie he got passes to from work; the three of them on the cool, wet sand with glistening water behind them their first week out here; and she'll realize as she closes her eyes tightly, trying to rest, sleep if only for a few minutes until the dizziness fades, that there isn't an image taken of their lives together, on her iPhone at least, when JW wasn't in the picture.

"I miss you," he says. "Miss you, miss you, miss you." His voice fades as he buries his face in her hair.

"Why?"

"Jesus. You feel good."

"I don't do anything right."

He's pushing his soft hands under her top, wrapping them around her rib cage. He could squeeze and snap her in two.

"I can't keep doing this," she says.

He's kissing her neck. Then her chest and her breasts, then he's biting and lifting her off the floor until she's looking down at him and she drops her head and he tosses her to the bed.

He stands over her.

"I don't want this," she says.

"Of course you don't."

"We're not doing this again."

“Doing what?”

“All of it,” she says.

“No one’s holding a gun to your head.”

“Any of it.” She’s leaning back on her elbows, her hair a mess, her legs crossed, not meeting his eyes.

“You don’t want to be here?” he asks, unbuttoning his shirt. “You don’t want me here?”

“I’m going to fuck you for a job,” she snaps, and remains on the bed.

“That’s what this is?” he asks. He’s on his knees, sliding his hand between her crossed legs, urging them apart. The sliding glass door is open and the warmth from outside washes over them. She shivers in it, and when she closes her eyes, an image flashes across her mind: a fine mist falling softly on paper-thin mizuna leaves and kale in a nearby Whole Foods, everything organic and cleansed. Then: frozen cherimoya melting on her tongue.

When she opens her eyes, she sees the paint from the purple walls melt, and what she feels is his tongue, and she sees a new house in Laguna Beach close enough to hear the waves crashing and business cards with her name in raised lettering and a small office in a glass tower overlooking palm trees and the glistening water in the distance, and the last image she sees before closing her eyes once more is the statue, the man balancing on one hand, and she thinks of Nick climbing the wall.

Later, their bodies are intertwined on top of cool white sheets. From behind her, unseen, he brings something to her mouth. "Breathe in when I tell you."

"What is it?"

"Trust me."

The hissing sound is isobutyl nitrite. She inhales the compressed air, which is pungent.

"Hold it in." He slides his free arm around her hips, across her abdomen, and in one motion he's lifting her, positioning himself behind her. "Exhale until there's nothing left."

"Goddamn," she says, and the room goes white and she feels him again and all tension leaves her body as if Klonopin were a mist and she's drinking it.

42

Nick wanders outside and the stench of burning plastic greets him. Their neighbor has today's fire going. Nick walks to the fence, can't see through the cracks in it, so pulls himself up, looks over. The young neighbor is shirtless and pissing into a decent-sized fire. A plastic lawn chair melts in the orange flames. Of course Phoebe stays away for days. Who wouldn't? He snaps a picture of the young man and the fire, texts it to her: *Wish you were here!!*

Back inside he composes a to-do list on his iPhone: seven addresses for rent collection from properties in Lake Elsinore, Corona, and Chula Vista; the total amount of cash he'll collect from the seven houses ($9,475); block watch after that with Metzger and Kostya; Jackson's pediatrician appointment next week (*MEDS for his breathing*).

He drank too much to be driving. But

rents are due or overdue for most of the tenants and he can't sleep and he's on his own, Jackson at Mai's until tomorrow morning, so he'll collect what he can tonight. All the windows are rolled down and Nick's black T-shirt is tight, his jeans ripped above the knee from a recent job, a wrought-iron fence that wouldn't budge. He smokes a clove cigarette and turns up some mix on the hip-hop station. The full moon is yellow and rotting.

He sends Phoebe a text. *What if I knew where you were? What if I came by to say hello?*

His handheld vibrates. It's been three days. He's texted and called so many times. He's been enraged, worried, terrified. He's threatened, promised, and begged. He's cried. He's considered the deep end of the pool, plastic bags and ropes cinched around his neck. He held Jackson too tight. He took him to the zoo. They watched the elephants and lions. A dead white rabbit tossed to the cheetah. Some turned away. Nick and Jackson watched the clean white fur turn crimson and then disappear. No more rabbit.

You don't know where I am.

The fuck I don't.

Tell me

I don't have to tell you shit.

Go to bed. It's all good. Be home tomorrow.

Don't come home. Someone might mistake u for an intruder home-invading gangster and shoot u on sight.

Nick don't drink and text.

Not a game babe. I will pull the fucking trigger.

43

"Imagine a week together. A month," JW says, not looking up from his iPhone, tapping out a message.

Phoebe's dressed, her hair damp from a long shower. She sits on the edge of a low purple chair. She crosses her legs.

"Imagine seeing each other whenever we want."

"I do."

"We can't do that with you out here."

"We just did."

"You don't belong out here. You'll get restless. Bored."

"Maybe." She starts checking her own iPhone.

"All the driving."

Messages from Nick asking rhetorical questions about her likeness to her own mother and if she shouldn't just make her escape permanent and an offer to send her things wherever she lands. *Paid for with my sweaty cash,* he wrote.

"Didn't you almost kill your kid from driving too much?"

"What are you even doing out here?" she asks, slips her phone into her purse.

"Firing people," he says without looking up, reads a message, mutters something to himself, then slides the phone into the pocket of his linen pants.

"Suits you."

"So you really want this thing," he says. "D&C." He's staring at her, studying, his shades on his head.

"Yes."

"It's a career."

"Yes."

"Why didn't you take my advice?"

"Which was what? You talked a lot," she says.

"And you didn't listen. Business school. Something bigger instead of always playing it so goddamn safe."

"How safe am I playing it?"

"You drive ten hours a day. Come on, bathrobes and Caribbean cruises?" he says.

"And now I'm doing something about it."

He laughs. "So work me, then. Like you worked me before. And no, I'm not expecting you to pay me back anytime soon."

"Well, that was the deal. I agreed I would

and I will. End of discussion."

He shakes his head, changes the subject. "I wonder if you can handle it. This isn't just sitting at a desk with Hawaiian-shirt days and Secret Santa. You meet and exceed expectations or you're gone. Back behind the wheel. And that's not a transition I'd wish on anyone. And unlike in Boston or New York, out here I won't have your back."

Her head throbs. "What's my trajectory? Tell me specifically. You know me. Where do you see me?"

"Consulting, maybe. Financial services or analysis. A promotion track," he says with nonchalance. "That's what D&C will be. But it's cutthroat. No margin for error."

"Just like that."

"I think so. Yes."

"So D&C, then."

"Back east is easier."

"This is what I want."

She slides her hand into the front pocket of his loose pants and removes his iPhone. She opens the image files and pages through pictures of JW and his family: riding horses, skiing, on a cold-looking beach, making Belgian waffles with fresh strawberries and powdered sugar in a massive kitchen with Viking stoves and a black granite island.

"What do you think they'll offer?" she

asks. “Where can I expect to be in three years, five years?” She stares blankly at the knit royal-blue monogram on his shirt pocket. He moves closer, presses against her. He kisses her on the mouth. His lips are dry. Her eyes stay open and she doesn’t kiss him back.

“You feel what you do to me?”

The door is closed now. When did he close it? Was she asleep, passed out, at some point? She can’t be sure either way, is dizzy thinking about it. And his tight grip on her wrists. White heat radiates from the top of her spine, splitting her scalp and spilling out from her pores. She closes her eyes tightly. Let go, she thinks, or maybe she’s saying it. She’s going to be sick.

“I think,” she says, “I actually need you to leave.”

He laughs. She pulls her wrists from his grip.

“I need to rest. I can’t with you here.”

He does this thing to her earlobe with his index finger and thumb, gently massages, then pinches it. “That’s why I love you,” he says. “Unafraid to bite the hand.”

Hardly, she thinks.

Later, having slept dreamlessly for hours, Phoebe is on the freeway. She doesn’t see the blue Boxster flashing its headlights at her in the rearview, trying to get her out of the way because she's going too slow, reading another text from JW: *Your optimism is heartening.*

She changes lanes, then again. She accelerates toward a looming exit sign. She doesn't read it but follows it, pulls off the freeway and onto surface streets, turns in to a strip mall parking lot, and stops.

Is it unfounded?

A long pause between text messages. Phoebe taps one out, quickly, sloppily: *D&C. That's it and you know it.*

De Bent.

I know. I did. Haven't heard.

Will take care of it.

Tell me when you call him.

You're welcome ;)

This isn't a game.

Laguna's pretty far.

She taps out a response: *We'll move.*

You're not messing around.

No. I'm not.

Was SO good to see you. Forgot how insane you make me.

I feel like shit.

You shouldn't.

Her cell rings. It's him. She doesn't pick up.

You're too hard on yourself.

This will kill me.

At dusk the next day, while Nick gives Jackson a bath, Phoebe sits alone by the pool, sips Maker's Mark. She and Nick haven't spoken except for four words since he got home from work. He saw her, shook his head, said, "I'm going to sleep," and walked upstairs, closed and locked the bedroom door. She returned that day, midafternoon, to a hushed, empty house. It was cool and smelled clean. And there was order where there had been chaos: clothes folded and put away, the laptop desk cleared of mail and empty cups. It made her tired for some reason. Her legs make intersecting circles in the glowing water, the cicadas crying out at the end of a hot, clear Monday in October, four months since Nick pulled the steering wheel of the dirty white Subaru sharply to the left, almost missing the turn in to a deserted sunbaked Carousel Court. A new phase is taking shape, coming into focus: the life they came out here for, by other means.

So I may need you closer than Laguna Beach.

She waits. He wants her to ask. She won't.

He sends three texts in quick succession:

Aren't you going to ask?
Closer to what?
Me

44

Phoebe complied with Nick's request: Don't be home when I get there.

He doesn't know where she is today, if she'll stay away for three more days, but he's leaving in an hour, after Jackson is down for his nap and Mai arrives. Nick texts: *Can't stand to be around you. Violently sick inside to share the same space. Will text when Mai arrives and be here an hour after that. She works harder than you with OUR son and deserves a break.*

There's more to it, Nick.

It's him. There's not more to it. There never will be more to it.

You have no money Nick. Where are you even going?

You don't know shit. You don't have a clue.

45

When she arrives home from work, it's late, almost nine. Since her three days at Hotel Bamboo, they haven't talked. Tonight, her second night back, she finds Nick asleep on the couch with his boots on. He smells like stale cigarette smoke even though he doesn't smoke. It must be the guys he works with. She imagines they carried trash from a house today, then went somewhere and drank and smoked. On the dining room table is an expensive-looking juicer.

Her first night home from her hotel stay: wordless. Nick was feeding Jackson, took him from his booster seat and carried his tray of chicken tenders and mashed peas and juice past her, and she tried to take Jackson but Nick angled him away, burst past her, took Jackson upstairs to finish his dinner and play in his room, locked the door behind him. He does that again now. He hasn't kept Jackson downstairs the past two days when she's around. That's how it is now. Since she spent the nights away and since he doesn't believe her when she tells him she was alone.

46

Each day since Phoebe's three-day disappearance, Nick spends thirteen hours out of the house, working houses, performing initial assessments for the company, playing landlord for himself. When he finally returns, he finds Phoebe sitting by the pool, smoking a cigarette, a glass of wine sitting next to her on one side, Jackson in a diaper and nothing else on the other. She makes small circles in the water with her feet. Everything — the thick grass, the wet bar, the wilting palms and the brown fence surrounding the property, his wife and son — is bathed in sepia light. But Jackson sits perilously close to the edge, drinking from a sippy cup. It's jarring. Nick approaches his son, trying not to startle him, not wanting him to fall into the pool. He'll sink like a stone. In one athletic motion, Nick squats and scoops him up and pulls him to his chest. He turns and walks back inside the house, closes the door behind him. He waits there for a moment, watching her. She doesn't turn around, doesn't even seem to notice that her son is no longer there, that Nick took him away.

Nick sends her a text: *Where is Jackson?*

She reads it. She turns her head, left then right. Alarmed at his absence, she stands. Nick flicks the patio light off, the kitchen light on. Their eyes meet. He whispers to Jackson, who does what his daddy tells him to.

Jackson waves and they leave.

• •

The Monday before they were scheduled to leave Boston, they went to brunch. College Hunks Hauling Junk came and left a week before, took what wouldn't fit in the Forester. Nick and Phoebe slept on the air mattress for six nights, Jackson between them. Phoebe stopped working on Friday. That Monday morning she didn't take Jackson to day care, and this pissed Nick off. He expected, needed, it to be just the two of them, no distractions. It was overcast and humid; Nick's T-shirt stuck to his back. At the restaurant they sat outside with Jackson in a wooden high chair, with crayons and a paper place mat. They should have sat inside, cooler and less crowded. Jackson scribbled madly. Nick looked past his son, past Phoebe, at traffic that didn't move. The air was filled with exhaust and the day felt nothing like late spring, more like the dead of summer.

"There's no job," he said. "They emailed yesterday and called today. They're very sorry, though." Nick watched a stalled bus spew black smoke from the rear. "They're very sorry. I mean, so, so sorry." He drifted off, couldn't meet Phoebe's eyes.

Jackson dropped some crayons. Neither parent moved.

Phoebe wasn't hearing him, not processing. "You're not serious."

"They're very sorry," Nick said again, finally looking at his wife. He'd promised himself after he hung up on them that morning, after he found himself pleading for part-time, or for independent contractor status, or for severance, for recommendations for other work, that he'd project confidence with Phoebe, reassurance.

"Nick," she said. "Come on."

"Unprecedented times. That's what they told me."

Phoebe was scooping up crayons from the floor. "It's kind of funny. I guess." She handed the crayons to Jackson. "But not really. I mean, if you had no job, we would have — What would we have?"

Silence. Nick stared at Phoebe. He did this: He met her eyes and wouldn't look away when he was serious. He'd say nothing and would just stare into her green eyes until she got it. When he asked her to marry him; when he told her that his father had died; when he promised she'd be okay during the cesarean; when he told her she deserved time to be a mother.

"You have an offer."

He nodded.

"You accepted — come on. Enough." She smiled.

"I'll find work. I'm already talking to people." That was a lie, but now he didn't look away.

"You're serious," she said, swallowed. She hummed to herself and said, "Okay, okay," under her breath. She sat back and squeezed her eyes shut tightly. She was processing. She pressed two fingers to her forehead. She seemed in pain. "We have — We both quit our jobs, Nick," she said.

"I know."

"This is —" She stopped. Her lips disappeared inside her mouth. Her face was flush. "We have the house. A mortgage. Payments. We have those now."

Nick stared at her.

"Stop staring at me and say something."

"We're fine."

She exhaled and lost all pretense of holding up, keeping a brave face. She deflated. "I needed time with him, Nick. More than anything. Now there's no time."

"I can fix this," he said lamely. "We'll still come out ahead on the flip. I'll find something. We go. We go."

"I thought you were going to tell me something —" She stopped. She was going to bring it up this morning if he didn't, but for some reason that day she was convinced he was going to say it: They should try to get pregnant again. That there was no better time. That pieces were finally falling into place, a new phase was beginning, their adult life was coming together, and was there a more beautiful way to commemorate that golden time in your life than conceiving a child?

"We go, Phoebe. We just roll with it. It works out."

"I quit my job, Nick. I quit my job."

"I never insisted you quit. Look, we just do it differently for a while. There are other jobs. We're still doing it. You realize," he said, more to convince himself, "how many people wish they had the balls to do what we're doing? How easy it would be to just accept what we have and inch along, another fucking Boston winter? Another year and another and the next. No, we're doing this, and guess what? We're doing it right."

Nick scratched at the paper place mat where it was cold and soggy from his glass. Phoebe stared, dazed, at her son and tried to swallow, but her dry throat was tight and wouldn't let her.

Nick waited.

"We have nothing," she said, halting. "We have to be out of our place, Nick. You don't have a job?" She pushed her chair back and stood and it fell. Phoebe weaved through busboys and hostesses toward the bathroom inside the restaurant. A cloud drifted away from the sun, and its glare in the boy's eyes was blinding. His vulnerability was startling. Without sunscreen, he'd burn. Without a watchful eye and precise cuts, he'd choke on his food. Wasps would sting him, send him into shock.

Nick stood up, opened a large green umbrella over the table, moved Jackson from the glare and into the shade. They sat alone in the stillness. Crayons and ice water. Nick was numb. The two of them alone, just a father and son. Phoebe reappeared. She was back. Face clean and clear, no evidence that she'd been crying. No sign of distress. She was remarkable that way. She could pull her hair back in a ponytail, splash water on her face, adjust her bra or top, and like that, she was poised, sharp and stunning.

"Okay," she said resolutely. "Does he have sunscreen on?"

"Yes."

She unfolded her cloth napkin and placed it on her lap. "Okay." She exhaled. "We go."

Nick tried for her hand. This time she let him. His palm was wet. His grip awkward and uncertain, a hand wrapped around hers when their fingers should have been interlaced.

"We're okay."

"I know." She sipped her ice water.

In the bathroom, the text message Phoebe sent was to JW. The SOS he responded to so many months later.

Come save me in L.A.

• •

In the morning, Nick is awake before seven and walks outside. He turns off the power to the filtration system, shuts off the water-fill valve. It takes him twenty minutes of kicking through brush and dead mice to find the clean-out port. He connects one end of a cracked rubber hose to it, the other to a submersible pump that looks like a dirty bomb. He drops it in the deep end of the pool, and the splash is cool against his legs, the shadows stretching across the backyard.

Slowly, the water drains. It'll take a day at most.

"Why?" Phoebe asks him as he leaves the house with Jackson, on his way to Mai's, then on to three houses to collect cashier's checks.

"Because you're not paying attention."

47

Nick is climbing the wall again. Blackjack is in his crate, in the corner of the living room, watching Nick ascend.

At the front door, Phoebe runs her hand along the black iron bars and wire that give the new security door the feel of something from a medieval castle. "It doesn't mean anything," she calls up to him from the front door. "Do you think this does anything?"

He laughs too loud, mostly because of the exertion, clutching hard rubber, tendons and muscle fibers straining. "You know how many homes I've put people in?" he says, looking up, grasping the next red rubber rock. "How many families are sleeping tonight because of me? You're welcome, by the way. Who's looking out for your ass?"

"I thought you were leaving me," she says with mock disappointment.

"And I thought you were gaming your benefactor. Isn't he staking you?"

"You'll see."

"Not if we leave you," Nick says.

He's on his fourth or fifth ascent on the wall. He watches Phoebe pace, transform, a beautifully vicious caged animal. Disappearing for three days! His mind is this choked freeway of half-thoughts as he nears the top of the climbing wall, his last attempt at the silver and gold rubber rocks that mark the top. He'll do it without them, no witnesses, but he'll know. And he's shirtless and sweating and the seventh Corona didn't put him over the edge and there's too much anger, agitation, coursing through him when what's required is poise, calm, clarity in thinking.

He's racing, but there's no clock. His breath is shallow and he feels vibrations, his pulse. Is the water running? It's one o'clock in the morning and she's taking a goddamn bath. Beads of perspiration drop from the bridge of his nose and chin. "She's gone. One foot out the fucking —" The slip is quick, the moment a flash of white, like black ice. The distance between the ceiling, where he was within arm's reach, and the ground, is twenty-two feet. A single thought, an instinct he picked up from soccer, basketball, all the camps and teams and drills: Don't reach out to break the fall. That's how your wrists snap, compound fractures, bloody shards of bone that require multiple surgeries, pins, rehab. So he does one thing: keeps his arms at his sides and braces. They're turning on each other. His throat tightens and he gags, the convulsion like a seizure, dry-heaves until he's coughing, hacking up bloody mucous. He bit his tongue. It may have come off. He's running his hands across the thick cool carpet feeling for his tongue, which he's not sure is still in his mouth. He looks up. From where he lies, he can see her shadow. She's in the hallway, around the corner, just out of sight. And he's convinced he can hear her saying to herself, "Fall, Daddy, fall."

48

"Go to your mother's," he says to her in the morning. His mouth feels like it's stuffed with cotton, and his tongue burns. He may need stitches. His movement is slowed despite the eight hundred milligrams of Advil he took an hour ago. He can't draw a deep breath.

Phoebe wasn't supposed to be here this morning and wouldn't have been if he hadn't fallen. They agreed to avoid each other until further notice.

She's nude and so thin, and without makeup or her hair done, she manages to look at once like a teenager and an old woman, depending on the angle and shadows. It isn't healthy, Nick thinks.

"Take a week. Take as long as you need. I mean it. Go. Please."

She steps into the shower. Nick walks to the bedroom window, twists the blinds. Metzger's orange tent has collapsed in the winds, coyote blood still smeared, fainter now, on the asphalt.

Nick pisses and spits into the bowl, doesn't flush. Phoebe would usually remind him but doesn't this morning. The water shuts off. She slides the glass door open, steam floods the room. "Go somewhere," he says. "Go suck him off again."

Maybe it's the transformative effect of water and steam on a woman's body, or maybe it's because he swallowed two Vicodin on an empty stomach, but Nick is caught off guard by the raw beauty of his wife: the angular physique, the dark eyes, the cheekbones, and that jaw, and he wonders if they'll ever fuck again. But as the steam clears, he sees how skinny she is, the collarbones as sharp as her hips. "You should eat," he says. "Go somewhere. Get some room service and figure it out."

"There's nothing to figure out."

"Decide if you want to come back and why."

She's bending over, brushing her hair. "Let's drive somewhere this weekend," she says. "Maybe the beach."

He punches the bathroom mirror. An instant spiderweb of split glass. His eyes are closed and he grips the vanity, deep-breathing, riding her out. She's prodding him, sticking him, until he snaps and gets it over with.

"So what?" she says, staring at Nick's red face in the shattered glass. "It means nothing. There are opportunities and he can help me, which helps us. But I'm not going to explain it to you like you're fourteen. You understand. So get over it. Someone needs to man up and save this fucking thing."

He's in the kitchen. Harsh sunlight pours through the windows. It's too hot. His head throbs from the fall. Even with the thermostat lowered to sixty-seven, the house can't get cool enough. Phoebe perches on a stool, thumbs through her phone while she talks.

"I'd have more respect for you if you were afraid. Fear can be noble. Fear shows maturity. Fear would show you're thinking, maybe even about someone else, your son, what's best for him. About us, what's best for your family."

"You need to stop."

"Then again, if you were fearless, you'd show some confidence," she says.

The knife he removes from the sink is for show. He's looking for something to slice.

"Do I scare you?" she says.

He finds an apple.

"There's no fear in you at all. But there's

so little confidence. So what is it?" she asks.

The apples have been sitting on the windowsill since yesterday. They're hard and green, crisp.

"It's not stupidity. You're not an idiot. You have a heart."

"You do realize I'm not participating? This is just you pushing me, and I'm not taking the bait, Phoebe."

He brings the blade down with force. The apple splits. Juice spills onto the knife handle, blade, and counter. He cuts faster, with more force, at first to intimidate, then without forethought, simply reactive.

"Failure, Nick. Some people have special skill sets, talents, gifts. Most don't, though. Maybe that's it. You're a worker. You're a bill-payer. If you apply yourself, and push, and really put your balls on the line, you'll meet expectations. Maybe a pat on the head for effort. Nick will show up, do the job, clock out at five thirty, catch the bus, home by six to surf the net. Watch *SportsCenter.*"

The apple is all wedges now. Juice and pulpy bits spray the granite countertop. He stabs one of the larger pieces, turns to Phoebe, pops the wedge in his mouth, and chews. He turns away, gathers up the apple wedges. Does she want him to drive the knife into her thigh? Her shoulder or chest?

"You won't defend yourself? I could be wrong about you. It's possible you have secret talents or some as-yet-to-be-displayed heroic abilities, and you're just waiting for the last possible moment to save the day."

He slides the wedges into a plastic container and seals it. When he opens the refrigerator door, she pops up off the stool, squeezes in front of him. She won't relent. He looks past her. The coolest spot in the house right now is here, in front of the open refrigerator. It doesn't help. The knife is on the counter.

"But I don't think that's it. Am I wrong about you? Tell me I've got it wrong." She is inches from his face. She has new lines and dark swatches under her eyes.

His hand is open when it narrowly misses her jaw, connects with the refrigerator door instead. The force with which the blow lands rocks the stainless steel appliance; a shelf dislodges, a container of sliced mango, a gallon of fresh-squeezed grapefruit juice, and a bottle of sparking apple cider crash to the tile floor, the fruit and juice spill, the bottle shatters, Phoebe slips, falls awkwardly to the ground, lands on broken glass. She is bleeding from the back of her thigh where the shard stuck her.

They'll kill each other. He realizes this.

He used to see the stories, familiar cable news fillers about middle-class people stabbing each other to death, blunt objects, making up elaborate stories about home invasions or abductions when the body was actually rolled up in an Oriental rug and dumped in a nearby ravine or pond. They're not twenty-four, he thinks. They could have played this game when they were younger, had insane high-volume battles that spilled out into hallways or in bars and not worry about how it looked or long-term consequences because they'd be eating brunch two days later and have no recollection why they'd fought. Not now. Tonight he has no answer to the question: What separates him and Phoebe from cable-news killers?

49

The text comes from JW at two o'clock on the Wednesday before Halloween. Phoebe, between appointments, races through light traffic from El Monte to West Covina. She finishes her second caramel macchiato and sucks on an ice cube. Her eyes burn from dry air and lack of sleep. Last night she made two phone calls to her mother in Florida. The first ended badly, her mother hanging up when Phoebe asked her to turn down the volume on the television and her mother snapped, "It's my goddamn volume." When Phoebe called back, she didn't speak when her mother picked up on the first ring. The television volume was softer. Neither one spoke. Finally, her mother told her she would come to Boston to see her grandson. "We're not in Boston anymore, Mother."

Phoebe changes lanes without signaling, needs to pull over: The exchange requires her full attention. She will not let him go without an answer, something concrete. The parking lot of a Del Taco. A painfully thin woman in cutoff shorts and a dirty white tank top is accosting customers, demanding money or food, spitting at them as they pass.

She reads the message from JW: *Well, well ??*

Someone made quite an impression

And . . .

Stellar

That's only round one

You're fine.

Second round in couple weeks

You're good

The skinny woman, who has the sunken, sallow visage of a meth addict, is going from car to car, pulling on door handles. She's three parking spaces from Phoebe's idling Explorer.

This has to happen. Okay? I know there may be nothing more you can do at this point. Is there?

De Bent's a friend. He knows how high on you I am. It's a good fit for you.

Phoebe bites hard on her lower lip, stares through the smudged windshield at the five lanes of traffic and the hazy sky, and she's shaking, trembling. *This can happen?*

This is happening.

She considers Jackson, what he's doing right now: finished with lunch, in Mai's living room, drawing with those fat scented markers. She'll get him early. She'll skip the drop-in in West Covina and the sit-down with the general practice in Hacienda Heights at four.

The pounding startles her. The woman is smacking the driver's-side window with an open hand, screaming "Rich bitch" over and over. Stringy hair and open sores on her face and neck. She calls Phoebe a vampire and a bloodsucking cunt and then plants her open mouth against the window. A dirty mist appears. From her Coach bag, Phoebe removes a sterling-silver pillbox, drops eight yellow Klonopin tablets on a Starbucks napkin and a twenty-dollar bill under it, folds it carefully two times. She opens her window. This startles the woman, who doesn't know what to do, so she just kind of staggers back. Phoebe hands the napkin to the confused woman, who grabs it and walks wildly away.

How can I ever ever ever repay you ;)

JW's response: *rolling eyes*

I know what I said. Let me.

Congratulations.

Think of something.

Not necessary.

She presses: *Please. I can handle my shit. I'll be in touch.*

50

Nick is drunk. He's been drinking since noon. He does this lately. When there's no work, when all the jobs are solo or with Arik, initials or rent collection, he'll have the day to himself, and after he cleans, tends the lawn, secures the house, climbs the wall, he drinks.

Jackson is spending the night at the nanny's because Nick simply didn't have the energy to avoid fighting with Phoebe and knew he'd need to sleep it off the next morning. It's nine thirty and dark and Phoebe is still not home and the cable is out and the Internet is down so Nick starts to thumb through images of Mallory, recalling the girl from that one afternoon, wearing thin white boxer shorts, lightly scratching her ass as she reached across Nick's body for the remote control, in the apartment she shares with Arik, lingering, her breast resting on his arm, the sweet smell of her hair in his face.

Hey is the message he sends to her.

The response he receives isn't from Mallory. It's an email from Phoebe. She's forwarding a message from Serenos Montessori. In the subject line she writes: *Midyear maybe?*

Nick sends her a text: *You're kidding, right?*

We'll be here. So why not?

Are you high?

But it still works. Makes sense.

They won't have slots, Nick writes.

They will. I called.

Whatever. The school cannot know that now — how many slots they'll have.

They usually do. And he's #4 on wait list.

He calls her. His shirt is off, tossed on the floor, and his jeans are unzipped. Through the bedroom window, he watches Metzger on a tall ladder, installing a new floodlight.

"What is this?" he says to Phoebe. "Some game?"

"You're so paranoid."

"Schools? Plans to be here? Doesn't sound like Phoebe. You should be planning your escape."

"I'm tired of the negative vibes. I'm exhausted from being exhausted all the time." She laughs. She is high, Nick thinks. This isn't Klonopin or Percocet talking.

Maybe something new.

"Can't afford it," he says.

"Again with the negativity. News flash: Down-and-out Nick is not nearly as sexy as 'I got this' Nick."

Silence.

"Take off your shirt."

"Phoebe."

"Come on. Send me one of your buff bod."

"Are you driving? You sound high."

"Buzzkill."

"I work tonight. So you need to be home to get Jackson in the morning."

"Can we have the rest of the night together?"

"So if you could come home and pick up Jackson tonight so he's not sleeping over there yet again. It's not cool to keep doing that."

"One dick pic," she says. "Then I'll do whatever you tell me."

"Just sleep it off wherever you are. And don't drive."

His phone beeps.

"I adore you, Nickels."

"You're a nightmare," he says, ends the call. He calls Mallory, then drops it before she picks up.

The text that arrives isn't from Mallory,

and he's disappointed. It's from Phoebe: *don't fret, lovebug. igotthis ;)*

51

It's Mischief Night. Nick sits by the pool, legs dangling over the edge of the filthy, empty concrete. He notices one of their floodlights is out. He'll change the bulb tonight. There's a man yelling over the music from next door. Phoebe is actually home and putting Jackson to bed. Nick hasn't spoken more than a couple of sentences to her other than in passing, about Jackson, since she returned from her three nights away. The text that arrives on Nick's phone is from Boss:

Angel Duty. Need you. Time and a half.

Cool

Empty 5 br in Sunland.

Fine.

Couple of break-ins to be perfectly honest. But it's quiet now. We need a presence in the house. Keep lights on, car in the driveway.

Of course.

And you're on today with Arik @ the house

in Chino Hills.

Roger that.

And let me know if Sean shows up today or any other day.

Why?

He's no longer with the company.

Why not?

Call me if he shows. There was an incident.

Later, close to ten, Nick walks the block with Metzger. The men are waiting for Kostya, who can be heard singing loudly to his children, who squeal with laughter. Metzger carries the Mossberg pump-action by his side. The gun is the reason Nick is out here at all. He returned it when Metzger got home from his second Buffalo trip. Nick wants it back.

Metzger hacks something up, spits. He laughs as he says, "Dumped my father's ashes over Niagara Falls. Blew back and hit a buncha Jap tourists, thought it was spray from the falls. Dim sum dipshits."

"I need your gun."

"Of course you do." Metzger's eyes are yellow. He's heavier than he was, hair thinner. He looks ghostly in the dim orange light. "When?" he asks.

"What?"

"When do you need it, and who are you

going to shoot?"

He could take it now, bring it with him to La Puente where he's meeting Sean. "Tomorrow," Nick responds, and he's walking without seeing and the soft asphalt feels like it's giving way and he's sinking in it when he realizes he's no longer sure what he's capable of.

52

Sean is in the kitchen of the La Puente foreclosure. He's shirtless and sunburned, a sweaty beast whipping tuna cans at the hornets that have nested in the kitchen. He's not supposed to be here.

Sean keeps missing the nest but comes closer each time. The nest is a misshapen gray balloon. And it's humming. Arik is shaking his head, but he's smiling, too, because Sean is getting pissed and cursing. Each time he grabs a can of green beans or tuna or soup and whips it at the nest, his baggy jeans fall lower. He's agitated and so are the hornets, brown and yellow monsters, bigger than any Nick has ever seen. The hornets sense that they're under assault and grow louder. They come and go through a living room window that's been shattered. Boss warned Nick about the hornets. And Sean. Arik was supposed to bring Black Flag but forgot.

"Shouldn't you do this on your way out?" Nick asks.

He came for an initial assessment. It was supposed to be just him and Arik. Nick's plan was to show up, assess whether he could take some pictures and list the house after the trash-out. He didn't bother to check the location ahead of time — he's not as focused these days — and the house is a ranch-style in a gang-infested blue-collar barrio. He'll never rent it.

"Tell me this," Sean says, clutching a bottle of ketchup in his meaty right hand, an edge to his voice. "Do you think we're idiots?"

Nick says nothing.

"You think we're doing this for flat-screens and microwaves? Like we don't see what you see?"

Nick watches the hornets. Arik moves behind him, out of his sight line, which makes him even more uneasy, as though something's going to happen and he's not sure what: the hornets or these two men in this hot, empty house. But he's not in a mood to be dictated to. Nick hacks something up, spits on the floor, and wipes his mouth using a towel he grabbed from the granite countertop.

"My turn," Arik says, and reaches for the

ketchup bottle. Sean keeps it from him, stares at Nick for a beat. Nick swallows hard, stares at this insane long-haired man from Orange County who has a kid facing trial for putting another kid into a coma, whose Jet Ski business is failing, who seems to have some strange attachment to Arik. They are standing in a hornet-filled kitchen of a foreclosed house in La Puente, California. The room feels too small. Nick breathes in Sean's body odor and the stale marijuana from Arik, who has moved closer to Nick.

"Thing is, dude, we're doing this," Sean says.

"Doing what?" Nick says casually.

Sean turns to Nick. The hornets are going insane now, poised to attack. Sean looks older, his thin lips tight, deep lines across his forehead and around his eyes like cracked glass. "Stay out of the way. Better yet, find something else."

Nick is silent.

"You don't want this. We got this. You're too late."

Nick has the addresses to the foreclosed properties. It's a growing list. So many properties to rent. Sean and Arik see it and want it for themselves. Sean is here for a reason. This is the message they're sending: It's over, it's their thing now.

"Besides," Sean adds, "who's your muscle? You think no one's in these houses already? You think gangbangers aren't squatting in there? Can't believe you've made it this far. Who's going to clear and hold? You? It's mine now."

"We'll see," Nick says. Hesitant for the first time.

"Dude, look. I don't know you. But I'm giving you a chance to get out. Find something else."

"You're the muscle."

"Yeah, motherfucker, I am," Sean says. "And you need to pay more attention."

Sean pivots, whips the bottle of ketchup at the nest, and hits it. Ketchup splatters against the wall. The gray balloon falls, lands heavy on the floor. Nick curses him. The hornets move too fast. Nick slips on a wet spot, hits his head hard against the floor. He's being stung repeatedly. Sean is on his hands and knees, crawling toward a doorway that leads to the garage. Arik is gone. Nick stumbles into a hallway, toward a sliding glass door, the backyard. The hourglass-shaped pool is nearly drained; dead mice and garbage float on the surface of the thick dark water. He rolls in.

Only when he's leaving the property does

Nick notice the black Maxima parked in the driveway. He checks: Nevada plates.

53

Turning from the main road, Nick drives into the darkness of Carousel Court. Kostya and Marina have added to their Halloween decorations: A Frankenstein statue that resembles Kostya stands pitched to the right, on the verge of falling over; a couple of small black hooded things with glowing red eyes join the zombie corpse propped up against the base of a palm tree. Nick knows Marina will tuck her pink .38 in her waistband if anyone shows up. It's unlikely that anyone will venture out, especially children. Not on Mischief Night. Not these days, with cars casing neighborhoods and home invasions. All the more reason to carry the gun locked and loaded, Nick thinks. Which reminds him: He needs to check the house again, make sure Phoebe hasn't bought a gun of her own.

All the lights in the house are turned off. He sits in the idling Forester, headlights illuminating the garage door, the blue and red chalk doodles from Jackson: a cockeyed smiley face. "Leave some goddamn lights on," he says to himself, addressing Phoebe's negligence.

Inside, it's cold, and when he flicks the switch for the living room and foyer lights, he's surprised to see that it's clean. He hears the barking from upstairs. For an instant it occurs to Nick: She's gone. He calls out as he peels off his drenched T-shirt in the foyer. There's no response. Then he sees Phoebe's white Coach bag on the glass coffee table in the living room. He taps out a text: *Thought you left . . . damn*

Blackjack is barking upstairs. Maybe Phoebe's not home. Despite Nick's desire to keep the dog in the master bedroom, she left Blackjack in the bonus room without his water dish and with the lights off. He's whining and wagging his tail, ears pinned back, thrilled for any human contact. The room smells like urine and feces. He's been in here for hours.

Did u even walk him before you left? Or ask Kostya? You said you had nothing scheduled today. Would be home all day. And yet you're gone. Question: are you really this much of a self-centered cunt?

After feeding Blackjack and letting him

out back, Nick feels the headache from this morning returning. He is so tired. His teeth hurt and his bones feel leaden. Nick turns off the kitchen lights, watches Blackjack sniff the yard in the bright glow from the floodlights. Nick has seven messages on his burner cell, all tenants with questions about cashier's checks or utilities or the people who showed up claiming or reclaiming the house as their own. All of them want answers and help, and he has none and can offer nothing. Now he wonders how many of the same houses Sean will visit and claim. Does he have the addresses already? Nick considers calling all of his tenants and warning them about scams, men who pose as bank contractors hired to repossess the house. He decides that none of this means anything next to one fact: It's after nine and Phoebe isn't home. Again.

Nick deletes the messages, doesn't make any calls. He has their deposits and rent. He'll collect next month if he can. Or not. His head throbs; the sharpness of the pain in his lower back is acute. Images of Phoebe taking JW's cock in her mouth burst in from nowhere. Nick falls to the sectional, eyes wide and unfocused as his mind races. He can't resolve disputes over ownership, so he resolves to stay away, never return the calls or visit the properties in dispute; JW forcing himself deeper into his wife's mouth until she's gagging; her iPhone flooded with messages from clients asking for lewd JPEGs.

He's slouched against the back of the sectional, neck stretched until he's staring upside down at the climbing wall. She rolled her eyes when he fell. That's what he knows. Whether or not she's fucking JW, the night Nick fell from the wall to the living room floor, when she heard the sick, dull thud from his nearly two hundred pounds hitting the ground, her instinct was to roll her eyes. During a recent argument, he'd pressed a wooden salad spoon into her abdomen and demanded her answer to the question: "What did you do when you heard me fall? The first thing, the instinctive reaction when you heard me land, the whole house shook, because that tells us all we need to know."

Her response: "I don't know, Nick. What do you want?"

The house is completely dark, hushed. Only the refrigerator makes any noise: ice cubes tumbling from somewhere deep inside into the overflowing plastic bin. What he'd give to be back in Boston, in their old place, his old job, morning routines, predictability and stability. The doughnut store. The ice cream store. The Super Playground.

The Red Slide playground. They'd go back with a dog and wrecked credit. They'd do the work required to fix their marriage.

He showers. On the bathroom floor he finds a bulging brown spider, crushes it with a clenched fist. He leaves it smeared across the white tile floor. In the kitchen he finishes off half a container of fresh-cut mango, fills a tumbler with Grey Goose. Blackjack barks at the patio door. Nick lets him in and taps out a text to Phoebe: *Are you with him? Working him?*

She doesn't respond. He stirs the drink with his index finger, sucks it free of vodka. He's sent eight texts to his wife today and she's returned none. It's Thursday, almost eleven o'clock. Jackson is spending the night at Mai's because Nick has no idea where Phoebe is, when she'll be home, if ever. He's shirtless and pacing the living room.

He fires off another text to Phoebe: *Ha-haha. I mean, really?* The glow from the screen saver of Phoebe's laptop (a floating portrait of Jackson's face, brown eyes and tangle of brown hair, puffy pink cheeks) as Nick pops the bubble, tapping the keyboard. He rereads an old email from JW. Five paragraphs. His answers to her questions. Nick has read it a dozen times. He does some push-ups. Sends another text. *Love?*

Really. You "love" him? Still you think you love him??

He laughs out loud.

He rereads the message she sent to JW in August, the one she inexplicably left open on her laptop:

I don't sleep. It's eating me from the inside. I've lost 19 pounds this summer and none of it has anything to do with anyone or anything but you and what I feel for you. There's nothing healthy about it all but I love you and love thoughts of you and dreams of you and the tastes of you and the weight of your body on mine and I apologize for this much honesty but you asked and I've decided that there is no more time for pretending and misleading. I know what I feel and think I know what I deserve finally, after everything.

Nick is a lunatic laughing out loud alone in the house. If he had Marina's pink .38, he'd be shooting the light fixtures and the windows and the laptop. Tapping out a succession of four one-word messages to Phoebe:

This.

Will.

Not.

Work.

He drops to the floor and does eleven push-ups. The sudden burst of activity ignites Blackjack, who grabs the first object he can find, Jackson's green Croc, and charges Nick, wants to engage, cold wet snout pushing against Nick's face and neck. Nick shoves the dog away too hard, eyes the rock-climbing wall. He starts to climb, then hops off. Blackjack is circling, whining, still with the shoe. Nick taps out another text: *Not sure why you'd ever think this would be ok. What ARE you thinking? Are you thinking??*

Then again: *LOVE? Love. You Love him. That's what you think it is? Or is that more of the game? Your master plan.*

Okay. I love you too. I love him too. That's right. I love JW too.

The message from Phoebe is instantaneous and stuns him: *Not what it looks like, Nick. At all. Trust.*

FUCK THAT. Fuck you fuck trust. You blew that one babe. May as well not come home. I got this. You're not needed here. Not wanted. Still want the dick pic?

The sound of Nick's heavy breathing, exhaling through his nose, and Blackjack, circling still. Nick wipes perspiration from his forehead, and his eyes glaze over staring at the glowing screen, Phoebe's cryptic response to his rage. The dog gives up, slumps to the carpet.

Before he can decide whether to question her further, call her, or simply tell her he won't be here when she gets home, he's leaving for a few days, that their son is still with the nanny and the dog is alone in the house, she sends one last message: *I love us, Nick.*

54

It's two A.M. Phoebe sits in the driveway, listening to the end of "Heads Will Roll" on Alt Nation. The Forester isn't here. Nick is gone. Inside, the house is cool and quiet. Blackjack is nowhere to be found, must be with Kostya. Nick wouldn't leave him in the bonus room. She swallows three Klonopins with the last gulp of merlot she left on the fireplace mantel, walks barefoot upstairs, falls asleep without undressing on the floor next to Jackson's empty crib. "I've got this, sweet baby," she says. "Mommy's got it taken care of now."

Her iPhone wakes her. It's ringing. The display reads *Blocked.* She picks up. The call drops. There is no voice mail. It doesn't ring again. She messages JW, asks if he just called. There's no reply.

The next morning, Friday, Halloween. She has appointments. Jackson must be checked on. The dog. She needs Nick. She'll tell him what she knows: that she's getting an offer, one that will allow them to move, leave the house, get her out of the car, put them in a little house by the ocean where they belong. They'll mend things, stick the broken pieces back together, and time and routine and Jackson will heal them.

If Nick were home while she dressed, he'd ask what she was doing. "You're clearly not working today," he'd say. And she's not. She's skipping her appointments. Nick would say something about the sheer material and thin straps that keep slipping from her shoulders. If it were two months ago or even September, he'd watch her, and she'd ask if he liked the dress, and only then he might grab her and slide his hands under it and around her hips and tell her they had time, quickly. Or maybe he'd just stare at her and say nothing, too fatigued to care.

But now she's alone in the house and the wind is gusting outside, sunlight seeping through the blinds, and she has the day ahead of her, waiting for word, confirmation, from JW.

She makes herself a mimosa and sips it slowly. In the bright cold kitchen: a sink full of dishes, a bloody rag from Nick's most recent work injury. Her phone is quiet. She slips a strap from her thin shoulder and unbuttons the top two buttons of her cotton dress and snaps a picture of herself with her free hand pulling up the hem revealing her tan thigh, the yellow edge of her lace panties, sends it to Nick: *Off to work <3*

The man who answers the door at Mai's house is in his fifties and wears a white T-shirt and khakis. It's Mai's husband, who has a Vietnamese name Phoebe can't remember. Mai and Jackson aren't here. They've gone to the playground.

"Down the street?" Phoebe asks.

"The zoo."

"I thought you said playground. She took him to the zoo?"

"Yes. She ask your husband and he says is fine."

Phoebe is quiet. The woman took her son to the zoo. He's never been to the zoo. She wanted to be the one to take her son to the zoo for the first time.

"She took him to the zoo" is the message she's leaving on Nick's voicemail. "Why does that make me sad? I wanted to take him for his first trip to the zoo."

Nick doesn't call, he texts. *News flash: not his first trip to the zoo. Daddy took him. And he loved it.*

55

The first house she sees is a three-bedroom Craftsman six blocks from the beach in Laguna. The rent is high and the enclosed backyard is modest but lush. From the master suite she can see palm trees, wires, and the ocean. She takes pictures of every room. This is it. She asks the agent what it will take to close today. She considers Nick's sweaty cash and the leverage she'll have with D&C as JW's girl. Although the house is a rental and doesn't make financial sense, securing it will drive the point home to JW: She's moving to Laguna Beach, minutes from work. She is serious about D&C and ready to start now.

"How much?" she asks.

Rent is $3,950. Offers are in. The view from the second bedroom of the house, Jackson's room: the ocean. The image in her mind: a white rocking chair by the window, Jackson on her lap, a story, watching sunsets that light up the room like some kind of golden dream.

D&C is all she types, attaches an image of the house from the street: this little yellow home off the ocean.

No response.

This is Laguna. They're asking $3,950. Ten minutes from work. Thoughts?

Nothing.

Hmm . . . I love us.

The vibration is instantaneous. As though he were sitting with his legs crossed in the Virgin Clubhouse at Heathrow, wondering how far she would go. *Take it.*

Lots of applications.

Tough market.

How should I close this?

Aggressively

Offer what, 4,200?

Is it premature? There will be other places.

This is the place. This is home.

You don't have anything yet.

Amusing

Have you heard from anyone?

You told me I nailed it.

I'm sure.

Are you?

As sure as one can be in this environment

Don't make me ask

What?

It's a rental. Safer move.

What do you want?

Close this for me.

How?

First, last, deposit.

Co-sign??

Not funny.

Wait till things solidify. Right? When D&C is final and you can budget, then take the family house hunting. What's the rush?

You won't do it.

There's a long pause.

The agent is at his Audi convertible, on the phone. Phoebe stands on the front walk, unwilling to move.

Give me the agent's #.

Splendid ;)

There is no response.

They might need ID or my social, but I don't know, how do you plan to do it?

Her iPhone doesn't vibrate, there is no response from JW. She waits. Ten minutes pass. The Audi is gone. She is alone on the front lawn of the house by the ocean, shadows stretching across the grass. Laughter and shrieking, and a pack of tiny goblins, a zombie and one white ghost pass by, orange plastic bags in hand, adults snapping smartphone pics, trailing close behind. A year from now, she thinks, next Halloween, that will be her and Nick, Jackson in costume, going door-to-door, filling his bag.

In the Explorer, idling on the street opposite the yellow house, she makes three phone calls. The first is to Mai to thank her again for all she's doing and to apologize for the insane schedule and mention a family emergency and Nick's unconventional hours and ask if Jackson can spend another night there.

She sends Nick a text: *You're off the hook again. He's with Mai tonight. And he had fun at the zoo. She said he loves the elephants. I guess you knew that. Anyway, house is yours. Have a blast!*

And you'll be where exactly?

She doesn't have an answer yet. She's miles from home. It's almost six. Jackson will be asleep by the time she gets to Serenos. She considers Hotel Bamboo. She considers sleeping on the beach. She doesn't respond to Nick's question because she doesn't know.

The vibration of her cell is a text from Mai. A picture of Jackson. He's a Smurf.

Is ok to trick/treat?

Jackson wears a fluffy white nightcap and a blue top and a bright white diaper.

Pants. He needs pants.

Too hot for the pants.

She calls Kostya. He answers on the first ring.

"Boo!" she says. She feels an intimacy with him that may not be real, but her high is gone, so it could be. The days are shorter, darkness comes earlier. All these little kids marching around as Transformers and panda bears and Power Rangers with their parents close behind triggers a surge of loneliness, a longing for something she can't remember ever having.

"I know your number. You don't scare me," he says.

"You must not know me very well."

"Someone steal our Frankestein. Or he get scared and run off."

"Check Metzger's tent."

He laughs. "You a sneaky bitch, but I like."

She smiles because she knows he doesn't mean it the way it sounds; nuance is lost in translation. The connection is breaking up.

"Our dog is alone in the house," she says. "Can you take him for the night?"

"— dog is dead?"

The connection is lost. The call drops. She calls back but gets voicemail. She knows he didn't mean it and couldn't possibly know if something was wrong with Blackjack, who's in the house and can't get out. But still she's scared. Horns blare. She's parked legally. Headlights blind her through the windshield. She's blocking a driveway. An SUV's horn blares. Her cell rings.

"It is Kostya. Marina tell me to say that for Halloween scaring. It is a good scare, yes?"

She pushes the car into drive, lurches forward. The driver of the SUV calls her a bitch.

Costumed kids and their parents witness the exchange. Kostya is still on the line. Embarrassed, she drops the call. She drives home to Serenos. It takes her nearly three hours. She swallows two Klonopins in the kitchen. There is no wine in the house. She pours too much rum in a Spider-Man cup and drinks it all. She taps out a message to JW, the question she doesn't want to ask, doesn't want an answer to:

And what do you mean final? With D&C what's NOT final?

When she sleeps, it's on the sectional in her white cotton dress, waiting for word. She felt playful when the day started, a vague sense of anticipation about better days. Now her jaw aches; cramps are churning her insides. Her throat is dry and hurts when she swallows.

The vibration wakes her because the iPhone is wedged between her head and the throw pillow. She can't focus. The words are blurred, a blended mess of black characters. Finally, she makes it out. It's not JW. It's Nick: *Nice dress. He get that for you?*

56

The private road that leads to the Sunland house, the location of Nick's first night of Angel Duty, is unlit and narrow, and when the sun sets, the dry hills that wrap themselves around the house cast uneven shadows that swallow the place whole. Nick is about to text Phoebe again and ask what else she's blowing his sweaty cash on besides sundresses and yellow underwear when his iPhone vibrates.

The message is from Mallory: *You were in my dream.*

He's been sitting in his Subaru outside of this completely dark, deserted mansion for an hour. It's ten o'clock and none of the streetlights work and there's no one around. Despite the Mossberg, he's not sure he's capable or stupid enough to enter the house alone. He may sleep in the car.

Is it wrong to say that turns me on?

nope

Was it interesting?

It was great, I'm still thinking about it. Definitely not wrong. Now the thought of you turns me on crazy.

Nick taps out a response: *I want to do something with this*

What do you have in mind?

I want to know what you like. Then I want to facetime or skype or whatever.

That's all??

Nick turns off the ignition on the Subaru, pulls a white latex mask over his head. Mallory continues the exchange: *This morning I got off thinking about the dream. You had me over the hood of a car. I love it from behind. And sure lets skype.*

He leans against the warm hood of the car, taps out his response: *I came up from behind in my dream . . . you were over a granite countertop. Empty house looking back at me. I could smell you, taste you.*

They're texting over each other. Buzzing and tapping and sending and the soft hue of the screen and the erection he's getting from wearing the mask and imagining how this twenty-two-year-old girl tastes almost make him forget about the house he's about to enter.

That sounds amazing. I'm wet. With your hand around my throat or holding my hair . . .

starting off slow . . .

Just ease it in . . .

Super slow. I'd want you to put it in & then pull all the way out again . . . over & over, I'll feel so tight around you, you'll love it.

Let me know when you can connect.

Now.

Andwhereyouwantmetocome

A long gap. He's seeing himself from a distance: wearing a white mask, clutching a pump-gauge shotgun with a case of shells outside of a deserted mansion on Halloween night. The dark hills seem closer somehow. The warm air is thick and soft.

inmymouthiwanttotasteyou

Do you know where Sunland is?

57

The Spanish revival behemoth is cold inside and smells like bleach. It's unfurnished. The electricity is still on, as is the air-conditioning. Nick calls out. He doesn't want to surprise anyone, and he needs to hear a voice, even his own, which echoes through the downstairs and up to the vaulted ceilings.

All the clean modern lines of the interior only make the arched black-framed windows more ominous. He taps wall switches as he goes, illuminates each room until he's in the kitchen. Outside, a half-moon pool in the backyard lies empty. The kitchen quickly fills with moths and other insects, drawn to the light through the shattered glass door where entry was gained. A wrought-iron gate surrounds the backyard and pool, presumably to keep mountain lions and coyotes from the property.

Nick returns to the dual spiral staircase.

"Listen to this!" he's calling out as he climbs the stairs. He places two green shells in the barrel of the Mossberg and pumps it. "That's the Mossberg. It's a shotgun."

But all of the rooms are empty aside from some balled-up sheets and a few empty paint cans. He calls Papa John's, and when he tries to give the directions to the house, the kid laughs and says, "Don't think so, dude. We don't go out that far," and hangs up. Nick brought his phone and music and tablet. He has some Dos Equis and an ice gel pack, vitaminwater, cold cuts, and hard-boiled eggs in a giant cooler. He'll elevate and numb his swollen, bruised left ankle and right knee (the fall did more damage than he'd thought initially). He has an air mattress and a pillow and fifteen of Phoebe's Klonopins.

You inside? It's Boss.

Nick is limping around the back patio, staring into the hills. *Big house*

That's a $2.6 mil property you're protecting

Nick writes back: *Was*

Later, Nick finishes the last beer outside as a warm mist settles over everything and the cicadas scream as he holds his phone to the sky and starts to film his surroundings and begins to narrate. "Home sweet home," he says. A police helicopter passes low overhead. A zigzag of spotlights cuts across the terrain with urgency, pursuing or searching for someone. Nick lies down on one of three chaises left behind, the shotgun on the concrete patio next to him.

The message he receives is from Phoebe: *Are you working tomorrow?*

I work everyday.

Do you have a couple of hours?

Where?

It's a surprise

No.

Please.

No.

I'll do all the driving.

Whatever

Nick drifts off, fitfully, shifting his weight on the chair outside, the cicadas the last thing he hears.

He can't stay asleep so he goes inside, gets online, tries to focus on the story he downloads about street brawlers in Rio and their animalistic gang rituals. But he can't keep from hearing strange noises, the cries from animals in the distance, coyotes maybe, and the crickets that seem to be inside the house despite the cardboard he duct-taped over the shattered window, and cicadas, and something scraping against the downstairs windows that are all so sweeping and grand, he is sure at any instant something will crash through, glass exploding everywhere, the assault, the home invasion under way, and all he will be able to do is run the other way, trying to get to his car or disappear into the blackness of the hills.

The air mattress he brought is positioned on a gleaming hardwood floor in the center of the large living room, exposed dark beams and a massive stone fireplace. It's late and he's nearly drunk, lying on the air mattress, picking at a scab on his left elbow and trying to remember how he injured it and if he has enough money to take Jackson back east, start over there, when headlights appear, illuminate the dark living room. A black MINI Cooper convertible comes to a stop and idles in the gravel driveway and the music cuts off and the driver's-side door opens. It's Mallory.

Nick doesn't bother putting on a shirt and leaves the lights off. The doorbell chimes and echoes through the huge empty foyer and living room, and he runs his hands over his hair, which he cut short, almost shaved. He's got a warm, nearly empty bottle of Corona in his hand as he pulls the front door open a crack, peeks through.

"You are not really here," he says in a

sleepy voice.

"Orange Dream?" She offers a big white cup with a red straw.

He sucks the straw and the sweet cold citrus slides down his throat as he opens the door for her, keeps the cup.

"This place is ridiculous," she says, and sticks a plastic bag of weed in his back pocket. "Arik says you should quit this job."

She moves past Nick and toward the stairs, where she turns and sits, leans back, elbows on the stairs. She's all legs — tan, thin, with a large bruise on her left shin. She's not wearing shoes.

"Are you two a couple?" Nick sucks the straw.

"Would I be here if we were?"

"I don't need complications."

She laughs. "Says the married father to the girl he invited to the deserted house on Halloween."

"Why'd you come?"

She reaches for the smoothie. He hands her the cup.

"Thanks again for the house you put me in. It's perfect. Not all this, but better than Arik's place."

"You owe me rent."

"It's in your pocket."

"Stand up."

She's on the third stair, so when she stands and Nick moves closer, she's taller than he is. He takes her hands. Her chin is at his forehead. He breathes her in. He reaches into his back pocket and removes the plastic bag of marijuana. "Tell me where you want me to put this."

She takes his right hand, the one that holds the bag, guides it down the backside of her tight yellow shorts. Nick closes his eyes and rests his head against her chest but only for a moment, never quite stops moving, massaging her breasts through her shirt with his forehead, chin, until he's pulling at her shorts, which somehow fall to her ankles, and he drops to his knees and urges her back down on the stairs, removing her shirt, and even as he tastes her, he can't jettison images of Phoebe pressed against a wall, JW's hand pinning her head against it. In refracted kitchen light, the faded acne scars are visible on Mallory's chest, as are the red marks from the grip he's had on her shoulder and neck, and he finishes and collapses next to her on the stairs, reaches for the white cup and tries to take a sip, but it's empty.

Mallory doesn't ask any questions and doesn't stay. Nick walks her to the car.

They're both barefoot and he's still shirtless. The scent of smoke hangs in the air.

She stops at her car, keys in hand, and turns to him. "So I'm wondering something. You think Arik's an idiot, don't you?"

"I think he's young."

She's laughing. "He pays the rent. So there's that." She slaps Nick's chest for emphasis.

Nick puts it together: They're in some kind of dysfunctional relationship that is all too familiar. They're working through something and making a mess of things, but they have an advantage that Nick and Phoebe don't enjoy, and Nick envies them for it. What they have that Nick and Phoebe gave away, so long ago he can't recall, is some margin for error.

Low white clouds distract him. "It's smoke," he says, more to himself than to her. She kisses Nick quickly on the mouth, hard, then turns from him. She left the Sirius radio on and a familiar pop song blasts from the speakers when she starts the car and she doesn't bother turning it down, and when the MINI Cooper's red taillights disappear around a bend in the deserted private road in the gray dawn light, Nick sees for the first time the shattered second-floor window and the illegible black graffiti tags on the right side of the house. He wonders how he missed those details, if maybe they happened since he arrived, while he slept. He wonders what other signs he's missed. Inside, there is a slow leak in the air mattress and only cold water runs in the shower.

The next night, his last in the house, Nick sits shirtless on the edge of the empty pool, lighting long wooden matches he found in the kitchen, tossing one after another into the blackness and watching the dark hills, waiting for the winds to come and the fire with it. The wailing is the cicadas. They're dying, he thinks. Phoebe hears them, too, wherever she is. The alarm they've ignored for too long. He has enough money, nearly sixty thousand in cash, to take Jackson anywhere, back to Boston, somewhere different, some new adventure. Maybe New Orleans. The simplicity of a father and son. At some point the boy will ask questions and Nick will answer them all, honestly and without hesitation. Your mother did what she could to take care of you. Your mother made herself who she is, and everything she gave you and continues to give only happens because she decided it was important. But she was tired, it was work, and there is something in her that needs special attention, and sometimes people can only fix the broken parts of themselves alone. Sometimes it's safer that way.

Punk-ass bitch

The text is from Phoebe.

Then a winking emoticon.

Cleaned out the fridge and three loads of laundry and smoked a joint with Marina. Do you still think she's hot? She thinks you're hot. She asked if we MUCK around! I think she meant mess. Do you, Nick? Do you MUCK around? Because you can if you want to. It's not like we ever have sex anymore and I totally understand and wouldn't be upset because the bottom line is you're still here and in days, literally, you won't believe what's happening. So tomorrow, 8 am? Please don't be late.

Nick drags the air mattress out on the patio but doesn't sleep. He's hungry and missing his son and Blackjack, staring at misshapen dark patches where the clouds are thinning and the glimmer of faint stars and wondering if it's possible that he'll ever miss Phoebe again because tonight he doesn't miss her at all.

58

"Nora. Nora?"

"It's Phoebe."

"I want to call you Nora. Do you mind if I call you Nora?" The man asking her this is the physician who sat casually on a barstool an hour ago under recessed lighting and for six thousand dollars a month spoke convincingly into a microphone about the merits of GSK's latest erectile dysfunction remedy to a roomful of colleagues, sales reps, and managers. He's buzzed and standing too close to Phoebe in a crowded suite in the same hotel.

The room is restless, quieter than usual, more reps, Phoebe figures, sobered by the new corporate directive for managers: The bar has been raised to stay employed until further notice; the bottom half in sales will be terminated at the end of the year. Phoebe was in the bottom twenty percent and has been since she started out here.

"Why the long face, Nora?" the physician asks, grabs a full champagne flute from a passing tray, replaces Phoebe's half-empty one.

Attendance tonight is a box Phoebe needs to check and is the least she can do. She's here because she still hasn't heard from JW. This conversation with the physician, well-managed, should pay off. She'll make an impression that will give her an edge over other reps. She may not become his rep, but he can send her to colleagues with large practices and new patients, which will boost her sales numbers, secure her spot in the top half by year's end.

But he keeps calling her Nora.

All of the physicians here are men. So are most of the GSK managers, about six or so, and the dozen or more GSK sales reps are women. One of them must be Nora. Phoebe peels her name tag from her chest and sticks it on the man's forehead. "Phoebe Maguire," she says.

The company men are managers, and all seem to have sticky product in their hair and wear leather necklaces and probably wax their bodies. A few of the sales reps and managers are playing a game, a hold-over Phoebe recalls from orientation for new hires. A woman shrieks, then earsplitting laughter. The game they're playing is charades and becomes something pornographic when one of the reps allows a young man to lift her skirt while her friend pulls the pants of the same guy to his knees. Someone pours champagne on them.

Phoebe's district manager stands between two tan, waxed men, clutching a champagne flute. He's watching her with the physician. He insisted she come tonight. She met him once before, when he interviewed her. Big cheeks, twenty pounds overweight. His receding hairline gives way to a massive forehead that makes his green eyes appear even smaller. The manager grilled Phoebe during the interview about why she wanted to go back in the field: Was she doing it for the money or was she committed to the GSK army? Was she mercenary or soldier? He asked these questions with a straight face. The physicians don't respect him and the reps resent him. Still he tries. He wears a black silk shirt with zippers on it and a black leather necklace and he's staring at her. She meets his eyes. His expression doesn't match the mood in the room, or maybe it does. His gaze is distant, somehow lost. When he notices that Phoebe's staring back, he raises a glass in a cross-suite toast. She does the same.

Phoebe checks her cell: 11:02 P.M.

"Do you have a curfew, Nora?" the physician asks.

She ignores the question. Her manager is suddenly next to her, his chest pressed against her shoulder.

"They took a month longer than they planned, but it was worth it." The manager is actually trying to impress the physician with talk about work he says he had done on his condo.

"Your *rented* condo," Phoebe interjects.

The physician isn't listening. Despite standing so close to Phoebe's manager, the physician isn't hearing a word he's saying. He lingers instead on Phoebe's shoes. They're silver. "Those are something."

The manager checks his handheld and reads a message that isn't there.

The wedding band on the physician's hand is thick silver; despite its prominence, he leers at her. There's no subtlety in his approach. His right hand is dug deep into his pants pocket until he removes it, brings it to Phoebe's chin, and gently rubs something from her face. "Got it," he says. His eyes are set too close together and he has thin lips with a short neck and his stomach pushes against the buttons of his shirt, which is tucked too tight. "Where back east?"

She says Boston and looks away, and the image that comes to mind is from late last spring: Nick carrying Jackson on his shoulders through the community gardens at dusk, their backs to her. The physician says he went to Harvard, and when she hears this, for some reason it breaks the spell and she says, still distant, "I didn't."

The physician starts listing colleges and universities in greater Boston, from the most prestigious and highly selective to the less competitive schools until he gets to Boston University, where she stops him by grabbing his forearm. "It was a fun school."

He says he was surprised it wasn't BC or some other Jesuit school and asks if she's Catholic.

"She's a heathen," her manager says. "She was pleasant once, too. Warm even," he confides to the physician.

The physician is wretched with perspiration over his upper lip and on his chin and leans in to Phoebe and says she feels warm, sliding his arm around her waist, squeezing her. "Strong, too."

The manager says she was a pro back east. "Stellar," he says.

And then her manager has his hand on

the back of her neck. "Out here, not so much," he says.

She's up for auction. She is the prized piece of pharma meat tonight. Yet she's the hunter, too, and the big game in the room, this vile little mole of a man, may be gettable after all. She runs some quick numbers and concludes that she could land this pervert and ten more just like him and all their patients and she'd still be in the bottom third. Which means, come December, she'd be fired. She finishes her champagne and tosses the flute on the floor next to the sectional.

"Let me help." The physician takes her hand and holds it.

In this moment, two men, strangers to her, feel compelled to place their hands on her and keep them there.

The physician's breath is warm when he presses his small wet mouth against her ear. "I'll prescribe it all. Whatever you're selling. Come to my office twice a month." He takes her hand and places it over his crotch and holds it there.

There are forty-five strangers in this room, and her eyes find the red and orange impressionistic print on a wall over the desk. The image is fluid and at first is a compressed face winking at her in the din of the sloppy crowd and shrieks of laughter, and a hand clutching her ass too hard turns the benevolent face flattened on the canvas into a demon, red eyes and long teeth, and the blood in its mouth is her own.

When she hits the bend in the freeway, she accelerates. She weaves through traffic. She wants to drive home. She wants to slip off her shoes and pour a glass of South African wine and walk upstairs to Jackson's room and sit with Nick and listen to their son sleep. She wants to wake up in the room to the sound of his little voice and Nick opening the blinds and letting the soft morning light fill the room and start their day. She wants to apologize to Nick and admit she's not nearly as in control as she wants to be. She wants to come clean: She doesn't trust herself.

She's still driving, and the long thin silhouettes are skinny palms against the thick black sky she knows is choked with smoke from fires and smog, and the bleak dry hillsides are tinder for what's coming. She feels small and clutches the wheel too tightly and presses down on the gas and it's her alone on this stretch of asphalt hugging the sea, splitting the mountains and brush. She is dwarfed by the elements. From under the passenger seat she removes Marina's pink .38. The weight of it sends a chill through her. She laughs to herself. Jesus. Why did she bother asking for this thing? Marina has two more, so she didn't hesitate when Phoebe mentioned it. She could fire it into the sky and no one would hear. Aim high, Nora, she thinks to herself.

59

Phoebe opens an Evite and addresses it to Kostya and Marina, Mai and her husband (whose name she still doesn't know), and two of her coworkers. She checks the calendar and decides on the second Saturday in November. She calls it a holiday season party, then changes it to "just because," then changes back to a holiday gathering, then types: *Bon Voyage.* Because that's really what it is: a going-away party. She emails Marina separately, tells her to invite some friends. She'll tell Nick the same, to have some of his sweaty friends come by. Why not? She cranks Pandora on a Led Zeppelin station that reminds her of college. There's no one home: Jackson is at Mai's, and Nick is at the house in Sunland. She considers going. She might. She could drive out there and surprise him. They could fuck on the air mattress and she could tell him everything: precisely what she's been doing with JW and why, and that within a month, weeks, days, their lives will be their own, the way they're meant to be, if not charmed then glistening by the sea, Jackson sleeping in the orange light of spectacular sunsets.

She doesn't know Metzger's email address and doesn't want him in their house, so she won't mention the party to him, though he's sure to wander over uninvited.

It's dusk and she sips her glass of Terra Blanca outside, stares at the fading orange lights lining the wall of the empty pool, the clear message from Nick that she's not to be trusted, not only with their commitment to each other but also with the well-being of their son. She walks back inside, closes and locks the sliding glass door, crosses the kitchen, and stands at the rock-climbing wall, gazing at her reflection in the blackness of the kitchen door, waiting for it to explode, something to burst through. The only sound is the icemaker churning, dropping cubes into a plastic bin. Everything is still. There are no more pills to take tonight, no messages to send him, questions to ask, demands or false promises, angles to play. All she can do is wait. She can't take it.

60

Phoebe meets Nick in the driveway on Carousel Court. She messaged him and he told her he got a late start and instead of anger she responded with nonchalance and sympathy. She wrote: *You must be exhausted.* He ignored it and texted Mallory instead. He's been collecting rent checks this morning. It's been days since he saw her at the Sunland house. He texts her too often and is unsure why. She hasn't been responding. At first she would reply an hour or two later. Then a day. Now she doesn't respond at all. Nick asks her what the deal is again. He started texting like this when he was drinking. Now it makes no difference whether he's sober or not. He asks her how he should interpret her silence. Once she responded six hours later: *What is your deal?* He fired back immediately: *No biggie either way.* She didn't respond, which made him insane. He accused her of judging him.

Then said she was just some random girl and who the fuck was she to judge him. Then he apologized. Now, this morning, on his way to pick up Phoebe, he is having an entire conversation with her even though she contributes nothing. Somehow it's cathartic for him.

At the last red light before reaching Carousel Court, he taps out a succession of manic messages: *I dig you, ok? That night was epic.*

Let's be friends. Let's start over.

Disregard everything I've said to date and pretend we just met. Hey. This is Nick. Thanks for giving me your number. Wanna grab a smoothie or something? Do you need anything? Some cash maybe? Wanna go shopping? Let me buy you something nice.

My wife is fucked. My kid's amazing tho, go figure.

Hello? Are you there? What the fuck? Respond. Once. Like common courtesy. K? I thought you were cool. Whatevs.

There is no response from Mallory.

Nick slows the Forester as he approaches the driveway. Phoebe holds a Starbucks tray with two white cups and an iced macchiato she's sipping through a green straw. Nick passes her, and when he does, he sees Jackson hiding behind her white sundress. They wave. Nick turns the car around and the two of them climb in.

"No, wait, I'll drive," she says.

"I got it," Nick says, but she's already out of the car and walking around the front to the driver's side, so he gets out and walks around the back to the passenger side, gets in, and slams the door closed. He'd rather be in the house, showering then sleeping, dreaming about Mallory.

Nick reaches into the backseat and tickles his son, who says through his laughter "Hi, Daddy" in his little voice. Nick glances reflexively at the face of his iPhone. No response from Mallory.

Phoebe drives west, toward the freeway. Her white sunglasses match her dress, and the brightness of the white accentuates her thin, tan legs and loose-fitting sterling bracelets and thick men's watch on her left wrist.

"We have the whole day," she says.

"To do what?"

"I want to show you something."

"There's nothing I want to see."

"It's a surprise."

She hands him her phone. A video is cued up. It's a backyard pool with clear blue water and voices and splashing and Jackson is wearing a red bathing suit and kicking and Mai is leading him, backing away a little farther the closer he gets, until she reaches the wall and he reaches her and she scoops him up, and his wet face and blinking eyes find the camera because Phoebe is calling out to him off-screen and Jackson is laughing, swimming.

"She taught him," Phoebe says.

Nick is moved by the image of his son flailing with purpose in the deep water. He swallows hard and averts his eyes as he hands the phone back to Phoebe. He exhales and the scenery is a blur and colors blend and for an instant he wonders if maybe it's not as bad as it seems. "Nice watch."

The watch on her wrist is not the one Phoebe bought for his thirtieth birthday. That one was thick and silver with a black face, not blue, and it was a Movado, not a Tag Heuer, and he sold it for four hundred dollars when they first got out here. It's his, JW's, he thinks. If it is, he might take her out to the Sunland house and throw her in the empty pool. It can't be.

They reach the freeway heading south. Black signs with orange lettering warn about wildfires. The sky is pale blue and stretched thin, wraps around them. Phoebe is in the left lane, trailing a red BMW too close.

"Let me see it," Nick says, and reaches across her body for her left wrist.

She nudges his arm, which stiffens.

"It's his?" He grabs her wrist too hard, wrapping his callused hand around the watch. She screams. The BMW slows. Nick curses. She swerves, narrowly avoids the BMW, horns sounding. Nick curses again. His coffee spills.

"Asshole," she snaps.

Nick has the watch. He studies it. "This is not my watch."

She's shaking her head. "I'm trying, okay?"

Jackson is crying out and Phoebe is reaching back, squeezing his leg, telling him everything is okay. She adds that Daddy got scared and that's why they both yelled.

"Tell me it's his or I will throw this" — he snatches her phone — "out of the car." He begins to lower his window.

"It's his."

He screams, throws the watch out the window. Jackson wails. Nick pounds the dashboard with a closed fist, then both fists, until he's unloading a barrage of punches. Exhausted, he drops his head on the hot dash, looks away from Phoebe, sweat burning his eyes.

"You should have left him with Mai," Nick finally says, exhaling. "You're a horrible mother."

At first she says nothing. Her eyes remain straight ahead, both hands gripping the wheel. Then she says distantly, "That's not true. I'm a good parent."

"We're leaving you."

Phoebe doesn't seem to hear him. She is talking to herself. "There's money for groceries. The house needs to be cleaned. It's coming together. We're getting there. And the laundry needs to be folded. Mai is there if we need her. It's good. We're better."

"When we get home," Nick says, "I'm packing his things and mine, and we're driving back to Boston."

She's talking to herself about orientation for new hires and her starting salary and a bonus she seems to think will erase their debts, and as she speaks she nods and leans forward in her seat, and instead of easing off the accelerator and coasting a bit she's gunning it, pumping the brakes, agitated as she talks about leaving behind neighbors in tents, and guns, and staying awake every night waiting for something horrible to happen to them, to Jackson, for the glass to shatter downstairs as they fall victim to their own home invasion because Nick insisted, refused, and she's stabbing the air in front of her with her right hand and Nick is reaching for his son's leg now but, too drained to turn around, leans back in his seat and watches the traffic.

"Refused to honor," she says, and trails off. "There are basic commitments. Expectations."

"Goddamn, you need help."

61

The yellow Craftsman in Laguna Beach sits empty. It's a Tuesday afternoon and no one on the lush wide street, dotted with purples and whites and reds, a few short palms, black wires and the Pacific in the distance, knows the young family in the white Subaru. No one knows that the man in the backseat with the young boy is a father reading him *Harry the Dirty Dog* for the third time in an attempt to console him or that the thin, pretty mother on her iPhone peering through the living room window is secretly terrified that she's making the mistake of a lifetime. It's just another breezy day off the ocean in Orange County.

Finally, the blue Audi pulls up. The agent lets them inside and waits in the living room while Nick carries Jackson, trailing Phoebe, from one sun-filled hardwood room to the next. In the upstairs hallway the floors creak as they walk. Phoebe has her hand wrapped around the dull silver knob on the white bedroom door, waiting to push it open in some grand gesture.

Nick's and Phoebe's eyes meet. They stand close to each other. He could grab her wrist and pull her hand from the doorknob and tell her, Not like this, I've got this. We're going home. Boston. I'll take care of it. He could hoist her on his shoulder like a plastic jug of water on a sweltering summer day and carry her out of here.

Her eyes shift before his. Heat radiates from her; she's tense, and a sheen of perspiration gives her thinning face a hollowed-out appearance, almost ghostly.

"Another house," he says more to himself than to her, exasperated. "Is he co-signing?"

She ignores the reference to JW and pushes the door open.

"Renting, Nickels. Renting." Then a look crosses her face, a question. "How much money have you made, Nick?"

Nick has never told her. He stopped talking about it when she insisted she wanted nothing to do with it. He made deposits in five separate accounts and kept cash. He's cleared over seventy thousand but has no interest in telling her. "What is he offering you?" he says.

The sunny room is all hardwood floor and

sweeping view, dark water and white surf in the distance. Nick puts Jackson down and the boy runs to the window.

"D&C in Laguna Beach. It's a ten-minute commute. There's a signing bonus."

"What's the job?"

"Consulting."

All Nick can think is what is unspoken, the expectation of this middle-aged man who has his wife on a string. All Nick can see is Phoebe averting her gaze when her cell rings and the call is him, and her leaving the room, walking outside to talk, lying when she returns, saying it was her mother, and Nick will seethe when he tries to resist the temptation to demand the fucking phone. And when she's home late and finds out later that he was in town for work he'll burn inside repressing every dark instinct that tells him to find out: Did she see him? Did she fuck him again?

"Tell me," he says, "how in the hell you think this can work."

"We need this."

He cocks his arm, ready to deliver a blow to the bedroom wall.

"It's the best option. It's the only option we have."

"For who? Not for me, it isn't. I have options. Jackson and I have options. I have money and a job and a house. I am living my options."

"Oh, come on, Nick. It's not sustainable. We both need to be earning. Unconventional is not turning this around for us."

"Unconventional?" He's laughing now. "That's very diplomatic, charitable terminology. You fucked this guy, Phoebe. While we were together. You fucked him. Do you not remember what that did to us? That we're still here, having this conversation, with Jackson existing, and your grand plan is to hitch our wagon to the star you *fucked.* And you didn't walk away, you kept it going, kept it alive." He's gritting his teeth and too close to her face. At her ear, resisting the overwhelming impulse to close his teeth around it until the skin breaks, until he's tasting the salt of her blood. He says, "For us, right? For us."

She tenses, her arm stiffens and meets the force of his body, which is pressing, leaning in to her. "We need it."

"You need it."

"Yes, I need it." She pushes him. "Back up."

"I don't need it. I don't want it. Don't push me."

"Step back. I will scream."

"Not like this. Not ever. Not him. We're

gone." He walks to Jackson, scoops the boy off the floor.

"Jesus, will you stop? Now it matters how —" Phoebe continues.

"Who. *Who* is making this happen?" He lowers his voice, holding Jackson to his chest, chin on his shoulder. The boy is tired or tired of them. "That matters. Yes, that matters a great deal."

"Not to me," she says, staring out the window.

"Well, maybe if he gives me a watch. Was that your signing bonus that I threw out of the car?"

"I haven't signed anything yet."

"So then tell me what in God's name occurred to you, Phoebe, what compelled you to put on his watch? And wear it? Are you that far gone? What are you even on these days? It's not just Klonopin."

She's next to Nick now, close enough to stroke Jackson's hair. "He's a factor. Would you rather I hide it? You know what I'm doing and why I'm doing it. The rest is up to us."

"You, me, Jackson, and JW. Happy shiny family. Your little surfside chalet." He's laughing for Jackson's sake. "Say it. Say it all. Right now. This is the time, because you'll never have a better chance, this room with this view for Jackson. If you're going to convince me, sell me, make me JW's bitch, you damn well better do it now."

Her iPhone vibrates and a chime sounds.

"Is that him? Does he have his own special alert? Is he ready for you now?"

She doesn't turn around. She removes her hand from Jackson's head and reaches into her carryall and removes her phone and checks it.

"Go ahead. Read it out loud." Nick stands behind her, close, making small circles on his son's back. "Let's see if it's good news."

62

Something for nothing. That's what he writes in the text he sends. JW says he's at Heathrow, on his way to Manhattan, then back to Los Angeles. That's what she wants, he says. Something for nothing. She's always been that way. She wants to be a mother but doesn't want to mother. She wants to be married but doesn't want to be a wife. He's referring to his second wife, the one suing him for emotional distress.

Listen to this. He sends a YouTube link to a song by Rush called "Something for Nothing."

Phoebe is brushing her hair, which is falling out, as she sits on the cool marble floor of the master bath. She's in mismatched underwear: black panties, pink bra. The laptop is on the bed, open to the D&C website, surrounded by printouts and highlighters, detailed financial analyses and reports, assessments and spreadsheets for

D&C clients that she's been immersing herself in for the past week. She asked JW to help her prep, and he sent it all.

Who is Rush? Phoebe writes.

Ouch. You're serious, which makes it sting.

So is that what you think about me? I want something for nothing?

Will you be there on Thursday?

Where else would I be?

Are you keeping an open mind?

She snaps a picture of the papers and highlighters and laptop that fill the king-size bed and sends it to him. *I'll be ready.*

Good girl.

I need D&C confirmation. The waiting is destroying me.

I can't make them do what they're not prepared to do.

What can you do?

I can bring you to New York.

And do what? Work for you?

Yes

That's impossible. You know it.

YOU can do anything you want. Bring your son. Hire help. Start over with real momentum. Trust me, I know all about starting over.

You know what I want.

What about what I want?

You have everything you want.

What do you have against NYC? A door-

man and grocery store and laundry in the building.

I have zero interest in moving to NY. We want to be here.

Where do YOU want to be?

Phoebe pulls a long silver hair from her scalp. *Okay. Fine. Let's play. I'll play along: three bedrooms on the Upper East Side, somewhere in the nineties, somewhere near you.*

For all three of you?

Two. Me and son.

Serious?

Sure.

Because I am. It's yours. But he can't come. That doesn't work.

For who?

For me.

That's what it's all about: what works for JW.

Don't be young.

West Side is fine too ;)

Tell me the thought hasn't crossed your mind: you and your beautiful boy in a sunny place in the sky overlooking the city. A whole new life.

Stop. Game's over.

That's the offer.

D&C weighs in. Then I'll choose.

See me Thursday.

A long gap passes between messages.

Phoebe turns off the lights. The pale glow is the laptop. She's pacing the dark room, relieved that Nick isn't home, that she can get on the phone if she needs to without sneaking out back or to the car. That she can have this out with JW right now.

So you're going to make me ask.

About?

Laguna Beach. The house. I gave you the agent's #

Didn't get it.

I texted it to you.

No. You didn't get the house. The room shrinks. She falls back against the wall, hard, slides to the floor. Her mind races back to the day she saw it, the messages they exchanged, the urgency and certainty she felt: That house was hers and the start of something. Now there is no house. She rips the comforter from the bed, sending the laptop and highlighters tumbling, stuffs the down blanket in her mouth, and screams. It was pivotal. That yellow house and that view for her son. There are pieces that must come together for this to work, and bedtime stories for Jackson in that room with that quality of light are essential.

There are other houses. Gorgeous sunsets in Manhattan too ;)

The emptiness becomes nausea. *How did*

you not? What did you offer?

It was gone. Got sidetracked with shitstorm called too late.

The view from the second bedroom. That was Jackson's view.

There are other views.

She knows the bottle in her Coach bag is still a third full, at least two or three days of Klonopin, maybe less if she keeps going at her current pace, consuming far too many far too often. The tingling is the blood in the veins near the surface of her skin, from her shoulders to her forearms to her fingertips. The thought of the medication released into her system makes her shiver. She scraped the concrete divider on the 110 yesterday, a sunny morning, orange sparks and horns sounding, and righted herself and kept going, drifting, high.

He messages her again: *No word from D&C?*

I just told you I'm still waiting. Why are you asking me that? Have you heard something?

How long has it been?

Phoebe massages her temples, lowers her head between her knees, and squeezes it, eyes open wide, locked on the iPhone screen and JW's questions. They've moved from the yellow house she won't be in, the view Jackson won't have, to the job itself, the company, the new life out here, what feels, rationally or not, like a last grasp at something. He's asking her, she thinks. Why is *he* asking *her*? It's his connection. He's the one who should be *telling* her. Like he did before. *I hear good things* or *Someone made quite an impression* or *You're golden.*

You're scaring me.

He responds: *No word.*

Call for me? Call De Bent? Find out?

Would look weak. Let it work itself out.

She taps out the message: *Oh well. There are other positions.* She's shaking.

Indeed

She asks the question: *Out here or only back east? The other options.*

See me Thursday. Make time. We'll discuss.

Just like there are other views.

She taps out messages as if she doesn't care either way. But they both know the truth — that she's dangling from the frayed cable that holds the elevator car in her nightmares, about to snap.

His response: *Always. Maybe it's time to cast a wider net.*

You mean NYC with you or nothing?

No response.

Hello? Is this it?

You're making your big move?

She continues to launch messages rapid-fire, one after the last, not giving him a moment to process or respond.

Forcing my hand.

You or nothing. Right?

This is your endgame.

Nothing. Another barrage:

Everything on your terms.

As if I won't stand up to you?

No one pushes you back, do they?

I call your bluff. You're thinking I have zero leverage. What can I do to you? How can meek little Phoebe touch the mighty JW? I'm going to send you a song. Listen to it closely.

She finds the track, the one she plays on repeat when she idles in traffic or can't force herself to get off the goddamn StairMaster at Equinox.

He ignores the track, "Heads Will Roll," the title offering a clue, a juvenile empty threat.

His response: *See you Thursday ;)*

63

Sean and two other men lounge in the shade of Nick's patio. One of the men stands near a mound of green sludge; Phoebe removed it from the bottom of the nearly empty pool he's pissing in. Nick drained most of the water but didn't get it all, and the water turned green, then congealed. Phoebe started the job of removing what might be toxic sludge but gave up after a few minutes. So there's just the small festering mound poolside.

Nick stands shirtless, sweating, in the kitchen, clutching the Mossberg. It's noon. It's as hot inside as it is outside. The power has been out since last night. The reason, according to Kostya, is the wildfires: They are only four percent contained. Evacuations have been ordered for Serenos and surrounding cities. Sean and his men are uninvited guests.

"Hey, guys," Nick says, slides the patio

door closed behind him. Sean passes a joint to the man sitting next to him. The man urinating turns his head. "Grab you a beer or something, Sean? You should have called. I'd have thrown something on the grill."

The men study the Mossberg.

"You know you have to clean these constantly?" Nick puts the gun front and center, holds it up with both hands, blows into the empty chamber.

Sean stands.

"This fucker next door," Nick says, and passes Sean, who is unshaven and smells like weed. Nick walks toward the fence separating his yard from his neighbor's. "Burning shit. Singing to himself. What if he feels like it's time to hop the fence?" He turns around, addresses Sean. "You know the drill. We have the family. We can't take any chances." He pumps the Mossberg for emphasis.

Sean reaches for the joint from his sweaty friend, takes a long drag. The urinating man has zipped and rejoined the other two. None of them moves. Sean exhales slowly, clears his throat. A chainsaw echoes from somewhere. Distant sounds of a helicopter. And the cicadas seem louder than ever. Nick knows it's lunchtime. Mai's routine with Jackson: She wakes Jackson after an hour nap, prepares his lunch, and wheels him outside in the high chair unless it's too hot. Nick knows it's too hot. It has to be. But still, she might very well slide the patio door open and come outside singing quietly to Jackson and step into the middle of this.

"You want to hit this?" Sean asks Nick.

Nick just looks at him. "Get to it," he says.

"The houses, asshole. They're mine now."

"They're yours."

The response seems to catch Sean off guard. He nods. Maybe he thought Nick would push back, seek some angle, keep a piece for himself. Sean is likely wondering what else he can snatch.

"Cash, I don't have. Spent it on this place and the pool your boy just pissed in." Nick turns to the urinator, who looks stoned out of his mind.

Sean flicks the joint into the pool.

"I'll text the addresses to you," Nick says, trying to wrap this up.

"I need the keys."

The patio door slides open. Mai is singing to Jackson. The men eye them both. Mai apologizes and looks at Nick, who quickly hides the gun behind his back.

"We're walking out now," Nick says to Mai, and motions the men toward the side yard, where Nick pushes the wooden gate open for them. In the street Sean laughs at something one of the other men says. Nick leaves them, finds the keys to nine properties in his dresser drawer, each with a piece of masking tape and the address scrawled in red, returns to Sean. "This shit wasn't necessary."

"Did I get what I came for?"

Nick watches them climb onto their motorcycles but isn't satisfied watching from a distance, so he approaches Sean, who straddles his bike, no helmet. Nick notices Sean's black cowboy boots with sterling tips. He's inches away. Sean's face is all deep pores and creases.

"Are we done?" Nick says.

Sean belches. "Who's to say? What do I know?" And the engine rips through the smoke-tinged air. They're gone. Nick waits until they leave Carousel Court before crossing the street, knocking on Metzger's door, and, when he opens it, handing him the Mossberg.

"You sure?" Metzger asks.

"Before someone gets killed."

64

She's in Jackson's room again, trying to sleep, when she hears the front door slamming shut, the alarm being set, Nick clearing his throat. The realization is this: All she has is Jackson. She wants Jackson but wonders if she needs him. She won't go back to Boston. She doesn't need to reconnect with people she knew. Instead she stands at the window, listening for Nick, watching for coyotes, ready this time, she thinks, to take them head-on. She'll shoot them from the window with Marina's gun. She'll walk outside and stand in the street and wait. They'll appear out of the shadows and mist, and she'll pick them off one by one.

If she does leave, she thinks, she'll do so without warning or goodbye. Otherwise Nick will fight it. He's angry these days. He has an edge and a toughness to him that she's never seen. If she didn't despise him, she might find it attractive. Regardless, if she tries to take Jackson with her, he'll come after her. He could open Jackson's door right now, and she might strike him without warning. She'll brush past him in the doorway and their shoulders will collide and she'll turn and knock the cocky smirk from his unshaven face. Shadows appear just out of range from the orange streetlight. The coyotes, she thinks, but doesn't wait to find out.

Nick is coming upstairs.

She walks to the door and locks it.

She can hear him in the hallway. He stops at Jackson's door, keeps going. Then he's talking to Blackjack. He's telling the dog it's time to go outside and do his thing. Blackjack was eating the green sludge Phoebe shoveled from the bottom of the pool. She needs to remind Nick.

The fourth pill she swallows sticks in her throat. She coughs and throws her head back and massages her larynx, takes another sip of wine. The thin sheen of perspiration is ever present now, a reaction to the meds, too many and too often. In her half-sleep she sees distorted images from recent days: the silhouettes of men lurking in the backyard, Kostya's dogs or coyotes in the living room. Nick on the wall, hung upside down and laughing at her. She can't focus for more than a moment on the papers in front of her, materials for the job, the career, the new track. It doesn't add up, none of it makes sense. And Jackson won't stop crying. It's the middle of the night and she's standing over his crib and she's shaking him, shushing him, pleading with him to stop, and the harder she shakes him, the louder he gets until everything goes quiet and his body goes limp and his head is deadweight and his arms and legs are rubber and when she wakes from the nightmare she's still next to her son's crib and he's still breathing, sleeping peacefully, dreaming.

She taps out a message to Nick: *I won't be home tomorrow.*

Neither will I.

You have to be. Jackson.

What about him?

You confirmed with Mai?

No

Then stay home with him or call her. Either way. I won't be here.

You're missing the point Phoebe: WE won't be here. Jackson and I.

Fine

We're leaving.

Fine

For good.

Fuck you.

Bye bye

Leave. That's fine.

I know. It is.

You take him anywhere though and there will be hell to pay.

You'd do that to him, wouldn't you? Put him in the middle of us. Use him like that.

If you take him I will follow you and take him back.

Unlike me, you have no money to fight this. I can afford the fight. You're unemployed and broke and some kind of addict. Good luck.

Minutes later she hears it: Nick is screaming. It happens so fast. She's downstairs and for some reason had picked up Jackson, carried him with her. The other sound she hears is sickening, a yelping that she's sure is the dog.

Nick is in the dark kitchen. Outside in the half-light from the one working floodlight, she sees what Nick does: misshapen shadows that move furiously, low to the ground.

Nick pounds the sliding glass door with a closed fist. She's sure the glass will shatter.

"What is it?" Phoebe is calling out, pleading.

Nick screams the dog's name as a question: Blackjack. He yells that he doesn't know. He cries out the dog's name again, this time with certainty. He slides the door open and they all hear it: savage and guttural sounds punctuated by a single piercing cry.

"Blackjack!" Phoebe cries out. She wraps Jackson in her arms, covers his eyes, rushes from the kitchen to the living room and back to the kitchen island.

Nick freezes in the open doorway. Slams the door closed. Pounds it again. The black head of the dog is slammed hard against the lighted edge of the patio nearest Nick. Phoebe can see the whites of the eyes and something pink and wet hanging from the throat, ripped out. She turns away as though struck by a blunt object. When she looks back, the eyes are black, shut. The animal is dragged back into the darkness. It's over.

65

There's nothing for Nick to bury. Just blood and clumps of fur and flesh to scrub clean from the concrete, which he does the next morning before Jackson is awake. They never got around to buying the dog a name tag, just a generic blue collar and a short leash. Nick drops both in the trash can that neither he nor Phoebe has bothered to bring in from the street since last week's collection. When he sees Kostya and tells him what happened, Kostya grips Nick hard between the shoulder and neck: "Lucky dog. Would have been dead a lot sooner."

He'd have died with dignity, Nick thinks. Instead he died with us.

66

White lights are strung from eucalyptus and short palms that line the long wide driveway leading to the hotel entrance. A handsome valet opens the door of the white Subaru and takes Phoebe's keys. It's Thursday, the middle of November, and still hot.

"Keep it nearby," she says playfully, willing herself through this part of it, the arrival she dreaded in Nick's dirty Subaru, and squeezes the young man's hand. The floral pattern at the center of her white cotton sundress draws eyes down, away from her gaunt face, the recent breakout on her chin, her puffy eyes, and the shitty car. She hears people talking about the fires. An elderly couple braces themselves against the wind. Someone shrieks and there's laughter and a fedora tumbles past. *Heads will roll:* The lyrics play in her mind and force a grin as the glass door to the hotel lobby is held open for her.

"Jesus," JW says when he sees her. He stands and they embrace and his fingers are cold against her back from the drink he held when she walked in. He steps back and touches the stone in her necklace. "Jade. I love this." Then he looks up. "Your eyes are ridiculous. Every time I wonder whether the shine is off . . ."

Phoebe sips from a glass placed in front of her. It's vodka. A young Asian man plays blues on a black grand piano. Behind it, a sweeping wall-mounted photographic montage of a celebrity in black and white. The woman in the display is familiar, but Phoebe can't place her: She's sequentially raging, pouting, laughing wildly, running, stumbling, and finally, in the last of six images, looking directly at the camera, at Phoebe, perfectly composed, all self-confidence and cool. Phoebe grips her glass too hard. She imagines hurling it at the wall.

"Where's my watch?" he asks.

"In a thousand pieces." She explains that Nick tossed it out the window of the car.

"He found it?"

"I wore it."

"Awesome."

JW slides a set of keys across the glass table in her direction. They slide to the edge, dangle just so. She stares at them.

They're silver and look new, with no key chain, simply a generic metal loop. Then, like Nick so many months ago the night of her thirtieth birthday in Boston, JW produces a laptop and turns the screen in her direction. It shows an apartment building called Post Toscana on East Eighty-Ninth Street in New York. Two bedrooms. Roof deck, residence club, twenty-four-hour doorman, fitness center, children's playroom, pool, spa, floor-to-ceiling windows, marble bath, hardwood floors.

"Pet-friendly," says JW, "so get a new dog."

"Are there views? I want Jackson to have a view."

"Thirty-third floor."

"I can't afford it."

"You don't even know the terms yet."

"Of what? What is this? Enough bullshit."

"Okay," he says. He reaches for his drink, pulls his hand back before touching the glass. "This is my final offer. The only offer. The only way I can do this and live with myself." He takes the drink this time, leaning forward in the leather chair, and stirs it with an index finger, stares at her.

"What about here? D&C. It's perfect."

"Those calls you made — maybe not the best idea."

She's brushing the jade stone in her necklace with her thumb. "I wasn't getting an answer from you. Or them. It's called being aggressive."

"Pressing a little too hard."

"If I were a man —"

"That's not it. There's a professional way to handle things."

"Who did you talk to? De Bent?"

"You'll be fine."

"What did he say?"

"It has no bearing on what I have in mind."

"Two calls is not a reason."

"It wasn't the calls."

"What, then?"

"Gorgeous. You are especially fuckable like this."

"Yes or no?" She massages the back of her neck and closes her eyes. "Yes or no?" She draws her words out. Her eyes remain closed. Then she opens her eyes and slaps the table with two open hands. "Answer me!"

A few heads turn toward their table; the pianist is between pieces.

JW's gaze is piercing, his voice drops. "It's done. D&C isn't happening. I'm sorry."

"They told you this."

"It's not the best fit."

"For me? It's fine for me."

"For anyone."

Her voice rises. "Because I made two calls?"

"Let's finish this upstairs."

"So you can fuck me again?"

"I want what I want, Phoebe."

"I mean, why not. That seems to be the arrangement here." There's a pause. She exhales and rubs her eyes, which are dry and itchy. She's talking under her breath, more to herself now. The nausea is a wave, her insides clenched, hands and feet tingle.

"Breathe, Phoebe. Get a hold of yourself. Hear me out."

The soft hum is the sound of Phoebe calming herself until the nausea passes. "Okay," she manages. "New York. New York, right."

"Okay?"

"Okay," she says, reaches for her water glass, takes a drink.

"You know one of the hardest things to do in life, the further on you get? Having the courage to give yourself a clean shot at happiness again."

"That's what this is?" she says. "My last chance at happiness?" She leans back in her chair. The pianist is gone. How long ago did he stop playing? The room is nearly empty. "I should go."

"Manhattan," he says. "A career. You and Jackson."

"Don't say his name like you know him."

"Your son will resent you for the rest of his life if you raise him in a toxic marriage."

"You'd know."

"I do. And he will respect you and learn from you when you empower yourself. Seizing opportunity and having the courage to make the toughest decisions."

"Deny him his father."

"You work it out. You both get him. Just not under the same roof."

"He'll follow us," she says.

"He can't live in the apartment. That's the only condition."

"Here we go. Do you have your own set of keys? Am I on call? The suite at the Regency again?"

"Nothing is irrevocable. Give yourself a chance. A break."

"And when he shows up?"

"Work it out. Just not together. I'm not staking your marriage. I want you in my life, untethered. No more messiness."

"Take it or leave it?"

"You get a safety net. A career track. Connections. A chance to prove yourself. Your MBA paid for by the firm. Nothing you don't deserve and won't earn. But you get no favors when you're there. The work has to be done and done well."

"I can't."

"There are no other options, Phoebe. Nothing at this level. Not now, not ever."

"When he comes?" she asks. "When Nick shows up. Which he will."

"He can live wherever he wants. Just not with you. Not in the place I put you. That doesn't work."

"Me and Jackson. That's it."

There's a long pause. JW finishes his drink. He extends his arm and holds a flat hand out over the table.

Phoebe stares at it. "What?"

"Your learning curve," he says. "That's my only real concern."

"It shouldn't be."

"The whole Laguna house thing. The rent on top of your underwater mortgage? On top of child care and a car? How did you plan to pay for it all?"

"Slowly," she says.

"You need to show some savvy. At this stage in your life, in this line of work. You're not a kid anymore. The stakes are different, and the expectations are here." He moves his hand a foot higher than it was over the table. "You're not playing for bathrobes anymore." He won't look away from her. "The hours are brutal. They don't care about you. Do you produce? That's it. That's all that matters."

"Like before," she says, and regrets the words as soon as they leave her mouth.

"No," he says. "Nothing like before. Unless you want to come in at a junior level or take on something administrative, but that trajectory is flat, with a low ceiling. Nothing about this will be like before. And you saying that gives me pause. More so even than your housing instincts."

"Enough," she snaps. "Don't lecture me. I am interested and am quite confident I can make it work or I wouldn't consider it."

"So you'll consider it."

"Do you want me or not?"

"Always have."

"Then enough with all the bluster. I know what I can handle and I know what's expected. It's a pretty big move and it's all a bit sudden." She fingers the shiny new keys. In her mind, she's holding Jackson in one arm, turning the key, and pushing open the heavy door of their new home for the first time. A week? Sooner?

"Come upstairs?"

She declines. He doesn't push, which reinforces what she's already feeling: that

JW is serious and nothing about this is frivolous.

"Tomorrow, then," he says.

"Sure."

"I've got a little place. Come with an answer."

"Not here?"

"Better. Charming. Rustic." He raises his eyebrows and smiles softly, and she feels the tension leave her body as she watches him get up and leave the lounge, checking his iPhone, not looking back over his shoulder.

She drives, slower than usual, the windows up. The car is silent so she can focus. The logistics and details of what is available to her come at her like so many reflectors on the freeway: day care, nannies, hours, travel, furniture, views, hardwood floors and plush throw rugs and Jackson's toys everywhere and she won't care when they're tucked away in their own little world thirty-three floors up in the sky, just the two of them, mother and son. And Nick: no more Nick. She's at the beach and walking barefoot across the cool sand until she feels the spray from crashing surf against her bare legs. She clutches the shiny keys in her right hand, could throw them into the black water. A particularly strong wave pushes her back, redirects her attention. When she looks inland, the sky is clear enough to make out the distinct orange glow from uncontained fires that won't be her problem, or a threat to Jackson, in a week or less because her mind is made up, the decision made.

67

The next morning. Nothing has changed. Phoebe's still leaving. She's moving to New York with Jackson. She's taking the position that JW is offering, the apartment he found for her. She's sitting upright on the bed. The house is quiet. Nick is outside in the front yard, spraying it with green dye. Metzger is talking to him. Kostya's black pickup truck approaches and slows to a stop and the three men talk and something is handed to Nick by Marina, who is riding shotgun. It's a Tupperware container. She must be asking about Phoebe, because Nick motions toward the bedroom window where Phoebe stands; she disappears before they can see her.

Phoebe looks at her phone: It's almost noon. She got home at two A.M. and was awake until five, online, reading about day care and pre-K and nanny shares on the Upper East Side of Manhattan. She drew up a budget on printer paper. A few extra Klonopins and she must have blacked out at some point, because at six she woke up on the back patio, wrapped in a white sheet on the chaise longue, only feet from the faded bloodstains Nick tried to scrub away. What woke her was the cicada crawling up the side of her neck.

This morning there's no message from JW. No follow-up to the instructions he sent her last night for meeting him tomorrow, the game he wanted to play: *Rent a car, follow my directions, meet me at the little shop off the beach near Malibu.* She pushed back, told him to stop. This was her life, not some inconsequential thing. He wrote: *Of course, gorgeous, but the car rental is obvious. How else do you plan to get to me? Doesn't your husband need the car? Do you want me to pick you up?*

She sends a message, says good morning, asks what happens after she arrives at the shop by the ocean. There is no response. She considers: What if JW left, went back to New York without her answer? What if she packs, books a flight, shows up in Manhattan with Jackson and the keys to the apartment on East Eighty-Ninth Street and lets herself in? What if, by the time JW calls her back or returns the text, she's already there, filling her refrigerator with kiwi and mango and organic kale and almond milk, waiting for the cable company and scheduling nanny interviews? He can't say no. She'll be there. She wonders if she can leave tomorrow. Tonight? A red-eye to JFK. Don't think. Just go. Now.

Jackson isn't in his room or downstairs. When Nick comes inside, he carries the Tupperware and his hands are green. He says nothing to her as he passes. He walks to the kitchen.

"Where's Jackson?"

He doesn't respond. He's washing his hands at the clean sink, all the dishes loaded into the dishwasher. She asks again. He opens the container, picks out a strawberry, pops it in his mouth.

"Where is he? Is he with Mai?"

He tries to leave the room. She grabs his arm. He knocks her hand away. She slaps his neck. He raises a fist. "Fuck! You!" he roars.

"It's my fault," she says. "All of it."

He shakes his head. He's sweaty and red. He walks away.

She follows him. "I know that," she says. "I own it. I have to live with it. Whatever happens, I realize is because of me and all of my exceptionally unreasonable expectations and conditions."

Nick stops, pivots. "Set by who?" he says. He struggles to pull his sweat-soaked T-shirt over his head. "You set them. For me. And what did you do? Drove a car full of pills around Boston? That's the ambition you're referring to? The expectations that weren't met?" The wet shirt is wrapped around his right fist and he punches the wall, four times in rapid succession. The last blow causes the wall to give way. The hole is surprisingly clean, the wall hollowed out, nothing behind the eggshell plaster surface.

Nick stands over the laptop, scrolls through email messages, double-clicking, scanning, deleting. He's refusing to engage on her terms, at her pace. Her urgency for resolution doesn't match his. She needs his full attention, and instead he put a hole through the wall. For what? To scare her? Intimidate her? At this point?

"You lost respect for me," he says. "I get that."

"I did," she says.

"At least we're being honest with each other."

"We are," she says.

"So I did fuck that girl." Nick closes the laptop. "And I may want to keep fucking her. I don't know what my point is other than to say since it's all on the table, we may as well see it through. What else?"

"I don't respect you as much as I need to," she says.

"Well, you can't stay married to someone you don't respect."

"And I don't expect you to," she says. She moves closer to him, at his face.

"Move away," he says.

"I am."

"Now. Step away now, before it gets bad."

She doesn't move.

"Ugly stuff," he says. "Move."

She takes a couple of small, careful steps back, grips the back of the dining room chair.

"For his sake. You and I can't go forward together," he says. "His dad can't be a punk. Some used-up taken-advantage-of little bitch."

"I know."

"You need to leave," he says, his voice rising again.

"I am."

Nick passes her, the chair between them. She tenses. He continues upstairs. "Now," he says coolly. Phoebe waits, exhales when she hears the bedroom door close and lock.

She should leave. She should take the

Subaru and go. But that doesn't make sense. She has to pack, plan. She has to get Jackson and check flights. She should follow JW's instructions and call Enterprise and meet him and lock this down. She can do it all now, not stop until she's airborne, heading back east with her son.

He's napping. That's what Mai tells her when she calls. Jackson just went down. Phoebe doesn't ask Mai to wake him. She needs everything to be as normal as possible until they're boarding the flight, if that's what it comes to, if she takes it that far. There is a JetBlue flight to JFK that departs Los Angeles at 10:50 P.M. She messages JW.

Think we're flying out tonight. Unless I hear otherwise from you. No point in waiting, right?

There's no response. She wants confirmation from JW that doing something rash, impulsive, is actually okay. If he's serious about the offer, and she has the keys to the apartment, why not now? What difference does it make when she gets there?

She walks quietly upstairs. The bedroom door is still closed. She goes into Jackson's room. She closes and locks the door. The clothes in his blue dresser are folded. She dumps them out. She's on her knees, carefully refolding Jackson's clothes, placing them in her own red suitcase.

The room, she realizes, is immaculate. Freshly cleaned. Mai must have done it. Nick brought her back last week despite Phoebe's insistence that she needed no help because she was free now, her days were hers again. Nick didn't trust her. He dumped a Whole Foods bag full of empty prescription vials on the kitchen island to make his point. She was out of control and needed help. "Nothing fatal," he said in a cool, detached tone as she scooped bottles up from the floor. "Just tidy up the frayed edges. Get off the meds. Get some rest. No shame in asking for help. We've all been there." His nonchalance and complete lack of condescension actually set her off. As though he was so far beyond the need for intervention that he could handle her crisis with the poise and maturity of someone whose life was in order. And she did kind of overreact, she recalls: throwing glasses, silverware, the casserole dish that was a wedding gift from Nick's aunt. She stood poised with the black crowbar that Nick kept under the kitchen sink, just in case. Held it over her head, ready to bring it down on something, on him. And he walked away from the fight. To her surprise, she let him.

■ ■ ■ ■

Standing in the hushed carpeted hallway, she hears Nick showering. She hears the television he's turned on in the bedroom. She hears him clear his throat and spit. He'll be ten minutes under the hot water, always too long in the shower, always too hot. The room will be choked with steam and he'll open the door and it'll pour out and he'll emerge with a towel around his waist and check his phone while the moisture and sweat dry under the ceiling fan. Then he'll collapse on the bed and close his eyes and lie motionless. She knows his patterns and routines. She knows how worn out he is. She can't recall the last time she heard him laugh. And there's no more adventure for her but her son.

He's startled to find her in the bedroom. She picked the lock with a screwdriver.

"You look tired. You should rest," she says.

He ignores her, walks naked, no towel, past her sitting upright at the foot of their unmade bed. "Believe me when I say you should leave."

"You haven't calmed down yet?"

He starts to hum.

"Want some?" She produces a small sterling silver pillbox, the head of a jaguar, that she knows Nick has never seen because she bought it on Etsy last week. It's filled with little yellow tablets, a few pink.

He applies lotion and deodorant and pulls on boxer briefs and walks to his side of the bed and sets the alarm on his iPhone. Phoebe starts to say something, but he cuts her off, looking down at his iPhone while he speaks. "Did I tell you the good news?"

"No."

"I got an offer," he says. "I accepted an offer. Salary, benefits, no more nights."

"Doing what?"

"Management."

"With who? The same people?"

"It's stable and they like me."

"If that's what you want," she says.

"I'll be earning more and working less. Jackson can have Mai until *next* fall and then Serenos Montessori." He slaps the dresser with an open hand for emphasis. "With or without you, babe. We'll be fine. I know that's not nearly enough for you: getting by, making ends meet. That doesn't cut it. But you know what? Jackson's going to be fine. He's going to thrive. Because of what I do."

"Your utter lack of imagination and ambition."

"Jackson is thriving," Nick says. "He can *swim.* He's not even three and he's keeping himself afloat. That is only because we came here, found Mai, made that happen."

"You're not hearing me at all."

"I can't shut you up."

"Don't you get tired of yourself?" she says. "The manic running around. Aren't you sick of yourself yet?"

"If I could fuck my way to prosperity."

"Avoid it. Keep avoiding."

"I'm salaried now. I did what I had to do."

"Congratulations."

"Answer this for me: When do *you* make something happen? Aside from nearly killing our son last year, when does Phoebe Maguire do something of consequence in this world?"

"We set completely unreasonable expectations for each other."

"I didn't."

"There was no way. That's my fault."

"This is poisoned. We're toxic."

She stands at the doorway. She trembles when she hears herself say it: "You can have him." Her voice cracks. Silence.

Nick says nothing. He stands at the window overlooking Carousel Court. Deserted.

The orange tent. The dim orange hue. Another dry windy night.

"For now," she adds haltingly. "Until I'm settled."

"Once you go," he says, and turns around to say more.

She's gone.

68

Nick is home alone with Jackson, who is sleeping while Nick is drinking and texting Mallory. It's not going well.

You don't think very highly of me do you?

Idk

I love being a father.

I don't care. Just stop dude.

There's more going on you know. It's not just me being a pig. You know? There are other factors. You don't believe me. How old are you?

Why are you doing this?

Respond.

Stop texting me.

No.

No?

Answer the question.

You've sent me an INSANE amount of messages.

Answer the question. Tell me how old you are.

A few minutes pass. She doesn't respond. *You can't even comprehend how complicated it becomes.*

After another five minutes and no response: *And you can fuck yourself you little whore. Ignore me. Who the fuck are you? I know where you live.*

The message that arrives minutes later is from Mallory's number, but the language isn't hers. *Bad move, dude. We know where YOU live and what time your viet nanny shows up and leaves.*

A JPEG arrives next. The image is Nick's own lewd picture he sent to Mallory. Another arrives: Phoebe and Jackson in the Explorer in the driveway, Metzger's orange tent clearly visible.

The last message: *We know where YOU live.*

He sends a text apologizing. He calls and gets voicemail. He leaves no message. He texts again. He asks her to stop. He explains that he's drunk and there's so much going on in his life right now and he's not in a good place and to please disregard his stupidity.

Finally, a photo in response: scrawled in red Sharpie on a piece of cardboard, their address on Carousel Court.

Nick walks upstairs, glances at Jackson,

who clutches a stuffed black dog in his crib. Nick stands at the window, pulls back the curtain. The street below is empty. Metzger's tent is dark. Nick listens, watches for what's coming.

69

When Phoebe returns, Nick and Jackson are asleep. She drove to the beach and sat on the pier and watched teenagers smoke weed and board the Ferris wheel and win cheap prizes. She considered the water, slipped off her sandals, and placed one foot on the railing. It was cool, like the wind off the ocean. If they'd just lived here, she thought. Instead she looked inland and saw the orange glow along the edge of the horizon, hillsides burning, and the Ferris wheel was turning and shimmering and the pounding surf was speaking to her. It's midnight when she gets home. She undresses and drinks wine on the patio under a white sheet. The message that chimes is from JW at last and is in the form of an email, not a text. There is no note or comment in the body of it, only a single word in the subject line: *Thoughts?*

Phoebe reads the first few lines. It's a joke.

It's a job description cut and pasted from Monster.com: *Brand ambassador (55k) Saks Fifth Avenue*

Phoebe stops reading after the section that reads: *The Brand Ambassador is responsible for driving their business and creating their own success.*

She sends a text message: *haha*

He responds: *Thoughts?*

About what?

The position.

What position?

I know it's not remotely connected to what we've discussed but I think it's all I can do for you now. My situation is in flux, turned upside down and back again. Will explain.

Who is this? Who are you trying to reach? JW, this is Phoebe. You're messaging the wrong person.

I know who I'm messaging, Pheebs.

You're fucking with me and I don't know why? :)

It's Saks. I figured you'd enjoy the perks. HUGE employee discounts ;)

How drunk are you?

Sadly sober.

Saks in NYC? That's a job you think would suit me.

Greenwich, CT.

You're not serious so will ignore this.

It's pressure-free. Easy living.

Who did you really mean to send the email to? One of your other girls?

I've figured something out.

What IS this really?

Will discuss. Maybe a bad idea. Maybe just stupidity.

You offered me something. Are you rescinding it?

Forget it. Shouldn't have sent. Some chaos in my world none of which has anything to do with you.

It very well does have to do with me if — fucking SAKS?!

It'll all be fine.

She taps out *Fuck you* and deletes it. She taps out *You fucking dick.* She taps out more crude terms and deletes them all.

Cicadas are falling from the trees into four feet of green sludge in the pool. The air is all smoke and burns her lungs. Phoebe wonders how long it takes to drown. Could she fall face-first into the pool and stay under until she passes out? She wonders if Nick would dive in after her. For the first time since she's known him, she's unsure of the answer. He might very well let her drown.

There is no D&C for Phoebe. She called

again. She reached the same sympathetic administrative assistant who knew her by voice. There was no conversation to arrange with De Bent. He wouldn't take or return her calls. She'd made five. Today was the sixth and last. The admin confirmed: The position she'd interviewed for had been filled. There was nothing for her at D&C. And there was no Laguna house. There was an apartment in New York City that was either available or not. If the position JW emailed her about, at Saks Fifth Avenue in Greenwich, Connecticut, is the offer, there is no path forward, no quick fix. There is the here and now: the thick smoke, the suicidal cicadas, and a life further from anything she ever imagined for herself than she can take.

Phoebe stands in the wind on the edge of the pool, arms by her sides, cicadas and debris swirling around her. If she raised her arms and held them aloft, she might look like something out of Revelation.

70

From under a white sheet next to Jackson's crib, Phoebe watches the rotating blades of the ceiling fan until she's too dizzy to keep her eyes open. This is how she starts the day.

She's talking sleepily to him. She sings his name quietly as she sits up. She turns to him when he doesn't respond. The crib is empty.

The note Nick left on the kitchen island reads: *He's at Mai's.*

She has the day to herself. The house feels bigger, emptier, than when they first arrived. She checks her phone. There are no messages from JW, though she wasn't expecting any. She considers it, decides not to text or call him. There are no messages from crude physicians or her district manager because she no longer works there. She stands alone at the kitchen island. The curtains and blinds are open. Harsh sunlight pours through. She walks from window to window, closing each set of blinds, pulling all the curtains closed until the house is dark. Everything shakes in the winds. The loose bedroom window rattles, the trees bend in it. Over the hum of the central air is the sound of her own breathing. She feels as empty and still as the house itself.

71

Nick says "No thank you" when the man in the orange apron behind the register offers him a Home Depot account. He moves through stores like IKEA and Bed Bath & Beyond with purpose. He arranges deliveries and pays in advance for assembly. He registers and interviews and submits background check information to the agency. He is granted access to the website and surveys profiles, sends emails and has conversations with four women, arranges successive meetings at Starbucks with two of them, and chooses one.

The woman, Jackson's new nanny, leaves the Starbucks and Nick finishes entering her contact information into his iPhone. She can start in a week. He sets reminders and deletes items from a list. He sends a text message to Phoebe: *How is he?*

Her response is immediate. *Fine.*

When do you leave?

Stop Nick

It's NYC, right, that's where you're following him to? Quite the trail you're blazing. A real example for our son. There's a term for what you do, what you've been doing for years.

Stop.

Whoring. Piece by piece you've whored yourself out.

Not true.

I need another day or two. Can you wait that long? Before the wind pisses you away?

Fuck you

Glad he's with Mai and not you. Just called her. He'll spend the night there.

Not necessary.

Actually, I'm coming home. I'll be there soon.

And then?

Then you're free. Gone. Go.

So you'll stay?

Only when you leave.

You're being ridiculous.

I don't know how I missed it. All the signals. From the start.

Don't blame yourself.

I was young and stupid. I was insecure Was?

That's it. I needed affirmation and you were good at that. That's a skill you've lost for sure. But you always managed to pump me up. That's your con. That's why they keep you around. The pharmas and the JWs. That's my wife. The corporate fluffer. Fuck me. How did I miss that?

Don't come home.

Stop me.

Changed the locks.

Bullshit.

Will call police if you try to break in.

Shoot me.

An hour later, he forwards her the picture Arik sent from Mallory's phone: Nick and Phoebe's address on Carousel Court, scrawled on cardboard.

Some assholes might pay a visit. Blame me if they do. They may show up looking like this. Shoot them instead.

He attaches an image of a white latex mask.

72

It's almost noon. She is supposed to meet JW at a country store in Malibu. From her rental car, she calls Mai.

"Is he awake?" He is. "Can I say hello to him?"

Jackson says, "Hi, Mommy! Froggy looking at me," about a frog in a small koi pond Mai has in their backyard.

"I'll see you very, very soon, precious, okay?"

The little shop off the beach is closing early because of the fires. A man stands on the roof, douses it with water from a hose. The store is nearly empty and smells like pine. The floor creaks beneath Phoebe's sandals. The tan bohemian woman behind the counter wears a crochet top and jean shorts and is watching local news coverage of the fires. Phoebe hears the rushed urgent tones of the two other customers; they're escaping to Santa Barbara.

Phoebe picks out a twelve-dollar pastel sea-glass key chain for the keys to the Manhattan apartment. The woman behind the counter gives her a sympathetic look, her gaze falling to the torn collar of Phoebe's stained white cotton dress. Phoebe's sunglasses fall from the top of her head when she reaches for the credit card that was declined. She hands the woman a ten-dollar bill, and as she's reaching into her bag to search for more cash, the woman says, "That's fine."

Phoebe awaits word from JW, the only reason she's here. His condition for seeing him. He likes the game. He sent her instructions: *Rent a car. Directions: Take the 110 West, then PCH to Malibu, the little shop at the first exit past the 76 station, text me when you're there.*

From the front seat of the car, she dangles the apartment keys and new key chain from freshly manicured fingernails. She snaps the image and sends it. The response is immediate: *Those aren't real. The keys.*

?

I was making a point. Closing a deal.

Of course, she writes back.

She didn't know. Of course she thought the keys were real. A set of three silver keys to the heavy oak door that opened up to her thirty-third-floor three-bedroom with a glimpse of Central Park and rooftop deck and the fresh start. A golden opportunity, a leg up, a clean break that, if she didn't fully deserve, she would surely earn.

If I'm in NYC tomorrow, where can I get a real set of keys?

See you soon.

She buries her feet in the cold wet sand of the beach. The spray off the ocean is foamy and has a polluted pink tinge, wraps itself around her as the tide moves in. She closes her eyes. The surf is pounding. Her head throbs from no sleep. Gray and white gulls idle in strong gusts off the water, cry out. She won't move until he calls.

"Where are you?" JW's voice is rushed.

"Where you told me to be."

"Stay put. Almost there." He's driving. Phoebe can barely hear his voice over the wind.

"Then where?"

"You'll see."

"Why this secrecy?"

"It's a surprise." Everything goes quiet. She waits a beat, wonders if he dropped the call. He clears his throat.

"I want to go tonight. I can fly to New

York tonight."

There's no response.

The black BMW that arrives an hour later is his and the only other car aside from hers in the gravel lot. He doesn't get out; the windows are tinted. The message on her phone is from him: *Follow me.*

The main house is ranch-style, midcentury, and lies beyond a massive stone archway. It's deserted. JW says, "I have keys," dangles a set of two brass keys in front of Phoebe, who refuses to get out of her car. A helicopter, the third she's seen, passes low overhead. They park in a deserted circular gravel lot. JW slings a leather bag over his shoulder and grabs a *Financial Times* and his iPad, sets the alarm of the car, and approaches Phoebe, who sits in the idling rental car, still gripping the wheel, the air-conditioning blasting. He motions for her to come, follows a cobblestone path leading down a dry ivy-covered hillside, dotted with eucalyptus and short palms, which becomes dirt until they reach the guest cabin: yellow, small, but neat and clean.

The air-conditioning has been turned off and the place is only a white king-size bed, a low whiskey-colored leather sofa and matching armchair, and a white plush throw rug. Candles are everywhere and JW immediately turns on the thermostat and the cool air is instantaneous and flows through black metal teeth in the hardwood floor. On the wall over the bed, Phoebe sees them: three bronze men ascending braided iron ropes. They're nude, muscular, and determined.

"Bruschetta," JW says, standing over a mini refrigerator. "Brie, pinot, Pellegrino, roasted cashews." Then he makes a sound of deep satisfaction. "She didn't. She did. God love her." He produces a silver tray of oysters. The note he reads is from the proprietor of the bed-and-breakfast: " 'Fresh today from Water Grill, per your request.' " He hands the rice-paper note to Phoebe. What he didn't read: *Be safe!* Phoebe assumes it's a reference to the fires.

"Sit," he says. "Open wide." He holds a shell to her mouth. It requires every ounce of will not to slap it from his hand. The grip of her interlaced fingers is too tight. She offers a tight smile, keeps her mouth closed, shakes her head.

"More for me," he says, and slurps the oyster, spilling some on his chin, wiping it with the back of his hand. "I'm not some kind of monster. I know you're ascribing all sorts of motivations to what must seem like schizophrenic plotting and replotting."

She watches. He won't stop moving, checking out the room, pulling back the sheer white curtains, rechecking the thermostat. "And I know you're here for some clarity, and we'll figure it out. As we always have." He ducks through a narrow doorway that must be the bathroom, then dips back out. "Oh, Jesus, I am wrecked," he announces as he stretches, and when his arms extend, the hem of his oxford rises to reveal some extra weight around the middle. "Eat, eat. Come on." He's walking back to the silver oyster tray.

She grabs his left forearm and squeezes. "How do these assholes do it?"

Their eyes lock. His are bloodshot and tired, the creases in his forehead pronounced, his stubble more gray than brown.

"I used to ask you," she says. "How all the young assholes who worked for you could afford million-dollar homes before they turned twenty-nine."

He pulls his arm from her grip. If this were New York, the suite at the Regency Hotel, or even his office in Boston, he'd hang on to her hand, play with her fingers. Instead he moves to the bed, sucks down a third oyster — eyes closed, head back, two big swallows — then wipes his chin.

"A leg up," she says.

He stares at her. Finally focuses exclusively on her: Phoebe Maguire, thirty-two years old, from Claymont, Delaware, via Boston via Carousel Court in Serenos, California. She is, according to the person in the world who knows her best, a broke, unemployed whore. She is a mother failing her child. She is a wife who quit on her husband. She broke every promise, explicit and implied. Tonight she believes it all.

JW's eyes are glassy and his gaze is distant, his mind somewhere else, not on her. He snaps out of it. "You're wasting away." He sits up. "There's nothing to you." The musculature is gone from her shoulders and neck. She knows this because the straps of this dress, which held it in place once, don't any longer. "Co-signing some rental house in Laguna before you even have an offer? Serious letdown, Phoebe. I'd hoped you'd come further."

Her laugh at this moment is unnerving. She stops at the window looking down the canyon and places her open hand on the glass. It's hot. She knows something now that she didn't before she followed him through the door: There are only a few places she should be, and this remote cabin with JW is not one of them. She's needed at home. Jackson. Not here with JW, her benefactor for eight years, who lost more money in the last year than she'll earn in a lifetime. She remembers that night in Boston six years ago, what he said he saw in her, the reason he would give her the leg up. He stares blankly at her when he looks up from his tablet, and it's the emptiness of his look that ignites the flash of fury she can barely contain.

"So what did you do with it? The money I invested in you," he says.

"The most responsible investment you can make," she says flatly. "The house."

He shakes his head, points a remote control toward the television, clicks on local news coverage of the fires. "That was the play." She'd wired it to Nick's account last year, when they decided on the cabana and the landscaping upgrades, the rock-climbing wall, the hourglass pool.

Nick asked and she told him: The money was from her dead aunt.

She stares at aerial shots of a single home that lies in the path of the advancing fires. The camera zooms in on the deserted house: massive, white, with acres of land and a pool and children's toys scattered across the dry turf.

"Fucking Saks?" she says.

"Bad idea," he says. "Horrible. The worst." Their eyes lock. "What is it with me? I do these things . . ." He trails off. "Have — something," he says, and glances at her knees. He could slide his hands between them in this instant, and she's not convinced she wouldn't let him. "You're so skinny."

"Saks," she repeats. "The offer." Her eyes are trained on his loafers. "I'm ready now. The apartment, I can make it work."

"Believe me when I tell you," he says. "Let it go. The whole Saks thing. That was me being a dick. I was playing with you. I was certainly not in the best shape when I did."

"Just let me get there. Let me get settled and figure it out as we go."

"Things are a mess for me right now."

Phoebe leans back on the sofa. Her arms are folded over her chest as tightly as her legs are crossed. The four Klonopins she swallowed on the way here are kicking in, but her stomach is empty and the nausea starts. She speaks in order to hear her own voice, hoping to move through the disorientation. She is here, meeting him, for a reason that seemed sound at one point but not now.

• •

He's up from the bed, turns the television off. He unbuttons and removes his shirt. His body is less taut than before but more tan. The faded blue T-shirt he pulls from his bag looks new and clean when he pulls it over his head. Written across the chest in bold white letters: *Why Always Me?* "A consolation prize from my divorce lawyer," he says about the shirt.

He falls to the sofa, throws his feet up on the coffee table, knocks a glass votive candleholder to the floor. It lands with a thud. Phoebe instinctively reaches for it. JW's eyes close and he rubs his face with two hands. Heavier than it looks, the thick glass rectangle is larger than her hand, is chipped, and has sharp corners. She rests the glass thing on the table, stares through it, her fingerprints clouding it. An inexplicable urge to clean it overwhelms her. She leans forward, reaches for it.

"So I will say this, Phoebe." His voice rises, startles her. "Something isn't sitting well with me. It's not your imagination."

She looks away from the candleholder to him, leans back on the sofa, and adjusts herself. The sudden tingling in her spine sharpens, needles her as he speaks.

"The whole house thing in Laguna," he says, then stops. "What were you thinking?

Asking me for that? For help, to what, co-sign, put you and your family in a house?"

She speaks quietly, her voice even, if not soft. She knows something now: Decisions have been made by JW, avenues forward cut off, including the last one, which may never have been real — a clean break and a fresh start for her and Jackson in New York. "You gave me the keys to an apartment in Manhattan," she says. "You can't complain about me asking for some help renting a house."

"I'm not saying it's logical or makes sense."

"It isn't. It doesn't."

He's still got his legs on the table, bare feet crossed, twitching. She watches his big toes; his nails are yellowing and need to be trimmed. One is all black, dried blood. Maybe from hockey, she thinks. Maybe from sailing or riding or stubbing it against the base of the new Caruso acrylic Japanese soaking air tub he sent her a picture of in September, an invitation.

"It's a gut thing," he says.

"Do you mind?" she says, and in one motion pushes his feet from the table.

The move startles him. He sits up, laughs a bit. "Yes," he says. "I do mind." He returns his feet to the table. Their eyes meet. "It's the dynamic. You asking instead of me offering. It's one thing when you're starting out and I can cut you a check. Give you a leg up. I get that. I loved doing that. And I was actually happy to do it again, when you reached out and asked me to come 'save' you out here. Okay, I thought. I've been there. You do what you must when you're up against it." He removes his feet from the table and leans forward, massages his knees as he speaks. "But this whole business of asking me to call some Orange County Realtor?" He's shaking his head. The disdain is genuine.

She blinks, rapidly. She processes his words and his body language, and she's no longer as cool as she thought. He's no longer questioning or even criticizing, she thinks. He's exposing her.

"Of course you're not moving to New York for a retail job at Saks. That was juvenile, sending that. Besides, how could you afford the rent?"

"I thought —"

"That I'd pay for you to live there? I knew that's what you were assuming. First month, maybe. But come on."

She swallows. Her throat is dry.

"I was a little pissed," he says. "Even disappointed. I have to be honest with you: That really turned me off."

"One call." Her voice is halting and she hates herself in the moment, not for what she did, the call she made to JW about the house, the play she made, asking too much, but for her voice cracking. She clears her throat. "A single call doesn't —"

"Hear me out, Phoebe. And promise me" — he stands and walks toward his overnight bag on the bed, his back to her — "that you won't blame yourself." He's removing items, clothing, toiletries. He's unpacking. "You're actually not the only reason this isn't happening."

• •

She was okay with it, or she thought she was, seconds ago. Of course the move, leaving Nick, was unreasonable, and flying tonight ludicrous. But hearing it confirmed that the last of JW's offers is off the table, no Manhattan apartments or consulting careers or clean starts with hardwood floors and a French-speaking nanny for Jackson. Of course the 10:50 P.M. flight will leave without her.

Phoebe is checking her iPhone, walking around the cabin, the hardwood creaking under her feet.

JW watches her run her fingers lightly

across the cool bronze backs of the muscular naked climbing men. Three little Nicks, she thinks. Nickels, she thinks. But there's nothing funny. The ropes the bronze men hang from are nooses.

He suggests a moratorium on contact.

"After tonight," she says.

"Of course. Then let's lock in some clarity to our relationship, as it were."

"As it were," she echoes, mocking him.

He says they can always be together, that it can be fun like it was.

"Like it was," she repeats.

"The favors. Just stop asking." He studies her as if assessing. "You're better than that. You're not twenty-six anymore." She pauses at the doorway to the bathroom. His hand hovers over his abdomen, slides under the waistband of his pants. "Smartest girl in the room," he adds.

She slips into the bathroom. She spills some pink and yellow pills from her bottle into her hand and throws them back, swallows them down.

When she returns, she hears him say the divorce is taking forever. He complains about financial disclosures and settlements and the financial hits he's taking, and then Phoebe's calling asking for him to co-sign on a rental property. "And I'm looking forward to hearing your voice —"

"And?"

"— during the shitstorm raining down on me, and it's you, but you're not asking how I am or when I'll be out here so we can be together. You're asking me for more."

She's nodding, hearing him out.

He's back to the call she made to him, its impact and how it threw him off and surprised him and how the extent of their totally unanticipated negotiations and the totality of her unseemly pushback and angling and neediness kept him from sleeping that whole night. Is there something wrong with him, he thought, some vulnerability she senses, some weakness all the women in his life see and try to exploit? "I mean, do you understand the nuance in what I'm spelling out here?"

She laughs. He doesn't smile. He's taking it too far, taking it out on her. She needs to leave. The nausea is a thick taut rope pulled through her gut. She closes her eyes as she considers the heat pushing in from outside and is unsure she can remain standing when it occurs to her: She wants to go home.

"God knows you work hard and have expertise in your field, and there's no shortage of effort. You were so good in Boston. Industrious." He gestures, implies a ceiling with his free hand, the one not idling in his pants. She's just not cut out for it, financial advisory work. The hard-core quantitative skills. The cognitive abilities. He's being honest now, and he's grateful that she's willing to listen, to hear him out. A lot of people couldn't sit for a real outside assessment, especially from someone they care about.

"By the way," he says, "I will not accept that this somehow ends today. I want us to continue when you're ready." He brings a leg up, crosses it over his raised knee. "I love us."

"You were assessing my ceiling."

"I value what we have."

She examines one of the climbing men on the wall: The rope is this thick hard metallic thing, sharp at the end. She turns toward him. He waits a beat, until their gazes are locked, then casually unbuttons and unzips his pants. "God, I want you right now."

"That's fine," she says, fading. "We all have our roles."

"Bringing you to New York to do a job I think could overwhelm you? That's not fair to you."

The wall feels cool against her bare shoulder as she leans against it, fingers the sharp point of the broken bronze rope.

"You know where I think you went

wrong?"

"Tell me," she says.

"The extra mile. The leg up. You didn't see it through. It almost feels like a failed investment. I loathe failed investments."

"You're right." Her voice is distant, and she's considering all the investments she made to get to this point. She's suddenly not here, no longer in this room. He's not sitting up in front of her, beckoning her to the bed. She's not putting the bronze man down.

"Come lie with me."

"I let people down," she says, echoing his words as statements of fact. Her throat catches a little less than the last time, though the words pose questions she can't answer.

"You're the one you let down."

"I let myself down," she says. "I did." Shapes in the room blur as if submerged in dirty water. The bedside lamp merges with JW's blue T-shirt, and the question it's asking is no longer legible. Blinking does nothing. (She says the words aloud to herself: *go home.*) When she doesn't move, it only intensifies her disorientation. Her body isn't responding to her mind. What is home now? Not *where* but *what* is it anymore?

"You are home," he says.

She reaches for her bag, the pink and yellow pills that will turn the haze into vapors. No more disappointments or disappointing. Simply rest. Finally. This is the vague new goal that's forming. She knocks the bag from the table and his voice is sharper, louder: "At a certain point, if there isn't that voice coming from somewhere deep inside you, directed at yourself, screaming, *This is intolerable,* demanding that you do something, take control, then to hell with it, why even bother?"

"Shh," she says, but not to JW.

"You never seemed the type, Phoebe. I worked under the assumption that there was always another play for you, some move you'd make."

"You don't think so anymore."

"You're predictable. You did what was expected when you called me about that rental house. When you made calls to D&C. When you told me you could fly to New York that night, just like that."

"I see" is all she manages. She draws her fingertip lightly along the smudged surface of the votive candleholder, delicate precise lines through her own fingerprints. She writes her own words, her last response: *I see.*

What she sees are ropes and climbing men

no longer ascending but holding on, straining, muscles burning, fatigued, their final trembling moments. She sees how small they look over JW.

"You should sit. You don't look so hot. Better yet, come here."

"My neighbor gave me this pink gun," she says. "I've never fired a gun."

"Do you want to shoot someone?"

With each glimpse of the bronze men, she sees not Nick's faded promise but her own.

"Lie down with me."

She goes to him and, without hesitation, swings the heavy glass votive candleholder, connects with his temple. He recoils and curses, but his voice, or the way she hears it, becomes something else, softens. She sees her father and Nick and so many men on that wall and the bloated giant on the king-size bed is laughing at her, at all of them. She's nowhere. A million miles from the little brick twin in Delaware, the abandoned drive-in theater, her first and only fight as a child. The last time she hit someone until she met Nick. She swings again. He blocks her. She may be swinging again, but she's not sure. He is holding her by the jaw, squeezing hard. His fingers sink into her dry skin. She stops. All at once she deflates. She laughs.

"Oh shit," she says to herself. "Come here," she says, still with her eyes closed. She pulls him close, wraps her free hand around the back of his bleeding head.

"What the fuck, Phoebe?" He pulls her hand from his head and it's red with his blood. "You're so fucked."

He tries to pull her down, but she resists and he falls instead. She says she's leaving. He's mumbling, holding his head with both hands. The blood streaks down the back of his neck. It's worse than he knows. She stares at the exposed beams of the ceiling. She hears him breathing. He's asleep. She closes her eyes and listens to the winds and the debris pelt the walls and roof and feels the earth move beneath her as her eyes close and she falls into darkness.

She wakes with a start. A door slammed or something rocked the house. Her mouth is dry and the room is blackness. She feels around the bed for her cell phone, a habitual tendency to check for messages from JW. But he's here, next to her, facedown on the bed. There are no messages from JW. No invitations or promises of new careers or apartments for Phoebe. This is her life, awake in the darkest hour of night next to a man who is not her husband, unsure where she'll go next, fires bearing down.

The breeze washing over her is too warm. The window is open or broken. The wind is the heat from outside. The dress she wore last night remains on, though she can't find her shoes. She tries to recall what they did and can't. She finds her phone. It's 1:13 A.M.

She pushes the door open. The heat and wind are a black storm she's braving barefoot, up the cobblestone path to her car. Only when she starts to drive and descend the narrow two-lane road deep into the canyon does she realize she has no idea how she got here, where she is, or how long it will take to find her way home.

73

She's been knocking on Mai's front door because her calls have gone straight to voicemail and she's not going in the house tonight without Jackson. She's not living another day without her son.

She is apologetic to Mai's husband when the door opens. "Can I get him?"

She is told to wait. The door closes. Phoebe knocks again, and this time when the door opens, it is Mai and she's holding Jackson, who is asleep with a pacifier in his mouth. Phoebe reaches for her son. Mai hesitates. She asks Phoebe if she knows what time it is.

Phoebe apologizes, but Mai still refuses to hand Jackson over. "May I?" Phoebe says. There is no movement. "Is there a problem?"

Mai suggests tomorrow may be better. She says Jackson is better off sleeping through the night at her house. She says she'll bring him over first thing.

"Is this Nick? Did Nick tell you to do this?" Phoebe flushes. "It's time for him to come home." She grabs Jackson, pulls him from Mai's arms, and the blanket he was wrapped in falls to the ground, but Phoebe is walking across the lawn and not looking back.

Only after laying him down in his crib and turning on the bathroom light does Phoebe see the handprint on her face from JW, the smeared lipstick and mascara, the tangled hair, a tragic clown of a mother.

74

Morning comes with a blast of white light. Jackson is standing up in his crib. Phoebe is facedown on his floor, wearing last night's dress. She can open only one eye, a migraine splintering her skull.

She reaches for and opens her small black bag, digs out the sterling jaguar head. Jackson was jumping up and down, saying her name, but has stopped now, watching her hand, wondering what's in it.

She wraps her hand around it, tells herself not today, she can handle one day with nothing in her system.

Mai is gone. Phoebe calls her cell and gets voicemail, so she calls the house and is told by Mai's husband that Mai is in Houston for two weeks, left this morning.

She messages Nick. *You didn't tell me Mai was leaving.*

Nick is contacting Phoebe or responding

to her texts only when it has to do with Jackson.

How is he?

Why didn't you tell me? What if I have things to fucking do?

Is he okay?

When will you be here?

Soon.

Today?

Nick?

Oh fuck you.

The eggs are cold and the juice is warm. The coffee she brews is too watery. She dumps it and tries again. The milk is expired. The whole refrigerator is rotten. Jackson is crying. He's hungry and wet, the show she put him in front of ended, and he's staring at previews for upcoming movies available on demand.

She heats up the eggs and changes his Pull-Up and she's thinking about money. She has none. She has the rental car, which she can't pay for but needs if she's going to leave, go anywhere. But where can she go? She's home.

She has three bottles of sauvignon blanc in the house and allows herself one full glass from the first bottle. The kitchen island is clear and clean. She stares at her cell phone. It's midnight. She sends Nick messages and finishes her wine and pours a second glass. She asks him to be honest: Did he ever really think they would survive this marriage? She adds, *You couldn't handle it. You weren't mature enough, Nick, to process the shit people go through to get somewhere.*

Her fourth full glass finishes the first bottle.

I'm not claiming purity. You're justified in leaving and not coming back. It's not as though I didn't give you reasons. I GET that. But you kept coming back. You tried and tried and no, Nick, you weren't the only one trying.

When she's sitting outside on the patio, she lights a cigarette and finishes her first glass from the second bottle.

Did I hold you back? Is that what you think? I think we held each other back. I think you underestimated yourself and I overestimated me and us and it's just shitty to feel that way but it's real.

She walks to the edge of the pool.

Will you fucking respond?

The wind shifts and the stench rises from the floor of the pool.

How do you even calculate whether Jackson will be better off with us together or apart? Would he learn a better lesson seeing us fight for something instead of quitting? What kind of lesson is that? How damaging is that?

His response comes, finally, when she's on her back, dizzy, next to Jackson's crib.

The point you're missing, Phoebe, is that the decision is made. And the answer is obvious: no, he's not better off as it is or has been. He's better off now. Now that this is over.

75

The floodlights are out. Phoebe borrows a ladder from Kostya. Jackson sits in his high chair eating Cheerios in white sunglasses and a floppy hat. She should wait until later in the day, when it's not so hot and bright, but she's bored and has been awake since five this morning and has the bulbs and Kostya needs his ladder back. Only when she is near the top does she feel it bend. She can see Kostya's backyard from the top, and the batting cage and pool, and the kids are throwing firecrackers into the wind. The bulb in her hand is too large and the one she tries to unscrew is rusted to the socket and she's squeezing it too hard and it explodes in her hand and white residue and glass shards drift to the ground and Jackson. When she looks down again, the bright white of Jackson's hat blurs with the garden hose and concrete. She sways, steadies herself, and the ladder shifts at its base and she plants an open hand on the side of the house and is frozen there, cursing Nick over and over.

The lights don't come on outside when she flicks the switch. She doesn't know whether it's the bulb or a short. But it's after nine and Jackson is still awake, waiting for stories, and the only light outside the house is the single patio bulb.

Jackson is restless and she tells herself it's all the noise from the wind or because he's overtired, but as she makes small circles on his back, she knows he senses what's happening — his father is gone.

There's four hundred dollars between her checking and savings accounts. Her mother calls back. Phoebe lets it go to voicemail. Her mother tells her she always knew Nick was a prick. She says Phoebe should take him to court. She says that her new boyfriend is ten years younger and is taking her to Atlantic City for the weekend. In the message, she asks Phoebe if there are any numbers she wants her to put money on at the roulette table. Phoebe doesn't call her back.

76

She can't sleep, and according to her phone, it's 2:29 A.M. She opens the blinds in Jackson's room and sees Metzger's orange tent, dark inside, and the trash spread out over Carousel Court is hers, the plastic bins on their sides from the wind or coyotes or Kostya's dogs. She pulls the string, slows Jackson's ceiling fan. She refills his humidifier and closes his bedroom door until it clicks. Her closet is a mess. She pulls dirty clothes from the floor and the hooks and throws them on the bed until the pile tips and spills. The black box is from Dolce & Gabbana. She removes the pink gun, cold and heavy in her hand, and gently flicks at the base of the handle, tries to remove the chamber. She checks the safety switch and turns it off and then on again. She slaps the base and feels it unlock. The chamber slides out easily. She holds the smooth steel thing and studies it. She marvels at the tip of each bullet as she empties the chamber into her palm. In the glow from the face of her cell phone, she reads the word *Winchester* and *40 S&W* as she rolls the cold copper thing between her thumb and forefinger. She places the single bullet in the empty chamber and slaps the chamber back into the butt of the gun, where it clicks. She cocks it. She releases the safety. She closes her eyes and exhales but can't manage a deep breath. The cracks in her skull are real. The spiderwebs of shattered bone are the nerve endings crying out for chemicals. She's wincing from the pain. She holds her head in her hands and rocks on the bed until she falls back on the pile of dirty clothes. The gun is in her hand. The disease is in her head, scraping the paper-thin layer of bone and scalp until it escapes. She'll blast it back in with overwhelming force. She screams so loud and long that her throat burns and she's no longer on the bed when she finishes. She's slumped on the floor with her head between her knees. She wakes Jackson. She hears him crying out for her. She lifts him carefully, clutches him tightly to her chest, managing to keep the nose of the gun, which she holds by her side, toward the ground as she shushes her son.

77

"I changed my mind," she says when she calls her mother. Her mother asks about what. Phoebe pauses, watches a cicada bouncing wildly against the inside of the wineglass, struggling. Phoebe trapped it on the kitchen island and hasn't decided what to do with it. Her mother says her name, her tone nurturing and filling Phoebe with nostalgia. She wants to be lying on her mother's bed, watching her mother's hands massage her thin little-girl feet. She wants to feel her mother's fingertips massaging her scalp, warm hands breaking an egg over her head until she's somewhere safe. She drops the call and turns off her phone. There is nothing anyone can say to her now. The cicada is frozen. Its swollen red eyes see nothing.

"Look at it." She holds Jackson in her arms. All the lights are on in the kitchen and living room. The cicada remains trapped, buzzing loudly. Jackson is confused, sleepy, unable to process the details: upside-down wineglass, cicada, his mother's voice with an unnerving edge to it. All he likely knows is that it's not time to be awake. "Isn't it amazing?"

Phoebe turns music on, hers and not Jackson's, so the vibe is off, too loud and rough for the hour, for any hour with Jackson. She turns the television on and props Jackson up in a small throne of throw pillows on the sectional. She puts on a cartoon, but she's unable to focus on any one task longer than a minute, her heart racing, and she's reacting to the meds because she took too much too fast, and she drank too much wine and gulped the last of it to empty the glass she used to trap the cicada.

She opens the refrigerator. She'll scramble eggs. The container is empty except for one egg. She can't scramble one egg. That's not enough for him. Is he even hungry? "Are you hungry?" she calls out. He doesn't respond. One egg is not enough. She reaches for it and curses herself. She grabs a bowl and a fork and cracks the egg, but it's a mess, with too many bits of eggshell in it, and she's trying to focus, to pick the little white bits of shell from the yellow, and she hears a thud and Jackson cries out. In one motion she whips the bowl of egg across the granite island and shatters the wineglass and bowl and the sticky shards of yolk and shell coat the cool kitchen floor. A burst of heat surges from her abdomen. She rushes to the patio door, slides it open, staggers outside, breathing away the nausea.

Back inside, she hears his cries, which are somehow simultaneously muffled and piercing. Jackson's head is wedged between the two disconnected pieces of the sectional Nick promised to reconnect but never did. He's bawling. Snot and tears cover his face. The television volume is too loud and so is the music she's playing, and they blend together and it's some form of sleep deprivation torture for her son and she's the veiled monster holding the blade to his neck.

Only when they're lying together, lights dimmed, television off, music turned nearly all the way down, does she relax her grip on Jackson. He's finally sleeping. Her eyes are heavy. The cicada buzzes from perch to perch, dining room table to the top of the television screen to the rock-climbing wall, where her gaze locates it on a red rock near the top. She studies it, doubts its existence, questions whether she's really seeing it, whether it's there at all, until her eyes give out, lids close, and blackness comes.

78

The house glows like a monstrous Japanese lantern. A Ford Escort is parked haphazardly in the driveway. Metzger's tent and house and all the others are dark. Nick scoops up plastic bottles and trash and stands up the trash bin, wheels it to the side of the house.

She didn't change the locks. He eases the front door open and it catches on the pile of mail in the foyer. The lights are all on, as is the television, and there is music coming from the Bose box, which has been moved to the dining room table. There are pillows on the floor and papers spread across the desk and coffee table. A warm draft is coming from somewhere. Nick finds Phoebe curled under a white sheet on the sectional with Jackson's stuffed black dog, a bottle of wine, and her iPhone and a bag of potato chips at her feet. A series of numbers, dollar signs, phone numbers, and names are scrawled in red marker on construction paper. She has written Nick's cell, social security number, and birthday along with his middle name. She drew a picture of Jackson inside a giant sun.

Nick is at the foot of the stairs when he notices: The sliding door that leads from the kitchen to the patio and pool is open. The warm air is coming from outside. The noise he hears when he reaches the door is Jackson, some high-pitched blend of laughter and surprise.

Nick rushes outside, calls his son's name in the darkness. In the glow from the dirty pool lights, he sees his son's silhouette. Jackson is on the opposite side of the pool, inches from the deep drop into the thick sludge. When Nick reaches him, Jackson is poking something with his little finger. It's a cicada, trapped and squirming, buzzing loudly, working to free itself from a deep poolside crack.

Inside, with his son watching him from the bedroom floor, Nick empties all of Jackson's clothes from his drawers into a small suitcase. Downstairs, Nick stops at the living room sectional, picks up Jackson's stuffed black dog, and says nothing to Phoebe before they leave.

79

The arched front door of the house on Juniper Street is thick white oak with a wrought-iron knocker. The greenery that surrounds the cottage is lush from the steady cool breeze off the ocean. The house is a foreclosure in Redondo. It took them forty minutes to get here through light traffic. Nick signed a six-month lease with Bank of the West just after Halloween. Jackson is asleep and doesn't see the glistening white lights Nick strung up on the short palms and eucalyptus trees that line the sidewalk and the front of the house. Jackson doesn't see the soft orange recessed light inside or the yellow leather Formula One race-car bed Nick claimed from a miniature mansion during an initial assessment in Calabasas (two days after Phoebe left and didn't return home for three nights). He doesn't see the billowing sheer curtain or smell the cool fragrant wind or the fresh sky-blue paint on the walls. He opens his eyes only when Nick draws the blanket over him. He asks if he can have a story. Nick says it's late, but then he picks up *Harry the Dirty Dog* from the nightstand, and before he turns the second page, Jackson is sleeping again.

80

"Where is he?"

"With his nanny."

"Mai's in Houston," she snaps.

"His new nanny."

"I'd like to know where my son is."

"He's with me."

"And where are you?" she presses.

"Gone."

"You're not taking him from me."

Nick is thumbing through the countless images of his son stored on his iPhone until he finds the picture he's looking for: Mallory. "You're asking where *he* was last night? I'll tell you where the hell he was —"

"I'm not letting you take him."

"— when you were passed out at one o'clock in the morning —"

"You won't get him. You'll never get him. I will never let you have him."

"— our son was on the verge of falling into the goddamn pool!"

81

If she could sleep in Jackson's crib without breaking it or feeling insane, she would. Instead she curls up next to it as she has in the past, since they arrived here, and pretends he's in it. She hums a couple of the songs she used to sing to him and keeps one arm raised, her fingers between the smooth wooden slats.

"Where are you?"

"It doesn't matter," Nick says.

"I'm going to find you."

"I doubt it."

"Come home," she says after a long pause.

"You're high," Nick says. "I can hear it."

"Bring him home."

"Are you scared now? Now that you realize how unnecessary you are?"

"Nothing scares me," she says.

"You know what I just realized? You're alone. In that house on Carousel Court. No husband. No son. No dog."

"I'm fine."

"No benefactor. No one," he says.

"I'm just getting started. I don't need a thing."

"You don't even have a job. You're neck-deep."

"I'll find you," she says.

"Do him a favor: Keep your distance."

"He needs his mother."

"He has what he needs."

82

The pounding is the front door. The chiming is the doorbell. The noise is simultaneous, and when she sits up, she hears it: laughter. She peers out the window and sees five vehicles: an SUV, three motorcycles, and a Nissan Maxima. She calls 911. She's put on hold. The house shakes from whatever bursts through the front door and lands on the floor downstairs. Seconds later it reaches her: a putrid egglike stench, and she sees the thick blue haze of smoke when she moves through Jackson's doorway to the hall. From the top of the stairs Phoebe sees the white masks: three, four? The head of a sledgehammer comes down on the coffee table, splitting and splintering the oak.

"Moving day!" a voice announces from under one mask.

From the top of the stairs, she rushes the men. Four of them. "No. No," she's saying, her voice rising. "No!" She's cursing and pushing and hears laughter. She kicks and she's pushed and she staggers back, collides hard with the head of the banister. She screams and charges again and swings wildly until a gloved hand grips her neck, tosses her aside, flips her over the sectional.

Another explosion, the sickening cracking sound of the sledgehammers on the living room furniture. Two men stomp upstairs. There is so much noise. Phoebe is covering her ears. The front door. She could walk or crawl to it, leave the house. Furniture is tossed over the winding staircase, crashing on the floor. Jackson's dresser, rocking chair, lamps. Two other men haul the stuff out the front door and toss it on the lawn.

That's when she feels it. The cold metal tip of something pressing into her neck. A thick hand around her mouth. The smells of latex and stale cigarette smoke. The man is breathing through his nose, pressing his mouth to her ear, behind her. He says nothing. The hand drops to her breast, over and then inside her dress.

The sectional is in pieces; foam and springs spill out like guts. A masked man takes a chainsaw to the ottoman, rips through it, pauses only to look at Phoebe and the man with his hands on her, then continues.

The man forces her to the floor. His knee and body weight grind her face into the carpet. She's flipped over and two men pull duct tape forcefully across her mouth. Her arms are ripped behind her back and wrists bound. The house is suddenly hushed.

Two other men watch as the two who have hold of her hoist her to her feet. One of the men has Phoebe by the jaw. She is still. He squeezes too hard. She tries to wrest herself free. Her white sundress is lifted over her underwear, then torn from her body.

She gags. The nausea is a wave. A surge she can't swallow. The vomit has nowhere to go. The tape forces it back down. She's flailing, vomit burning as it passes through her sinuses and out of her nostrils. She kicks violently until a fist lands on the side of her head, which hits the wall, where she collapses.

From the floor, the blur of faint yellow light is the glow from the pool. She tries to sit up. Shadows close in. They drag her through the kitchen, where two more men — she has counted five so far — stop using crowbars to pry loose the granite countertops and watch the other two pick her up and press her too hard against the sliding glass door. One of them slaps her ass. She's nude, cut, and bleeding.

A decision is made. They drag Phoebe from the kitchen, through the smoke, up the stairs. The question that forces its way through the vapors is this: What are you fighting for? The answer is instinctive and comes as they lift her body from the floor: Jackson. At once she is weightless and free.

Someone says, *Enough.* Someone else says, *Go.* She is dropped. She is deadweight. She slides down, awkwardly, along the winding staircase until she comes to a stop against the wall. She is stepped on by one of the men on his way down to join the rest, who convene in the foyer.

She frees her wrists and ankles and moves quickly up the stairs. In the bedroom closet she is reaching for and loading Marina's gun. It feels heavy and cold in her trembling hands, and at the top of the stairs she's lying on her stomach and squeezing the trigger. The earsplitting blasts ring out, and with each round, a shock of white light until there is nothing but a thinning bluish haze of smoke, echoes, and stillness.

The ringing in her ears from the rounds fired and the blows she's taken begins to fade as she moves through the hushed house without thinking, her hands brushing lightly along broken pieces of furniture, the wires jutting out like severed tendons from where the flat-screen hung. She's pulling a loose piece of plaster from the wall where the head of a sledgehammer punched through. Then another piece and another until the hole is gaping. She moves to the kitchen, and the granite is cracked and loose atop the island, so she grips the edges and wrenches it free and the slab crashes to the floor. She opens the refrigerator and freezer doors and, one after the other, top to bottom, rips the shelves out, jars shattering at her feet, and she's still nearly nude except for the underwear, which is torn, and a loose oversize flannel shirt she pulled from the back of an overturned chair. In the half-light from the refrigerator, she sees the floor and the shards of glass, knows that a step in any direction will slit her feet open. She is stuck in the punishing glare of her own nightmare.

The shard of glass she steps on is from a shattered wine bottle, and slices open the heel of her right foot like soft fruit. An artery is punctured, which is why the foot bleeds as much as it does, but after she pulls the glass from her foot, which takes more effort than it should, the shard hooked and catching somehow on flesh, she grabs her keys and phone and the address she finds next to the laptop, which she assumes is where Nick took Jackson, and she leaves a trail of blood from the kitchen, across the living room carpet, to the foyer, where she left the gun. She tells herself the address in her hand is where they have to be. She can't stay here, in this house, alone. The front door swings open wildly and she tries only once to pull it closed behind her but doesn't. The sky is translucent black and feels so low that if she punched the air, it would wrap itself around her fist and pull her through to some other place. The car starts and she wipes the sweaty, sticky hair from her face and drives, outrunning the darkening skies toward something luminous.

83

Nick's feet hang over the edge of Jackson's yellow race-car bed, but it doesn't matter because Nick is curled up around his son as he sleeps. *Blood is red, the sky is blue,* Nick's voice is hushed, *the clouds are high and the heart is full.* Jackson's breathing is easy and Nick's head is heavy, becomes one with the pillow as his voice fades, and the scent of his freshly bathed son is enough to make him dream of bright mornings and full days of laughter and games, stories and tricks and birthday parties, and the two of them making one seamless golden life together.

84

The ranch-style house is dark and sits well back from the street. A soft orange patio light seems brighter than the streetlights on the deserted narrow strip of winding asphalt she's been on for a mile or more. She doesn't see the Subaru in the empty driveway. She idles and grabs the slip of paper Nick wrote on, and checks the number and street name against the numbers painted on the edge of the concrete patio, and they match. The bottom of her right foot is sticky and wet with blood when she touches it. She drove here for many reasons, some of them sound, though now she can remember only one: Jackson. She's here for him. What she does now is for him. She sent Nick a text from a red light on the way here: *He can't have a mother he's ashamed of. I won't do that to him ever.*

She doesn't try the front door. Instead she

walks around to the side, scales the waist-high wrought-iron gate, stumbles to the ground. She stands and follows a stone path to the back, where she can see the soft white glow from the microwave-oven light in the kitchen. She gazes up at the second floor; the bedroom windows are open and dark. It's difficult for her to focus. She's dizzy, so she'll sit for a moment, she tells herself. She'll rest and she'll wait for it to pass. She'll make a plan. There is momentum now. She faced the wind and turned it. She is not some woman trudging listlessly through the vapors. She is the vapors.

She'll pick up a small stone and toss it at the window. She'll do that until a light comes on, because Nick refuses to respond to her messages.

The modest weathered house, temporary as it is for them, seems an ideal place for father and son to ride out the storm. Even now, at their worst, Nick is providing safe harbor for their son, while she is half-dressed and bleeding in the dry grass.

I'm here, she wrote. *I found you. Please let me in. I just want to rest and tomorrow wake up together.*

Her eyelids feel heavy, her eyes burn, and she drops her right hand to the thick dry grass of the backyard and eases her grip on the handle and trigger of the gun. She'll sit and rest. She drifts off to the steady, throbbing rhythm of her sliced-open foot, familiar, like Jackson's heartbeat.

85

The owners found her in the backyard of their pale yellow Craftsman house on Livingston Street in Calabasas. They called the police and reported a woman with a gun, facedown in the grass, motionless and bleeding.

86

Her father watched the motorcycle races Saturday afternoons on the only channel they had out of Rome on a small color set that came with the house. He'd taken Phoebe to a couple of live races since she'd arrived, but the noise from the engines made her cry the first time because they'd stood so close to the serpentine track and she was sure they'd be killed. But the colors, brilliant reds and forest greens, golden yellows and majestic blues, thrilled her, and from her father's muscular shoulders, she was mesmerized by the spectacle.

"How do they keep from tipping over?"

"Practice," he said.

"How fast are they going?"

"Faster than a cheetah," he told her.

"What happens if they crash? Do they die?"

"Depends."

"Che palle!" She grinned when she deliv-

ered the phrase she'd learned on the beach one night, out late alone with friends again. *What balls!*

He didn't react. He never reacted anymore. His time in Sardinia was over. His two-year contract not renewed. It was time to leave. He would return to the States — to Claymont, Delaware — to face his old life: work, Phoebe's mother, debt, and no way back here or anywhere like it.

And Phoebe's adventure, like his, was complete: a two-year vacation with her father at his best.

In the last month she'd followed an eleven-year-old boy named Paolo one night to the beach, where they kissed and shared his cigarette and there was a bonfire and older kids who gave them wine. She routinely stayed out after eleven, even though she was only ten. She didn't worry because she knew her father wouldn't be home, and if he were, he'd have had two bottles already and be passed out.

It hadn't always been like this. She'd watched Tom Petty on a humid day in Philadelphia from his shoulders. He'd grilled chorizos outside for just the two of them and he'd played his records and let her sip his beer. When she was seven and spent ten days in the hospital because her nose wouldn't stop bleeding and her platelets were all screwy and she dreamed of angels visiting her, she'd fall asleep to her father's voice telling her stories and wake up to find him wide awake in the same chair. She asked if her mother had come or planned to, and the response was the same as it had been the night before and the night before that. His expression gave her the answer she expected.

"Why doesn't she see a doctor, too?"

"She's trying, princess."

It had always been the promise of something better that fueled him. He was a young man with energy who knew there was still time to make things happen for himself, to see the world, to "breathe new air," he used to say. And he had been right. The assignment he'd pitched himself for, pursued on and off for years, came in: two years diving for the Merchant Marines in Sardinia. They knew it would end. But the finality and the realization of what lay ahead were deadening: work without adventure or the promise of it.

Most mornings were clear and breezy, and when they were, the two of them rode their bikes together over cracked hillside streets through the bright sunlight, a cooling wind off the ocean. She tried to keep pace. He took turns too fast. He lost her once at a fish market near the docks. Then again at the monastery. She always caught up to his bright red ten-speed. They reached Challenge Hill. He smoked a cigarette and stared off through aviator glasses at short palms and the small village of shops and small cars that lined the streets to the shoreline. She was sweating through her Rolling Stones tank top. She saw her father, head down, cigarette still between his lips, careen down the hillside without her.

She launched herself. Hurtled after him. Wind screamed in her ears. She heard nothing else. She'd catch him. The handlebars shook. She was going too fast. If she stopped, she'd crash. If she kept going, she'd lose control, get hit or hit something. Streetcars and taxis and motorcycles fed the intersection at the bottom. She screamed, but no one heard. He was gone. Turned off, left or right at the bottom, she didn't know. She was doing this for him, but he wasn't here to see it. At the edge of the small park with the fountains and pond, from the corner of her eye, she saw a flash of red, his bike, his hair. She screamed for him. He waved and she heard it, over the wind and her own panicked cries, *"Che palle!"*

All at once a blast of light, sunlight, and she tucked her head low, like the motorcycle racers did, and steadied the handlebars, swerved, and slalomed, then braced herself as the tires hit the cross street at the bottom of Challenge Hill. She was rocked, stood upright by the impact, bounced twice, then steadied herself, tucked again, but loosened her grip and coasted, looking back over her shoulder to see her father closing in, beaming.

• •

When they returned to Delaware, the plan was to try again with her mother. She was better, or so they said. Chemical imbalances were corrected. But her mother couldn't manage to get Phoebe to school on time with regularity or even at all — within four months she'd missed nineteen days — so it was decided that her father would take her. Again.

He was back and living in a redbrick twin in Claymont, waking at six, smoking two cigarettes, wearing his tan pants and white polo shirt and work boots for another ten-hour shift at the Franklin Chemical warehouse, shipping and receiving, safety and oversight. She knew this only because she studied his laminated photo identification, its slick neon-green borders giving it a futuristic flair she couldn't resist. She asked once anyway what he did for a living. Or maybe more than once. But the only instance that Phoebe recalled was the time he answered without hesitation: "I don't do shit for a living."

On Thursday nights he'd come home too late, after ten. He'd have stopped somewhere to drink. He'd collect Phoebe from the neighbor's, where she'd be woken up from the couch and walked home. If it was a really bad night, it would be midnight or later. When he drank too much, she locked her bedroom door, the dresser pushed up against it, because he'd start yelling, and she always hoped he was on the phone, maybe fighting with her mother or his girlfriend, just not himself, because that was the scariest. Work made monsters of men. He became something awful when he returned from Sardinia. Work without promise did horrible things. Ground him into dust. Silenced him. Confined him to dens and garages and dark bars and depression. An unsalvageable appendage. From her bedroom window, she watched her father rage on the patio and was filled with an unexpected calm. There were no good options, no safe harbor. Only the promise of something better, golden, made it bearable. She lay still and awake, became the cool jagged eye of the storm as she sank into the center of her bare mattress and somehow drew strength from the ruin around her.

87

The first few questions they pose here are direct and without nuance or emotion. Legal questions, technicalities, to get a handle on what they're dealing with: Who is Phoebe Maguire? She is a married thirty-two-year-old mother of one. She is unemployed. She is from Boston by way of Claymont, Delaware. She has never been arrested. Her presence facedown in the backyard of a stranger's house with a firearm is the reason she's here. She knows this: She hurt no one, posed no threat. The chamber was empty. The door locked from the outside and the canvas straps they finally removed from her wrists, the bars on the window, are overkill. She peed in a cup. They stuck her with a syringe and took her blood. The larger issues are the ones that require more than the mandatory seventy-two-hour stay.

A woman whose job it is to assess patients

at this stage sits next to her bed, out of arm's reach, asks if Phoebe wanted to hurt someone. When Phoebe doesn't respond, the woman looks over her glasses at her and mentions Nick's name. Then Jason's.

"Jackson," Phoebe corrects her. "This is fucking ridiculous. I went to the wrong address. The wrong house." She's agitated and hasn't slept longer than an hour since they brought her here. She gave them Nick's cell phone number when they asked if there was family they could notify. She had to tell them yes, she had drugs in her system. No, she could not tell them how much, but she could list them all.

What about her? she is asked. Did she want to hurt herself last night? Is she responsible for the cuts on her wrist? She didn't know they were there. She holds up her thin wrist, draws a finger lightly along two dark red slits. "I had a gun. Why would I slit my wrists?"

She is reminded that it was empty.

"Only after I fired it five times."

But why bring the gun to the house? the woman is asking. She doesn't like Phoebe. She resents her, Phoebe thinks. The woman is heavy, and Phoebe can see her alone in an apartment on weekends, watching movies and wondering if she should post another image of her cats on her profile page. Phoebe can picture the woman studying the adoption agency websites. She'll do it only if the kid is white, Phoebe thinks, or Russian.

"Nick and Jackson?" the woman asks. "You weren't going to hurt them?"

"You're taking this far too seriously. I had a rough night."

She is asked to lower her voice. A large man in burgundy scrubs appears in the doorway.

"We got this," Phoebe says, and waves him off. She apologizes and returns to lightly touching the area of her face that feels as though a hammer were brought down on it with full force. The gun, she says, had everything to do with the men dragging her by the hair up the stairs of her house. The ones who ripped the dress from her body. "There's something about near-death experiences that can trigger irrational behavior. Okay? PTSD. Write that in your tablet and let me go the fuck home."

Her levels, she is told, are off the charts. For a woman so slight to have so much in her system and manage to put one foot in front of the other, much less get behind the wheel and drive, is remarkable.

Phoebe brings her hands together, touches

her fingertips to her dry lips. She stares at her toes, the foot wrapped in so much blue, white, and yellow gauze that it looks like some kind of piñata. Her toes move when she wiggles them, but they feel cold or numb, she can't tell the difference. "I feel nothing," she says.

You must feel something, she is told. What about Jason?

"Jackson."

She is asked if it is her intention to drift through her son's childhood feeling nothing. Missing the whole thing.

"I miss nothing."

"You're missing something right now," the social worker says, staring at her pointedly.

Later, when they bring her orange juice she doesn't drink, she asks how long she'll be here. She is reminded that this is a seventy-two-hour mandatory detention. What lies ahead for her is to be determined.

"By who?" she asks. "Nick?"

No answer is given.

The skyline visible through her barred window shimmers through in the twilight. She is twenty-two stories up, alone in a spare, cold room, watching the sun drop from the sky. She is no one's wife or mother. She's a patient surrounded by strangers. She is Room 7B. She is elevated levels and dependency and withdrawal and emotional and psychiatric assessments. She is hungry and malnourished, and as the last light fades and the glint of sunlight off the steel and concrete becomes glistening lights set against a violet haze, she pulls the stitches from the bottom of her swollen left foot, staining the white sheets with blood.

"I want to go home," she says to the woman with the glasses.

She is told that her husband said differently, that she was moving to New York.

"What am I obligated to do after this? After I leave?"

Nothing, she is told.

"So there's nothing required of me?"

In forty-eight hours, she is told, she is free to go.

She wants to watch Jackson wake up. She wants to hear him laugh and wrap him in a soft towel and smell his clean hair after a bath. She wants to go home but doesn't know where or even what that is anymore.

88

Nick stands in the doorway, staring at his wife. Her feet stick out from under a white sheet. A plastic cup and a box of tissues and a small light rest on a bedside table. The room is gray and white with two metal folding chairs and a large window that has been sealed shut. Her eyes are closed, and with her hair pulled back and the sheet under her chin, she looks like a twelve-year-old girl. He saw her like this once before, after the accident in Boston. But now, unlike then, he is the reason.

"Do you want this on?" Nick finally says. A small television bolted to the wall is turned up too loud. She doesn't respond, so he turns it off and she says nothing. "Are you thirsty?"

Nick's eyes move from her feet, one in a white slipper and the other wrapped in gauze, to the handprint around her neck, to the purplish bruise under her right eye, which is swollen. She wears a plastic name tag around her wrist. He reaches first for her hand, then notices the cuts and considers her hair or face, but she's propped up and it would be awkward, so he wraps his hand lightly around her left forearm, which is warm from the sunlight that glances off her waxy-looking skin and white sheets.

Nick explains what he knows about who came to the house and why. None of it seems to come as a surprise to Phoebe. None of it matters.

"I shot at them, Nick. I fired a gun. Inside our house."

The words *inside our house* wash over Nick, somehow release tension from his burning shoulders. Something in the way he hears Phoebe refer to their house feels cathartic.

She was leaving, he suddenly thinks. She was gone. She was leaving their house, their son, behind. He slides forward in his chair, then pushes it back, farther from her bed. "You were going to leave him. You were gone."

She closes her eyes again. She says her head hurts. Nick touches her thigh and she flinches. "Don't," she says.

She's been here for twenty-two hours. The next fifty hours are mandatory because of what they found in her system, the trespassing charges, and driving under the influence. Where she goes from here is an open question.

Nick has her forearm now, and she has her eyes on the grated window.

The next time he speaks, the sun has set behind the skyline, the ocean somewhere just out of sight. Nick wears leather sandals and feels the sand between his toes from the hour he spent with Jackson chasing seagulls on the beach.

"Do you want to see him?" She doesn't move and Nick continues, "He won't know the difference."

Finally, she shakes her head and tells him no.

From the hallway, Nick calls the house and speaks to Jackson. He's in bed and Gloria, the new nanny, has read him three stories. He says he built a castle with these giant multicolored foam blocks Nick bought for him last week.

"And then what?" Nick asks.

Since he brought the blocks home, Nick and Jackson have built and destroyed too many castles to count, so his son knows exactly how to respond to his father's cue.

"Knocked it down!"

89

Nick comes to see her again. It's the second full day. The seventy-two hours are almost over. It's a bright clear morning, and she sees him standing in the doorway with his hands shoved deep in his pockets. He's unshaven and sunburned. She keeps her eyes nearly closed so he'll think she's asleep. She wants to see him as he is in his natural state. Not reacting to her gaze, her glare, her expression of disdain or disappointment.

And what she sees is extraordinary. He looks strong. His arms are thick, and the bright white T-shirt is stretched from a physique he lost and regained since Boston. He's here today for someone else, she thinks. He's passing through. He's full of pity for her, yet somehow he's decent enough to keep it to himself, to wait at least until the bruises fade.

Later, he's still there, sitting on the edge

of a metal chair, his hands wrapped around her foot, watching her. This may be the closest she's felt to him since they left Boston.

90

She sits on the edge of the steel-framed bed, dressed in the clothes Nick brought from home: faded jeans and a white T-shirt and sandals. She asks where Jackson is. She's ready to go. Nick doesn't respond.

"Can we go now?"

Nick says nothing, pulls the folding chair around, sits down, and faces her. He says the decision is hers. She can go home if she wants to go home.

"But you won't be there. Jackson won't be there."

Nick says nothing. The day is clear, the sky crystalline blue. The room is so bright, he draws the curtains closed so they can see each other's eyes without squinting.

"You can't take him from me," she says. "I mean permanently, you can't."

"Yes, I can," he says. "Right now, at least."

"So that's it."

"You have options."

"Apparently not."

"I can take you somewhere."

These are the words that make her eyes close tightly, her head turn in the direction of the grated window, the drawn curtain. Her feet twitch and she pinches her nose between her eyes, her neck and ears bright pink. She's not breathing.

91

The crackling sound was from the beige speaker in Phoebe's third-grade classroom. The voice was familiar and cold, that of the assistant principal, whose only job, it seemed, was to summon delinquents to the office. When "Phoebe Vero" rang out, her insides dropped and every head in the classroom turned and her eyes were wide and she left the hushed room, the gray tile floor seeming to give way beneath her.

She knew her father was taking her back. She hadn't known it would be that day, from school. She'd been with her mother in Cherry Hill for less than a year, and again it wasn't working out.

However, in the office waiting for Phoebe wasn't an unshaven man in yesterday's jeans, but her mother, radiant, holding wildflowers, laughing with the assistant principal. They were smiling for some reason. The assistant principal said something that seemed inappropriate for the moment: "Have fun." Phoebe's mother smelled like she did on Thursday nights, when she would leave for bridge, or the nights when she didn't have to work the next day and left Phoebe with the neighbors. She took Phoebe's hand and led her from the office, out the side door of the redbrick school, and into the parking lot.

It was a bright, cool spring day and Phoebe's mother turned the radio on before answering the question: "I want to spend the day with my daughter. That's why."

The Oldsmobile was clean and her mother smoked a long thin cigarette and, with bright red lipstick and her Coke-bottle sunglasses, looked like someone else entirely. She looked at ease and content and asked Phoebe to choose. There was a play in the city or they could go to the zoo.

Phoebe asked if they could do both.

They ate lunch in the city. Phoebe's mother ordered one martini. She asked Phoebe about summer and if there were camps she wanted to try, or maybe summer club at the school again, and Phoebe drank two Cokes with no ice and said she didn't know, and her mother stared at her for such unusually long stretches that Phoebe thought she'd done something wrong.

They stopped for manicures, and after the play, Phoebe said she wanted to be an actress. Maybe in the summer, her mother said, they could find a theater camp.

The traffic was backed up and they never did make it to the zoo. Her mother was sullen, somewhere else. The radio stayed off. Her mood had shifted.

"I don't want to go home," Phoebe said. She was near tears. "I don't want to go to Dad's." Her mother said Phoebe wasn't happy anywhere.

The next morning would come, which meant Tuesday would be gone, and her mother's lipstick would come off and Phoebe's nail polish would chip, a fading reminder of something rare and elusive. Her mother would work tomorrow and the next day and night and middle shifts and long weekends and she'd wait for the calls and checks that came from Phoebe's father with no regularity and every time after that Tuesday in May when the speaker in her classroom crackled, Phoebe's pulse quickened, though a little less each time until she felt nothing at all.

92

Most of the women here garden; they grow arugula, kale, snow peas. The only woman Phoebe speaks to with any regularity, Lucy, tried and failed at heirloom tomatoes, but her boyfriend bakes hashish into his chocolate chip oatmeal cookies; Phoebe has eaten a couple, gotten sick each time. She feels no need to avoid Lucy, though, or the other women here, because none of them poses a threat to Phoebe's sobriety. They asked her what she had in mind her first morning in the woodworking studio, and she said something comfortable that she could bring home, that provided some utility. Something her husband would appreciate, she said.

The only time she cries is when she sees Jackson. The first time, Nick has him dressed up: little khakis and a white button-down shirt and his light-up sneakers. He keeps slapping the bottom of his shoes to show her, but it's too bright outside on the hillside to see anything. She pulls a tag from the left sleeve of Jackson's shirt, which Nick must have just bought for him. Jackson's fingers grip the back of her neck, and he drops his head and all of his body weight easily against her chest. Nick sits forward, elbows on his knees, hands clasped together, fingers at his mouth. Phoebe wears a white blouse and yoga pants and short chopped hair and no makeup. Forty minutes pass. She closes her eyes for most of the time, breathing in Jackson, whispering to him. He wraps and rewraps his fingers around her thumbs.

She asks if they're back home on Carousel Court and Nick shakes his head, says there's some straightening up that needs to be done. "And I think we need a new fridge," he adds, laughing.

A bell chimes. Phoebe glances at the white hillside cottage with pale blue shutters. Other women, all in white blouses and yoga pants and slippers, make their way up the grassy slope along winding cobblestone pathways to the building.

"This is so good. Okay?" he says, looking around. "See it through."

"Why don't you answer my question?"

He says nothing.

"What is your inclination?" She draws out the last word of her question.

"Not now. I don't know what's best. Finish this and we'll figure it out."

"Oh, fuck that," she says, her voice rising. She closes her eyes. She stands and kisses Jackson's forehead and hands him to Nick and walks away.

93

The path to the beach is narrow. She looks over her shoulder once. The lights are bright in the main cottage; her bungalow is dark. She's alone and burning up. The wind off the water makes the wet cotton gown feel cold as it sticks to her sweaty thighs and chest. She chews her fingernails raw, digs her pulpy fingertips into her abdomen, which is tight and quivering.

She shares a bright-white-and-honeydew room with a stranger. She is sweating through a blue cotton gown because her cells and nerves and vital organs crave chemicals. They're greedy, expect more of the same if not better, a new high, more, always more.

The staff here helps her with the process of weaning. They try to help with expectations and perspective. Stay in the moment, all that Zen shit. The moment is the reason she may just walk to the end of the driveway instead of the beach, find the main road, and walk until someone picks her up and drives her home or wherever Nick has him now.

Instead she's barefoot on a stretch of beach staring at the black water, buried up to her chest in cold, wet sand. Let the tide come in, she thinks. Let nature do what it does. Who is she to resist?

94

Three weeks have passed. Nick is holding a Tupperware container of cookies. "Some woman named Lucy gave these to me." They're close to a ledge; the ocean wind is cool. Sunlight burns off the last of a thin gray mist. Phoebe leans in to Jackson and says sternly that he cannot eat these. "They're poison," she says. "Let's be superheroes and save the day." And one by one Phoebe and Jackson start chucking the cookies over the cliff.

Her eyes are fierce, Nick thinks, as she whips the things out over the water. She's barefoot and, without makeup, looks pale and raw.

"So you delivered," she says, glancing sidelong at Nick, barely suppressing a half-smile. "The regenerative time you promised when we came out here." She hands Jackson the last cookie and compliments his throw. She hands the empty container to Nick.

"When you're done here," he says, "just come home."

Her hair has grown back. Nick says he likes it short. With her finger, she twists a long curl in Jackson's hair. "I like this."

"He needs a cut," Nick says as they walk.

"Let it grow," she says.

"Are you sleeping?"

She holds her hands out in front of her, spreads her fingers. She studies them, says nothing. "I slept for twenty-two hours. Then I was awake for three days." The fevers, she says, come when she sleeps. In her dreams she throws herself over the cliffs into the crashing surf for relief. One night, she admits, she sneaked down to the beach in her nightgown and stripped naked, buried herself in the sand for relief.

"This is costing a fortune," she says.

Nick doesn't respond. They can afford it for now. But not much longer.

There's a moment when they're finished throwing cookies into the surf and Phoebe is holding Jackson and they're all standing too close to the gravelly edge and Nick is tense, the drop at least forty feet, his hands clenched into fists and inching closer to her, wondering if there's something in her eyes, some distorted fun-house-mirror version of her own purpose in this moment, or some bleak morass of a life she can't possibly slog through, that might make her consider the edge.

Nick grabs her arm. "Can we walk a little?"

She laughs. "I'm not jumping."

"That would be a huge waste of money."

She puts Jackson down and they walk.

Phoebe has moved on from woodworking. She's gardening now. Growing amaranth, because unlike kale and spinach, it can thrive in the heat. Nick returns his attention to the thing between them, the reason she walked them to the woodworking studio.

"So," she says. The white Adirondack chair is misshapen and awkward-looking.

"It's the angle, maybe?" Nick says, and adjusts it, starts to sit down, to test it.

She grabs his arm. "You don't want to do that. They want it out of here. It's depressing people."

"It's abstract."

"Like it's about to collapse," she says.

"Can we bring it home?" Nick says.

She says only if they can keep it in the backyard.

"Have you thought about the email I sent?"

She nods.

"Can you do it?"

"My bones feel like lead." She rubs her left arm, then her right.

"Do you want to at least try it?"

She says she does and runs her hand lightly over the edge of the chair. The paint is still drying. She tries to brush the white from her fingertips. She sighs and says she's more tired than she thought. "Tell me something we can't handle, right? That's what I keep saying to myself," she says.

Nick pulls a small, neatly folded cotton T-shirt from his pocket, hands it to her. It's Jackson's. Nick brings one, unwashed, each visit. She brings it to her face, breathes it in.

95

Nick finishes his third beer and studies the dark shadowy hillside beyond the house, where the winds and the beast that devoured Blackjack came from. His gaze falls to the glowing pool and Phoebe's patch of soil where she'll try again. Out front, the orange tent is gone from Metzger's lawn. Folded up and put away, Metzger said, because whatever deterrent effect it may have had is gone, given what happened to Phoebe in their house.

She's been home for a month. The ninety days reduced by half when Phoebe and Nick decided it was time.

Nick passes the pool, its soothing chlorine scent, and the fresh topsoil Phoebe spread this morning. He slips through a parting in the hedges they recently planted, heading up the hill. He's been doing this at night. He waits until she's asleep because she'd tell him not to, that it's dangerous and there's no need. They're fine, she'd say.

He climbs the hillside and gazes down from where it levels off. The homes on Carousel Court and identical tracts of houses stretch out until they become a blurry field of lights. Blazing. Who's next? he wonders.

Nick throws empty Corona bottles at the moon from the hillside behind their house. Tonight he carries only a small knife. Tomorrow he may be empty-handed. The next night he may not come up here at all. In some of the houses he sees tonight are his former tenants, scared families whose money he took and spent on his own family. He stands on a hill with a small weapon and his family, somehow, intact.

Pieces of Phoebe are gone, ripped away and replaced by something new. He's not entirely sure what. There is a depth to her eyes that wasn't there, as though they've sunk. He won't treat her like a patient, a martyr, or some kind of monster. Nick knows she is none of those things.

The secret he shares with no one because they'd never believe him. The reason he comes up here now, tonight, is this: He can hear Phoebe and Jackson. The cicadas have come and gone, their shells ground into dust, the air finally still and free of smoke, and the helicopters and sirens less frequent, which means for Nick, on nights like this, he's sure when he closes his eyes and concentrates, he can hear them both as they sleep, his family, breathing.

96

The email that arrives is from JW's email account. It's dated April 1. Phoebe is in the new Serenos Whole Foods and staring at her iPhone and checking the day's date and it's the same as the one on the message.

And there's an attachment, a PDF. She clicks the link and opens an invitation to a company retreat in Boothbay Harbor, Maine. The event is next week. *You guessed it. Awash in Chilean sea bass and mint juleps. Come! As a wise man once said: all can be forgiven or at least momentarily forgotten.*

When she gets home, she shows Nick the message on her phone, then deletes it.

Walking the hillside later that night, he wonders if something was proved. Some grand test passed. Some crucible endured. The fire season is over. The talk on Carousel Court has shifted to the seasons ahead, new threats, rain and flooding and landslides.

Someone moved into the house next to Metzger's. They seem to have kids, a soccer ball on the lawn. As Nick sorts through the avalanche of unopened mail, he stops when he sees a bill from the window-and-door-replacement company addressed to the Maguire Family. For the first time he can recall, the term carries weight, feels significant, sobering and inspired at the same time. They arc, for better or worse, the Maguire Family.

97

Phoebe leaves the water on for Nick's shower. She's drying off with a clean white towel. Nick is naked and brushes lightly against her when the towel drops. They linger there. He kisses the back of her neck. She reaches back, rests her hands on his legs, and closes her eyes.

"I'm excited," he says.

"Me too."

She feeds Jackson. Nick sets the ADT and turns on the sprinklers. She wears a yellow cotton dress; he's in olive pants and a crisp blue button-down. Her silver bracelets, rings, and turquoise necklace are all new. She did her own nails last night with clear polish, and the reading glasses soften her further. Nick shaved and his haircut is conservative, sideburns trimmed. He has two cups of coffee already made, so no need to stop.

They arrive twenty minutes early, which is

their intention. They want a few minutes to walk around, take in the surroundings, the vibe and energy of the place.

They sit in five tiny blue chairs. Nick, Phoebe, and Jackson. Tea and cake are served. They're asked to talk about Jackson. Neither of them hesitates, but each pauses thoughtfully before responding to questions about Jackson and their priorities for him, their assessment of his personality. Nick and Phoebe each credit the other for Jackson's most impressive personality traits; each takes responsibility, with self-deprecation, for areas that need work.

Two women sit across from them, jotting things down, asking Jackson gentle questions about stories he likes to be read and favorite foods. One of the women offers her hand and asks Jackson to walk with her around the classroom. The walls burst with color from student art, and sunlight floods the room.

As new parents, they're asked to describe the greatest challenge they've encountered thus far. Something that none of the parenting books or the wise counsel of family prepared them for. Something they never saw coming.

An enormous orange sun is painted on the classroom floor. Jackson circles it. The women watch him. Around and around. Jackson is giggling as he picks up speed. He's nearly running now. Is this a bad thing? Nick and Phoebe worry that Jackson may be blowing his chance with too much enthusiasm, not responding as he should to direction, lacking control over his instincts, unable to contain his exuberance.

"He's a runner," Phoebe says finally, laughing.

Admit him or not, they think. What the women here don't understand, what no one else knows or could ever fully appreciate, is that wherever the resilience comes from, however perverse, it's their own. Tell them no, dismiss or reject them, burn their house to the ground. They've put themselves through worse. Yet here they sit, perched on little plastic chairs, never more comfortable together, this crisp bright morning the beginning of something.

ACKNOWLEDGMENTS

First and foremost I'd like to thank Jennifer Joel of ICM for her support, guidance, infinite patience, and wisdom. I'm not sure where this project would be without her. Jofie Ferrari-Adler of Simon & Schuster has been more than an extraordinary editor and advocate, he's been a friend. Thank you as well to Julianna Haubner of Simon & Schuster for her responsiveness and kind words throughout. I'm enormously grateful to Jonathan Karp and Marysue Rucci for their support and stellar editorial insights. And enormous gratitude for the tireless work Richard Rhorer, Erin Reback, and Stephen Bedford have done and are doing. I'd also like to thank the following people who offered invaluable help along the way: Beth Thomas and Ciara Robinson of Simon & Schuster; Josie Freedman of ICM; Katharine Cluverius, Gita Kumar, Anna Louisa Yon, Leeya Mehta, Morgan Macgregor, and

Eric Reid. And of course, Morgan Entrekin, who gave me a chance and published my first book so well.

And for my family: my mother who reads and appreciates fiction in a way that fills me with so much happiness (I have another Roland Merullo novel for you!); my brother James who inspires me with his decency and talent and his superstar wife Kate Malone, bringing out his best, no doubt. Nancy and Matthew, Suzy and Chrissy: thank you for being so good to me.

Jeanine and Julien, there are likely words that express what you've given me and made me, but I can't find them. You truly are my golden age.

ABOUT THE AUTHOR

Joe McGinniss Jr. is the author of *Carousel Court* and *The Delivery Man.* He lives in Washington, DC, with his family.

The employees of Thorndike Press hope you have enjoyed this Large Print book. All our Thorndike, Wheeler, and Kennebec Large Print titles are designed for easy reading, and all our books are made to last. Other Thorndike Press Large Print books are available at your library, through selected bookstores, or directly from us.

For information about titles, please call:
(800) 223-1244

or visit our Web site at:
http://gale.cengage.com/thorndike

To share your comments, please write:
Publisher
Thorndike Press
10 Water St., Suite 310
Waterville, ME 04901